BOW STREET SOCIETY:
The Case of The Curious Client
By
T.G. Campbell

TABLE OF CONTENTS

ACKNOWLEDGEMENTS

Thank you to Karen McDonald for her proofreading skills and the support she patiently gave me through this entire process, especially during "camera gate." Thank you also to Pashen and Thayne for their support in this endeavour.

While researching the historical context for this novel, I had assistance from certain individuals and organisations. The assistance they gave me, and the information they provided me with, was both invaluable and appreciated beyond measure. Those individuals who assisted me included Peter Lane at the London headquarters of The Magic Circle, who gave me a guided tour of the museum, imparted his expert knowledge, and made a generous offer to have this manuscript considered for the Magic Circle's Library, and Paul Robert of The Virtual Typewriter Museum, whose enthusiasm and generosity were both charming and appreciated. He sent me electronic copies of the operating instructions for the Salter 7 and Blick 5 typewriters. Also, Neil Handley, MA, AMA+, FRSA, Curator at the British Optical Association Museum, The College of Optometrists for taking the time to answer my questions. Also, the staff at the Metropolitan Police's Heritage Centre for their time to give me a tour of the collection, for their patience, and for signposting me to other invaluable sources.

I'd also like to thank Lee Jackson for creating, arguably, the most comprehensive collection of contemporary sources from the Victorian Era, *The Victorian Dictionary* (see the Sources of Reference section at the end of this book for the full website address). I found this website invaluable. I'd also like to thank Mr Jackson for answering my questions in both a swift and polite way.

Finally, I'd like to thank Yahari for the fantastic Bow Street Society logo design, and all my friends and family for their continued support and encouragement.

PROLOGUE

"Victoria is on her way," Mr Joseph Maxwell said in a hushed voice as his deep-set green eyes betrayed both apprehension and excitement. A man of average stature, but of slender form, he had broad shoulders, freckle-covered, sunken cheeks, and high cheekbones. His distinctive red hair was neatly combed and parted to the left. An apprentice journalist with the *Gaslight Gazette* newspaper, he had an overall well-turned-out appearance. This consisted of a black frock coat over a dark-grey waistcoat accompanied by a high-collared white shirt, and black, silk cravat. The last had its tiny bow tied over his Adam's apple. The scents of lavender and carbolic soap lingered around him.

When his two companions reacted with a mere polite smile and subtle nod, though, he rested his clasped hands upon the table and twisted around in his chair. He watched as a waitress carried sliced Victoria Sponge cake to a couple sitting on the opposite side of the crowded tearoom. He wore the respectable attire of a middle-class gentleman, whilst she was adorned in a burgundy bustle dress and feather-topped hat which mimicked the fashion worn by ladies of a similar class. Both were in their twenties, despite the fact his brown hair was duller than her blond, and both were around five feet nine inches tall. Rubbing his thumbs together, an ache in Mr Maxwell's back then obliged him to face his companions once more.

The tearoom was housed above a branch of the *Aerated Bread Company* with its only access being a set of stairs leading from the rear of the ground-floor shop. Located on the Euston Road, the *A.B.C. Tearoom*—as it had come to be known—was a favoured refreshment stop for many a Londoner. Northbound travellers on their way to the London and North-Western Railway's Euston Square terminus were also daily regulars. Due to its popularity, there was often a queue down the stairs. Yet, the staff could be relied upon to clear the tables discreetly and efficiently. Thus, ensuring one was seated in no time at all.

A four-foot-high counter faced the door with a tin sign affixed to its front announcing all customers must 'Enquire here.' To its left was a tall, wooden-framed display cabinet containing a vast array of delectable goods, including freshly baked aerated bread loaves and scones. In addition to allowing one to see what was on offer, the cabinet's glass panes also protected the goods from being contaminated by the bad smells of the city and 'germs.' The remainder of the room's furniture consisted of ebony tables covered by white tablecloths and high-backed chairs with firm, dark-green cushions. With regards to décor, exposed floorboards were preferred over carpets due to the high rate of footfall the tearoom experienced. The walls, meanwhile, were papered with a dark-green, curving plant design on a slightly lighter green background. The low winter's sun poured in through sash windows, adding to the already welcoming glow of the wall-mounted, gas lamp sconces. Their sashes were open to provide the reassurance of fresh air from the street, thereby negating a customer's concerns about the possible build-up of carbonic gas.

"Are they the couple we're waiting for?" Mr Maxwell enquired. "Miss Dexter, may I see your sketches again?"

Miss Georgina Dexter offered a gentle smile and pulled her satchel onto her lap. From it, she took two drawings: the first of a male, the second of a female. Her posture remained impeccable as she held them across the table to him. At only five feet tall, she was considerably shorter than he. Yet, her petite form was nevertheless in perfect proportion. There was also an age difference of three years between them, with her being the younger at eighteen. Like him, she was fair skinned with red hair. Hers was two shades darker and several inches longer than his, though, and kept tightly pinned beneath a midnight-blue bonnet with black edging. The plain straight-lined dress she wore matched the bonnet in colour. With her entire chest and part of her neck covered by its material, Miss Dexter felt as comfortable as she could in the company of two bachelors—neither of whom she courted.

"Yeah," Dr Percy Weeks replied. His Canadian accent was in stark contrast to those of his English companions. Unlike them, he was slouched with his head leant back and his hands resting upon the backs of their chairs. A lit cigarette, perched in the corner of his mouth, bobbed as he exhaled smoke in their direction and warned, "So, stop gawkin' at 'em." Miss Dexter pressed a handkerchief to her mouth as she coughed, whilst Mr Maxwell crumpled his nose and moved his head back. "Dunno why I'm here anyway."

I must agree with you, Doctor, Miss Dexter thought. The man reeked of liquor and, despite being in a tearoom, had refused to purchase a cup, citing the fact he didn't drink "such shit" and much preferred coffee. As if hearing her thoughts, he retrieved a silver flask from his overcoat and took a swallow of Scotch whisky without a hint of shame. Her concern regarding his Bow Street Society membership—born from behaviour of this kind— wasn't of real note, however, when one considered his affiliation with the Metropolitan Police at Scotland Yard. Yes, police officers were often exposed as drunks, but Dr Weeks was allegedly a man of *medicine,* one upon whom the Yard relied (or so she was told). It left her feeling utterly bewildered whenever she tried to fathom how such a man as he could be granted such great responsibility.

Aside from his vulgar choice of vocabulary, lack of manners, and distinct accent, Dr Weeks' other remarkable traits could be said to be his short, slick-backed hair, small, waxed moustache, and long, short-haired sideburns, all of which were jet black. The fine quality of his attire meanwhile was in blatant contradiction to his behaviour. A dark-green, tailor-made, three-piece suit was accompanied by a matching tie with gold pin, and a white shirt with starched collar. His knee-length, black overcoat hung from the back of his chair, whilst a black, felt trilby sat upon the table. At twenty-nine, he was the eldest of the three.

"Miss Trent said we'd need a doctor when Miss Johnson faints," Mr Maxwell said.

His words pulled Miss Dexter back from her thoughts, and she offered him another smile as she rested her charcoal smudged hands in her lap. Though he'd seen the sketches earlier, she was reluctant to point this out when he studied them for a second time.

"She seems to know what she's doing," Mr Maxwell added. "Miss Trent, that is."

"Put the damn things outta sight," Dr Weeks growled, pulling the sketches from Mr Maxwell's grip and tossing them back to Miss Dexter. "*Jesus.*" He shook his head.

"Sorry," Mr Maxwell muttered as he felt his cheeks grow hot and his mouth turn dry.

Miss Dexter quietly cleared her throat and slid the sketches back into her satchel. "Miss Trent's instructions, to me, were to watch Miss Johnson and Mr Eddows, and to only act when the time is right." She cast an awkward glance between them as she lifted her teacup to her lips. "I intend to do that."

The scrape of a chair against the floor then pulled their attention back to the young couple. Miss Johnson was doubled over with her face contorted in pain as she gripped her corseted stomach with a lace-clad hand. Upon seeing this, a passing waitress stopped at once to enquire, "Are you unwell, Miss?"

"Of *course* I am unwell!" Miss Johnson snapped, her outburst garnering further attention from those at nearby tables. "I feel positively *foul*!"

"Here, darling." Mr Eddows spoke softly as he pushed her half-eaten slice of Victoria Sponge towards her. "Have something to eat. It may help you feel better—
"

"I *shan't* have another bite!" she cried and, much to his dismay, shoved the plate across the table before she gripped the table's edge and turned her wrath upon the waitress. "*You* must have baked with rotten eggs."

"No, Miss," the waitress began, "I can promise you we don't—"

Her words were cut short by Miss Johnson suddenly toppling backwards, however. Both the waitress and Mr Eddows leapt forward to catch her, the latter succeeding. Looking at those around them, he cried, "Is there a doctor in the house?!"

"That's my cue," Dr Weeks said, stealing himself with another swig of whisky and getting to his feet.

Those sitting at the tables around the couple's strained their necks and delivered hushed commentaries to their immediate neighbour. Miss Johnson's faint had also garnered horrified gasps from customers elsewhere in the tearoom, but even they couldn't pull their eyes away.

Upon reaching the couple, Dr Weeks stepped in front of Mr Eddows and delivered several firm taps to Miss Johnson's cheeks.

Mr Eddows rose at once to lean across Miss Johnson and shield her. "Stop that." He glared over his shoulder at him. "What do you think you're doing? Who are you?"

"I'm the doctor ya called for," Dr Weeks stated and half-turned to drop his cigarette into the vase of flowers in the table's centre. Gripping Mr Eddows' arm, he encountered a greater degree of resistance than he would've expected when he yanked it away. "And I'm tryin' to help yer friend, so get outta the way."

Mr Eddows stepped back and, watching Dr Weeks recommence his tapping of Miss Johnson's cheeks, muttered under his breath, "Americans."

"Canadian, actually," Dr Weeks corrected as he pressed the back of his hand against Miss Johnson's forehead.

"Is there a difference?" Mr Eddows enquired sardonically.

"Canadians are more refined," Dr Weeks retorted as their eyes met.

"Not this Canadian," Mr Maxwell remarked into Miss Dexter's ear as they joined them. Her cheeks immediately flushed crimson, obliging her to bow her head as she took a bottle of smelling salts from her satchel and passed it to Dr Weeks. Pulling its cork out with his teeth, he then spat it onto the table and wafted the bottle's contents under Miss Johnson's nose. Within seconds of inhaling the salts' pungent aroma, Miss Johnson was brought out of her faint with a sharp gasp.

Despite this seemingly happy event though, Mr Eddows eyed Miss Dexter and Mr Maxwell with suspicion. "Who're you?"

"Just friends of Dr Weeks. We were taking tea with him when we heard your call for help," Mr Maxwell explained.

Mr Eddows responded with a blunt hum, but the suspicious glare remained.

"Let's get ya outta 'ere," Dr Weeks said as he helped Miss Johnson to her feet.

"I'll just fetch your bill, sir," the waitress informed Mr Eddows.

"You *honestly* expect us to pay for this poison?" Mr Eddows challenged. The waitress' mouth opened, but Mr Eddows halted her voice at once by exclaiming, "Don't be ridiculous, woman! The cake made her ill! Look at her!" He gestured to the trembling Miss Johnson who, despite her apparent illness, maintained a healthy pink glow. "I utterly refuse."

"If you'd permit me to fetch the manager, sir—" the waitress replied.

"You already have my answer," Mr Eddows interrupted and picked up his coat and hat along with Miss Johnson's. Mr Maxwell had brought Dr Weeks' things which he now proceeded to put on. "Come on, we're leaving," Mr Eddows instructed once they were ready.

"B-But sir, you can't—" the waitress stuttered with her hands outstretched as Mr Eddows strode out the tearoom. Dr Weeks followed, supporting Miss Johnson who held onto his arm for grim life. Wide-eyed at the sight, the waitress went to chase after them but was blocked by Miss Dexter who'd stepped into her path. "Pardon me, Miss—"

Miss Dexter took her hands in hers. "Don't worry."

"Miss?" the waitress enquired, confused.

"Your manager already knows of this," Miss Dexter replied. Offering a smile of reassurance, she parted company from the waitress to take her place in the pursuit of the others.

"Tell him the Bow Street Society was here," Mr Maxwell instructed the waitress as he passed. Catching up with Miss Dexter by the door, they both then took deep breaths as they crossed its threshold and descended the stairs.

Parked outside was a two-wheeler, highly varnished, hansom cab. It had both the inside and outside plates and stencilled certificate on its back, to show it had passed its examination by the inspectors at Clerkenwell. Furthermore, whomever owned it, in this case the Bow Street Society, had paid the two shillings for the licence to drive it around London. Further expense the Society had incurred was fifteen shillings carriage duty to Somerset House and five shillings to the Metropolitan Police for a licence and badge to drive. Though the cab was inspected annually, a cabman's ability to drive was only assessed once. At the end of each year, the cabman took his current licence to New Scotland Yard who would issue him a clean licence that was valid for a further twelve months. His length of service had to be recorded on the back of his current licence by his employer before he could have it replaced, however.

Pulling the cab was a single, brown horse, brown being the more fashionable colour and the one most preferred by cab customers. The wheels, meanwhile, were approximately four feet wide. Between these wheels, resting upon the axle, was the main body of the cab; a wooden bench within a two-sided box with a ceiling that also doubled as a canopy over the passengers' heads. The front edge of this canopy was carved into a curved arch whilst, attached to the edges of the left and right walls by hinges, were heavy, wooden doors with pointed middle sections to accommodate passengers' knees. These, coupled with the wooden canopy, provided some shelter from the elements and from any mud and spray the horse's hooves kicked up. Glassless windows in the cab's sides enabled passengers to see where they passed, as well as providing the much-valued free flow of fresh air. Finally, candlelit lamps hanging from the top corners of the front of the cab enabled passengers to see when climbing into the cab at night.

The driver was sitting upon a narrow seat, attached to the outside of the cab's back wall, elevated enough so he could see over both the cab and horse. This seat also had iron railings on three sides to prevent him from toppling out when the cab was in motion. His broad shoulders were hunched over his calloused hands which in turn held the horse's reins. These reins ran along the top of the cab, through the hollow tips of a V-shaped attachment mounted upon the canopy's front edge (to keep the reins in line) and down to the horse's harness. Aside from his face, the driver's hands were the only other parts of his body visible beneath a heavy, black cape. Even his scuffed, and slightly torn, black-leather boots were concealed, though they rested against the back of the cab. Having pulled down the brim of his brown hat, to block the low, winter's sun, he now pushed it back up with a fat thumb as he enquired in a rough voice born from London's East end, "You wanna cab?"

Mr Eddows and Miss Johnson looked up into his brown, beady eyes which were set deep into his weathered face. Middle-aged with bushy sideburns, his intimidating appearance was softened by the warmth of his smile.

"Yeah, we do," Dr Weeks replied.

"Hop in, then," the driver replied, pulling his hat's brim back down over his eyes and clearing his throat. "Plenty of room inside."

Though a cab this size sat two persons comfortably five was out of the question. Dr Weeks therefore perched upon a narrow step at the cab's rear and gripped both the roof's edge and the driver's seat. Meanwhile, Miss Johnson, Mr Eddows, and Miss Dexter in turn climbed inside and settled themselves upon the bench. Mr Maxwell hesitated, however.

"Get in," Dr Weeks ordered.

Mr Maxwell swallowed hard and inched closer to the cab. "Right… yes, let me see…" He hoisted himself onto the cab's edge, thereby causing it to tilt, and held his breath as he slid into the narrow space beside Miss Dexter and the wall. As he dropped down onto the bench, though, he accidentally placed his hand upon her knee and cried, "Oh!" He felt his cheeks burn. "Please, forgive me." Glancing at Miss Dexter, he saw her face had also turned crimson. Yet, rather than bring him comfort, it served to increase his embarrassment. Feeling his hip was wedged against Miss Dexter's, he tried to press his body against the cab wall as much as possible. "Fortunately, the journey isn't a long one…"

Mr Eddows slammed his door shut, prompting Mr Maxwell to do the same. Faced with the problem of where to put his hands, though, he searched around before finally deciding to rest them upon the door's top edge. The sharp lurch of the cab as the horse trotted forward caused him to fall back, however. His left hand gripped the cab's window at once, whilst his right was dropped to the bench to steady himself. When he felt Miss Dexter's dress, though, his eyes widened as he realised he'd no clue upon which part of her anatomy his hand was resting. Yet, to his greater surprise, he felt Miss Dexter's hand not only rest upon his own but give it a gentle squeeze. "Oh." Mr Maxwell looked from their hands to her reassuring smile. "Erm… thank you, Miss Dexter."

"How are you feeling, darling?" Mr Eddows enquired.

Miss Johnson had her fingers pressed to her temple as she replied, "Foul, still. I shall be relieved when we reach the hospital."

"We're taking them to the hospital?" Mr Maxwell enquired, addressing Miss Dexter.

"Yes," she replied, trying to use her eyes to warn him against saying anymore.

"Where else would you be taking us?" Mr Eddows enquired as he leant forward to eye Mr Maxwell suspiciously once more.

"Endell Street—" Mr Maxwell replied, only realising his error after the words had left his lips.

"*Endell Street*?" Mr Eddows challenged in disbelief.

"Yes… you see… erm…" Mr Maxwell stumbled.

"What the bloody hell's going on?!" Mr Eddows demanded and struck the cab's back wall. "You said you were a doctor!"

"I am!" Dr Weeks shouted back "Maxwell, keep yer damned mouth shut!"

"But I—" Mr Maxwell began.

"Let us out!" Mr Eddows demanded as he struck the roof.

The driver cracked the whip instead, though, driving the horse into a gallop and sending the cab into a series of violent lurches to the left and right as it weaved through the chaos of London's traffic. Omnibuses, cabs, carriages, and vans all sped past in a blur of colours and smells. Faces of pedestrians rushed by the windows as they darted around the cab without warning. One stepped out in front of the horse, only to leap back again. Miss

16

Johnson and Miss Dexter simultaneously covered their mouths and held their breaths at the sight.

"Get off the road!" the driver yelled above them.

"Are you coppers or sumin'?!" Mr Eddows shouted over the din. His once refined accent had now degenerated into that of a slum dweller. When neither Miss Dexter nor Mr Maxwell replied, he reached across the ladies to grab Mr Maxwell's lapel and pull him as close to him as the doors allowed. Within the gloom of the cab there then appeared the glint of something metallic in Mr Eddows' other hand. When he looked down at it, Mr Maxwell saw the unmistakeable shape of a revolver. "Either you let us out, or I'll have to do sumin' stupid."

"Don't be thick, Toby!" Miss Johnson warned upon seeing the gun. "Put it down!" She gripped his arm with one hand and tried to prise the gun from his fingers with the other.

"Oi, ge' off me!" Mr Eddows growled.

The cab leapt up into the air as it struck something in the road and, as it landed, everyone inside was thrown upward from the bench. Dropped as violently as he was thrown, Mr Eddows landed awkwardly, his hand slamming against the door's top edge as a result. He immediately lost his grip upon the gun and it clattered down the door's smooth exterior, struck the horse's galloping hooves, and fired.

The horse gave a blood-curdling shriek as the bullet lodged itself in its thigh. Its leg at once collapsed and the horse toppled sideways at full speed of the remaining galloping legs. The cab, with no way of stopping, collided with the body of the stricken horse and its left wheel was lifted clean off the ground whilst its right was stopped dead in its tracks. Everyone inside lifted their arms to shield themselves as the driver ducked, Dr Weeks leapt onto the road, and the cab flipped and rolled into oncoming traffic. Those vehicles' horses shrieked and tried to rear up onto their back legs as their drivers fought to keep control and swerve out of the way. Yells and

17

screams of pedestrians fleeing for their lives then filled the air when the cab rolled across the road and threatened to mount the pavement. As it struck the curb, though, it tilted forward and fell back onto the road with a loud thud, its wheel spinning and its panicked horse shrieking.

ONE

A slender finger lifted the curved, brass arms of a W.B. copy holder to free the page of the notebook it had been gripping. This was flipped over the notebook's top, and the arms allowed to drop into place. With this task complete, the fair-skinned hands set about commencing a new sentence with a pressing of the Improved Salter 5's shift key, followed by swift striking of the QWERTY keyboard as the notes were transcribed. Within moments the brief ring of a bell signalled the end of the line and the typewriter's carriage was released by the left hand before being pushed back by the right.

Another high-pitched, yet quiet, bell then cut through the typist's tapping. This one was mounted on the front of a narrow, vertical, wooden box attached to the wall beside the desk. The typist plucked the curved-lipped cylinder from its metallic cradle on the box's side and pressed it to their ear. Speaking into a black cone jutting out from beneath the bell, the typist said, "Good afternoon, Miss Rebecca Trent of the Bow Street Society, Endell Street, speaking, how may I help you?"

On paper Miss Trent would've been considered 'old' at twenty-eight. Yet the youthful rosiness of her complexion, enhanced by a hint of blusher and ruby-red lipstick, often deceived others into believing she was far younger. Corkscrew ringlets of chestnut brown hair cascaded from her head to hang between her shoulders with a few strays permitted to frame her face. A tight corset accentuated the slender curve of her waist beneath a long-sleeved, dark, and light-brown checked top with dark-brown fur trim on the cuffs and squared neckline. Her dark-brown, layered cotton skirts had a small bustle at their rear and hung over her black-leather, high-heeled boots.

"Ah, hello," a rather pleasant-sounding, deep voice replied into her ear. "You say this is the Bow Street Society on *Endell Street*?"

"Yes." Miss Trent rolled her dark-brown eyes. Based upon the location alone, the Society's name made little sense unless one knew the significance of Bow Street in the annuals of crime and punishment. "To whom am I speaking?"

"Mr Thaddeus Dorsey. I need your assistance, but I can't speak for long. My friend is missing; I'm greatly concerned about him."

"I see. If I could have your address, I'll make arrangements for some of our members to call upon you to discuss the matter further." She retrieved a second notebook from her desk and rested it upon the slanted shelf beneath the mouthpiece with her pencil poised.

"It's Bow Street, the house with the white door."

"What're you doing on that?" a quieter but angry voice interrupted.

"I'm not unsafe," Thaddeus insisted and ended the call with a click.

Miss Trent quirked a brow and stared at the earpiece a moment. Putting it to her ear once more, she held the cradle down for several seconds and waited for the operator's voice. "Hello, this is the Bow Street Society on Endell Street. I've just received a call from a gentleman on Bow Street, but the line failed before he could give me his telephone number. Could you supply it to me, please?" She wrote down the number as it was dictated to her. "Thank you, goodbye." She replaced the mouthpiece into its cradle and lifted a thick book from the floor beneath.

Dropping it onto her desk with a thud, she swept the dust from its cover to read the word 'Phonebook' and the current year of 1896 printed upon it. Flipping through its 1,350 pages, she scanned the single columns on each for the number. Covering the entire country, the book had a total of eighty-one thousand entries. Eventually, though, she found what she was looking for and placed a sheet of paper beneath the entry to note down the accompanying address.

The door struck a chair on the opposite side of the desk, distracting Miss Trent from her task. Seeing Miss Dexter's dust-covered skirts first, followed by her arm, as she attempted to squeeze through the gap between door and chair, Miss Trent stood and dragged the latter away. Leaving it in the corner, she allowed Miss Dexter to enter and cross the compact space to join her. The next to enter was Mr Maxwell who, upon giving her a tight-lipped smile, lingered at the threshold with sheepish eyes.

"Keep goin'," Mr Snyder said from behind him.

"Oh, sorry," Mr Maxwell replied and stepped to the side. Running a heavily scratched hand through his dishevelled hair, he straightened his collar and patted the dust from his coat.

Mr Snyder, unable to find sufficient room within the office for his broad frame, remained in its doorway. He, like the others, had dust covering his clothes, scratches to his face and hands, and tears to his cloak.

"What happened?" Miss Trent enquired, having become more concerned by the appearance of each new arrival.

"Cab's knackered," Mr Snyder replied.

"*How?*" Miss Trent's lips parted as she looked between them in disbelief. "And the horse?"

"Too hurt to survive," Mr Snyder replied.

Miss Trent gave a sigh of regret. "We've only *just* had that cab approved."

"Yeah, I know," Mr Snyder replied as his eyes locked upon Mr Maxwell.

"What happened?" Miss Trent enquired, following his line of sight. "Mr Maxwell?"

Mr Maxwell cleared his throat and toyed with the bow of his cravat. "We watched Mr Eddows and Miss Johnson as instructed…"

"Yes," Miss Dexter interjected as she rested her clasped hands against her skirts and looked to Miss Trent's feet.

"And saw them feign sickness, *just* as the coffee house owners' testimonies said they had in the past," Mr Maxwell continued in triumph.

"And then…?" Miss Trent probed.

"Dr Weeks approached them. He spoke to Miss Johnson and convinced them both to be escorted to Mr Snyder's cab outside," Mr Maxwell replied and hastily approached her. "I didn't know he had a gun, Miss Trent, I swear to you."

"A *gun*?" Miss Trent stared at him.

"Mr Maxwell let slip we woz bringin' 'em 'ere and Mr Eddows got out a shooter," Mr Snyder explained. Mr Maxwell immediately shrank back as Miss Trent glared at him. "Mr Eddows dropped it and shot Blue-Tie. Dr Weeks jumped off the back and the cab rolled. We woz okay, but Eddows and Johnson woz out cold. Sergeant Bird from Holborn took them in but a-nuva cabbie had saw Eddows holdin' the gun, so Bird sent us off."

"You could've gotten everyone killed with your stupidity," Miss Trent scolded Mr Maxwell.

"I'm sorry…" Mr Maxwell mumbled, turning aside and rubbing his mouth to soothe his nerves.

"But, as it is, you're all fine aside from a few scratches," Miss Trent conceded with a soft sigh as she went behind her desk and picked up a file. "And we achieved what we were commissioned to do: catch the coffee house con artists. The consortium of proprietors will be pleased, at least. I'll have the case file sent to Sergeant Bird so he may bring the additional charges against Mr Eddows and Miss Johnson." She replaced the file and addressed Mr Snyder, "Can the cab be repaired?"

"Yeah. I'll take Freddie to ge' it and hire one from a bloke I know. We've got Red-Shirt to pull it," Mr Snyder replied.

Miss Trent exhaled and felt the tension dissipate from her shoulders. "Good." She held up the address copied from the phonebook. "It's fortunate our next commission is within walking distance then, isn't it?" She held it out to Mr Maxwell who, taken aback, hesitated before gingerly taking it. "But do anything so stupid again, Mr Maxwell, and I'll have no choice but to consider the immediate cancellation of your Society membership. Understood?"

"Y-Yes, thank you," Mr Maxwell stammered. "Whom should we ask for when we get there?"

"Mr Thaddeus Dorsey," Miss Trent replied. "You may encounter some resistance as there was a second, angrier voice on the line just before Mr Dorsey told me he wasn't unsafe and hung up his telephone."

"So that means he probably is, then," Mr Maxwell remarked.

"No, it means we must investigate further," Miss Trent replied, "Miss Dexter, you may accompany Mr Maxwell. Mr Dorsey's friend is missing so we'll need a sketch made of what he looks like to distribute." The two nodded their agreement. "I'll contact another Society member to assist you. Wait for them to arrive before you knock on the door and ensure all three of you return here afterwards to let me know what happened."

"We will, Miss Trent," Miss Dexter replied and headed down the stairs ahead of Mr Maxwell.

Miss Trent, meanwhile, turned to a large, wooden filing cabinet standing to the right of her desk. It had seemingly hundreds of shallow, square drawers which filled the entire wall. She opened one labelled 'J-L' and it was full of index cards. Flipping through them until she came to the one she needed, she pulled it out and copied its address onto an envelope with a black capital 'B' printed in its corner. The 'B' was surrounded by vines and framed by a thick, square border. Returning the index card to the cabinet that was then locked, she next typed a brief note and slipped it into the envelope. Once it was sealed, she passed it to Mr Snyder and the two bade farewell.

As he emerged onto the street and hailed a passing cab, though, Mr Snyder didn't notice a figure loitering on the opposite side. The stranger's dark-blue eyes watched Mr Snyder until he had secured his transportation and climbed inside. Whilst he was then driven away, the stranger tossed a lit, hand-rolled cigarette onto the pavement and crushed it beneath their scuffed, black-leather shoe. Stepping off the curb a moment later, the stranger waited for another cab to pass by before they crossed the road, entered the open doorway, and climbed the stairs.

Miss Trent, having returned to her typing, expressed her disbelief at the cab's destruction in the form of incomprehensible mutterings under her breath. She therefore failed to hear the footfalls on the stairs and the soft creak of the door's hinges as it was opened. It was only when she heard the floorboards complain under the stranger's shifting weight that she noticed the shadow cast across her typewriter. She immediately looked up and into the watchful eyes. Recognising the crooked nose and dark-red eyebrows which accompanied them, she settled back in her chair and rested her hands upon the desk.

"Please, sit," she invited.

The stranger removed a black trilby from his head to reveal neatly combed dark-red hair beneath. He was a man in his early forties with calloused hands, weathered features, and a well-maintained moustache and beard that matched his hair in colour. At five-feet-nine he dominated the space. He smiled and, dropping his hat onto the desk, closed the door with a soft click.

* * *

"How long have you been a member of the Bow Street Society, Miss Dexter? If you don't mind my asking?" Mr Maxwell stepped around a fellow pedestrian whilst Miss Dexter kept her distance behind him.

"I don't mind." She kept her eyes fixed upon the pavement in front of her. "It has been about six months in all."

"Do you enjoy it?"

"I don't take joy from others' suffering, Mr Maxwell."

"No, no, of course not." He pressed his chin against his chest, deepening his voice. "Perish the thought." Coughing, he slowed his pace to fall in step beside Miss Dexter and rubbed his chest. "I'm not like others in my profession." He frowned. "Might be why I've been an apprentice for the past three years." He looked sideways at her, but her eyes remained downcast. "No, what I meant was; do you enjoy the hunt for the truth, the exposure of villains?"

"I create sketches."

"Yes," he made a downward sweep with his hand, "I know, but those sketches may very well be crucial in the identification of criminals and ne'er-do-wells. Also," he turned and walked backwards to see her whole face, "you take descriptions from witnesses to create those sketches. That is a talent in itself."

She stopped and met his gaze. Mr Maxwell, having done the same, smiled with hopeful eyes. Rather than acknowledge the compliment though, she enquired, "May I see it?"

"Pardon?"

"The address Miss Trent gave to you. May I see it?"

"Yes, of course." He rummaged around in his pockets. "It's here somewhere." Yet, when his hands were withdrawn, an avalanche of papers toppled onto the wet pavement. Crouching, he picked up and inspected each in turn. "Those are my notes… erm, more notes… a fellow's name for reasons which now escape me… a-ha! Here we are." He straightened and gave it to Miss Dexter.

"Thank you." She read the address and compared its number to that on the house they were standing beside. "I believe we're here."

The four-storied, semi-detached, red-brick building was the epitome of domesticity. Its oak front door was painted white with a round stained-glass window depicting a large, yellow flower in its upper panel. Its lower had floral carvings within a circular frame. Above the door was a second, squared, stained-glass window depicting smaller versions of the yellow flower. A scuffed brass plaque etched with the house number, a doorknob, and letterbox caught a lantern's candlelight as it hung from a short chain in the porch's centre. The walls of the porch were covered by wood panelling painted to match the door. A set of steep, stone steps led to the uneven pavement of Bow Street below. To the left and right of the porch were tall, white-framed windows which appeared to fade into the near pitch blackness of the house's shadow.

It was five thirty p.m. in mid-January so, naturally, it was already dusk. Mr Maxwell gave a polite nod to the lamplighter who was igniting the lamppost they were standing under. The lamplighter looked at him with mistrust but nevertheless, moved onto the lamppost on the corner. Once there, he watched the pair until Mr Maxwell watched back. At which point the lamplighter lit the lamp and headed toward Endell Street.

"I hope whoever it is arrives soon." Mr Maxwell shivered and wrapped his arms around his chest. "Who does she usually send to these initial client meetings?"

"I really couldn't say. Miss Trent sends whomever she feels would be most appropriate."

The sound of horses' hooves against the cobblestones then filled the air, heralding the approach of a four-wheeled carriage pulled by a couple of chestnut-brown mares. Painted in black lacquer with gold leaf adorning its handles and framing its door's central panel, the carriage had the letters 'P' and 'L' intertwined beneath its window. The apparent wealth of the carriage's owner was further denoted by its red-velvet curtains and the impeccable uniform of its driver.

As the carriage slowed to a stop beside Mr Maxwell and Miss Dexter, a slender, black, leather-clad hand appeared from behind the curtains and lifted the external handle. Unlatched, the door swung open and a highly polished shoe was lowered onto the metal step before its counterpart found the pavement. As the passenger emerged from the carriage, he was revealed to be a handsome gentleman in his late twenties. His slim face had an unblemished, fair complexion, high—yet delicate—cheekbones, and a perfectly formed nose. Emerald-green eyes, which were at once warm and arrogant, complemented the slight lift of his chin to create an air of superiority. A few golden-blonde curls poked out from beneath his brushed, black top hat, whilst long, closely cut sideburns lined his jaw. His tailor-made clothes consisted of black trousers and a pristine frock coat, cinched in at the waist, coupled with a maroon waistcoat and matching silk cravat.

He gripped the silver handle of his ebony cane and leaned upon it as he extended his hand to Mr Maxwell. "Mr Percival Locke, at your service."

Mr Maxwell blinked as he took his hand. "Not *the* Percival Locke, the magician at the Paddington Palladium?"

"The one and the same," Mr Locke replied.

Mr Maxwell's jaw dropped. "…I," he cleared his throat, "Mr Joseph Maxwell—journalist. That is, I am an, um, apprentice journalist for the *Gaslight Gazette.* And this is Miss Georgina Dexter, freelance artist."

"Pleased to meet you, sir," Miss Dexter interjected with a brief one-sided curtsey. Unacquainted with the newcomer until tonight and unmarried besides, it would've been improper for Miss Dexter to mimic Mr Maxwell by offering her hand.

"As it is my pleasure to meet you but, please, such forms of address are neither necessary nor expected," Mr

Locke replied as he attempted to free his hand from Mr Maxwell's grip.

"Oh!" Mr Maxwell cried, releasing Mr Locke's hand. "Sorry."

Mr Locke cast a disapproving glance in his direction. He then ascended the steps with Mr Maxwell and Miss Dexter behind him. No sooner had Mr Locke lifted his cane to knock on the door, though, was it opened by a man with short—yet, unkempt—dirty-blond hair. He was in his mid-twenties with a thin build swamped by the shin-length, dark-brown coat he wore. Patches upon its sleeves and elbows covered where the material had ripped or worn away. Their stitching was sparse and crude. Stepping out onto the porch, he slammed the door behind him and turned its key. Upon coming face-to-face with Mr Locke, he halted in his tracks. "Who are you?"

"I am Mr Percival Locke, and these are my associates—"

"What do you want?" the man interrupted.

Having turned aside to indicate Mr Maxwell and Miss Dexter, Mr Locke now looked sideways at the petulant man. "We have been invited by a Mr Thaddeus Dorsey, are you he?"

"No," the man replied.

"Is he here?" Mr Locke enquired.

"I've never heard of you. What he want to see you for?" the man enquired, looking amongst them with a constant, cold glare.

Mr Maxwell raised his hand. "His friend is missing."

"What friend?" the man scoffed.

"That is what we are to here to establish," Mr Locke replied. "Mr Maxwell, Miss Dexter, and I are from the Bow Street Society, sir. And you are?"

"Jack Colby; Mr Dorsey's only mate, so you lot can bugger off." Mr Colby moved but was halted a second time by Mr Locke standing in his way.

"My good man," Mr Locke said. "Earlier today Mr Dorsey telephoned Miss Rebecca Trent, the clerk of the Bow Street Society, and expressed a desire to enlist our services in locating a friend of his that he was most concerned about. If it is indeed you of whom he was speaking, we shall be only too delighted to 'bugger off,' as you put it. Yet, I am sure you shall understand when I insist we hear it from Mr Dorsey himself."

"Get lost," Mr Colby barked, moving forward a second time.

Again, Mr Locke stood in his way. "*Mr* Colby, we may continue this conversation until dawn, or you could save us all some time by informing us of Mr Dorsey's whereabouts."

Mr Colby glanced back at the door.

"If it's another friend that's missing, Miss Dexter can take his description from Mr Dorsey and draw a sketch that we can use to find him with," Mr Maxwell explained.

"Not bloody likely," Mr Colby sneered.

"I can assure you the Society has more resources than you think—" Mr Maxwell said.

"*Nah*," Mr Colby barked. "Not likely you'll get a description."

"We certainly shan't if you do not tell us where he is," Mr Locke replied.

"Mr Dorsey can't tell you what he can't see," Mr Colby retorted.

TWO

"P—pardon?" Mr Maxwell enquired with wide eyes.

"He's blind," Mr Colby said and forced Mr Locke aside by driving his shoulder into his. Mr Maxwell and Miss Dexter also parted, thereby allowing Mr Colby to reach the steps. "As well as wasted your time." He went down to the street but turned to look up at them. "So bugger off, or I'll get a copper."

Mr Maxwell and Miss Dexter descended the steps to join him, the weight of his glare pressing heavily upon them as they did so. Mr Locke lingered on the porch for a moment, longer though. During which time he slid his cane between his fingers and caught its handle.

"Please accept our apologies for delaying you, Mr Colby," Mr Locke said as he strolled down the steps.

Mr Colby grunted and strode away in the direction of Covent Garden.

Mr Locke rested his left arm against the crook of his back as he watched him leave.

"That's that then," Mr Maxwell remarked.

A patrolling police constable appeared from around the corner and headed toward them. Mr Maxwell greeted him with a nod when he passed, and the constable bid him a good evening with a touch of his hat's brim. Mr Locke returned the pleasantry and, waiting until the constable had put several yards' distance between them, pivoted upon his heel and went back to the porch.

"Mr Maxwell," Mr Locke called, tossing his cane to him.

Mr Maxwell's arms flailed, and his hands stumbled to catch it, however, and it landed on the pavement with a loud clatter. Both Mr Maxwell and Miss Dexter held their breaths as they looked down the street at the constable who'd stopped to investigate the source of the noise. Mr Maxwell collected the cane and held it up as he said, "I'm forever dropping it!" The constable studied him a moment but then continued on his way.

"What are you doing, Mr Locke?" Mr Maxwell hissed up the stairs as he saw him retrieve a small, black-velvet roll from his frock coat and unfurl it.

"There is something more going on here," Mr Locke replied. "Mr Colby knew very well where Mr Dorsey is; he is inside."

"Inside?" Miss Dexter echoed and climbed the steps to join him.

"Yes," Mr Locke replied as he laid the roll upon the floor. Glancing back at Mr Maxwell, he instructed, "Do be so kind as to keep an eye out for the return of our friend the constable." He checked the time on his pocket watch. "We have nine minutes."

"For what?" Mr Maxwell enquired.

"To gain entry," Mr Locke replied and inspected the lock. It was a steel-cased lock with a smooth, brass knob of around three inches wide and a brass plate around the singular keyhole. Mounted into the door frame was another steel fixture that formed the second half of the lock. Having recognised the make and mechanism at once, Mr Locke knew the key had thrown the bolt into a state of dead lock, thus preventing the door from being forced open. Furthermore, that this design included an internal, smaller knob to draw back the bolt and a compressible snib to prevent the bolt locking when the door was closed. Selecting a long, silver pick from the roll, he inserted it into the lock and attempted to manipulate its mechanism.

"But Miss Trent said breaking and entering is forbidden by the Society!" Mr Maxwell cried and bounded up the steps.

"Unless there is a sufficiently justifiable reason for doing so," Mr Locke replied, selecting a second pick and inserting it into the lower part of the lock. "And do you not think the welfare of our client is a sufficiently justifiable reason, Mr Maxwell?"

"His welfare?" Mr Maxwell enquired.

Miss Dexter had moved closer to Mr Locke to watch what he was doing. Having heard what was said between the two gentlemen, she whispered, "Do you suspect some harm may have come to Mr Dorsey, Mr Locke?"

"I do not know," Mr Locke replied, "but Mr Colby was *very* keen we should not speak with him. Furthermore, Miss Trent's note stated Mr Dorsey abruptly ended his telephone conversation with her when another, angry voice, spoke." There was a sharp click as the bolt sprang back into the lock's casing.

"Our constable friend is back, and it's only been a minute!" Mr Maxwell cried, panic stricken.

"Ah, that will be the Bow Street police station," Mr Locke replied and turned the doorknob. "The police tend to keep a closer eye upon the more affluent residences; greater targets for thieves, you know." He pushed the door open and ushered Mr Maxwell and Miss Dexter inside. Slipping in after them, he closed the door as the constable reached the bottom of the steps. He watched him pass by through the stained-glass window and turned the lock's interior knob to slide the bolt back into place. "He is walking away."

The vast hallway they found themselves in had a grand staircase leading up to a narrow landing that encircled the room. The stairs' smooth, oak handrails were polished to a shine and supported by rounded oak balusters. Their steps were covered by a burgundy carpet whilst the hallway's floor was black-and-white checked tiles. The landing and hallway's walls were adorned by a light-red paper embossed with a burgundy, repetitive floral pattern. At the far end of the hallway, to the left and right of the stairs, were a further two doors with more in between. Only the second on the left was ajar, however.

"Hello?!" A voice suddenly called from it. "Mr Colby?!"

Miss Dexter stifled her startled gasp.

Mr Maxwell, who'd turned toward the door at the sound, pressed his finger to his lips as he looked to the others. With great care he crept around the staircase and locked his gaze upon the door. In doing so, though, he didn't see the small table and knocked it with his hip. The china vase standing upon it tilted at the impact and spun on the edge of its base. Mr Maxwell thrust out his hands but, unlike the cane, succeeded in catching it. He kept a tight grip as he moved it back to the table's centre and breathed an audible sigh of relief once he'd stepped back. Miss Dexter also exhaled and placed her hand over her racing heart.

"Mr Colby, I… I need to use the chamber pot…" the voice said.

Mr Maxwell crept over to the door and put his back to it. Taking its handle, he eased it open and peered into the dimly lit room. Mr Locke and Miss Dexter watched from the other side of the hallway but, when Mr Maxwell hadn't ventured in after several moments had passed, Mr Locke crossed the room to join him. Yet, despite the floor's hard surface, his footsteps made no sound. Thus, his sudden presence beside him startled Mr Maxwell. Meanwhile, Miss Dexter, who was reluctant to be left alone, hurried along after Mr Locke with a distinct rustling of her skirts. Upon reaching them, she stood behind Mr Locke and peered around him, into the room.

The part visible to them had dark-olive paper with a high-grade, embossed scroll design covering its walls. The floor was exposed, wooden boards painted in a dark-brown varnish. This was in stark contrast to the white enamel of an iron bed frame standing perpendicular to the door.

Miss Dexter, realising she was looking into someone's bedroom, turned away with crimson cheeks, whilst Mr Maxwell and Mr Locke explored further. As their gazes ran down the bed frame's straight lines, they came across a man in his mid-forties with an immense beard covering his jaw and neck. His fair complexion was made paler by the blackness of his hair and the creaminess of the Nottingham bed spread pulled up to his chin. It had a floral design with an Irish point finish to match the cases upon the plump pillows piled up beneath the man's head.

A kerosene lamp, lit to half its capacity, was standing upon a table between the bed and the door to illuminate the man's face. Its rotund brass and nickel-plated base and plain, white-frosted glass dome shade with chimney would've been more at home in a study than a bedroom, however. Even the scratched, round-top table beneath looked like it belonged elsewhere.

"Mr Colby?" the man enquired as he turned his head. Yet, his eyes failed to focus upon either of them, prompting Mr Maxwell to push the door open a little further.

"I know who you are," the man said.

Mr Maxwell froze.

"Why do you never speak?" the man enquired with a frown as he looked to the foot of the bed.

Miss Dexter clung to Mr Locke's sleeve whilst he tapped Mr Maxwell's shoulder and pointed to the other side of the room. Mr Maxwell's mouth ran dry and his heartbeat echoed in his ears as he swallowed hard and pushed the door wide. When he did, though, he was stunned to discover the man was the room's sole occupant. Confused, he looked to the bed to question the man but was further taken aback by the sight of rough ropes, tied to the frame, which disappeared beneath the bedspread and moved whenever the man did. Unable to look away, Mr Maxwell kept his eyes upon them as he moved around the bed until he reached a large fireplace at its foot. Mr Locke, having noticed the ropes the moment he'd entered the room, quirked a brow and cast a curious glance at Mr Maxwell. Miss Dexter, meanwhile, had decided to err on the side of propriety by staying on the other side of the threshold.

"Palmer, is that you?" the man enquired when he seemed to at last notice Mr Maxwell. Hearing the creak of a floorboard to his left, he then turned his head toward Mr Locke. "Mr Colby, are you there?" His lips quivered. "Please, I need relief…"

"Unfortunately, I am not he," Mr Locke replied.

"Wh—who are you?" the man demanded. To Mr Maxwell, he enquired, "Who is this man, Palmer?"

"I'm not 'Palmer,' sir," Mr Maxwell replied in a meek voice. "My name is Mr Joseph Maxwell, an apprentice journalist with the *Gaslight Gazette.*"

Fear contorted the man's features as he opened and closed his mouth several times before he found his voice, "A—a journalist?!"

"He is here in his capacity as a member of the Bow Street Society," Mr Locke explained. "As am I. My name is Mr Percival Locke, an illusionist, and this is our associate, Miss Georgina Dexter, who is an artist in addition to being a Bow Street Society member."

"Good evening, sir," Miss Dexter said as she gave a half-curtsey.

"Am I correct in assuming you are Mr Thaddeus Dorsey; the man who requested the Society's assistance?" Mr Locke enquired.

"Yes," Mr Dorsey replied. His features relaxed and he turned his head from Mr Locke to Mr Maxwell and back again. "Yes, I am." A broad smile swept across his face then as he exclaimed, "I am!" He chuckled. "You came! You *really* came! And Mr Colby let you *in…* I can't believe it. You're here to find Palmer, yes? I'm so very worried about him. He stopped visiting me, you know. And he was always so good at keeping his word. Fetch him. Fetch him and bring him to me."

Mr Locke moved closer, but Mr Dorsey's eyes continued to stare, unblinkingly, past him.

"That's our intention, Mr Dorsey," Mr Maxwell replied.

"I draw sketches based upon descriptions and hoped I could create one for your friend," Miss Dexter said. "Though we've now seen the signs of your physical impairment for ourselves, Mr Colby did inform us of it whilst we were outside. If you don't mind my asking, how much of your sight is lost?"

"For most of the time, I'm able to see only vague shapes and colours through a thick, white fog. There are times when I'm able to see with crystal clarity, however," Mr Dorsey replied, and the Bow Streeters exchanged surprised glances. "Though what I see can't always be relied upon. I know," Mr Dorsey patted the bed. "Palmer was here because he spoke to me. The rest don't do that." He frowned. "He was always so very kind to me."

"The rest?" Mr Maxwell enquired.

"Of what I see when I see clearly," Mr Dorsey replied, absently.

"But you saw 'Palmer' clearly?" Miss Dexter enquired.

"No, he was blurred, as all of you are now. So, he must've been there," Mr Dorsey replied with a shake of his head. "No, he was here." He gave a sad sigh.

"We will find him," Miss Dexter reassured. "Though it's highly irregular, will you permit me to enter your bedroom?"

"Of course," Mr Dorsey replied with a lifting of his fingers beneath the bedspread.

Miss Dexter hesitated, though, as she recalled his earlier request to use the chamber pot. Uncertain how to phrase such a delicate subject, she enquired, "Is there anything else you need to do before we begin?"

Mr Dorsey frowned as he tried to fathom what she was referring to. His eyebrows then sprang up as he cried, "Yes!" He turned his head toward Mr Locke. "Sir, would you be so kind?"

Mr Locke quirked his brow for a second time at the request whilst Miss Dexter left the room and closed the door. Nevertheless, Mr Locke pulled back the bedspread, released Mr Dorsey's wrists from the ropes, and turned his back. Mr Maxwell, feeling embarrassed on behalf of them all, copied Mr Locke in turning his back to face the fireplace. To distract his attention from the sound of liquid pouring into the chamber pot, he inspected contents of the mantel shelf. There was a brass and ceramic-faced mantel clock running five minutes slow, and a pile of books with torn, leather bindings. Their titles, authored by prominent legal authorities, covered various aspects of criminal law. Standing at either end of the mantel shelf was a brass candlestick with no candles, whilst an ornament of two lovers sitting upon a bench sat to the clock's left. A thin layer of dust had accumulated upon the entirety of the shelf.

To the right of the fireplace was a dark-oak, dining room chair with flat-topped arms positioned at an angle to a washstand standing against the wall. A rough, cotton towel was folded and placed upon the shelf beside ingredients to make camphorated dentifrice. These being finely ground rock chalk, camphor to create a medicated taste, and spirit of wine to moisten the camphor enough for grounding. On the top of the washstand was a matching ceramic bowl and jug filled with cold water, a cut-throat razor, a bar of carbolic soap, and tooth and shaving brushes with horsehair bristles.

"Thank you," Mr Dorsey muttered behind him, followed by a soft thud as the chamber pot was replaced under the bed. "Could you retie me, please?"

"If you insist," Mr Locke replied.

Mr Maxwell cleared his throat and ran his finger across the mantel shelf whilst Mr Locke secured their client's wrists and pulled up the bedspread.

"We are finished," Mr Locke announced and opened the door. "You may come in, now, Miss Dexter." He went to the washstand to cleanse his hands, prompting Mr Maxwell to face the bed once more.

Miss Dexter stepped inside and, with a subtle nod to Mr Locke, enquired, "May I sit, Mr Dorsey?"

"Yes, yes, of course," Mr Dorsey replied.

"Thank you," Miss Dexter said and perched upon the edge of the bed. Readying her sketchbook and pencil, she went on, "Please, tell us as much as you can about Palmer's physical appearance, Mr Dorsey."

"He has fair skin… is quite tall—I think—and has dark hair, though it might be the light in here," Mr Dorsey mused aloud.

"Was there anything else about Mr Palmer which may help us to find him?" Miss Dexter enquired. "Did he have a working-class accent, or perhaps one more akin to your own? Was slang commonly used by him when speaking, and was his voice quite deep, raspy, or, perhaps, more effeminate?"

"He *never* cursed, and I never had any reason to tell him not to; he was a *good* man—a *genuine* man," Mr Dorsey replied. "He spoke clearly, but his voice, and vocabulary, weren't what you'd call 'sophisticated,' but it didn't matter—not to him and certainly not to me. His voice… was young sounding; he wasn't a man of my age, not even close. Though I'd say he was mature beyond his years. Oh! And he always had a rather contradictory smell—a combination of carbolic soap, a mustiness that reminded me of my old books, and a slight hint of bitter almonds."

Miss Dexter finished her sketch and noted the additional points down its side. She frowned as she concluded the likeness was too vague to base a search upon. After a moment's consideration, though, she recalled a memory that could provide an answer to their problem. "I once witnessed a blind man gently touching the face of his friend; he said it was to allow him to 'see' him. Did Palmer ever allow you to touch his face in such a way, Mr Dorsey?"

"Yes, he did; the last time I saw him. It was his suggestion," Mr Dorsey replied, his eyes remaining static as he recalled that last meeting.

Miss Dexter bit her lip and said, "I have some knowledge of clay modelling… I could create a basic model of a man's head and bring it to you to touch and adjust accordingly."

"What a marvellous idea!" Mr Dorsey exclaimed with happy surprise. His smile then vanished, however. "Mr Colby really doesn't like strangers visiting me, though—for my own good. I've not told him about Palmer; he wouldn't like it. He does so much for me, you know." A worried expression fell upon his face. "You didn't tell him why you were here, did you?"

"We did…" Mr Maxwell replied. "We really had little choice, Mr Dorsey. He wouldn't let us see you."

"He has not permitted us to see you, still," Mr Locke interjected as he folded the towel and returned it to the washstand. "We were obliged to let ourselves in."

"Oh, dear…" Mr Dorsey's frown deepened. "Where is he now?"

"He went out," Mr Locke replied.

"Oh… He won't be pleased." Mr Dorsey swallowed hard. "He puts up with so much from me."

"You are our client, Mr Dorsey, not Mr Colby," Mr Locke said. "Thus, *you* are our primary concern."

"Did Mr Colby know of Palmer previously?" Mr Maxwell enquired.

Mr Dorsey shook his head.

"You said Palmer allowed you to touch his face the last time you saw him. When was that?" Mr Locke enquired.

"Two nights ago," Mr Dorsey replied.

"Have you seen him since?" Mr Locke enquired.

"No. He promised he'd visit last night but didn't; he has *never* broken his promises to me before," Mr Dorsey replied. "I'm afraid something foul might've befallen him."

"What is Palmer's Christian name?" Mr Maxwell enquired and held the top of the bedframe at Mr Dorsey's feet.

"I don't know," Mr Dorsey replied. "He only told me to call him Palmer. I never thought to ask him his full name."

"Did he only ever visit at night?" Mr Locke enquired.

"Yes, after Mr Colby went out," Mr Dorsey replied.

"Does Mr Colby go out every night?" Mr Maxwell enquired.

"Mhm. He says it gives him a much-needed break from me," Mr Dorsey replied, lamenting, "The night would go by so very fast when talking to Palmer."

"Does Mr Colby always leave at the same time?" Mr Locke enquired.

"I never know what the time is these days," Mr Dorsey replied. "I'm only able to judge the approximate time of day by the routine Mr Colby has put me in."

"Does Palmer have a key to the house?" Mr Locke enquired as he moved around the room, taking in every minute detail of its size, location within the house, and decoration. Clearly, it was never intended to be a gentleman's bedroom but a parlour or study of some sort.

"No," Mr Dorsey replied.

"How does he enter the house, then?" Mr Locke enquired.

"You know... I have no idea," Mr Dorsey replied, his features contorted by confusion.

Mr Locke pulled back the heavy curtain hanging at the sash window and found small, round nails embedded into the frame at regular intervals. An attempt to open the window confirmed the nails were preventing it from being slid upward. He peered through the dirty pane and saw it overlooked a small garden at the house's rear. When he stepped to the left, he could see into a second window belonging to another part of the house. Built onto its rear, this second area appeared to be a kitchen from what he could see. "Can Mr Palmer pick locks?"

"Not that I know of. At least, I don't remember hearing any locks being picked," Mr Dorsey replied.

"Perhaps you were asleep?" Mr Maxwell suggested.

Mr Dorsey shook his head. "No. Once Mr Colby leaves, I know it won't be long until Palmer arrives, so I lie here, wait, and listen. I've never heard anyone doing things to the lock whilst I've been lying here."

"If I may be so bold, Mr Dorsey, why is your bedroom on the ground floor?" Mr Locke enquired.

"It's safer this way—for me," Mr Dorsey replied. "Stairs are perilous for one who's blind. The bulky, and the exceedingly small, pieces of furniture I possess have also been placed upstairs so I don't trip over a table or catch my foot upon a leg. They're antique, you know, handed down to me by my father, who inherited them from *his* father. Mr Colby and dear Timothy put only the essential pieces in here, the parlour, and the library— though I only use the last if Mrs Bonham visits. Literature is one of the great passions I mourn the most. She reads to me often."

"Who are Timothy and Mrs Bonham?" Mr Maxwell enquired, stepping aside as Mr Locke crouched in front of the fireplace.

"Timothy is my brother and Mrs Bonham is a good friend of mine," Mr Dorsey replied. "She lives next door with her brother, Mr Lanford Glasgow, who was my former business partner in my law firm before this wretched blindness descended upon me."

"You—" Mr Maxwell begun but cut himself short when he noticed Mr Locke poking his head into the fireplace. Bewildered as to the reasoning behind his fellow Bow Streeter's actions, but deciding there must be some, he resumed, "You are confined to the ground floor rooms, then?"

"Not *confined,* exactly," Mr Dorsey replied. "I can't go upstairs on my own, yes, but Mr Colby has been good enough to escort me to the upper floors and guide me around in the past. He's even described the furniture to me, though he isn't the most eloquent of men, you know."

"Is there any way Palmer could have gained access to the house via the upstairs rooms?" Mr Locke

41

enquired as he finished his inspection of the chimney and fireplace.

"Oh, *no*," Mr Dorsey replied. "All the windows are kept locked. Besides, anyone attempting to break in through a window would be seen by Mr Glasgow's household, if at the back, and by Constable Grey if at the front; he patrols far more than he's required to."

"We noticed," Mr Locke replied, leaving the room to look up the staircase.

"You said Mr Colby does a great deal for you. In what capacity?" Mr Maxwell enquired. Seeing Mr Locke move out of sight, though, he headed for the door but reconsidered when he realised Miss Dexter would be left alone with their client.

"He's my attendant," Mr Dorsey replied. "It was the only solution my brother gave me when I said I wanted to stay at home. I'm not unsafe."

Mr Maxwell and Miss Dexter looked to the restraints with equal concern.

"The ropes are only used at night, when Mr Colby is out, so I don't hurt myself."

Mr Maxwell and Miss Dexter exchanged worried glances, but it was the former who straightened, cleared his throat, and began, "Well—"

"I think we have enough to be going along with," Mr Locke interrupted as he strode back into the room and looked between his fellow Bow Streeters. "Do you not agree?"

"I do," Mr Maxwell replied, relieved the illusionist had returned when he did.

"Me too," Miss Dexter added, putting her sketchbook and pencil into her satchel and rising to her feet. She laid a gentle hand upon Mr Dorsey's shoulder and whispered, "I will create the model tonight and would like to return at ten thirty tomorrow morning so you may make the adjustments. Would that be convenient?"

"Oh, yes," Mr Dorsey replied with a warm smile. "Thank you for coming here this evening and taking on my case. I appreciate it greatly."

"You know how to contact the Society again if you remember anything further about Mr Palmer," Mr Locke said and retrieved the chamber pot from under the bed. "I shall dispose of this for you, Mr Dorsey." To Mr Maxwell and Miss Dexter, he added, "I shan't be a moment."

"We'll wait for you in the hallway," Mr Maxwell replied. "Good night, Mr Dorsey."

"Good night!" Mr Dorsey cried, beaming from ear-to-ear.

Miss Dexter bade him a quiet good night also and left the room ahead of her fellow Bow Streeters. Whilst Mr Maxwell then walked with her to the front door, Mr Locke took a sharp left and entered the kitchen. He emptied the chamber pot into the sink and worked the water pump a few times to wash away the urine.

Rather than returning the pot to Mr Dorsey, though, he left it in the sink and went to the back door instead. Examining both it and the windows, he discovered the latter had been nailed shut whilst the lock of the former was rusted beyond use. The door's frame was also sturdy and windowless. The garden wall wasn't high enough to prevent one from scaling it, however.

Collecting the chamber pot, he returned it to Mr Dorsey's bedroom and bid him a final goodnight before joining the others. "There is something amiss about all of this," Mr Locke whispered as he opened the front door for them. "I simply cannot put my finger on what it is." He allowed them to leave ahead of him and gave Mr Dorsey's bedroom door a final glance. Stepping onto the porch, he heard the hall clock strike the hour of seven thirty as he closed the door and secured it with his picks. His carriage had returned and was waiting by the curb. He gestured toward it as he descended the steps. "Let us return to Miss Trent."

THREE

Thick, sulphurous smoke poured along the underground railway platform, ushered forwards by the engine as it pulled in. Doors of the first, second, and third-class carriages were flung open even as the train slowed, and new and old passengers swiftly exchanged places. Yet, the late hour meant their numbers weren't as considerable as one may expect. The clock, suspended from an iron chain, announced it was a quarter past nine. There were two platforms at the station. The current one was for trains destined for Bishop's Road in the eastbound direction, whilst the other opposite was for trains heading in the westbound direction for Farringdon Street. Both lines formed part of the Metropolitan Railway, originally opened in 1863. At the platforms' rears were curved walls covered by cluttered collages of posters advertising Maskelyne and Cooke's astounding magical feats at the Egyptian Hall, Sunlight Soap, and everything in between. The slapdash way advertisements were pasted over one another—often by rival companies—also meant frequent travellers on the line had little hope of reading them all.

Another remarkable feature of the eastbound platform—and others like it at some of the Metropolitan Railway's other underground stations—was the compact bar. There a weary traveller could moisten their throat dried by the smoky confines of the train's carriage. These bars, referred to as "subterranean hotels" by Miss Beale in her pamphlet *Called to the Bar*, were staffed by first-class barmaids, sub-manageresses and manageresses who'd work upwards to eleven hours a day. They earned Miss Beale's nickname from the fact they included rooms which often slept six of the staff members at a time. Naturally, they could've gone home once their shift was over—some lived only a mile or so away—but men, referred to as "hangers on," would often follow. This, coupled with their usual home time being midnight once the clean-up was complete, led most barmaids to remain at their place of work. The eastbound platform's bar was typical of its kind; small, draughty, unventilated—despite being engulfed in clouds of engine and tobacco smoke on a near constant basis—and soaked in the combined stench of stale alcohol and sulphur. Due to its underground location, daylight into the bar was impossible. Thus, its gas lamps were kept lit twenty-four hours a day.

The barmaids stood, rather than sat, behind the bar for the entirety of their shifts. This inevitably led to great physical exhaustion and the partaking of drinks. Each barmaid was given a drink allowance, with the teetotallers amongst them being permitted to drink ginger beer or lemonade instead. Regardless of their preferred tipple, though, they were expected to take it from the different-coloured glass measures standing upon a shelf behind the bar. These measures were used to store the dregs poured from customers' glasses once they were finished. The white measure was for brandy, the blue for gin, the green for whiskey, and the red for rum. The barmaids would often switch their customer's order for this waste, though, and drink the order themselves. As Miss Trent took her place amongst the customers at the bar, she saw one of the barmaids doing just that.

"Brandy, please," Miss Trent said to her, laying a timetable on the bar and taking out a purse. "And *actual* brandy; none of that muck you've got in there." She gestured to the white measure.

"Evenin', Miss Trent," greeted a second barmaid who'd leant across the bar to set down a gentleman's whisky. She was in her late twenties with loose-curled, blonde hair hanging about her shoulders. Her hair had a fine layer of soot upon its strands, courtesy of the many engines which had passed through that day. Her fair-skinned cheeks were also smudged with dirt.

"Evening, Polly," Miss Trent replied with a warm smile.

"I'll do this one," Polly told her fellow barmaid as she stepped in front of her. Pouring some brandy from a bottle on the shelf, she put the glass down before Miss Trent, and brushed her hand against hers. "Been a long time since we seen you down here."

"It has," Miss Trent replied, momentarily resting her hand upon Polly's. "It wasn't intentional."

"It never is," Polly remarked with a hint of contempt. Sensing the sub-manageress' eyes upon her, she glanced over her shoulder to see the disapproval on her face. "Best be getting on," Polly muttered and moved down the bar to serve another customer.

Miss Trent took a well-earned sip of her brandy as she caught sight of a brown bowler hat being put onto the bar out the corner of her eye. Its owner was on her other side smoking a pipe. The distinct odour of its tobacco drifted into her nostrils but soon became lost in the station's miasma of smells.

"How bad was it?" the pipe-smoker enquired in a softly spoken, male voice.

"'Knackered' was Mr Snyder's exact wording," Miss Trent replied and turned toward the tunnel as if awaiting a train's arrival.

"And the others?" the pipe-smoker enquired with a deep sigh.

"Unharmed." She lifted the glass to her lips. "No thanks to Dr Weeks." Taking another sip, she then cradled the glass in her brown-cotton gloved hands whilst her gaze returned to the tunnel. Hearing the pipe-smoker's footsteps move around her, then, she turned back to the bar.

"You told John it was Mr Maxwell's slip of the tongue." The pipe-smoker's hushed voice said from behind her. Hearing the snapping shut of a pocket watch, followed by a soft sigh, she next heard the pipe-smoker's footsteps move back to his original place at the bar. Putting her drink down, she retrieved a brass case from her purse and took a cigarette from it. As soon as she'd placed it between her lips, the pipe-smoker's hand appeared holding a lit match. He enquired, "May I?"

"Thank you, sir." Miss Trent allowed him to light her cigarette. "It was." Imbibing the smoke for a moment, she then leaned closer to the pipe-smoker to dispose of the excess ash into the ashtray at his elbow. As she did so, she whispered, "But Dr Weeks abandoned the cab, and them." Placing her elbow upon the bar's edge, she leant upon it and looked squarely at the pipe-smoker for the first time.

He was in his early thirties with short, dark-brown hair parted to the right, sideburns which framed his slender face, and a neat moustache that dominated his upper lip. Warm, hazel-brown eyes crowned the high cheekbones of his fair complexion. A hand-knitted, burgundy scarf hid his cream-coloured shirt and dark-brown tie, whilst the shin-length, black overcoat did the same to his three-piece, brown-tweed suit. With his pipe still lit, he rested the heel of that hand upon the bar's edge whilst the other rested in his pocket. He was a couple of inches taller than her, making him just shy of six feet.

"Waiting for a train, sir, or just got off one?" Miss Trent enquired.

"Waiting for one," the pipe-smoker replied and ordered some lemonade. As he counted the money, he added in a soft voice so only Miss Trent heard, "Dr Weeks has to be careful."

"Won't be long to wait," Miss Trent said and watched the barmaid set down the glass and take his money. When she'd walked to the bar's other end, Miss Trent leant across him to add more ash to the ashtray. As she did so, she whispered, "I know, but he should've checked they weren't hurt."

"Yes, I know," the pipe-smoker replied in a casual tone. Holding the glass to his lips, he added in a hushed voice, "Holborn received the file." Glancing sideways at her, he caught her questioning look but gave a shake of his head before he took a mouthful of lemonade.

She sighed. "I should've known Bird would take the credit." She drank some more of her brandy. "*This* time will be *our* time."

"Hopefully." The pipe-smoker emptied his spent tobacco into the ashtray. "John passed on your message about Mr Dorsey. What did they find?"

"Him—tied to a bed," Miss Trent replied as she leant over him, again, this time to crush out her cigarette.

The pipe-smoker's brows lifted in unison but, to any onlooker, he appeared to be concentrating on the final scraping-out of his pipe.

"For his own safety; he's blind and left alone at night," Miss Trent explained.

The pipe-smoker's hand stilled as his lips parted. After a moment's pause to consider the situation, though, he remarked, "Not a straightforward one, then."

Miss Trent smirked. "No." She drained her glass and placed it within the barmaid's reach. "But we'll play our parts, as we always do, and get to the bottom of it."

"I have no doubt," the pipe-smoker returned her smile and glanced down the bar. "How is Miss Polly, by the way?" Though he had a knowing look to his eyes, he kept his voice hushed to ensure only Miss Trent heard him.

"Fine, as far as I can tell. I hadn't seen her until today."

"Is that because—?"

"No, it's not," Miss Trent interrupted. "I've been busy—as you well know." The rumble of a train within the pitch-black tunnel momentarily distracted her. "And you also know she doesn't let him visit her here."

The pipe-smoker hummed and looked to the tunnel, too. "I don't suppose you know how one might get to Charing Cross?"

Miss Trent slid her timetable toward him. "You're on the right line, sir. If you check the timetable, I'm sure you'll be able to gauge your progress."

The pipe-smoker lifted the timetable's cover and saw some folded pieces of paper tucked inside. Smiling, he replied, "Ah yes, I see where I must go."

The sound of the approaching train was almost deafening as its engine burst forth from the tunnel like a demon flying from the gates of hell. Several of the bar's customers covered their mouths with their handkerchiefs as the platform was once again engulfed by sulphurous smoke. The shrill grinding of metal against metal followed as the engine came to a halt, the doors of its carriages once again flying open as the exchange of passengers recommenced.

"That's my train," the pipe-smoker announced and put on his bowler hat. Indicating the timetable, he enquired, "May I keep this, Miss?"

"Be my guest, sir," Miss Trent replied.

The pipe-smoker thanked her with a smile and was soon on his way. She watched him until he'd climbed into a third-class carriage and, as the train rolled forward, debated with herself about having another drink. Deciding against it, she left the station via the stairs with a discreet wink to Polly as she passed.

FOUR

"Georgie!" Mrs Dexter called through the locked door of her daughter's bedroom. "Are you in there?!"

"Yes, Ma-Ma," Miss Dexter replied as she put pencils and paper from a battered, paint-covered table into her satchel.

"Breakfast is ready."

"I shan't be having any Ma-Ma, I have to go out."

"You have to eat, Georgie. You ate hardly any dinner before you went to your teaching last night. Then you locked yourself up in this room of yours for the remainder of the night. It's not healthy." Mrs Dexter knocked. "Will you open this door, please, and speak to me face to face?"

Miss Dexter unlocked and opened the door to reveal a man's disembodied head sitting upon the table.

Mrs Dexter gasped and pressed her plump hand against her broad bosom. "*What* is that?"

"It's a clay model, Ma-Ma." Miss Dexter put on her satchel to hang across her body and lifted the wooden board upon which the head stood.

"I can *see* that, but what is it *for*?" Mrs Dexter insisted as her daughter shuffled around her with the board precariously balanced against her body. Mrs Dexter was a short woman in her late forties. She had brown eyes, fair skin which sagged from her cheeks and chin, and dark-grey hair streaked with white, pinned into a bun at the base of her skull. A black, A-line skirt hung over her wide hips, protected by a white apron showing signs of her early-morning cooking. The remainder of her attire comprised of scuffed, black shoes and a dark-blue, long-sleeved blouse with a high neck. "Is this for another of your cases?" Her daughter nodded, and Mrs Dexter followed as she moved towards the stairs. "That Society should pay you for all this work you're doing."

"I'm a volunteer, Ma-Ma," Miss Dexter replied as she descended with careful steps. "Besides, it's good for my work." Relieved when she'd reached the bottom of the stairs, Miss Dexter placed the model upon a short, square-topped table just as someone knocked upon the front door.

"It's good for George Dexter, you mean," Mrs Dexter retorted and stepped past her daughter to open the door. The moment she saw who it was, though, her scowl vanished, and she beamed at the visitor. "Good *morning,* Mr Snyder."

"Good morning, Mrs Dexter," Mr Snyder replied with a lift of his hat. "Miss Dexter." He looked between them. "How is Mr Dexter this morning?"

"He's well, thank you," Mrs Dexter replied and leant around the parlour's open doorway to address her husband. "Aren't you, Henry?"

"Mhmm, yus," Mr Dexter replied without lifting his gaze from the *Gaslight Gazette's* morning edition. He was an inch taller than his wife and considerably slimmer. In his mid-fifties, he'd lost almost all his hair. The little that remained sat around the base of his head in a closely cut, light-grey line. He did, however, have rather impressive grey whiskers, moustache, and beard. A senior accountant at a City of London firm, he wore a three-piece, black suit of acceptable quality, a pressed, white shirt with a starched, Eton collar attached, and a black tie.

"Want me to take that?" Mr Snyder enquired and pointed to the model.

"Yes, please. Thank you," Miss Dexter replied as she and her mother stepped aside to allow him the space to collect it. Following him outside, she then put her hand upon her mother's shoulder and kissed her cheek. "I'll be home for dinner, Ma-Ma."

* * *

"Sergeant Bird wants the usual for the story," Mr Baldwin said over the din of many typewriters and conversations in the *Gaslight Gazette*'s office. At thirty-five he was one of the newspaper's most experienced journalists. He was standing before the desk of its editor, Mr Morse, holding Bird's scrawled note alongside a lit cigarette. The sleeves of his off-white shirt were rolled up to his elbows, whilst the remainder of his attire consisted of a dark-grey waist coat, black trousers, and dark-green cravat with brown, floral print. His mousy-brown, thick goatee beard and moustache complemented the dark brown of his short, unkempt hair and shallow sideburns. "Want me to give it him?"

"What's he offerin'?" Mr Morse enquired as he smoked his own hand-rolled cigarette.

"Full details of the crash and arrest of the coffee house con artists," Mr Baldwin replied.

"Bloody coppers," Mr Morse muttered and flicked ash into an empty mug beside his typewriter. Seeing Mr Maxwell in the doorway of his office, he growled, "*What?*"

"P—Pardon the intrusion, sir," Mr Maxwell stuttered, toying with his cravat's bow. "But, well, if you're speaking of the accident yesterday, I, er, I have a first-hand account."

"Yeah, I know: Sergeant Bird," Mr Morse replied.

Mr Maxwell's eyes widened, and he shook his head. "Oh, no," he said, "That's not right. He wasn't there, at least not until *after* the crash. *I* was there though, along with Miss Dexter and Mr Snyder. *We* were the ones who caught the con artists."

"*You?*" Mr Morse scoffed.

"Well, not *me* on my own, but the Bow Street Society," Mr Maxwell replied and held up a typed document. "I have the full account here, sir."

Mr Morse snatched it from him and read it over. Once he was done, his gaze shifted to Mr Maxwell as he enquired, "Is this true?"

"Ev—every word of it, sir," Mr Maxwell stammered. Clearing his throat and wiping the sweat from his palms when Mr Baldwin was given the article to read, he went on, "I'd like it to be included in the evening edition, along with a piece asking for information on the whereabouts of a missing man named Palmer."

Mr Morse crushed out his cigarette and glared at Mr Maxwell as he replied, "We'll put it in 'cause you saved us a few bob, but if you've lied to me—"

"I haven't," Mr Maxwell interrupted. "You have my word, sir."

Mr Baldwin gave the article back to his editor with a nod of approval.

"And the other article, regarding the missing man?" Mr Maxwell enquired. "I shall have more information in the next couple of hours."

Mr Morse glanced at the clock on the wall. It was nine-thirty in the morning. He settled back and rested his arms upon those of the chair. Scratching his nose, he replied, "That can go in, too." He pointed at Mr Maxwell. "But *only* if you get the copy to me by midday."

"Thank you, sir!" Mr Maxwell exclaimed, stepping backwards into a colleague's desk. Apologising to them over his shoulder, he then sidestepped around it and hurried back to his own, shabbier one in a narrow corner of the office. Slipping a sheet of paper into his typewriter and winding it into position, he then glanced out the window and saw a cab pull up with Mr Snyder in the driver's seat. Leaping to his feet, he gathered up his coat and strode to the door, knocking a pile of papers off a desk as he went. Unable to assist with their retrieval, he apologised profusely to his colleague and ran downstairs. Bidding farewell to the man behind the printing press there, he soon emerged into the hustle and bustle of London's Fleet Street. With only one arm in his coat, he opened the cab's door and beamed at Miss Dexter sitting inside with the model upon her lap.

* * *

"No!" The woman cried, rushing toward her husband, but it was too late. A spark erupted into the gloom of the gas light as the flint-lock pistol fired, and Mr Locke tumbled over a large trunk behind him. The distraught woman was shoved aside by her irate husband who approached the chest with his pistol held high. Her desperate pleas were stifled by her violent sobs as she fell to her knees and clutched her trembling hands to her mouth.

Suddenly, Mr Locke leapt up from behind the chest and drove his fist into the underside of his would-be murderer's jaw. A pair of cymbals crashed in the instant he made contact and the husband reeled backward, collapsing upon the floor. When he didn't move, Mr Locke ran a hand over his hair and spat the shot into his palm. Violins burst forth in a wave of triumphant harmony as he turned to the unoccupied auditorium and held the shot aloft. He held his pose long enough to imagine the roar of the applause and cast the shot aside in perfect timing with the violins' crescendo. Stepping onto the chest, he unfurled his arm and reached out to the woman as the violins quietened.

The lifting of her head followed their gradual build into a second crescendo as a romantic flute accompanied them. Upon seeing Mr Locke was alive she rose to her feet and opened her arms to him in a sweeping, graceful motion. She then bounded across the stage and leapt toward him, his hands catching her by the waist and lifting her prone form above his head. Holding her there for several moments, he lowered and held her close as she wrapped her leg around his waist and arched her back in a feigned faint. With the continued accompaniment of the violins and flutes, he took her hand, and eased her upward to rest against him. With his arm tight around her waist he lifted their hands above their heads and rested his forehead against hers. Their hands descended in time with the fading of the violins, followed by the final burst of flutes as their eyes met and their lips closed the distance between them. Yet, just as they were about to kiss, the curtain fell, and the rehearsal was over.

"Clear the stage!" A man yelled, emerging from the wings on stage left.

Mr Locke allowed the woman to stand upon the chest and, after jumping down, took her by the hand to assist her in doing the same. She appeared to stumble as she stepped off, though, obliging Mr Locke to catch her.

"Are you hurt, Amelia?" he enquired.

"No," the woman replied with scarlet cheeks. "Thank you, Mr Locke."

"Good." He set her down. "I am glad to hear it."

"Bring the Paris set for the chorus line!" The man from the wings yelled.

Amelia's blush deepened as she pulled away and left the stage, fanning herself with her hand as she went.

A veritable army of stagehands descended upon the stage to change the scenery and props whilst a group of can-can-inspired female dancers gathered in the wings.

"Pardon me, ladies," Mr Locke said as he slipped through the middle of them.

"Certainly, Mr Locke," one replied with a giggle.

"Splendid rehearsal, Mr Locke," complimented another.

"Thank you, Miss Cotton," Mr Locke replied to the second as he walked backwards to face her. This caused the first to giggle again, but there was longing in all their eyes when he turned back around and walked away.

"It's such a shame he's married," Miss Cotton remarked to the agreement of the others.

"How was I?" the on-stage husband enquired as he fell into step beside Mr Locke.

"Excellent." Mr Locke shook his hand. "Do that tonight and we shall bring the house down."

"I will, sir! Thank you!"

Mr Locke gave him an appreciative smile, unlocked the door to his dressing room, and slipped inside. Due to his elevated status as the Paddington Palladium's owner and headline act, his dressing room was both the closest to the stage and the largest. Its walls were adorned by a plain, dark-blue paper whilst the floor was polished oak boards covered by a floral rug of varying shades of blue. An oak desk with three deep drawers at either end occupied the entire right-hand wall. Its surface was polished to a shine whilst its edges and drawers were decorated with hand-carved stars, moons, and signs of the zodiac. In its centre stood a matching ceramic bowl and jug set with a hand-painted, Chinese-style design. Lined up on its left were combs, scissors for both hair and nails, and nail files. To its right was a bar of lavender-scented carbolic soap, a box of powdered talc, a round, ceramic tub containing chalk dentifrice, and a horse-hair toothbrush. Tubes of grease paint and bottles of black hair dye lined the desk's back edge beneath an immense mirror. Its gold gilt frame depicted two women, barely attired in togas, holding vases of grapes, simple scrolls, and leaf embellishments. Standing to the left of the door, opposite the desk, was a five-panelled, oak, folding screen with Chinese dragons, lotus flowers and bamboo carved into it. Beyond this were an immense trunk and a dark-blue chaise lounge standing against the wall.

He removed the cheap frock coat he'd worn on stage and draped it over the chair tucked beneath the desk. Retrieving a key from on top of the mirror, he unlocked a drawer and took from it a brown, leather-bound box. Opening it to check its contents—a vial, needle, and tourniquet—were present and correct, he then took it behind the screen and deposited it into the interior pocket of a tailor-made, black frock coat that hung there. A sudden knock upon the door prompted him to emerge, though, and relock the drawer. Yet, only once the key was back in its hiding place did he call, "Come in!"

The door opened and a man in his late twenties wearing a valet's uniform entered.

"Good afternoon, James," Mr Locke greeted. "I require my stage coat to be cleaned and pressed for tonight's performance."

"Yes, sir," James replied as he followed Mr Locke behind the screen to assist him in dressing.

"Also, my dinner jacket and shirt. I shall be dining with Mrs Locke before we open tonight."

"Will you require your other shirt pressed, too, sir?"

"Yes," Mr Locke considered. "Have it ready for after my performance, along with a bouquet of roses and a box of Turkish Delight."

"Very good, sir," James replied, holding up the tailor-made frock coat for Mr Locke to slip his arms into. When he had, he lifted it onto his shoulders, gave its bottom a gentle tug, and smoothed out the creases with his hands. "When should we expect you, sir?"

"Four o'clock. I have some Bow Street Society business to attend to and then some other appointments," Mr Locke replied, putting on his top hat and taking up his cane. "Good day, James."

"Good day, sir."

FIVE

Mr Colby glared at Mr Locke, Mr Maxwell, and Miss Dexter the moment he saw them standing on the porch. His grip tightened on the front door as he sneered, "I should put the coppers onto you lot."

"Is Mr Thaddeus Dorsey at home?" Mr Locke enquired.

"You know full-well he is," Mr Colby threw back. Nevertheless, he stepped back and opened the door wide. "He's in there."

Mr Locke stepped inside and, removing his top hat, stated, "You shall have to be more precise than that."

"In *there*." Mr Colby pointed to the first door on the right that was standing ajar.

"*Thank* you," Mr Locke replied with a dip of his head.

"Thank you, sir," Miss Dexter echoed in a timid voice as she passed Mr Colby upon entering the house.

Having been given the unenviable task of carrying the clay model inside, Mr Maxwell grunted under its weight whilst navigating the lip and sides of the doorframe. Peering over it once he'd managed to get it into the hallway, he began, "I don't suppose you could—"

"No," Mr Colby interrupted. "I couldn't." He slammed the door and almost walked up Mr Maxwell's heels as he followed him across the hallway. When they neared the other door, though, Mr Colby stepped around and in front of Mr Maxwell, causing him to veer sharply to the right. It was only by wedging the board's front edge against the nearest wall that Mr Maxwell was able to avoid disaster. Breathless from the shock, and suffering a racing heart besides, he glared at Mr Colby whilst he shoved Miss Dexter and Mr Locke aside. Entering the room ahead of them, Mr Colby announced, "The housebreakers are here."

Mr Maxwell shook his head in disgust and eased the board away from the wall. Mr Locke and Miss Dexter were standing just inside the room, so he stood at the threshold. An armchair opposite had its back to them, but Mr Maxwell presumed its occupant was Mr Dorsey. Mr Colby was stood over him, speaking close to his ear.

"Yes, I understand," Mr Dorsey mumbled.

Mr Colby momentarily squeezed his shoulder in a vice-like grip and collected a tray of tea things from the low table in front of him. Departing in the same bullish manner in which he'd arrived, he then disappeared into the kitchen.

Although it was morning, the day remained overcast. The chill of outdoors had also penetrated the room due, in large part, to the meagre amount of coal in the wrought-iron hearth. Mr Dorsey's armchair was at least the closest to it, but both he and the room were enshrouded in gloom. Despite there being gas lamps mounted upon the walls, the space was partially lit by a single lamp standing upon a table at Mr Dorsey's elbow. Additional weak light also came from the window opposite the fireplace. Overlooking Bow Street, its thick, heavy curtains were tied back.

"Good morning," Mr Dorsey greeted without facing them. "This is Mrs Esta Bonham. Esta, this is Mr Percival Locke, Mr Joseph Maxwell, and Miss Georgina Dexter from the Bow Street Society."

As they ventured further into the room, they were surprised to find a rather beautiful-looking woman perched upon a two-seater sofa across from Mr Dorsey. The light was so dim they'd failed to notice her before. She was in her early-thirties with shoulder-length, dirty-blonde, curly hair which was lifted and pinned at the back of her head. Positioned vertically upon her head's summit, with its tip brushing against her forehead, was a narrow, boat-shaped, navy-blue hat with upturned, velvet brims on either side. Fabric flowers in varying shades of blue were intermingled with cream behind the hat's brims. Her attire, meanwhile, comprised of several components. The first was a bone inlaid corset undergarment that kept her waist narrow and her breasts lifted. The second was a long-sleeved jacket with two sets of pearl buttons running from her bust to her waist, a white lace panel to cover her bosom, and navy-blue lapels. Finally, her bustle skirts completed the ensemble. Both her jacket and skirts were adorned with baby-blue and navy-blue vertical stripes.

Sitting with perfect poise and posture, Mrs Bonham inclined her head and said, "Good afternoon, sirs, miss. It is an absolute pleasure to meet you; Mr Dorsey has already told me all about you." Her pale-blue eyes turned to Mr Locke. "I'm curious, though, sir. Are you the same Mr Percival Locke who performs magic at the Paddington Palladium?"

"I am," Mr Locke replied with a warm twinkle in his eyes. "And the pleasure is all ours, Mrs Bonham. Mr Dorsey speaks very highly of you and, now that I have met you, I can see why."

"You are very kind, sir," Mrs Bonham replied as her cheeks flushed pink.

"We've brought the clay model," Mr Maxwell announced as he approached Mr Dorsey. "Where should I put it?" he grunted. "Sooner rather than later, please."

"On the table here should be fine," Mr Dorsey replied. As he reached to touch the dark, blurry mass, though, he winced, and his hand went to rest upon his side instead. Mrs Bonham leant forward at once but withdrew again a heartbeat later when she remembered they weren't alone.

Mr Maxwell, who'd been in the process of putting the model down, noticed their odd behaviour and enquired, "Is something wrong?"

"No—" Mr Dorsey and Mrs Bonham simultaneously replied, stopping at the realisation of their error and exchanging nervous glances. Mrs Bonham's cheeks had also flushed a deeper shade of pink.

"Muscles are just a little stiff this morning," Mr Dorsey continued. Holding his ribs, he settled back into his armchair with a soft sigh.

"It's a rather impressive model," Mrs Bonham complimented.

"Thank you," Miss Dexter replied.

"*You* made it?" Mrs Bonham enquired, stunned.

"Yes, I'm an art teacher and artist in addition to volunteering for the Society," Miss Dexter explained. "Mr Dorsey, I've sculpted the clay to mimic as much of your description as possible, but, as we discussed, we need you to inspect it with your hands and make any adjustments you feel necessary. We'll then have a photographer capture its likeness so we may distribute it and the description of Palmer's other mannerisms as widely as possible."

"Have you ever met Palmer, Mrs Bonham?" Mr Maxwell enquired.

"Certainly not," Mrs Bonham rebuffed with offended eyes.

"Palmer only visits me at night," Mr Dorsey reminded him. "Whilst, on most days, Mrs Bonham visits me for an hour or two in the afternoon." He traced the contours of the model's face with his fingertips and pinched the bridge of its nose. "By the way, how is Malcolm, Esta?"

"Still frightfully unwell, I'm afraid," Mrs Bonham replied with a sigh. "He can't seem to keep anything down."

"Who is Malcolm, if I may ask?" Mr Locke enquired as he strolled over to the window. Though appearing to look out onto Bow Street, his focus was in fact the window's frame. It, like the bedroom and kitchen windows, was nailed shut. *Curious*, he thought.

"My cat. I've had him since he was a kitten," Mrs Bonham replied.

"Esta usually brings him for me to stroke; I find it very calming," Mr Dorsey interjected whilst his fingers worked to make the model's lips smaller.

"Lanford detests him," Mrs Bonham remarked as she watched Mr Dorsey's hands.

"Mr Lanford Glasgow is your brother, correct?" Mr Maxwell enquired.

Mrs Bonham turned cool eyes to him and, in a cooler tone, replied, "Yes, that's right." To Miss Dexter, she said, "You mentioned earlier you intend to have a photographer capture the model's likeness. Lanford has a photography business in addition to his law firm—"

"The law firm you were a former partner of, Mr Dorsey?" Mr Maxwell interrupted.

"Yes; Mr Glasgow bought my half of the business when I lost my sight," Mr Dorsey replied. He pushed up the model's cheeks and smoothed down its cheekbones to make them more refined.

"As I was saying," Mrs Bonham continued with a glare to Mr Maxwell. When he edged away with a sheepish expression to stand beside Mr Locke, she went on, "Miss Dexter, Lanford may be able to take the photograph if he hasn't any other appointments today."

"If you could ask him, Mrs Bonham, we would very much appreciate it," Miss Dexter replied with a smile.

"Yes, for I have never met a photographer amongst our members," Mr Locke interjected and touched Mr Maxwell's elbow to get his attention before pointing at the window frame. At his confused expression, Mr Locke put his hand on the windowsill to indicate the nails whilst half-turning to the others and saying, "Mr Dorsey, it only occurred to me after our parting last night that we did not ask what you and Mr Palmer spoke of when you met. Could you enlighten us now?"

"Spoke of?" Mr Dorsey enquired. He and Mrs Bonham looked to one another, but he cleared his throat, shook his head several times, and replied, "Nothing... nothing at all."

"You spoke of nothing?" Mr Locke probed.

"Nothing of import," Mr Dorsey snapped. "What does it matter, anyway? It shan't help us find Mr Palmer any sooner. Speaking of which, I'm done." He pulled his hands away and they all moved forward to inspect his work. Prior to his input, the model was plain enough to pass for any man in London. After he'd made his adjustments, though, the model had only gained a minor degree of refinement. There were no scars or deformities; nothing to distinguish Palmer from the crowd. Still, all they'd wanted was a starting point and now they had it.

"That's very good, Mr Dorsey," Miss Dexter said. "Mr Maxwell, would you take the model, please?"

"Hm?" Mr Maxwell enquired as her voice roused him from his stunned reverie. Mr Dorsey had done considerably better than he'd expected. "Oh, yes… yes, of course." He lifted the model with a soft grunt and carried it to the door. As soon as he'd reached it, though, he was halted by Mr Dorsey's frightened gasp. Thinking their client may have forgotten to add a detail to the model, Mr Maxwell therefore turned back around but was confused to find Mr Dorsey staring at an empty corner of the room.

"Get out of here," Mr Dorsey commanded as he rose to his feet. "I said *get out*!" He swiped at the air above Mrs Bonham's head, causing her to shriek and be pulled out of harm's way by Mr Locke. Miss Dexter, also frightened by the sight, retreated to the door and both ladies sought refuge in the hallway.

"Don't you laugh at me!" Mr Dorsey yelled. Flipping over the table, he then approached the corner like a cat stalking a mouse.

Mr Colby, having heard the ruckus from the kitchen, shoved the ladies aside and ran into the room. Without hesitation, he punched the back of Mr Dorsey's head to daze him and hooked his arms under his patient's. Clasping his own hands against the back of Mr Dorsey's neck, Mr Colby thereby forced Mr Dorsey's shoulders back and threw him face first upon the sofa. This was swiftly followed by Mr Colby pinning him down with a knee between his shoulder blades whilst he retrieved a length of coarse rope from his pocket. Gripping Mr Dorsey's wrist, he tied it to the other and secured them with a tight knot. A second length of rope was then retrieved from his other pocket that he used to secure Mr Dorsey's ankles.

"*Release* me!" Mr Dorsey demanded.

"Shut up!" Mr Colby growled with a smack to the back of Mr Dorsey's head. Glancing at Mr Locke and Mr Maxwell as he made a make-shift gag from a dirty towel hooked through his belt, Mr Colby ordered, "Get out!" Though they were reluctant to do so, the two Bow Streeters obeyed whilst Mr Colby applied the gag and climbed off his patient, panting. The curtains were closed with a couple of harsh tugs and Mr Colby slammed the door behind him as he joined the others. "Got what you wanted?" he sneered at the Bow Streeters. Locking the door and depositing its key into his pocket, he dismissed them with a sweep of his hand. "Clear off!"

"We are going," Mr Locke replied, escorting the others outside.

Mr Colby followed them, though, and ensured the door was locked after they'd left. Upon returning to the locked one and hearing Mr Dorsey's yells, he kicked it and ordered, "Shut up!" The yells fell silent in an instant and Mr Colby went back into the kitchen, muttering, "Selfish fool…"

* * *

The footman who answered Mrs Bonham's knock was tall, around six feet, and of slender build. He wore the traditional uniform of an open black, waist-length jacket with tails over a pale yellow, button-down waistcoat with black, horizontal stripes. The remainder of his attire was the more ordinary black trousers and white shirt with matching bow tie. He was around twenty years old with high cheekbones, a narrow-bridged nose, and electric-blue eyes. These features, combined with his age and short, neatly combed black hair, made him rather handsome. The faint scent of carbolic soap lingered around him as he allowed his mistress and her guests to enter the considerable hallway beyond. He said, "Good afternoon, ma'am."

"Good afternoon, Perkins," she replied. "Is my brother available?"

"He has a client sitting for him, ma'am."

"Ah, I see. When he is finished, could you tell him he has some new clients in the waiting room?"

"Certainly, ma'am." Perkins held his arm out to the others. "Please, may I take your coats?"

Superficially, the size and layout of the Glasgow-Bonham household was identical to Mr Dorsey's. Polished, mahogany handrails swept down the grand staircase opposite the front door and ended in a couple of brass columns. Mounted upon each was a brass-vase kerosene lamp with a frosted glass, domed shade, and cylindrical chimney. Rather than a series of balusters, the stairs were framed by three-dimensional, bronze-sculpted panels depicting complex vine and leaf designs. Both the stairs and hall floor were covered by a Nile-green carpet, whilst the walls were adorned by a heavy, Nile-green paper with gilt bronze vertical stripes. High-grade mahogany pieces comprising of a grandfather clock, a three-legged side-table with semi-circular top, and coat stand furnished the room. These were complemented by smaller items such as a brass umbrella stand with floral embossments and an exquisite statuette of a young woman on the table. She was sitting upon the ground with her elbow upon a rock, a bundle of wheat tucked into the crook of that elbow, and a sickle in her spare hand. Finally, a telephone identical to Miss Trent's was mounted upon the wall to one's left.

Mr Locke and Miss Dexter allowed Perkins to take their coats, but Mr Maxwell declined on account of the clay model in his hands. Yet, as Mrs Bonham led Mr Maxwell upstairs, Mr Locke and Miss Dexter stayed behind to scrutinise Perkins as he hung their coats upon the stand. Noticing their peculiar behaviour, Mrs Bonham paused on the stairs to enquire, "Is something the matter?"

"Not at all," Mr Locke replied but continued to linger even as Miss Dexter joined the others in climbing the stairs. Only once he was confident Mrs Bonham was beyond earshot did he enquire from the footman, "Have you ever visited Mr Thaddeus Dorsey's home, Perkins?"

"No, sir," Perkins replied with a contrived smile.

"What is your given name, Perkins?" Mr Locke enquired.

"Arthur, sir," Perkins replied and left the room.

Intrigued nonetheless, Mr Locke went upstairs to find their hostess and his fellow Bow Streeters.

Again, similarly to Mr Dorsey's house, the first floor had a landing encircling the hallway with décor mimicking the downstairs. All its doors were closed except for two on one's left and right upon reaching the stairs' summit. The door to the left had a brass plaque that read *Lanford Law Waiting Room*. Beyond it was a green-carpeted, high-ceilinged room with leather wing-backed armchairs and sculpted marble fireplace. Meanwhile, the door to the right had its own brass plaque that read *Glasgow Photographers Waiting Room*. Beyond it was a cluster of chairs in mismatching designs from the humble wooden stool to a fabric-covered armchair that had lost some of its stuffing. The room's polished floorboards were scuffed and covered by a worn, floral rug, whilst the only feature it shared with its counterpart was the sculpted marble fireplace. Unlike in the first, though, this one was lit.

Mrs Bonham led them into the room on the right to find it was unoccupied. There were signs of it having been recently inhabited, however. A smouldering cigarette rested in the ashtray upon a low oak table in the room's centre and a copy of that morning's edition of the *Gaslight Gazette* was lying on the armchair. Well-thumbed magazines were also strewn about the table and chairs. She said, "If you'd like to wait here, my brother will be with you as soon as he can."

When she turned to leave, though, Mr Locke stepped forward to stay her. "Pardon me, Mrs Bonham, but I would like to discuss what happened at Mr Dorsey's house, if I may?"

There was deep sadness in Mrs Bonham's eyes as she fought to supress a scowl. "No," she replied through rigid features. "You may not."

"Mr Dorsey is our client," Mr Maxwell reminded her. "We have a right to know if he's in danger."

"Thaddeus—" Mrs Bonham flinched and corrected herself, "Mr Dorsey is only a danger to himself." She went to the door and gripped its handle. With her back to the others, she added in a quieter voice, "as much as it grieves me to say it." She took a deep breath and, with greater composure, continued, "But I shan't discuss him without his permission or his presence. If you wish to know more, you must ask him. Good day to you." She moved forward with her head bowed only to be halted for a second time by the sight of another's feet. Looking up into their face, she said, "Lanford, these people are from the Bow Street Society. They'd like you to take a photograph of their head."

"Pardon?" Mr Glasgow replied with a forward motion of his own. Yet, Mrs Bonham stepped around him and hurried away without offering any further explanation. Confused, he offered them a contrived smile, wiped his hand on a grimy-looking cloth and extended it to Mr Locke in the first instance. He said, "Good morning, sir. I'm Mr Lanford Glasgow of *Glasgow Photographers*. My sister said you wish me to photograph a head; whose head is it?"

He was in his late thirties with a slender, toned frame, piercing brown eyes, and a distinctively large nose with flat tip. His short, dark-brown beard met his sideburns of the same colour, whilst a well-maintained moustache echoed the neatness of his other facial hair and that upon his head. He wore a plain black waistcoat with wide lapels over a white cotton shirt whose long-sleeves were rolled up. Black bands were tied around his arms, just above the elbows, whilst the dark-grey of his pressed trousers was complemented by the light-grey of his cravat. The top of which was tucked into the waistcoat.

"This chap's," Mr Maxwell replied. His arms were trembling under the model's weight.

Mr Glasgow stared at it in disbelief. "I see," he muttered.

Mr Locke gave his hand a firm squeeze and said, "I am Mr Percival Locke, and these are my associates, Mr Joseph Maxwell and Miss Georgina Dexter. We are here in our capacity as members of the Bow Street Society."

"My sister mentioned the name," Mr Glasgow remarked as his frown deepened. "I'm sorry; what is the Bow Street Society?"

"We are a group of morally minded individuals who assist those with cases which need investigating, cases the police either cannot or will not consider," Mr Locke explained and indicated the model with his cane. "*This* is a man by the name of Palmer. Do you recognise him?"

"No," Mr Glasgow replied, shaking his head. "Should I?"

"Not necessarily," Mr Locke remarked and settled into an armchair by the fire. "He had been paying nightly visits to your neighbour and, I believe, your former business partner, Mr Thaddeus Dorsey until two nights ago."

"What was the nature of these visits?" Mr Glasgow enquired.

"We'd rather not say," Mr Maxwell replied with a sheepish glance to the photographer. Unable to sustain his grip upon the board for much longer, he set it down upon the table and breathed a sigh of relief. Adjusting his frock coat, he then opened and closed his sore hands several times. "Mr Dorsey just wants to find him because he's worried about him."

"And you want me to take a photograph of this model?" Mr Glasgow enquired.

"Yes, please, sir," Miss Dexter replied.

"Miss Dexter is an artist of great skill," Mr Locke said. "It was she who created the model for Mr Dorsey to adjust. Are you able to take the photograph we require, Mr Glasgow, or should we take our business elsewhere?"

"No!" Mr Glasgow cried as he rushed forward. Staying himself a moment, though, he then continued, "That is; of course, I can take it. Please." He stepped aside. "If you would be so kind as to carry it to my studio next door, I can take the photograph immediately."

Mr Locke and Miss Dexter looked to Mr Maxwell with expectant eyes.

"Very well…" Mr Maxwell conceded. Lifting the model with a deep grunt, he shuffled along behind Mr Glasgow as he led the way.

"I shall accompany you, sirs," Miss Dexter interjected and followed them out of the waiting room. Meanwhile, Mr Locke remained where he was aside from checking the time on his gold pocket watch and pressing his breast to ensure what he needed was still there.

SIX

Mr Morse glared at Mr Maxwell over the top of the photograph. A thin wisp of smoke rose from his cigarette and dispersed into the office's choked atmosphere as he growled, "What am I supposed to be bloody looking at here?"

"It's the clay model of Palmer, sir." Mr Maxwell wiped the sweat from his palms onto his frock coat and leant over the desk to point out the various features on the photograph. "There's his nose, eyes and, ears—"

"It looks like something you've dug out of the privy! I won't have it in my paper." Mr Morse tossed the photograph at him and, whilst Mr Maxwell scrambled to catch it, took a typed document from the pile. "And *this* is as much a piece of shite as that; you don't say how the accident happened, who'd hired the Society—"

"I can't break client confident—"

"*Don't* interrupt!" Mr Morse slammed his fist down upon the desk.

"S—Sorry, sir…" Mr Maxwell muttered, his voice barely above a whisper, as he toyed with his cravat's bow.

"You want to be a journalist for this paper?!" Mr Morse ripped the article in two. "I've read better things by illiterate children!"

"That's impossible, sir, because being illiterate means—"

"I *know* what illiterate means, you idiot!" Standing, he waved the two halves in Mr Maxwell's face. "*This* is *worse* than what they could've put together, is my point!" He tossed the pieces at him and yelled, "Baldwin!"

"I—I can rewrite it, sir," Mr Maxwell timidly suggested as Mr Baldwin joined them.

"Pay Bird whatever he was asking for and get a story I can actually print," Mr Morse ordered the newcomer.

"Yes, sir," Mr Baldwin replied and hurried away.

70

Mr Morse's hard glare shifted to Mr Maxwell and he growled, "What are you still doing here?"

"I was happy to rewrite it, sir."

"But I wasn't."

"B—but, sir—"

"Get back to your desk, Maxwell, or you won't have *anything* to write!"

Yet, Mr Maxwell didn't move. Instead he shifted his weight from one foot to the other with nervous hopefulness in his eyes as he held the photograph up.

Mr Morse's eyes narrowed. "Didn't you hear me?!"

"Y—yes, I did, but… what of the photograph?"

Mr Morse clenched his hand into a fist as he moved around his desk and advanced upon his employee. When he took a firm grip of his arm, though, and pushed him through the door, Mr Maxwell stumbled and cried, "I'll pay for the column space, sir!" Straightening, Mr Maxwell smoothed down his frock coat and added, "out of my own pocket."

Mr Morse's glare remained, but his proverbial hackles appeared to ease as he considered the proposal. "Fine," he agreed in a calmer tone. "But you'll pay double for the privilege."

"Of course, sir." Mr Maxwell swallowed hard. "And I'll give you a far superior article next time; you have my word." *If this new case provides such a story,* he thought.

"Get back to work," Mr Morse muttered and returned to his desk to read the proofs for the evening edition.

"Y—yes, sir," Mr Maxwell replied, beating a hasty retreat to his own work area.

* * *

The *Turk's Head* public house on the corner of Edgware Road wasn't what one would call sophisticated, or clean, even. The unstable stools and squat, rounded tables crammed into its small interior boasted all manner of stains, rips, and burns. Knife notches were also visible on the tables' edges; remnants of near nightly brawls fuelled by cheap gin. Sparse and grimy sawdust, soaked with stale alcohol, covered the floorboards, and stained the wood. Entry was via a door on the pub's angular corner. Two large, dirt-covered windows were set at right-angles to the door with the promise of 'fine ales' and 'tobacco' written in chipped, peeling white paint upon their glass. Directly beneath these windows, on the inside, were sun-bleached pews which had been purportedly 'reclaimed' from an 'abandoned' church by the pub's landlord.

Polly peered through a window as she passed and pulled her shawl tighter about her shoulders to fend off the night's chill. A lamp lighter ignited the lamp on the corner and Polly heard voices and laughter drifting through the pub's door as she neared it. Upon entering, she was greeted with warm smiles and fond hellos by many of the patrons who invited her to join them. Yet, she declined them all in favour of another who was sitting in the far corner.

"Sorry I'm late, luv," Polly apologised as she slid onto the stool beside Miss Trent's and found a glass of gin and water waiting for her. Removing her shawl, she folded it and laid it upon her lap. If her hand happened to stray to squeeze Miss Trent's under the table, the action went unnoticed by those around them. She picked up her drink and locked her gaze upon her companion as happiness filled her eyes.

"It's fine," Miss Trent replied with a soft smile. "However, that's not the only reason why I invited you here."

The happiness vanished from Polly's eyes as she put down her untouched drink with a thud. "I should've known," she remarked, coolly. Draping her shawl back across her shoulders, she rested one hand upon her hip as the other beckoned Miss Trent to continue as she said, "Come on, then. What is it you want this time?"

"Don't be like that."

"Like *what*?" Polly retorted. "What's going on, Becky? You told me—" She glanced at the two men sitting at the table close to their own. Resting her elbows upon the table and leaning forward, therefore, she continued in a hushed voice, "You told me you loved me and then nowt since, 'cept that feeble excuse at the bar the other night. And who was that bloke?"

"No one you need to concern yourself with," Miss Trent replied. "Besides, you're a fine one to talk."

"Don't go bringing that up again."

Miss Trent picked up her own drink. "Why not? I was just talking to the bloke; you're doing a lot more with Dr Weeks."

"A girl's gotta eat, ain't she? And dun' change the subject! You only ever come to me when you want something," Polly pointed out and took a fair gulp of gin and water.

"You agreed to be a part of the Society," Miss Trent reminded her.

"Yeah," Polly replied with a momentary wave of her hand. "'Cause I thought it would bring me closer to you, didn't I?"

"I'm sorry," Miss Trent said, knowing Polly was telling the truth since neither she nor Weeks were aware of the other's membership to the Society. Those were the rules they'd agreed to upon joining, after all. Yet, the shake of Polly's head and scrutiny of her glass told Miss Trent the feeling of belief wasn't mutual. Reaching for Polly's other hand beneath the table, she whispered, "I *do* love you." When Polly accepted her touch, she continued, "But, we must be careful, mustn't we?"

Polly kept her eyes downcast.

"*Mustn't* we?" Miss Trent repeated.

"*Yes,*" Polly replied bluntly and pulled her hand from Miss Trent's to tighten her shawl around her shoulders.

"Will you at least hear me out, please?" Miss Trent enquired. "You don't have to agree to anything if you don't want to."

Polly took another mouthful of gin and water, rubbed her forehead, and gave a deep sigh. Scrutinising her companion's face for any hint of deceit, she then folded her arms across her chest and leant against the wall behind her. Her fingers strummed against her arm and her tongue pressed against the inside of her cheek as she considered the request. Finally, she said, "*Go on, then.* But you've got to do more, Becky."

"I will, I promise." Miss Trent pulled out the evening edition of the *Gaslight Gazette* from where she'd kept it tucked beneath her on the stool. Opening it at the relevant page, she placed it in front of Polly and tapped the dim photograph of Miss Dexter's clay model. Beneath it was a basic, hundred-word description of Palmer. "Recognise him?"

"Nah," Polly replied and, leaning her elbows upon the table, rested her chin in the palms of her hands. Fortunately literate, she read the description and mused aloud, "Palmer... I know loads of blokes called Palmer. This is not one of them though."

"I need you to pass the word around to the girls at the other station bars," Miss Trent explained. Seeing the alarm in Polly's face, she held up her hand and went on, "You don't have to take this. Just tell them to look in tonight's *Gaslight Gazette* and let you know if Palmer's been in their bar in the past week." She put her hand on Polly's arm as reluctance crept into her eyes. "*Please,* Polly. We have to be sure he's safe for the sake of our client."

"It'll take me a while... A day at least."
"That's fine."

Polly scrutinised Miss Trent once more. This time, though, her head was showing her all the trouble she could get into with the manageresses, whilst her heart was replaying all the intimate moments she and Miss Trent had shared. Feeling her love overwhelm her logic she released a deep sigh and replied, "Okay. I'll do it."

"Good," Miss Trent said with a broad smile. Closing the newspaper, she folded it in half and tucked it under her arm. "I've got something else I want to talk to you about."

Polly rolled her eyes. "*What*?"

"Follow me and I'll tell you," Miss Trent replied and drained her glass.

"Where—?" Polly enquired, but her companion was already on her feet and halfway to the door. Hurriedly drinking the remainder of her gin and water, Polly then navigated her way through the crowded pub and back outside. Seeing no sign of Miss Trent, though, she cursed under her breath and wrapped her shawl around herself as tightly as it would go. *That woman!* She thought as she walked down the street in the direction of her lodgings at the station. When she passed by the service alleyway for the pub, though, a hand grabbed her by the arm and tugged her into the shadows.

"Hey, get off—!" Polly yelled, but another hand covered her mouth to stifle her words. As their weight pinned her against the damp wall, Polly felt her heart race and the warmth of their breath against her cheek.

"I love you," a familiar voice whispered from the darkness.

Polly's body relaxed against the wall in relief. Feeling the hand lift from her mouth and be replaced by the delicate brushing of lips, she stepped closer to her would-be attacker. Giving their lips a gentle kiss, she whispered, "I love you, too, Rebecca."

* * *

For the more discerning traveller in London, hansom and hackney cabs were the preferred choice because of their relative privacy and social status. For those with lighter pockets though, such an option didn't exist, especially when one had to make twice-daily journeys between the suburbs and employment in the city. Walking, though healthier and cost-free, was impractical in such situations. Thus, many turned to the London Omnibus Company and its many vehicles for a financially sound travelling alternative. Most fares started at 1d (one penny) or 2d (twopence) for part journeys and didn't exceed 4d (groat) or 6d (sixpence) for the whole distance of a route. Even if one were returning home after dark, the omnibuses could be relied upon as they ran from about eight o'clock in the morning until midnight. Thus, it wasn't an unrealistic notion for Mr Snyder to pay Charing Cross a visit at seven o'clock in the evening. Counted amongst the central points from whence omnibuses were boarded in all directions, Charing Cross was also one of the stops closest to Bow Street. As such, it was an excellent starting point for Mr Snyder to seek out Palmer's movements on London's transport routes.

The Society could only obtain a single print of Mr Glasgow's photograph of the clay model, and Mr Maxwell had used it for his article, so Mr Snyder was obliged to take the latest edition of the *Gaslight Gazette* with him instead. Entering the crowd of would-be travellers jostling for first place on the pavement's edge, he soon caught sight of a red omnibus parked at its official stop several yards away. It formed part of a line of omnibuses that stretched back as far as the eyes could see. A pair of horses pulled each, whilst open-air upper floors provided additional passenger seating. The formal destination written upon the front of the red omnibus was Royal Oak and Charing Cross despite its actual final stop being Bayswater. Deciding he should enquire at this red omnibus first, he attempted to ease his way through the crowd but was met with considerable resistance by those around him.

Aside from the fact everyone refused to relinquish their spot on the pavement, the medley of cargo they carried—from new-born babies to bulky laundry baskets and caged parrots—made it impossible to move around them. Thus, he was forced to wait as his desired omnibus was filled and sent on its way. Many others also underwent the same routine at different times, which resulted in the crowd shuffling a few inches forward every few minutes. By the time the red omnibus returned, Mr Snyder was close enough to read the other stops adorning its façade. These included Regent Street, Oxford Street, and Edgware Road. He still wasn't close enough to board, however.

He therefore looked to the couple which had pulled up to the stop nearest to him. They were both yellow and counted Camden Town amongst the stop listings painted on their sides. Their announced destinations differed, though, with the first being Bull and Gate and the second being Duke of St. Alban's. Yet, regardless of what their façades said, Mr Snyder's intimate knowledge of the London omnibuses and their routes told him the actual final stop of the first yellow omnibus was Kentish Town, whilst the actual stop of the second was Highgate Road. Furthermore, that both were merely passing through Charing Cross in order to commence their respective routes from Victoria Station.

As both vehicles had arrived, Mr Snyder had heard their conductors, or cads as they were informally known, yell out the fares in spite of the fact they were written on both the interiors and exteriors. The cads also declared the reasons why their omnibus was the better choice as they jumped off their narrow ledges at the omnibuses' rears. After opening the rear door—the only means of boarding and departing the vehicle—the cad of each omnibus began taking monies from those lucky enough to secure a place at the front of the crowd. Mr Snyder watched as both men pocketed a portion of the fares they were given in full view of the crowd without a hint of shame. Deciding to speak to them about Palmer, despite their conduct, Mr Snyder waited as those who'd paid boarded the omnibus and climbed the steps to its open-topped deck. It was apparent most passengers preferred to squeeze onto the narrow benches there, or even stand, rather than take their chances in the enclosed confinements of the lower deck.

"Oi, mate!" Mr Snyder shouted over the din of hooves, yells, and chatter. When one of the cads looked up, he held the newspaper aloft and pointed to the photograph of Palmer. Though it was after dark, the glow of a nearby lamp post provided sufficient light for the cads to see the image. Mr Snyder enquired, "You seen this bloke?!" The cad shook his head, so Mr Snyder showed it to the other who gave him the same response. Ushering their last customer into the lower deck, both men then slammed the doors, climbed back onto their ledges, and gave the omnibus a swift thump. Upon hearing this signal, the drivers geed their horses and both omnibuses lurched forward into the immense throng of vehicles attempting to depart Charing Cross.

By this time, the crowd at the stop for the red omnibus had diminished and Mr Snyder was able to get close enough to speak to its cad. In line with the fashion of the time, the cad had short, combed brown hair and a brown moustache of a respectable bushiness. He was attired in a dark-brown tweed suit with matching waistcoat, a pair of scuffed, brown-leather boots, and a brown bowler hat. He also carried a whip that was leant against his shoulder whilst resting in the crook of his arm. When he held out his hand, Mr Snyder informed him, "I don't need a ticket."

"Then I'm not int'rested, mate," the cad replied. Ignoring the newspaper Mr Snyder then held aloft, the cad reached over his shoulder to take the fare of another customer.

"Jus' take a look, yeah?" Mr Snyder requested, raising the newspaper higher. "Won't take a mo.'"

"I've not got a mo'," the cad replied and issued a ticket to the other customer. Once the customer had boarded and the cad reached for the door, though, Mr Snyder stepped in front of it. "*Oi!*" the cad cried.

"This bloke's got to be found; his Mum's worried sick," Mr Snyder lied. "Jus' want to know if you've seen him these last couple-a days."

"You wot?" The cad stared at him in disbelief. "You know how many I see?" The cad shook his head and thumbed over his shoulder. "Sling your hook!"

"*One* look," Mr Snyder said without moving. "Then your 'bus can leave."

The cad's eyes narrowed but one glance over Mr Snyder's broad frame told him his own leaner one wouldn't be enough to force him out of the way. Mr Snyder's crooked nose also hinted at an experience of fisticuffs that the cad didn't want to be on the receiving end of. He therefore took the newspaper, cast his eyes over the photograph, and read the description. "Not seen him," he said and passed the newspaper back to Mr Snyder who, satisfied with the answer, moved aside. Relieved to be getting on his way, the cad slammed the door, slapped the omnibus' rear twice, and leapt up onto his ledge to grip the top of the omnibus as it, too, lurched forward to join the throng.

Mr Snyder was far from finished, though. Without waiting for the red omnibus' departure, he headed for a set of green omnibuses. The announced destination on their fronts was "Atlas," but Mr Snyder knew their actual final stop was Camberwell, (specifically Camberwell Gate). This was reached via Westminster Bridge, Westminster Road, London Road, and Walworth Road. Though it seemed like the figurative needle in a haystack, Mr Snyder was almost certain Palmer must've travelled on *one* of these omnibuses during the past week.

* * *

"I like the description," Miss Dexter said as she lifted meek eyes from the newspaper to look at Mr

Maxwell. "And you included Mr Glasgow's photograph." She cast her eyes downward and held out the newspaper. "I'm sorry the model wasn't more distinctive."

"You did your best," Mr Maxwell reassured and slipped the newspaper into his jacket. "It's not your fault Mr Dorsey's recollection wasn't as comprehensive as we'd hoped it would be."

They began the short walk from Miss Trent's office on Endell Street to Bow Street.

"Perhaps." *I should've garnered more details about Palmer from Mr Dorsey*, she thought. *Yet, what further questions could I have asked?*

"Someone will recognise Palmer from your model, I'm sure of it." Mr Maxwell reached for her arm to reassure her, but Miss Dexter shrank back in alarm. Stunned by her reaction, he withdrew his hand and realised his faux pas. "S—Sorry. I, er…"

Miss Dexter kept her distance, and her head bowed as they stood on opposite sides of the pavement. "It's… I shouldn't have moved away so quickly—"

"No, no, it was my error." Mr Maxwell cleared his throat. "Forgive me, I…" Noticing someone lighting the lamp outside Mr Dorsey's house, he enquired, "Isn't that our fellow?" Without waiting for her reply, he strode down the street toward the figure with Miss Dexter walking a few paces behind. She preferred it that way, whilst he didn't want her to hear him muttering under his breath as he scolded himself for being so stupid.

"Good evening, sir," Mr Maxwell greeted the lamplighter once they'd reached him.

"Evenin'," the lamplighter replied as he used the long, metal rod he was holding to close the door of the lamp's glass casing.

"My name's Mr Joseph Maxwell and this is Miss Georgina Dexter, what's yours?"

"Ralph Bell," the lamplighter eyed them both. "You needin' a lamp lightin'?"

"No," Mr Maxwell replied. "But we would like to know: do you light the lamps here every night?"

"Nah, just on Sundays," Mr Bell said in a sardonic tone.

"But today's Wednesday…" Mr Maxwell replied, confused.

Mr Bell pointed at Mr Maxwell as he enquired from Miss Dexter, "Is your bloke bein' serious?"

"*Very*, and I don't like being made a fool of," Mr Maxwell warned despite his expression lacking the conviction of his voice.

Mr Bell shook his head. "I've got work to do."

"As do we," Mr Maxwell retorted. "We're looking for someone."

"Who?" Mr Bell enquired.

"A friend of ours," Mr Maxwell replied and retrieved the newspaper. Showing the photograph to the lamplighter, he enquired, "Have you seen him?"

Mr Bell took the newspaper and squinted at it under the lamp light. "Can't say if I have or not; he looks like most blokes I know." He looked between them. "Wait, didn't I see you both here last night?"

"No," Mr Maxwell replied at the same time as Miss Dexter replying "yes." Clearing his throat, though, Mr Maxwell glanced at Miss Dexter's sheepish smile and corrected, "Yes… you did. We were waiting for him, but he never arrived."

"Sorry, I can't tell you anything more," Mr Bell replied and allowed Mr Maxwell to take back the newspaper. "Good night, sir, miss."

"Good night," Mr Maxwell replied whilst Miss Dexter offered a polite smile. Watching Mr Bell move onto the next lamp, Mr Maxwell put the newspaper away and mused aloud, "Maybe we should ask the coal and milk men in the morning."

"Mr Dorsey said Palmer only visits at night," Miss Dexter reminded him.

Mr Maxwell hummed as he saw the usual police constable on patrol in the distance. Having noticed a narrow alleyway running adjacent to the left of Mr Dorsey's house, he waited until the constable was shining his lamp at another house before he hurried into it. Miss Dexter, startled by her fellow Bow Streeter's sudden movement, decided she had little choice but to follow. The alleyway was in complete darkness, however, so she was obliged to remain closer to Mr Maxwell than was proper. He led her into the service alleyway running perpendicular to the row of houses and their rear yards. Though curious to know why Mr Maxwell had brought them there, her fear prevented her voice from sounding. Instead, she waited as he looked up at the houses of Mr Dorsey's direct neighbours, and then hurried after him when he approached Mr Dorsey's back gate. A sudden bang from the darkness then caused her to gasp in fright.

"Locked," Mr Maxwell lamented from somewhere in front of her.

She listened to the rattle of the gate as he gave it a violent shake before his voice once again spoke from within the darkness.

"I can't see a lock on this side so maybe it's on the other?" Mr Maxwell mused aloud.

"I can't see anything," Miss Dexter whispered. "And you frightened me besides!" She wasn't keen on loitering at the back gate of a blind man's house, either. *Surely this sort of thing was more Mr Locke's area of expertise than Mr Maxwell's?* She thought. *And to be found here with a gentleman who's neither my fiancé nor relative would be unthinkable!* How this would assist them in locating Palmer, she had no idea.

"Mr Locke said the back door was rusted shut…" Mr Maxwell mused, only to realise what she'd said a heartbeat later. "I frightened you? Oh, I'm sorry. I didn't mean—"

"Who's there?!" a third voice cut through the darkness.

Mr Maxwell immediately pressed his back against the gate. Gripping Miss Dexter by the arm, he pulled her against him and stifled her startled gasp with a hand over her mouth. "Shhh…" he whispered into her ear and lowered his hand upon feeling her nod.

They held their breaths and listened as the footsteps came down the service alleyway toward them.

"I know you're there! It's the police!" the voice shouted as the footsteps grew closer. "Come out now and I won't have to put the derbies on you."

Miss Dexter closed her eyes and gripped Mr Maxwell's frock coat.

Several moments passed without a sound from any of them. Then, the scrape of a boot against dirt sliced through the silence as its owner moved closer. Miss Dexter pressed her head against Mr Maxwell's chest to brace against their seemingly inevitable discovery. Yet, to her surprise and relief, she heard the boot scrape across the dirt away from them, followed by footsteps which grew quieter as their owner departed. It was only when they'd died away, completely, though, that she released the breath she'd been holding, and Mr Maxwell did the same.

"I think he's gone," Mr Maxwell whispered, his warm breath caressing Miss Dexter's face.

"I think so, too."

"You may let go of me now, Miss Dexter."

Miss Dexter gasped and released his coat at once. Taking several steps back, she was grateful to the darkness for hiding her flushed complexion. "I apologise, Mr Maxwell."

"No apology needed." Mr Maxwell took a gentle hold of her arm to guide her from the service alleyway but, this time, she responded by moving closer.

"Will you escort me home, please?" she enquired once they'd emerged from the alleyway and saw the constable wasn't anywhere in sight.

"Oh… Yes. Of course, I will." Mr Maxwell released her arm and offered his own.

"Thank you, Mr Maxwell," Miss Dexter replied with a soft smile as she slipped her hand into the crook of his arm.

"It's my pleasure, Miss Dexter." He returned her smile as they headed down Bow Street in search of the nearest omnibus stop. "But…" His smile faded. "Please don't tell Miss Trent we were nearly arrested though."

"I shan't," Miss Dexter chuckled in relief. "I only ask you don't put me in such a predicament again."

"Now I can't promise *that*. But I'll promise to always protect you when I do."

"I think that's acceptable," she replied, smiling up at him.

Relieved and embarrassed by his own antics, Mr Maxwell gave a bashful smile in return.

SEVEN

It was early the next morning and Mr Snyder was once again on the hunt for the elusive Palmer amongst London's omnibuses. He'd spoken to yet another cad at a Charing Cross stop who'd given him a glimmer of hope when he'd pointed out a customer matching Palmer's description in the crowd. Unfortunately, upon closer inspection of the individual, Mr Snyder found several dissimilarities which made the possibility of him being Palmer unlikely. This suspicion was then confirmed when the man replied in what Mr Snyder assumed was French after Mr Snyder had addressed him as 'Palmer' and asked if he knew a Mr Dorsey. Disheartened but not dissuaded from his mission, Mr Snyder had made enquiries with the cad on the next omnibus to arrive, then the next, and the next. None of them would commit to having seen the rather mundane-looking man depicted in the clay model's photograph.

Mr Snyder was pondering his next course of action when he saw an omnibus bound for Westminster Bridge. Reaching it just as the cad was about to slam its door, he paid the fare—ignoring the cad's partial pocketing of it—and climbed aboard. Passengers were sparse on the lower deck, so he took a seat close to the door and felt the top of his hat brush against the ceiling. As the vehicle lurched forward, he gripped the edge of his bench and listened to the creaking of the upper deck under the weight of its numerous occupants. Resolving to make the best use of his time, though, he made enquiries about Palmer amongst the other passengers. He paid attention to men whose attire suggested they worked in the City of London as this increased the likelihood of them making twice-daily journeys. Just like the cads, though, no one could say for definite if they'd seen Palmer or not.

When the omnibus arrived at Westminster Bridge a short time later, Mr Snyder disembarked and pressed on through the throng of people vying for a place on his 'bus.

Yet, rather than continue his search amongst the other omnibuses parked there, he instead walked to the tram line. Transporting passengers to stops such as Clapham Common, Peckham, Battersea, and Wandsworth, the trams were like omnibuses in appearance but operated on a set of rails. They were nonetheless horse drawn, but Mr Snyder could remember a time when London's trams were entirely steam-powered. Since tram fares were also similar to omnibuses'—either 1d. or 2d. for part of the journey, and between 2d. and 4d. for the whole—it was viable Palmer had made a connection from one to the other as Mr Snyder had.

For the next hour he visited tram after tram, speaking to person after person, but no one could recall seeing Palmer, let along remember hearing his name. Dejected, Mr Snyder took an omnibus back to Charing Cross where he changed to another—a blue omnibus bound for Waterloo Bridge—and travelled as far as the Strand. Walking from there to Ludgate Hill, he spoke to the cads on the omnibuses bound for Blackfriars' Bridge. When they, too, couldn't help him, he paid the fare and journeyed to Blackfriars' where he made enquiries amongst the trams bound for stops in the south, such as Deptford and Greenwich. Yet, even these efforts failed to provide him with the answers he sought. Fearing he may never find a trace of Palmer, he took an omnibus back to Ludgate Hill where he changed to a dark-green Holloway one. Travelling to Gray's Inn Road, he focused his attention on trams bound for Kingsland Road and Stoke Newington via Clerkenwell Road, Dalston Lane, Mare Street, Hackney, and Hampstead via King's Cross. He was keen to keep his search parameters quite small, at least for the time being. Again, though, his efforts bore no fruit and he was obliged to double back on himself to make enquiries amongst the trams departing from Moorgate. This would ensure the stops north and northeast of that terminus would be covered. He also thought a visit to a few of the cab shelters wouldn't go amiss. Some of his fellow cab men might've picked up Palmer, after all. Thus, with a pocket full of pennies courtesy of Miss Trent, he continued his search.

* * *

The skies had opened by the time Mr Snyder brought his loaned cab to a stop behind another outside St. Clement Danes church. Torrential rain bucketed down upon him as he climbed down from his seat and told an enquiring gentleman his cab wasn't available to hire. Infuriated, the gentleman hurried away to locate another cab elsewhere. Mr Snyder shook his head in amused disbelief at his behaviour and headed toward a compact, rectangular structure made of wood. Painted green, it had a black tiled roof and narrow, glass windows all around it. Each window had a solid, square panel beneath, and the entire structure was raised a few inches off the ground. A wooden box with open slats in its sides was mounted onto the roof. A narrow, cylindrical, tin chimney stuck out from behind this box where a constant stream of coal smoke could be seen pouring out.

Upon opening a door in the structure's side, Mr Snyder was met by a wall of warmth and the enticing smells of stew and coffee. The origin of all three was a small stove a little to the door's right in the middle of the room. Standing behind it was a man in a shin-length apron, thick trousers, and a dark, cotton, long-sleeved shirt. He cast an indifferent glance in Mr Snyder's direction but continued stirring the immense pot on the stove's top. Five cab men were huddled on benches around a long, wide table running down the room's centre. The compact size of the structure meant those in the middle would have to wait for those on the outside to move before they could stand. Having been engaged in quiet conversation whilst reading the newspaper or eating when Mr Snyder had opened the door, they then fell silent when it closed with a thud behind him. For several long moments, the only sound was the barrage of rain against the hollow roof as all eyes were on him.

"Wot you doin' 'ere, Sam?" one of the men enquired.

"Come to ge' a warm, Wilf, like the rest of you," Mr Snyder replied.

"Dis is jus' for cabbies, and you're not a cabbie," Wilfred retorted.

"Just leave it, Wilf," a second cab man urged.

"I've got my licence," Mr Snyder replied. "Not that I've gotta justify myself to you, mind."

"You gonna let 'im in 'ere?" Wilfred growled as he looked to the man at the stove. He seemed more interested in his stew than Mr Snyder, however, so Wilfred turned to his fellow cab men for support. Yet, each time his eyes met theirs they looked down or pretended not to have noticed. Wilfred's eyes narrowed. "Damn you all, then. Lemmie ge' out," he ordered as he stood and moved along the bench. The couple of cab men who were sitting beside him did the same and Wilfred left with a scowl to the man at the stove and a violent slamming of the door. The entire structure shook as the cab men returned to their seats and, within moments, they'd drifted back into quiet conversation once more.

Mr Snyder gave a soft sigh and ordered a cup of tea from the man at the stove. Having spent half his day on the omnibuses and trams, he'd then spent the other half visiting the cabman shelters in High Holborn and Archer Street near Bow Street. He was chilled to his core, soaked through to the bone, and suffering from painful throbbing feet as a result. None of it had been worthwhile, either. His hopes therefore rested on the occupants of this shelter due to its location. Being on the Strand it was within walking distance of Bow Street and, more importantly, open during the evening hours when Palmer visited Mr Dorsey. Palmer could've hired a cab from here rather than risk meeting someone he knew at the High Holborn or Archer Street shelters. Mr Snyder took his tea, sat on the end of the bench, and blew across the surface of the steaming-hot beverage to cool it.

"Hello, Joe!" Mr Snyder called to his friend who'd emerged from a door marked lavatory at the other end of the shelter, behind the stove. Lifting his cup when Joe saw him, Mr Snyder then stood and extended his hand to him as he approached. "How've you been keepin'?"

"Still breathin'," Joe replied, giving Mr Snyder's hand a firm squeeze. He was in his late fifties with grey eyes and a greying moustache. "It's good to see you, Sam. How do's?"

"Can't complain, y'know," Mr Snyder replied, sitting back on the bench but sliding along so Joe could join him.

"You still got the fare with that Society lot?" Joe enquired as he eased his aching bones onto the hard bench.

"Yeah," Mr Snyder replied with a smile. "Cab's a wreck though."

"*Bloody* hell, you just got that passed last week. What happened? Will it fix okay?"

"Yeah, think so." Mr Snyder took a sip of tea. "Horse got shot."

"Blimey…" Joe replied, stunned. "How?"

"Long story…" Mr Snyder retrieved the *Gaslight Gazette* from his coat and put it down in front of Joe. Tapping the photograph with his stubby, cold finger, he said, "We're looking for this bloke. Have you seen him? He calls himself Palmer."

"Yeah, I've seen him," Joe replied, lifting his hand to indicate Palmer's height. "Tall bloke, yeah?"

Mr Snyder shrugged his shoulders.

"He takes a cab, regular like, to Chelsea, he does," Joe added.

Mr Snyder was so surprised someone had *finally* remembered seeing Palmer that he appeared shocked by Joe's revelation about the destination. Taking a large mouthful of tea, therefore, he echoed, "Chelsea?"

"Yeah."

"When?"

"Coupla days back. Why, he trouble, or sumin'?"

"Dunno yet." Mr Snyder leant closer to his friend. "Can you remember where you dropped him off in Chelsea?"

"The same place I always drop him—Brookbond House on the King's Road," Joe replied.

Mr Snyder at once visualised the map of London he'd first memorised years ago and amended every few months since. "Brookbond House…" His mind's eye homed in on the area. "Bit posh 'round there," he mused aloud. Recalling a set of buildings, then, he enquired, "That's one of those flat buildings up by Sloane Square, right?"

"Yeah," Joe replied and picked up the newspaper to inspect the photograph further. "If this bloke's trouble, I've never seen it. Always been a good fare, a right Gent; tips well, too."

"He always ge' in at the same place?"

"Nah; picked him up 'ere once or twice, or on the corner of Bow Street."

"How'd you know his name's Palmer?"

"He told me, didn't he," Joe said and put the newspaper back down in front of Mr Snyder. "He said he thought me and him were friends as we saw enough of each other; picked him up four times in five days once. He likes to chat out the window when the cab stops a bit and when he gets out. Yeah, nice bloke he is."

"He ever travel with anyone?"

"Nah, always on his own, he was."

Mr Snyder drank the remainder of his tea and slipped the newspaper back into his coat. "Thanks, Joe," he said as he stood and gave his friend's shoulder a gentle squeeze. "You're a good mate."

"You're not too bad yourself," Joe replied and the two bid their goodbyes.

Yet, despite his relief and delight at finally making progress in his search for Palmer, Mr Snyder knew his class of person wouldn't get further than the door at a place like Brookbond House. What he needed was a gentleman of wealth. What he needed was Mr Percy Locke.

EIGHT

Akin to the other apartment buildings on the King's Road, Brookbond House was constructed of red brick with immaculate symmetry to its Gothic architecture. Each floor had identical couplings of three-sided bay windows—one on the left and one on the right—with intricate vine designs carved into the brickwork. These designs were beneath the wide stone stills of the sash windows which made up the bays. Sitting on these sills were boxes of pansies and roses, whilst a fan of red bricks crowned the windows' arched frames. The spaces between the bay windows were occupied by identical couplings of single sash windows on each floor. On the ground floor, an arched, white stone porch led to the building's immense, oak front door that was varnished in a dark lacquer. Hanging from the arch's centre was an iron-framed lantern containing a lit candle to illuminate the black-and-white checked floor below. Two white stone steps led from the pavement to the porch where several iron letterboxes were mounted on the wall to the door's right. Organised into rows, each had a number and removal brass plaque engraved with the apartment owner's surname.

Whilst Mr Snyder stayed with his cab, Mr Percy Locke climbed the steps and suspended a slender finger over each plaque in turn as he read the names. Finding Palmer's amongst them, he turned upon his heel and approached the door whilst taking the velvet roll of lock picks from his frock coat. After casting a cautionary glance over his shoulder, he inspected the lock. It was a model he'd commonly found on the front doors of wealthy homes where he'd attended dinner parties. Its inner workings were therefore familiar to him, so it didn't take long to manipulate it into opening. Upon hearing its tell-tale click he put away the tools of his, arguably questionable, skill and slipped inside.

The hallway was devoid of furniture and had a flight of stairs running up the right-hand side to the first floor. A dark-blue carpet ran up their centre and complemented the dark-blue, cream, and light-blue floral runner rug lying to the left of the stairs. The remainder of the floor was exposed boards covered by a layer of pristine varnish. The door to apartment one was situated at the foot of the stairs with the door to apartment two directly opposite. In addition to its number, apartment one also had a plaque with 'Housekeeper' engraved on it.

Mr Locke listened. The sounds of female voices accompanied by the clatter of various pots and pans drifted through the housekeeper's door, whilst a piano was being played somewhere upstairs. Given that it was early evening, it was possible Palmer was at home, so Mr Locke crossed the hallway and climbed the stairs to the second floor. Stepping onto the narrow landing, he peered through one of the two sash windows and saw Mr Snyder with his cab. The décor was simple; dark-brown wooden panelling covered the walls' lower halves and a cream and dark-brown wallpaper covering their upper. A cream dado rail formed a boundary between the two, whilst wall mounted gas lamps with plain glass shades and brass mounts illuminated the stairs and landing. Apartment five was on the landing's far end to his right, whilst his intended destination—apartment six—was to his left.

Using the edge of his cane's handle, he tapped twice upon the door and waited—no response. Applying an additional two taps with more force, he leant toward the wood and listened. Not so much as a creak reached him. Mr Locke knew some individuals were slow to answer their door so allowed Palmer a few moments' grace before deciding he wasn't home after all. He stepped back to peer up the stairs leading to the second floor. No one had emerged from their apartment to confront him over his presence there, or entered from the street, so he once again retrieved his picks and set to work on the lock.

It was a simple keyhole with brass surround beside a dull, brass knob. Yet, Mr Locke suspected there was an iron casing fixed to the other side of the door with a bolt that slid into the door frame. In his experience, places like Brookbond House had less sophisticated locks on their interior doors due to the owners' assumption the external door and housekeeper's lodgings at the foot of the stairs provided sufficient security from house breakers. It wasn't necessarily true, of course. For where there was a will there was, often, a way. As he proved with his manipulation and breaking of the second lock since his arrival.

Putting his picks away once more, he cracked open the door, peered inside, and listened; nothing. Opening the door wide, he went inside and closed it behind him with a gentle click. He was standing in a darkened lounge that also served as a dining room. To the left of the door was a short wall. He crept over to it and peered around its corner to find an open doorway leading to a bedroom. A kerosene lamp stood on a table in the corner of the lounge to the right of the bedroom door. Both it and the apartment's gas lamps were extinguished but, as he placed a gloved hand upon the shade of the kerosene lamp, he found its glass was still warm. Turning his attention to the fireplace, then, he used a poker from the stand to rummage around in the iron hearth. Though there weren't any embers, the damp consistency of the ashes told him it had been recently extinguished. Wiping the poker clean with his handkerchief afterward, he replaced it into the stand and explored the rest of the apartment.

Its décor was as luxurious as the communal areas of the building. Wood panelling painted cream adorned the walls lower halves whilst cream wallpaper with an embossed, brass-coloured stripe covered the upper. In between was a plain, beech dado rail. Two wing-backed armchairs upholstered in soft, brown fabric stood at opposing ends of the fireplace looking inward. A gentleman's shirt was draped over the arm of the chair to the left and a lady's purple shawl was on the seat of the chair to the right. It looked like it had fallen from her shoulders and crumpled into a heap behind her whilst she'd been sitting. Each chair had a wine table beside it with a wine bottle and glass standing on the one to the left and a wine glass standing on the one to the right. All three were empty. The remaining furniture consisted of a low-backed, two-seater sofa stood in the centre of the bay window, a round dining table with two chairs stood in the middle of the room, and a writing desk in the far-left corner. Prints of paintings depicting generic subject matter, such as vases of flowers and bowls of fruit, hung on the walls, but Mr Locke couldn't see a single photograph anywhere. Approaching the fireplace for a second time, he examined the contents of the mantel shelf. There was a clock housed in a gold-plated casing, a china ornament of a couple sitting on a bench, and brass candelabra at each end. Tucked behind the ornament were letters addressed to Palmer. Since their envelopes had already been torn open, he picked up the first and pulled out the letter. At once the strong scent of lavender filled his nostrils. Sniffing the paper, he discovered it had been covered with the scent. Reading the letter's first few handwritten lines, he concluded it was a rather sweet love letter. A check of its bottom revealed a space where the signature should be. He therefore examined the envelope and saw the postmark was Holywell Street. *Interesting*, he thought, and returned the letter to its proper place.

Finding nothing else worth investigating, he moved his search to the bedroom. There he found a pair of gentleman's trousers lying on the floor directly inside the door and a woman's dress draped over the bottom of a brass-framed double bed. The bed's blankets and pillows were twisted and strewn all over it. Two wardrobes stood against the wall opposite the bed, so Mr Locke went to them next. In the first he found numerous sets of clothes belonging to a gentleman. In the second were mostly women's clothes, a few towels, and some clean bed linen.

A dressing table was conspicuous by its absence, but a lady's horsehair, silver handled hairbrush sat upon a cabinet to the left of the bed. The brush had a ceramic panel on its back decorated with hand-painted pink roses and daisies. It was accompanied by an ornate perfume diffuser, a pair of delicate pearl and gold earrings, a lady's pocket watch, and a copy of Jane Austen's *Pride and Prejudice.* Within the cabinet's drawers was a pair of black, lady's gloves, a pearl necklace in a red-velvet box, ribbons, hairpins, and various hat and hair adornments. A lady's boned corset and pair of silk bloomers lay on the floor in front of the cabinet.

In the corner behind him, to the right of the wardrobes, was a washstand with an intricately decorated ceramic jug and bowl standing on its top. Behind these was a ceramic cup containing two horsehair, wooden-handled toothbrushes with a round, ceramic pot of ready-prepared dentifrice beside it. On the pot's lid was the stamp of a local pharmacist. On the other side of the bowl were two closed cutthroat razors and a large bar of rose-scented carbolic soap. Mr Locke examined each razor in turn and found they showed equal amounts of wear. This surprised him as he would've expected one to be a replacement for the other.

Returning the razors, he then went back around the bed to examine a second cabinet. Unlike its counterpart its surface was free of clutter and its drawer was locked. Mr Locke therefore called upon his picks for a third time to gain entry. Inside, he found a further pile of love letters, a plain, wooden box, and a gentleman's solid gold pocket watch with a hand-painted ceramic face and brass hands. Again, the letters weren't signed, but their contents were far more explicit than the one he'd found on the mantel shelf. Furthermore, the author described positions Mr Locke thought were physically impossible, even for someone as flexible as he.

Putting the letters onto the cabinet's top, he next opened the box and found a pile of five-pound notes. It was a large amount of money by most standards but, judging by his surroundings, Mr Locke suspected Palmer was a man of some means. Returning the money to the box, he then put it beside the letters before continuing his search of the drawer. At its bottom was a copy of the apartment's lease. Mr Locke picked it up and read its contents. When it came to the name of the renter, though, he stopped. To his surprise and curiosity, it wasn't Palmer but a Mr Arthur Perkins...

* * *

Miss Trent opened her office door but didn't enter; she *knew* she'd locked it when she'd left to get some supper. Allowing her eyes to adjust to the gloom, she made out the outlines of two silhouettes. The first was behind her desk whilst the second was standing to its left. The individuals' heights and builds had a wisp of familiarity about them, but the shape of a cloak around the shoulders of the second convinced her. "There is a lamp, you know," she remarked as she walked across to her desk, lifted the glass shade from a kerosene lamp on its corner, and lit it with a match. As she increased the amount of oil feeding it, the light grew and fell upon the faces of Mr Locke and Mr Snyder.

"We've not long got here," Mr Snyder informed her.

"And I shan't be staying for much longer," Mr Locke remarked as he checked the time on his pocket watch; it was almost six thirty. Snapping it shut, he slipped it back into his waistcoat and moved around the desk. "Palmer is renting an apartment at Brookbond House on the King's Road in Chelsea. Though 'Palmer' is on the letterbox outside, the apartment's lease records Mr Arthur Perkins as the tenant."

"Isn't Mrs Bonham's footman called Perkins?" Miss Trent enquired.

"He is. When we visited the Glasgow-Bonham residence, Miss Dexter and I were struck by Perkins' similarity to the clay model. When I enquired if he had ever visited Mr Thaddeus Dorsey's home, though, he told me he had not. The apartment's lease is proof he was lying," Mr Locke replied and put on a black scarf. "According to the lease, 'Palmer' is his second surname, but he nonetheless requested it be used on his letterbox. Mr Glasgow's address is also recorded in the lease as Mr Perkins' former residence. When we visited Brookbond House, Palmer, slash Mr Perkins, was not at home. Further investigation of his apartment revealed he had been there recently with a woman, however. Evidence of this was in the empty bottle of wine and glasses by the fire. I presume she is his lover, rather than his relative, on account of some sweet, and some very explicit, love letters I found. Though they were all unsigned, the paper upon which they were written was covered in a lady's lavender perfume. Furthermore, I believe his lover resides with him at his apartment for there was lady's clothing in one of the wardrobes, feminine items on one of the bedside cabinets, and female undergarments on the floor. Her dress was also flung over the bed frame, whilst the blankets and pillows were askew. Thereby suggesting she and Palmer had shared in some spontaneous but rather passionate lovemaking. Now, if you would excuse me," he walked toward the door, but Miss Trent closed and stepped in front of it.

"I trust you'll be happy to go to Mr Glasgow's house first thing in the morning to confront Mr Perkins?" Miss Trent enquired as she folded her arms across her chest. "Mr Maxwell, Miss Dexter, and Mr Snyder will be with you, of course."

"I have a prior engagement I cannot cancel," Mr Locke replied. Yet, despite his cool tone, his fingers had instinctively pressed against the needle-containing box concealed within the inside breast pocket of his frock coat.

Miss Trent caught the motion and frowned with grim understanding. Not wishing to confront him in front of Mr Snyder, though, she said, "You're a volunteer, Mr

Locke, and the Society appreciates the time and skills you give us. I therefore can't force you to attend Mr Glasgow's home tomorrow—"

"No, you cannot," Mr Locke interrupted.

"And nor would I wish to," Miss Trent finished in a hard tone. "However, you are the only one who's stepped foot in Mr Perkins' apartment and seen the lease. We have only your word to rely upon."

"And my word is as honourable as it should be," Mr Locke retorted and reached for the door handle. Miss Trent sidestepped in front of it, however.

"Then you won't mind recounting what you saw in person," she replied. "Nine thirty tomorrow morning, Mr Snyder will pick you up from the Palladium and take you to the Glasgow residence, along with Mr Maxwell and Miss Dexter. Agreed?"

"Will you let me leave if I do?" Mr Locke enquired.

"Of course," Miss Trent replied.

Mr Locke gave a soft sigh. "Very well. I shall be there."

"Good," Miss Trent said and moved away from the door. As he opened it, though, she intentionally delayed him further by enquiring, "Another dinner party tonight, is it?"

Mr Locke suppressed the urge to roll his eyes as he replied, coolly, "Not that it is any of your business but, yes, and I do not wish to be late."

"Heaven forbid," Miss Trent retorted in a sardonic tone. "Did they ever find the pearl necklace stolen from the Baroness de Hartier's home?"

Mr Locke's brow lofted. "Unfortunately not," he replied in a dry tone. "Good night, *Miss* Trent." He then went down the stairs to the street where his private carriage awaited him. Although he'd hurried, his step was so light neither Miss Trent nor Mr Snyder had heard his footfalls as he'd descended.

"He is so arrogant," Miss Trent muttered as she closed the door and perched upon the desk of her desk. "Still," she rubbed her temple, "we have something to tell Mr Dorsey at least. My enquiries at the bars on the underground stations didn't turn up anything beyond some poor souls getting mistaken for Palmer."

"Yeah, I got the same on the 'buses and trams," Mr Snyder replied with a smile. "Got Brookbond House from my mate, Joe, at the St. Clement Danes Church's shelter on the Strand; Palmer got his cab from there or the corner of Bow Street. Joe said he was a good bloke who tipped well; talked to him, too."

Miss Trent hummed as she became lost in thought. The sudden, shrill ring of the telephone brought her back with a start, however. Cursing under her breath for being startled, she twisted around upon her desk to pluck the receiver from its cradle. Leaning across as far as she could, she then said into the cone, "Hello, Bow Street Society, Miss Rebecca Trent, Society clerk speaking."

"Thank goodness you're still there! Something truly awful has happened!" a woman's panicked voice exclaimed.

Miss Trent winced as she attempted to twist further to gain better access to the telephone. Fortunately, Mr Snyder had the presence of mind to move her immense typewriter, though, and she was able to swing her legs over the desk to dangle them over its other side. It was unladylike, certainly, but practical problems often required practical solutions.

"Please, take a deep breath and tell me *exactly* what has happened," Miss Trent said into the cone.

"There's been a murder!" the woman's voice cried.

"Pardon?" Miss Trent replied in disbelief. "In that case, you need to call the police—"

"I have, but they refuse to investigate! *Please,* Malcolm was absolutely everything to me, and Mr Dorsey told me you would help," the voice explained.

100

"Mr Dorsey?" Miss Trent repeated for Mr Snyder's benefit as their gazes locked. "And your name is?"

"Oh, didn't I say? Mrs Esta Bonham; I met three of your members yesterday. *Please,* someone has murdered my cat—they *must* be found!"

"Did you say your *cat*?" Miss Trent enquired, stunned.

"Yes, he has been brutally slain!" Mrs Bonham cried. "Will you help me?"

Miss Trent was silent as she tried to gather her thoughts.

"Hello?" Mrs Bonham enquired with panic in her voice.

"I'm still here," Miss Trent replied with a frown. Considering the request based upon the fact Society members were already scheduled to visit the Glasgow residence the following morning, she said, "I shall send Mr Locke, Miss Dexter, and Mr Maxwell to you in the morning."

"Oh, thank you! Thank you so much! I shall expect them at ten o'clock tomorrow. Goodbye!" Mrs Bonham cried, followed by a soft click as she hung up the telephone.

"Now I've heard it all," Miss Trent said as she returned the receiver to its cradle. "Mrs Bonham's cat, Malcolm, has been murdered and she wants us to investigate."

"Wot?" Mr Snyder stared at her. "We gonna?"

"Of course," Miss Trent stood from the desk. "After all, that's what we're here for; to investigate the cases the police can't… or won't."

NINE

"I swear to *God* I didn't do it!" Mr Dorsey yelled as he was dragged from his home in handcuffs by two uniformed constables. Behind them was a broad-shouldered man of six feet with a large nose over an unkempt, brown moustache. His knee-length brown overcoat was worn in places and oversized for his frame. The dark-grey trousers, black waistcoat, and poisoned-white shirt he wore were also far past their prime. The knot of his dark-green tie was flat and askew along with the brim of his black hat. Standing on the porch, he imbibed some snuff as he oversaw the constables wrestling Mr Dorsey into a Black Maria.

Watching the scene unfold from their own door was Mrs Bonham and Mr Glasgow. The former turned to the latter with desperate eyes and cried, "This is absolute nonsense! We must speak to them, make them see sense!"

"No, we must let them do their jobs. They know what they're doing."

Mrs Bonham gave a soft sigh of exasperation as she looked back to the street and saw Mr Maxwell, Miss Dexter, and Mr Locke alighting from a hansom cab. All three had seen Mr Dorsey being taken away, it seemed, as they were taken aback when they approached the Bonham-Glasgow residence and Mr Maxwell enquired, "What's going on? Why are the police taking Mr Dorsey away?"

"They've arrested him for murder," Mrs Bonham replied.

Miss Dexter gasped.

The Bow Streeters had travelled from Miss Trent's office after a briefing at eight forty-five that morning about Mrs Bonham's case. Mr Maxwell therefore naturally assumed the obvious as he enquired, dumbfounded, "Of your cat?"

"No," Mrs Bonham replied. "Mr Perkins has been murdered."

"When?" Mr Maxwell enquired.

"The police think it happened last night," Mr Glasgow replied. "Mr Colby found him in the hallway this morning with his throat cut. Thaddeus was the only other person in the house at the time."

The moustached man with the snuff descended the steps from Mr Dorsey's house and struck the back of the Black Maria twice with an open palm. "Ge' 'im to the station!" He ordered the driver who gave a subtle nod of acknowledgement and spurred the horses into motion with a flick of the reins. The vehicle lurched forward and moved in a wide half-circle as the driver changed its direction and took it the short distance to Bow Street police station. As it left, Mr Dorsey's terrified face momentarily appeared at the barred window but was pulled out of sight by the constables accompanying him. Meanwhile, having seen Mr Maxwell and Miss Dexter gathered outside the Bonham-Glasgow house with a fellow he didn't recognise, the moustached man strode over and demanded with a scowl, "Wot you meddlers doin' 'ere?"

"We are here to investigate a murder," Mr Locke replied.

"Of Mrs Bonham's cat, Sergeant Bird," Mr Maxwell added.

Sergeant Bird's scowl didn't soften as he stared at the two of them. When neither showed any signs of deception or sarcasm, though, the mirth crept into Sergeant Bird's face and he chuckled. Hearing another cab pull up behind him, he turned and shouted to a shabbily dressed Dr Weeks, "Oi, doctor!" He pointed to the Bow Streeters. "This lot's 'ere to find a cat-killer!"

Dr Weeks' tired eyes showed no humour, however, as he enquired, "Where's the damn meat, Bird?"

"Inside, you can't miss 'im," Sergeant Bird replied through a chuckle and followed Dr Weeks into the house.

In the moment before the front door closed, Dr Weeks' voice warned, "Get away from the body!"

Mr Locke tutted at both men's conduct and said to the others, "Mr Maxwell, Miss Dexter, would you be so kind as to accompany Mrs Bonham to her cat, please?"

"Absolutely *out* of the question," Mr Glasgow stated in disbelief.

"Lanford, please—" Mrs Bonham began.

"*No,* Esta," Mr Glasgow interrupted. "Given the current events surrounding our neighbour, I think such an investigation would be very inconsiderate; I won't allow it."

"The deaths could be connected," Mr Maxwell suggested but cowered under Mr Glasgow's glare.

"Malcolm was *my* cat and it's *my* money." Mrs Bonham pointed out to her brother. "You might not allow them to investigate, but *I* will. I've helped you a great deal; all I ask is for you to help me a little now."

Mr Glasgow parted his lips to forbid her further, but the determination in her eyes dissuaded him. He therefore released a soft sigh instead and replied, "Very well, but don't disturb me. I have a great deal of work to do today." He then went inside before anyone could respond as a third cab arrived, this time at the current residence.

A man in his late thirties with a youthful face, pointed nose, and large, protruding ears alighted from it and paid its driver. When he then extended his hand to Mr Locke, the magician saw he had short, black, wavy hair and bushy eyebrows over chestnut brown eyes. As he gave Mr Locke's hand a firm squeeze, he enquired in a soft Scottish accent, "Mr Percy Locke, I presume?"

"Correct."

"Dr Rupert Alexander, veterinary surgeon, at your service. Miss Trent requested I examine the corpse of a cat by the name of Malcolm."

"Then you must speak with his owner," Mr Locke replied and indicated Mrs Bonham. "Mrs Esta Bonham, this is Dr Rupert Alexander, a veterinary surgeon and fellow Bow Street Society member. Dr Alexander, this is Malcolm's owner, Mrs Esta Bonham."

"Thank goodness you're here, Doctor," Mrs Bonham replied. "I've found Malcolm's death most upsetting; any light you can shed on the matter would be gratefully received."

"I give you my word as a surgeon, Mrs Bonham, to do all I can to give you the answers you seek," Dr Alexander replied.

"And this is Mr Joseph Maxwell, an apprenticed journalist with the *Gaslight Gazette*, and Miss Georgina Dexter, an artist. They are also members of the Bow Street Society," Mr Locke introduced.

"Hello," Dr Alexander greeted.

"Please, come in," Mrs Bonham said as she opened the door. Yet, as they made their way to the porch, a distraught man hurried down the street and bounded up the steps to Mr Dorsey's house.

"Poor man…" Mrs Bonham said when she saw him. "That's Mr Timothy Dorsey, Thaddeus' brother."

"Go on without me," Mr Locke said as he descended the steps once more and approached Mr Dorsey's house. Timothy Dorsey had knocked upon the door and was pacing in the porch when Mr Locke reached it.

Aged thirty-five years, Timothy Newton Dorsey was the younger of the brothers. Unlike Thaddeus, his chin was clean-shaven whilst his jaw was framed by sideburns which were narrower by his ears and broader by his mouth, thereby creating a fan-like shape. A moustache in mid-growth adorned his upper lip. It, his sideburns, and the thick, wavy hair upon his head were chocolate brown in colour. He was shorter than Thaddeus by a few inches and slimmer besides. His attire consisted of a double-breasted, dark-brown jacket over a pair of black trousers, a cream-coloured shirt, and olive-green tie.

As Mr Locke made the slow ascent to the porch, the door opened, and Timothy Dorsey moved back several paces at the sight of the constable who'd answered it. The colour drained from Timothy's face like water from a sink as he clapped his hands over his mouth and enquired in a voice strained by emotion, "Oh my God, so it's true…?"

"And you are, sir?" the constable enquired in return.

"This is Mr Timothy Dorsey, constable. Thaddeus' brother," Mr Locke said upon standing beside him. At Timothy's stunned expression, he offered him his hand and continued, "I am Mr Percy Locke from the Bow Street Society. We have been hired by your brother to investigate a private matter of his that, unfortunately, I am unable to elaborate upon at this current time. I can assure you, however, we have your brother's best interests at heart. If you would permit us, therefore, we are willing to do all we can to help him—and you."

"Bow Street… Society?" Timothy echoed, confused.

"Yes," Mr Locke replied. "Perhaps Mr Timothy Dorsey should speak to Sergeant Bird, constable? Naturally, inside would be preferable to the doorstep where anyone may hear."

The constable glanced between them but then half-turned to get the sergeant's attention. Yet, in doing so, he allowed the ghastly scene to be laid bare for them. Mr Arthur Perkins' body was lying chest-down and lengthways across the corridor to the left of the staircase. His head was resting in the open doorway of Thaddeus Dorsey's bedroom. and his bent arms lay either side of his head on the floor. A pool of blood had formed beneath the body from a gaping wound in the man's throat. From where they were standing, neither Mr Locke nor Timothy could see Mr Perkins' lower half. Nevertheless, the sight of blood and Mr Perkins' wide-open eyes was enough to send Timothy into a faint. Mr Locke lunged forward and caught him at once, however, and, draping his limp arm about his shoulders, dragged him inside.

"You can't come in here," the constable said. When it became clear Mr Locke had no intention of leaving, though, he took a firm grip of his arm and explained, "This here's a murder scene; public aren't allowed in."

"Take your hand off me," Mr Locke warned.

"I'm sorry, but it's the rules, sir," the constable replied.

"To hell with the rules, this man needs to lie down," Mr Locke retorted as he tugged his arm free and moved swiftly toward Thaddeus' bedroom. The fact this would lead him pass the body was far from coincidental but, alas, his plan was thwarted by a disgruntled Dr Weeks who rose to his feet and blocked his way. He'd been crouching beside the body whilst inspecting it through an immense magnifying glass attached to a strap around his head.

"Get yer goddamned feet away from the meat!" Dr Weeks ordered, causing the lit cigarette in the corner of his mouth to bob up and down as he did so.

Mr Locke looked down at their feet but glanced at the scene on his way up to meet Dr Weeks' gaze. As a result, he was able to make mental notes of the additional details he'd been unable to see before. These were: a small dagger with an ornate handle lying beside Mr Perkins' right hand, considerable blood splatter and spray on Thaddeus' half-open bedroom door and frame, and white fragments dusting Mr Perkins' legs and the immediate area around them. Curious as to what these fragments could be, he glanced at the scene a second time and saw a small table lying on its side with its top facing the front door. It was the same table Mr Maxwell had walked into during their first visit so, by association, the white fragments were probably the remnants of the white vase that had been standing on it. Mr Locke informed Dr Weeks, "My good man, our feet are nowhere near Mr Perkins' body."

"But they're still where they shouldn't be," Dr Weeks replied as he picked up a small, blood-stained kitchen knife from the floor. It was approximately six inches long with four of those being taken by the blade that was an inch wide at its broadest point. Taking it to Sergeant Bird, who'd emerged from the parlour, he said, "Found that in the guy's trouser pocket. Blood's dried; reckon s'round a day old." As Bird reached for it, though, Dr Weeks pulled it away and went back to the body with it.

"This gentleman refuses to leave, sir," the constable informed Sergeant Bird when he noticed Mr Locke's presence.

"Does 'e?" Sergeant Bird's gruff voice growled as he came around the stairs. Seeing that Mr Locke was holding up the unconscious Timothy, he pointed at him and enquired, "Who's that?"

"Mr Timothy Dorsey—Thaddeus' brother," Mr Locke replied as Timothy began to come round. "I will assume you shall speak with him in the parlour, Sergeant." Seeing Timothy put his weight on his feet but then sway, Mr Locke assisted him across the hallway to the parlour.

"Oi!" Sergeant Bird called as he went after them. Standing in the doorway, he glared at Mr Locke who was gently lowering Timothy onto the sofa and promising to fetch him some brandy. "I never said you could come in 'ere!"

Mr Locke ignored him, however, and spoke over his shoulder to the dumbfounded constable, "Could you fetch Mr Dorsey some brandy, please?"

Sergeant Bird nudged Mr Locke back from the door and growled, "You're not in charge here—"

"And neither are you," Mr Locke interrupted. "Unless the Metropolitan Police do not think the discovery of a body in a blind man's home is worthy of an inspector's attention?"

"We do," a rough, male voice stated in an East-end-of-London accent from the direction of the front door. Everyone apart from Dr Weeks, who had continued his preliminary examination of the body, looked that way as a result. The newcomer entered the house and shut the door with a thud. In his early forties and five-feet-nine inches tall, he had dark-blue eyes, a crooked nose, and weathered features. His calloused hands removed the black trilby from his head to reveal neatly combed dark-red hair beneath whose colour matched that of his eyebrows, well-maintained moustache, and beard. The remainder of his attire consisted of scuffed, black-leather shoes, a knee-length, black overcoat, dark-grey trousers and waistcoat with a light-blue pinstripe, white shirt, and light-blue tie. As he approached Sergeant Bird and Mr Locke, he held up a warrant card, and said, "Inspector John Conway of A Division."

"Scotland Yard?" Sergeant Bird enquired, taken aback. "Wot you doin' 'ere? E Division's got its own inspecta to look into this."

"Orders of Chief Inspector White," Inspector Conway replied. At Sergeant Bird's questioning gaze, he continued in a firmer tone, "You lads let a bloke break into a 'ouse and get done in yards from your station; it's bloody embarrassing. Your inspector's been stood down and I'm in charge. Now, get some brandy like this bloke asked for."

Sergeant Bird squared his shoulders and scowled. Nevertheless, he stomped off to the kitchen in search of some brandy whilst Inspector Conway turned his attention to the man in the parlour doorway. "Mr Percy Locke, yeah?" he enquired in a cold—yet calm—tone whilst extending his hand to him.

"That is correct," Mr Locke replied and gave his hand a brief squeeze. "Though I am not the one to whom you should be speaking, Inspector. Mr Timothy Dorsey, Thaddeus' brother, is presently in the parlour attempting, but failing, to recover from his shock at seeing a body in his brother's hallway. By the way, exactly what is it that connects this crime to a criminal gang? As I understood it, you were the head of the infamous—pardon me, *famous*—Mob Squad of Scotland Yard."

"And I thought you was just a magician," Inspector Conway replied. "What's a bloke that does magic doin' knowin' 'bout the workin's of the Yard? Unless he's got summin' to hide."

"Magic is all about secrets, Inspector."

"So's 'ouse breakin'."

"And slander is both a terrible, and terribly expensive, thing. I wouldn't recommend it."

The corner of Conway's mouth twitched. Keeping his gaze on Mr Locke, he called, "Weeks, when did this bloke die?"

"Between ten and eleven o'clock last night," Dr Weeks replied.

"I want a report on that body after Mr Locke here's gone," Inspector Conway said.

Dr Weeks grunted in response.

Unperturbed by the Canadian's rudeness, and still with his back to him, Inspector Conway enquired, "Who found the body?"

"Mr Jack Colby; e's in the kitchen," Dr Weeks replied as he stood and exhaled a cloud of smoke.

"Thanks," Inspector Conway said. To Mr Locke, he warned, "I want you gone by the time I get back."

Mr Locke watched and waited until Inspector Conway had stridden down the corridor into the kitchen before he returned to the parlour and closed the door ajar.

"Inspector John Conway of Scotland Yard will be here at any moment to speak with you," Mr Locke told Timothy. "You do not have to face him alone if you do not wish to. I will be here to support you, just as we are supporting your brother."

Timothy slowly lifted his head. The colour had returned to his complexion, but his eyes remained haunted. "Please, sir, if you would," he replied. "I need a friend right now."

"Indeed." Mr Locke looked to the door but heard no sign of anyone approaching. Leaning closer to

Timothy, therefore, he enquired in a soft voice, "How close are you to your brother?"

"Very close."

"But not close enough to live here with him?"

"No, I... Thaddeus is sick; he sees things that aren't there, and they make him react... harshly. He can't see very well either, making it worse. It's not... I never know what he'll do when he has an attack. He's a lot stronger than me..."

"But not stronger than Mr Colby," Mr Locke observed, recalling the incident they'd witnessed only days before in this very room.

"No, he makes sure Thaddeus doesn't hurt himself. He takes care of him."

"And he resides here on a full-time basis?" Mr Locke enquired, and Timothy nodded. "Forgive me, Mr Dorsey, but I must ask for your whereabouts last night when this most unfortunate incident took place."

"When did it happen, exactly?"

"Between ten and eleven o'clock."

"Well, I... was at work until five o'clock—I'm a clerk at the Bank of England—and then I took the omnibus home."

"Did you go out at all after you returned home?" Mr Locke enquired, and Timothy shook his head. "I see." Mr Locke adjusted his stance, so he had both Timothy and the door in his field of vision. "How well does your brother know Mr Perkins?"

"Not well at all."

"Then why do you think Mr Perkins was here last night?"

"I have no idea; he's Mr Glasgow's footman, not Thaddeus'. He has no reason to be here unless—" Timothy stopped as a look of dreadful realisation fell over his features.

Mr Locke faced him. "Unless...?"

"Thaddeus invited him over." Timothy swallowed hard and bowed his head. "I can think of no reason why he'd do such a thing though."

"You said he was sick and you did not know what he would do when suffering an attack. Using that reasoning, your brother inviting Mr Perkins here would not be completely beyond the realm of possibility, would it?"

"No, Thaddeus trying to invite him wouldn't be but Mr Colby letting it happen certainly would. As well as paying Mr Colby to keep Thaddeus from hurting himself, I also pay him to make sure he doesn't cause trouble for others. Besides, as sick as Thaddeus is, he wouldn't kill anyone. It's not who he is, not even the sick Thaddeus."

"Then who is he?" Inspector Conway enquired from the doorway. Both men looked at him in surprise at the sudden interruption. They then remained silent as he approached and took out his warrant card. "Inspector John Conway of Scotland Yard." Whilst Timothy read the card, he added, "I thought I told you to hop it, Locke."

"You did," Mr Locke replied but made no indication of leaving.

"I want him to stay, Inspector," Timothy interjected when he saw the policeman's glare. "He's a friend of my brother's and therefore a friend of mine." When Inspector Conway's eyes shifted to him, Timothy's face paled. "*Please,* I'd like him to stay."

Inspector Conway remained silent as he considered the request. After a long pause, he said, "Fine, but keep your mouth shut, Locke."

"But of course," Mr Locke replied.

"Please, be seated, the both of you," Timothy invited.

Whilst Mr Locke took the space beside him on the sofa, Inspector Conway chose to sit in Thaddeus' armchair by the cold hearth.

"And to answer your question, Thaddeus is a very sensitive, caring man," Timothy said once they were settled.

112

"That's not what Colby's just told me," Inspector Conway replied. "He said your brother's a raving lunatic."

"Yes, he is, but he wouldn't *hurt* anyone," Timothy replied with a frown.

Inspector Conway watched him closely as he said, "Colby said he's hit him b'fore, and hurt 'isself b'fore, and that's why he was tied to 'is bed when Colby went out last night."

"*What*?" Timothy enquired, shocked. "My brother is *never* tied down, Inspector." Timothy looked between them. "I would never allow it." Timothy's eyes narrowed as he saw the inspector's unconvinced expression. "My brother is *not* dangerous!"

"Your bruvver was the only one in the 'ouse last night, Mr Dorsey," Inspector Conway replied. "Mr Perkins' body weren't there when Colby left but was there when he got back this mornin.'"

"What do you mean '*when he got back*'? Mr Colby is *supposed* to look after Thaddeus all day and all night!" Timothy cried in disbelief.

"And why's that?" Inspector Conway challenged.

"Because that's what I pay him for!" Timothy yelled.

"Mr Colby also resides here with Thaddeus Dorsey," Mr Locke interjected.

"Nah." Inspector Conway shook his head as his hard gaze remained fixed upon Timothy. "It's because your bruvver's dangerous, isn't it?"

"No!" Timothy yelled as he leapt to his feet. "Where is he? I want to talk to him *right* now! This is all a complete and utter *lie*! Thaddeus is unwell, yes, but he's not a *murderer*! If—if anything, Thaddeus should've been the murder victim if Mr Perkins was stalking about the house in the middle of the night while my brother was tied, *helpless,* to his bed!"

"But he weren't, sir," Inspector Conway replied and rose to his feet.

Timothy stared at him in disbelief as he began, "But you said—"

"Colby tied 'im up b'fore he left, but that don't stop your bruvver from gettin' 'imself loose after," Inspector Conway interrupted. "There's no way Mr Perkins got in 'ere without your bruvver letting 'im in; Colby locked the front door when he left and unlocked it when he got back this mornin,' the backdoor's lock is rusted shut, the windows are all nailed down—"

"*What*?!" Timothy exclaimed and looked to the window. Yet, even with the distance between it and him, Timothy saw the nails in the frame. "No... no, no." He shook his head. "This is wrong. I would've *never* agreed to this! My brother's sickness does *not* warrant such measures!"

"You do not know for certain it was Mr Thaddeus Dorsey who let Mr Perkins into the house, Inspector," Mr Locke interjected, much to Inspector Conway's annoyance. "You only have Mr Colby's word for it that he left Thaddeus alone last night."

"And it's been sound so far," Inspector Conway pointed out. "Colby says that dagger by Mr Perkins' hand is Thaddeus' letter opener." To Timothy, he said, "Look at it and tell me it's not his."

"Very well," Timothy replied. "I *will*." Swallowing hard and straightening his back, he then walked briskly from the parlour and across the hallway with Inspector Conway and Mr Locke following. The moment he rounded the stairs and saw the dagger, though, he froze in shock.

"Is it 'is?" Inspector Conway enquired behind him.

The colour drained from Timothy's face a second time as he mustered a nod.

"It belonging to Thaddeus does not automatically equate to Thaddeus being the one who wielded it," Mr Locke pointed out as he stepped forward to allow Timothy to lean upon him. "Granted Thaddeus *could* have released himself from his bed, unlocked the front door, invited Mr Perkins inside, and murdered him but retie himself afterwards? Such a feat would be an incredible accomplishment for a sighted man, but for a blind one I would say it was as near impossible as one can get. No, *your* focus should be on Mr Colby, Inspector, *not* Thaddeus."

"Don't tell me what to do, conjurer," Inspector Conway growled. "Bugger off, both of you."

"Gladly, Mr Timothy needs to pay Thaddeus' lawyer a visit anyway," Mr Locke replied with a smile and led Timothy to the front door.

"But Thaddeus doesn't have a lawyer," Timothy said, confused, as they left.

"Is Mr Glasgow not his lawyer?" Mr Locke enquired once they were back outside.

"No, Mr Glasgow wouldn't hear of such a thing."

"I see," Mr Locke replied. Falling silent whilst they descended the steps, he then turned to Timothy at their base and said, "Do not fear, Mr Dorsey. Your brother is a client of the Bow Street Society; he *shall* have a lawyer."

TEN

Mrs Bonham felt sick as she led her guests across the hallway to a closed door. When they'd passed it, her gaze had drifted to the spot where Mr Perkins had often stood, and her stomach had lurched at the memory. Indicating the door, she said, "Malcolm is in the parlour, here."

"Thank you," Dr Alexander replied. "You don't have to come in if you don't want to. I'll need Miss Dexter to make sketches of the body, but Mr Maxwell can stay with you if you'd like?"

"No, Lanford wouldn't approve," Mrs Bonham replied with a cold, fleeting look at the apprenticed journalist. "I'll be in the waiting room for Lanford's law firm upstairs when you're done."

"One moment, Mrs Bonham," Dr Alexander said. "Is this where Malcolm was found?"

"No, he was in the kitchen but cook wanted to prepare dinner and I knew Lanford would want rid of him immediately if we didn't move him," Mrs Bonham replied.

"I understand, thank you," Dr Alexander replied, allowing the distressed woman to depart as he opened the door and went inside.

The parlour was a fair size and overlooked Bow Street through a large bay window to the far right as one entered. Opposite the window was a plain, polished oak surround fireplace with mustard-and-brown-checked tiles bookending its cast-iron hearth. It was a stark contrast to the ornate marble fireplaces of the waiting rooms in both colour and design. Light-yellow wallpaper with a curved leaf design in mustard covered the walls, whilst the floor was exposed boards varnished in a dark lacquer. A large, square rug of varying shades of green and cream lay in front of the fireplace as a much smaller, round rug of plain Nile-green lay beneath the window.

Hanging on the wall above the fireplace was an oil painting of an upper-class woman in a yellow gown. She

116

was sitting in a garden filled with flowers of every colour imaginable so, naturally, as an artist, Miss Dexter was drawn to the image. Additional ornamentations were a set of heavy, dark-brown curtains tied back either side of the window and an elaborate glass chandelier. The mantel shelf, meanwhile, held a clock in an engraved, brass casing, two uninteresting brass candlesticks, a bland, wooden, cigarette box, and a selection of poetry books.

The furniture included a display cabinet in the corner of the room filled with a hand-painted, pale green and yellow floral dinner service. Additionally, a three-seater sofa with curved arms and legs, Queen Anne feet, and Nile-green seat cushions, back and arm rests stood opposite the hearth. Its matching chair stood at an angle to the fireplace, looking inward, whilst a low cabinet stood to the right of the window. Finally, a plain fireguard was positioned before the hearth, and a round, oak table with two chairs, stood on the rug by the window.

In its centre was a wooden chopping board saturated with dried blood and, in the middle of that, lay the corpse of a cat on its back. Dr Alexander stared at the ghastly sight in disbelief. "My God," he muttered. "What monstrosity…" He neared the board with great trepidation and growing anger. Fearful he may utter a profanity in Miss Dexter's presence, he placed a loose hand over his mouth until he'd digested what he saw. Standing with his knuckles upon the table, he said with disgust, "We must find who did this."

Mr Maxwell came up behind him and swallowed hard at the sight as his fingers toyed with his cravat. Miss Dexter, meanwhile, had hesitated by the door whilst contemplating if she should go any further. Yet, her recollection of what Dr Alexander had told Mrs Bonham in the hallway persuaded her to venture over to the table. She was as disgusted as her associates by what she saw and both she and Mr Maxwell nodded in agreement with Dr Alexander's statement.

"Have you much experience of things like this, Doctor?" Mr Maxwell enquired.

"I've never been asked to attend a murder scene like this before," Dr Alexander replied. "But I've seen some things at the Poor People's Out-Patient Clinic, I can tell you."

"What's that?" Miss Dexter enquired as she took her sketchbook and pencils from her satchel and laid them out upon the table.

"A free veterinary service for the poor founded by the Royal Veterinary College in 1879; I volunteer there three or four times a week," Dr Alexander explained.

"Is that where you qualified from, then, the College?" Mr Maxwell enquired. Copying Miss Dexter's example, he pulled a notebook from his pocket to write down Dr Alexander's findings from the examination. Unfortunately, the notebook's corner caught a used handkerchief that was also in Mr Maxwell's pocket and, to his horror, fell onto the board. He plucked it up at once but grimaced when he saw the blood on it. "Sorry," he mumbled with a sheepish glance to the others as he stuffed it back into his pocket. Miss Dexter smiled in amusement at both his antics and flushed complexion, but Dr Alexander dismissed the mistake with a wave of his hand.

"Yes; I studied there for three years to become a veterinary surgeon," Dr Alexander said, pulling a chair out from under the table and putting his bag down upon it. "I now have my own practice in addition to my work at the clinic. Excuse me a moment, please." He left the room, and Miss Dexter started to sketch the unfortunate feline.

"Terrible…" Mr Maxwell remarked.

Miss Dexter hummed but continued her work.

The next few moments passed in silence between them until Dr Alexander returned. When he did, he removed his jacket and draped it over the sofa's arm, saying, "Apologies about that. I needed to ask someone to bring a bowl of warm water and a towel for after the examination." Rolling up his shirt sleeves, he approached

the table and leant over the corpse with a glance to Mr
Maxwell to ensure he was ready to take dictation.

"A short-haired *Felis Catus*. Male, with brown
fur," Dr Alexander said and peered inside the cat's mouth.
"His tongue is resting against the corner of his mouth; his
canine, incisor, premolar and molar teeth are all there, but
the jaw's been dislocated. A cut, about a quarter of an inch
deep, goes from the underside of his chin to his stomach,
where the cut is much deeper and has been pulled apart."
Dr Alexander eased his fingers into the cut on the cat's
neck and widened it look inside. "His pharynx is still
intact." He moved his fingers along the length of the cut
and opened it wider, still. "But his oesophagus is cut open
all the way down…" He moved his fingers further along
the cut. "…and pulled open." Removing his fingers, he
repositioned himself at the table and peered into the gaping
wound in the cat's stomach. Slipping his fingers inside, he
continued, "The small and large intestines have been taken
out and are missing. The pancreas, kidneys, liver, bladder,
and ureters have been cut from the body, removed, and
tossed back into the cavity." He lifted the flesh nearest to
the neck and slid his fingers underneath. "I *think* the lungs,
heart, bronchial tubes and trachea are all intact, but I'll
have to open him up properly to make sure. I'll do that
back at the clinic." He withdrew his hand just as the maid
entered carrying the bowl of water and towel. "Thank
you," he said. "Put it down here, please."

"Yessir," the maid replied, hurriedly doing as
instructed while trying not to look at the horrific mess.
"Will that be all, sir?"

"Yes, thank you," Dr Alexander replied. The maid
gave a shallow bob in place of a curtsey and hastily left the
room.

"So, what does all that mean?" Mr Maxwell
enquired.

Dr Alexander washed off the excess blood in the
bowl and took a bar of carbolic soap from his bag to

remove the rest. As he did so, he replied, "If I was a betting man, I'd say someone was looking for something."

Miss Dexter put the finishing touches to her sketch and moved away from the table.

"Such as?" Mr Maxwell enquired, his concerned eyes following Miss Dexter.

"Something small enough to be swallowed by a cat but too big to be passed," Dr Alexander replied and dried his hands on the towel. "Or something someone couldn't wait to be passed. This doesn't scream the actions of someone who cared about Malcolm."

"Looks like curiosity really did kill the cat, then," Mr Maxwell remarked, but then his eyes widened in horror. "I'm so sorry! I didn't mean to sound so heartless."

"I know," Dr Alexander replied. "But I think you're right. Whatever Malcolm swallowed is the thing that got him killed." He took some cloth from his bag and draped it over the cat's body. "We should speak to Mrs Bonham about Malcolm's health over the last few days."

"Mrs Bonham was there when Mr Dorsey was touching the clay model; she told him Malcolm had been unwell," Miss Dexter interjected in a quiet voice as she returned her sketchbook and pencils to her satchel.

Mr Maxwell pointed at her and exclaimed with a smile, "That's right!" His smile vanished when he saw the solemn expressions of his associates, though, and he wiped the sweat from his palms onto his frock coat. "Yes," he cleared his throat, "Let's talk to Mrs Bonham."

* * *

Mrs Bonham stood at the window clutching her handkerchief. Her features were contorted with a mixture of grief and unease as she stared into the distant horizon. She was alone in the Lanford Law waiting room when the Bow Streeters entered. The sounds of their feet therefore caused her to spin around at once. Upon seeing it was them, she enquired, "What did you discover?"

"Will you sit, please?" Dr Alexander requested in return and approached the armchairs. "What I've got to say might shock you."

Mrs Bonham's face paled as she looked between Dr Alexander and Miss Dexter with fear in her eyes. Nevertheless, she perched upon an armchair and held her handkerchief tightly in her lap.

Dr Alexander sat across from her and said, "I've examined Malcolm's body and, as you're aware, it was cut open. I'm afraid his organs were also removed, and his intestines stolen."

Mrs Bonham pressed her handkerchief to her mouth. "His *intestines* were stolen?" she half-whispered after taking a few moments to calm down. "Do—do you think he was killed by a violinist?" Her lips trembled. "To make strings for his instrument?"

Dr Alexander placed a gentle hand upon hers. "No, that's impossible. Violin strings are made from sheep, lamb, or goat intestines, not cat."

"Thank goodness," Mrs Bonham muttered.

"I do think the theft of his intestines is significant though," Dr Alexander admitted. "I believe he was murdered because he swallowed something someone was desperate to get back."

"Swallowed…?" Mrs Bonham echoed as her eyes glistened with tears she fought to hold back. "But… who? Why? What… what could they have been looking for?"

"Something small enough for Malcolm to swallow without choking; like a gem for example," Dr Alexander replied. "Has anything like that gone missing in the last few days?" He glanced at Miss Dexter and Mrs Bonham did the same as he continued, "Miss Dexter said you'd told Mr Dorsey Malcolm was ill. When was that?"

"A couple of days ago," Mrs Bonham replied, dabbing her eyes with her handkerchief. "I went to see him because he was worried about his friend. I would usually take Malcolm with me on my visits because he likes Mr Dorsey so." Mrs Bonham sniffed and bowed her head.

"But I left him at home because he'd not been himself. He'd wretched and coughed, but nothing had come up; he was just lying around feeling sorry for himself."

"Did you take him to see Mr Dorsey last night?" Mr Maxwell enquired, and Mrs Bonham shook her head. "So, you stayed at home?"

"Yes," Mrs Bonham replied in bemusement.

Dr Alexander and Miss Dexter shared the feeling as the former looked at Mr Maxwell with disapproval and the latter looked at him in confusion.

"Did you have a veterinarian examine him at all?" Dr Alexander enquired from Mrs Bonham.

"No, Lanford—my brother—said he'd be fine, and I shouldn't worry," Mrs Bonham replied, blinking several times as she looked to the ceiling. "Oh, if only I had listened to my instincts!" She dried her eyes, again, but the tears kept falling. "If only Mr Perkins hadn't visited Mr Dorsey... Oh, it's all so *horrible*!" She stood and went back to the window. "*Please*," she said, her voice strained with emotion. "I need to be alone."

"Of course," Dr Alexander replied, also standing. "I'll take Malcolm back to my clinic and prepare for his burial."

"You know where we are should you need us, Mrs Bonham," Miss Dexter added.

Mr Maxwell was urging her with his eyes, though. Confused, she gave a subtle shake of her head and brushed her fingers against his arm to encourage him to follow as she and Dr Alexander headed for the door. Mr Maxwell didn't move, however, and enquired,
"You were at home *all* evening, Mrs Bonham?"

"Yes," Mrs Bonham replied through a half-sob.

"Can you remember what you were doing?" Mr Maxwell enquired, ignoring the blatant displeasure of his fellow Bow Streeters.

Mrs Bonham took a deep breath to calm her emotions. "I embroidered for a time... then retired to bed wherein I read for an hour before taking my draught and falling asleep." She turned her head to glare at him with tear-streaked cheeks. "I didn't kill him. Now, *please,*" she looked back to the window, "leave me to my grief."

Mr Maxwell nodded with a solemn expression and closed the door as he left.

ELEVEN

Mr Maxwell joined Dr Alexander and Miss Dexter on the landing. The former's expression was one of condemnation as he folded his arms across his chest, whilst the latter attempted to hide her disquiet at Mr Maxwell's behaviour by looking anywhere but his face. "We've got to ask these things," Mr Maxwell said with resolve. "If Mr Dorsey didn't kill Mr Perkins, someone else did."

Miss Dexter lifted meek eyes to meet Dr Alexander's stern ones and their respective objections faded considering their fellow Bow Streeter's logic. Her avoidance of Mr Maxwell's eyes therefore ceased, and Dr Alexander lowered his arms. Yielding to Mr Maxwell's point of view, he replied, "I agree."

"So, while you're collecting Malcolm, I'll see what I can find in Mr Perkins' room," Mr Maxwell said.

"Don't be stupid, man," Dr Alexander hissed with a glance to the waiting room door.

"But you don't know where his room is," Miss Dexter pointed out, worried.

"No, but he was a footman, correct?" Mr Maxwell said.

"Yes," Dr Alexander replied.

"Then male servants' rooms in these townhouses are usually in the basement. My father's servants' rooms are anyway," Mr Maxwell explained.

"But what if you're caught?" Dr Alexander enquired.

"I won't be, not if you distract anyone from going down there," Mr Maxwell replied.

Dr Alexander and Miss Dexter exchanged concerned glances.

"The police are next door; it's only a matter of time before they come here to search the room," Mr Maxwell went on. "When that happens, we won't have any chance of doing the same, and therefore won't have any chance of helping Mr Dorsey."

Miss Dexter nibbled upon her lip as she toyed with the fabric of her skirts, unconvinced by the propriety of Mr Maxwell's suggestion. Yet, again, she couldn't find fault in his reasoning. Uncertain as to what should be done and lacking the confidence to either agree or disagree as a result, she waited for Dr Alexander to make the decision.

"I can't say I'm in agreement, but go on," Dr Alexander said.

"Thank you," Mr Maxwell replied with a broad smile. "I shan't be long, I promise!" He then hurried down the stairs, along the corridor, and through the basement door.

As Dr Alexander and Miss Dexter descended from the landing, he said, "Remind me, please; what it is he does for a living?"

"He's an apprentice journalist with the *Gaslight Gazette.*"

"Oh," Dr Alexander replied with a frown. When they reached the hallway, he instructed, "You'd best wait here and keep watch, then, while I collect Malcolm's remains. If you see anyone coming, faint and I'll come back to assist you."

"I don't faint," Miss Dexter replied in a surprisingly no-nonsense tone. "But I'll raise my voice so you can hear me."

Dr Alexander's frown lifted into a smile. "I see now why Miss Trent hired you as a Society member."

Miss Dexter felt her cheeks warm but stayed by the stairs whilst Dr Alexander went into the parlour.

Meanwhile, Mr Maxwell had changed to a more cautious pace in descending the dimly lit stone steps and emerged into a gas lit corridor. A door stood ajar a few metres in front of him. From it came the scent of baking bread and the sound of women conversing, presumably servants. The corridor continued into the darkness on his left so Mr Maxwell side-stepped along it with his back against its wall and his arm outstretched for potential obstacles which could give away his presence. Eventually coming to another door, he tried turning its handle and was delighted to find it was unlocked. An involuntary squeak escaped his lips and he slapped his hand over them to stifle it. With his heart racing, he peered back down the corridor but saw no one. He lowered his hand and licked his dry lips as he reached for the door handle once more. *What if there's someone inside?* He thought and froze with the door ajar. *What would I say?* He hadn't heard anyone ask who was there when he'd opened the door. *I am here under Mrs Bonham's invitation*, he recalled. *I could be lost?* His heart rate slowed as he smiled, *Yes! Lost, that's it!* He puffed out his chest and went in.

There was no one there. *My lying skills will have to be honed another day*, he thought with disappointment. Straightening his cravat and smoothing down his frock coat, he then walked a circuit of the room. It was the epitome of basic—exposed brick walls and stone floor with no decoration on either. A single-sized, rickety bed frame of dull brass stood in the corner. It was immaculately made with coarse, brown, woollen blankets over an off-white sheet and flat pillow. An unstable table was beside the bed with a candlestick standing upon it. The melted candle it held was unlit. In the far corner was a washstand with the usual articles for toilet laid out on its shelves. Mr Maxwell bent over and peered under the bed; nothing. *Nothing could be hidden in here*, he thought. *There's nowhere to hide it*. He sighed and was about to leave when he noticed a small, wooden chest standing at the foot of the bed. It was polished oak so was almost invisible in the gloom. Deciding he ought to look inside, but not wishing to be caught doing so, he pushed the door closed and crossed over to it. He'd underestimated the weight of the door, however, and it slammed with such a loud thud he almost leapt out of his skin.

Mr Maxwell held his breath and heard a muffled commotion of female voices, followed by a woman enquiring into the corridor, "Who's there?!" His heart ran a marathon in his chest as he prayed they wouldn't investigate. Alas, he heard the same woman say, "It sounded like it come from Perkins' room. I'm gonna look."

"Don't you be leavin' me 'ere alone!" A second woman said.

"Come on, then, but be quiet!" The first woman warned.

Mr Maxwell clasped both hands over his mouth to muffle his fast breathing as he spun this way and that in frantic search of a hiding place. Seeing the bed, he remembered there wasn't anything under it. He therefore threw himself onto the floor, lay on his stomach, and dragged himself under it as the women's footsteps grew nearer. He'd just managed to tuck himself in at the back, by the wall, when the door flew open.

"Who's in there?" the first woman enquired into the darkness.

"We'll fetch a constable if you don't come out," the second woman warned.

"I've got a knife," the first woman added.

"No, we don't, cook," the second woman whispered.

"They don't know that, do they, Betsy?" the cook hissed.

"*What's that*?!" Betsy cried and both women shrieked in terror as a mouse scurried across the floor toward them. "It's a *mouse*!"

"Fetch the master!" cook ordered, pulling Betsy out of the room with her and slamming the door. Mr Maxwell held his breath and listened to the women's hurried footsteps as they rushed back down the corridor and up the stairs. Knowing he had even less time to complete his search, he scrambled out from under the bed, beat the dust from his clothes, and opened the chest.

Inside were the usual set of clothes reserved for Sundays—a pressed shirt, clean suit, and polished shoes. A folded spare nightshirt, bed socks, and long johns were also present, alongside an old, well-thumbed copy of the Bible, a pair of sturdy boots, and a brown, knitted scarf with matching gloves. Mr Maxwell had put the items on the bed as he'd found them until he was left with an empty chest. He sat back on his heels and rubbed the back of his neck as he realised his efforts were for nought. Releasing a soft sigh of defeat, he put the Bible back into the chest but paused when he saw a finger-sized hole in the corner of the chest's base. Curious as to what it was for, he slipped his finger inside and felt a gap between the floor of the chest and its actual base. His heart leapt in excitement and he pulled up the false floor in an instant. Hidden beneath were some banknotes and a pile of letters tied with ribbon.

Yet, even as he loosened the ribbon's knot, he heard footfalls on the stairs and the voices of cook and Betsy. Concluding it was unwise to tempt fate any further, he pocketed the letters, put the banknotes back into the chest, replaced the false bottom, and bundled the remained items into it. Hearing the women approaching for a second time, he closed the lid and slipped behind the door just as they opened it. He held his breath as cook and Betsy crept inside holding a rolling pin and wooden spoon respectively. Waiting until they'd cleared the door, he then stepped around it and slipped into the corridor.

He needed a brandy by the time he'd made it back to the safety of Dr Alexander's and Miss Dexter's company in the hallway upstairs. His fellow Bow Streeters glanced over his dishevelled, dust-covered state with both curiosity and concern. Yet, Mr Maxwell went straight for the front door and held it open for them, saying, "I think it's time to leave." Glancing to Mr Snyder's cab outside, he saw Sergeant Bird approaching with a constable and a red-haired man he didn't recognise. He looked important, though. "*Yes*," Mr Maxwell said, his voice strangled by his fear that the police would recognise him as a thief as easily as if it was written on his forehead. "Definitely time to go."

Dr Alexander looked at Mr Maxwell, perplexed, but upon seeing the police arrive, left the house carrying Malcolm's corpse in a large box. Miss Dexter took Mr Maxwell's arm and followed their associate. As they passed Sergeant Bird and his colleagues neither group acknowledged the other; something Mr Maxwell was most grateful for indeed.

TWELVE

Mr Gregory Elliott. Solicitor read the card as it was placed upon a copy of the *Police Gazette.* The sergeant looked up from it but had to tilt his head back further to meet the solicitor's gaze. Mr Elliott was a man in his late twenties with dark—almost black—short hair and unfashionably clean-shaven cheeks, chin, and upper lip. The fair, almost translucent skin gracing his slender face meant he was often described as beautiful rather than handsome. His unflinching, green-brown eyes gazed down his narrow nose at the sergeant as he stood before the main desk in the entrance hall of Scotland Yard. In a monotone, he stated, "My client is Mr Thaddeus Dorsey."

"We've not sent for you," the sergeant replied.

"I'm acting under instructions from Mr Timothy Dorsey who holds the power of attorney over his brother's—Thaddeus'—financial affairs. He is also the party accountable for ensuring Thaddeus Dorsey is kept in a state of comfort within the confines of his own home, as a voluntary boarder, without the prospect of profit for Mr Timothy Dorsey. Such obligations are stipulated in the terms attached to the formal arrangement of a single-house confinement, as outlined by the Lunacy Commission, in accordance with the Lunacy Act of 1890. Now, if these terms are broken as either a direct or indirect result of your preventing me from seeing my client, you may rest assured." He glanced at the stripes on the man's cuffs. "Sergeant, I shall lodge a formal complaint with Commissioner Bradford and have you dismissed on the grounds of incompetence."

"He's in the cells."

"I shall speak with him there, then," Mr Elliott replied.

The sergeant hesitated as he contemplated refusing the request. Deciding it was wiser to grant it on the grounds of self-protection, however, he called to a constable in the back office to temporarily fulfil his desk duties.

"May I also enquire if there was a reason for my client being transferred here instead of remaining in custody at the Bow Street police station?" Mr Elliott enquired whilst they waited and the sergeant made a brief search of the solicitor's black, leather briefcase.

"Orders of Inspector Conway," the sergeant replied as he returned Mr Elliott's property. When the constable emerged, the sergeant lifted a hatch at the desk's far end, stepped through to join Mr Elliott on the other side, and lowered it again. "This way, please, sir," he invited, leading Mr Elliott through a door directly to the left of the desk and down a flight of darkened stairs.

At their foot was a low-ceilinged room with another desk across its back-left corner. To its left and right were locked, barred gates. Beyond these were long, narrow corridors with solid brick walls on one side and heavy, black iron doors on the other. Each door had a peephole set deep into its centre with a small, round cover slid over it, and a narrow, locked food hatch at its foot. A further three corridors branched off from the left-hand one, whilst the one on the right led to a dead end.

"Solicitor's here to see Dorsey," the sergeant told his equivalent behind the desk as he gave him the business card. "Custody Sergeant Smythe, here, will sort you out, sir," he informed Mr Elliott and returned to his post upstairs. In the meantime, Smythe read the card, scrutinised Mr Elliott for a moment, and read the card again.

"Caused us a lot of trouble he has," Smythe said, unhooking the bundle of keys from his belt and unlocking the gate on the right. When he pulled it open with a loud scrape of its metallic hinges, a cacophony of groans, complaints, hollers, and bangs erupted from the cells' occupants. Smythe struck the doors of the loudest prisoners with his truncheon and ordered them to be quiet as he and Mr Elliott passed. Some heeded the warning and fell silent whilst others took it as a challenge and yelled louder still with several profanities thrown in for good measure. When he reached cell number eight at the far end of the corridor, Smythe continued, "Was shouting when he arrived, shouting when he was measured, and shouting when he was photographed. He whacked Constable Tompkins good, too, so you can add assault of a policeman to his murder charge."

"Has he confessed?" Mr Elliott enquired.

"No," Smythe replied.

"Then it's suspicion of murder, Sergeant. As for his behaviour, he is a blind man sick in mind. Did you tell him of your intentions before you measured him?"

"No," Smythe scoffed, unlocking the cell door, and opening it wide enough for Mr Elliott to slip in. Once he'd entered, the door was slammed shut, filling the narrow, white-washed windowless cell with a deafening bang.

"Mr Thaddeus Dorsey?" Mr Elliott enquired of the prostrate figure on the narrow, wooden shelf masquerading as a bed. A long, low moan came back followed by sobbing. "Mr Dorsey, you must control yourself," Mr Elliott urged in a firmer tone. "I am Mr Gregory Elliott, a solicitor and member of the Bow Street Society. They, and your brother, have asked me to represent you. To do that, I must hear your account of what happened, however." He pulled him by his arm into a sitting position and leant forward to speak to him eye to eye. "You will be hanged if you don't tell it."

"The walls are bleeding," Mr Dorsey muttered as he surveyed his surroundings. "Red…" He stood from the shelf, thereby compelling Mr Elliott to move aside. "So much red." He went to the door and traced the cracks and bumps in the paintwork with his fingers, saying, "So much of it." His wrists were still bound by handcuffs and they jangled as he then spun toward Mr Elliott. Rather than focus on him, though, he instead looked at the empty space above his shoulder, muttering under his breath, before turning his head sharply this way and that as if watching an invisible object flying at great speed. "Red!" He shouted, lifting trembling hands to his face. "It flies and morphs before me! It won't stop!"

"*Mister* Dorsey!" Mr Elliott shouted above his yells and Mr Dorsey turned around at once. In a quieter, much calmer tone, Mr Elliott continued, "Either you sit down, control yourself, and tell me what happened or soon your hallucinations will be all too real. It will be *your* blood you'll be seeing."

Mr Dorsey stared at him as if he were the hangman.

"*Sit. Down,*" Mr Elliott repeated.

Mr Dorsey closed and parted his lips several times whilst the failure of his eyes to focus on Mr Elliott continued. He clasped his hands together, shuffled back to the shelf, and dropped down onto it.

"Thank you," Mr Elliott said. Sitting beside his client, he retrieved a notebook and pencil from his briefcase. "Now, tell me *everything* that happened last night. Don't leave out any details either, however small or trivial you think they may be."

"There are blinking purple circles on my hands," Mr Dorsey mumbled and closed his eyes. "I was tied to the bed. I heard someone coming toward my bedroom door, then a scuffle, and finally the smashing of the vase in the hall. I shouted out, I did!" He opened his eyes and wiped them with the side of his hand. "But no one answered. I listened and heard someone walking away. Then it was quiet. I didn't know Mr Perkins was there, dead, until Mr Colby came back in the morning and yelled I was a murdering lunatic who needed to be hung. Then I heard him run into the street and shout 'murder.' But I didn't murder him, Mr Elliott, I *didn't*. How could I? I was tied to the bed *all* night, the same way I'm tied to it every night. Ask Miss Dexter, Mr Locke, and Mr Maxwell; they'll tell you how they found me."

"Miss Trent gave me a brief account of their prior meetings with you. Was Mr Colby in the house when you heard someone coming toward your bedroom?"

"No, he'd gone out quite some time before. I don't know when… You said you're a solicitor; do you know Hamish McGraw?"

"The old fellow who's perpetually sitting by the fire at the Law Club?" When Mr Dorsey nodded, Mr Elliott continued, "Yes. I was just a clerk when I saw him successfully defend Mr Ashley."

"The fellow accused of being the Kilburn Killer?"

"Yes. In the end, it was revealed to be the boutique owner from Oxford Street, Mr Albert Wentworth."

A smile crept across Mr Dorsey's lips as his facial features relaxed with the reminiscence of the Law Club; a place he greatly loved but was forbidden to go.

"Did the person near to your bedroom speak at all?" Mr Elliott enquired.

"No. As I told you, they came toward the room, there was a scuffle, the vase smashed, I shouted out, and someone walked away." Mr Dorsey gripped his arm. "Wait a moment, I *did* hear some grunting during the scuffle and then…" He became downcast, and his voice trembled under the weight of his terrible realisation. "…A thud of something hitting the floor."

"In which direction would you say the footsteps were headed?"

Mr Dorsey's features contorted with frustration as he shook his head and replied, "I'm not certain." He took a moment to replay the memory in his mind. "I heard their footsteps for longer than if they'd simply gone into the kitchen though; that door is next to mine. I *thought* I heard a door opening, but I don't know which." He sighed. "I was probably looking straight at them when they were scuffling in my doorway but these *blasted* eyes!" He rubbed the offending organs with his thumbs. "I saw nothing but darkness."

Mr Elliott stopped his notetaking as a question posed itself in his mind. He watched his client return his hands to his lap and, seemingly, stare into space. Wishing to have an answer to his question, he held up his pencil in line with Mr Dorsey's eyes and moved it left and right along his disputed line of vision. As he did so, he scrutinised his facial muscles for any twitches which may betray an underlying effort to refrain from looking at the pencil. There were none. He therefore moved the pencil closer to Mr Dorsey's face and withdrew it several times to gauge his eyes' responses. Neither appeared to follow or even focus upon it.

"What are you doing with that pencil?" Mr Dorsey enquired.

Mr Elliott held it directly in front of his client's face and, in his usual monotone, replied, "It's not a pencil. It's a pen."

"It's a pencil."

"How do you know it is?"

"I know a pencil when I see one!"

Mr Elliott withdrew the pencil and poised it over his notebook as he challenged, "When you *see* one?"

Mr Dorsey gave a soft sigh and replied. "Well, not *actually* see it, of course. It's a figure of speech." He then turned toward Mr Elliott and demanded, "Are you testing me?"

"Yes."

Mr Dorsey's jaw momentarily fell open before he clenched it tight and rubbed his hands in his lap. Easing the tension in his jaw as his features creased with worry, he then enquired, "But *why*?"

"Because Miss Trent told me you were blind. Yet since I've been here, you've spoken of seeing 'purple spots' and 'red' and have displayed only a fraction of the clumsiness I would expect to see from a blind man. Furthermore, you informed me of your blindness at the point in your story where you may have been forced to admit you recognised the victim had you full sight—did you recognise him?"

"No!"

"You know as well as I do eyewitness accounts are never one hundred percent reliable; facts are altered, skewed, or withheld altogether, for both accidental and intentional reasons. I have to put your claim to the test if I'm to protect your interests to the best of my ability."

Mr Dorsey's lips trembled as he enquired in a meek voice, "D—Did it pass?"

"It did until you insisted it was a pencil," Mr Elliott replied.

"I… I smelt the wood of it when you brought it closer to my nose."

"And your reference to being able to 'see' it?"

"I wasn't born blind," Mr Dorsey pointed out. "I don't use the correct terminology all of the time, but that *doesn't* mean I can see."

Mr Elliott considered the point and concluded it was a valid one. "Very well, I believe you."

"*Thank* you," Mr Dorsey replied with blatant relief.

"How strong *is* your sense of smell?" Mr Elliott enquired.

"Reasonably strong."

"In that case, what did you smell last night?"

"Carbolic soap followed by burnt almonds."

"When did you smell each scent and, on a scale of one to ten, how strong were they both? One being very weak and ten being very strong."

"I smelt the soap as soon as the first person approached my bedroom door. The burnt almonds scent was intermingled with the soap. Then I only smelt the burnt almonds after the vase smashed. The soap was certainly the most powerful of the scents, a nine. The burnt almonds were weaker, a six or seven."

Mr Elliott made short-hand notes of Mr Dorsey's account whilst fresh questions formed in his mind as he began to build a picture of the previous night's events. Having completed his transcription, he enquired, "Did you smell anything else?"

"No."

"Did you know at the time it was a vase that had been smashed?"

"Yes."

"How?"

"As far as I'm aware, it's the only item on that side of the hallway that would make such a noise. Also, smashing china has a very distinctive sound to it."

Mr Elliott noted Mr Dorsey's swiftness of response and the clarity of his answers. If this had been a criminal court rather than a police cell, Mr Elliott would've been confident in his client's ability to persuade the judge and jury of his innocence. Nevertheless, he'd witnessed eloquent men walking free despite their evident guilt and uneducated men sentenced to death despite their evident innocence. It was a fine line and Mr Elliott had yet to settle on which camp Mr Dorsey belonged to. Referring to the notes he'd made during his earlier conversation with Miss Trent, he said, "The deceased's name was Mr Arthur Perkins; is that name familiar to you?"

"He's Mr Glasgow's footman. Do you know Mr Lanford Glasgow, Mr Elliott?"

"I can't say I do. You've met Mr Perkins, then?"

"Possibly… I really can't remember. It's been so long since I've been in Mr Glasgow's home."

"You never knew him beyond his capacity as Mr Glasgow's servant, then? Perhaps under an alias?"

"I never go anywhere or receive any visitors aside from Mrs Bonham and my brother."

"So, you have no idea as to why Mr Perkins was in your house last night?"

"Absolutely none! That's what makes me being here so utterly ridiculous!" Mr Dorsey struck his knees with the base of his fists. "What reason would *I* have for murdering a servant?! And not even my own servant!"

"The police are far from infallible, Mr Dorsey. Some more intentionally so than others," Mr Elliott remarked.

Mr Dorsey hummed and replied, "Trial of the Detectives."

"Indeed," Mr Elliott said and referred to his earlier notes for a second time. "Who is Mrs Bonham?"

"Mr Glasgow's widowed sister," Mr Dorsey replied. Forlornness descended upon his features as he thought aloud, "the poor woman... She's been upset so much already with Malcolm's death."

Mr Elliott caught the change of tone in his client's voice and enquired, "Mrs Bonham is a close friend of yours then?"

"Only as close as is respectable. She visits me because her brother intimidates any other man who shows the slightest interest in her. He knows I have money of my own. Mrs Bonham was bequeathed a handsome monthly allowance from her late husband's estate."

"Does she have any reason to place the blame for Mr Perkins' murder on you?"

"No... none whatsoever."

"Does Mr Glasgow, Mr Colby, or your brother, Timothy?"

"*No*. None of them would want to see harm come to me."

Mr Elliott's past professional experiences of criminal murder trials told him such a rose-tinted scenario was both unrealistic and practically impossible. The complexities of human nature intermingled with the infinite variations in personality and sensibilities didn't make a pleasant cocktail where groups of people living near to one another were concerned. Disagreements and irritations were inevitable, and it was when these things intensified to unmanageable levels that the temptation of removing one's enemies became real. With all this in mind, he shifted his focus onto the man who spent the most time with Mr Dorsey daily as he enquired, "What is your relationship with Mr Colby like?"

"He looks after me."

"He ties you to the bed at night."

"He looks *after* me," Mr Dorsey insisted. Standing, he then paced back and forth across the small space the cell provided.

Mr Elliott recalled Miss Trent informing him of the nailed-down windows, but he decided against questioning Mr Dorsey about those for the moment. Instead, he moved onto the next person Mr Dorsey appeared to have a close connection to as he enquired, "And your brother, are you close?" Interested in his unconscious physical reaction as much as his verbal, he watched for the minutest twitch of a muscle or movement of his eyes.

"Yes," Mr Dorsey replied and dragged his fingertips down his face before pushing them back up it. It made Mr Elliott wonder if his client suspected his scrutiny. "I would've gone to Bedlam if not for Timothy."

"You owe him a great deal, then."

Mr Dorsey stopped pacing and turned toward him as he exclaimed, "Indeed I do!" Rubbing his hands together, he recommenced his pacing but at a slower speed as he went on, "And the same goes for Mr Glasgow. He bought my half of the law firm because he knew how much it meant to me, how important it was to keep its success going." He frowned. "He was very understanding, despite my having kept my deteriorating eyesight from him."

"How did he find out?"

"I… had a particularly frightening hallucination in the office one day and reacted very violently. Some of my clerks—Mr Farthing, Mr Pertwee, Mr Campbell, and Mr Starling—had to call upon Mr Glasgow to help restrain me."

"How many clerks did you have?"

"Ten altogether in the end; they really did everything for me aside from standing up in court. Though I'd stopped doing even that in the month or so before it all came out."

"None of them had any suspicions, then? Not even Mr Glasgow?"

"No. I always said I was above paperwork and even research. I was so well respected by them, and my esteemed colleagues at the Law Society, no one questioned it."

Mr Elliott spent a few moments updating his notes as conclusions began to form in his mind alongside further questions for both his client and fellow Bow Streeters. Having been a clerk himself, he was familiar with the process of how they were trained. He therefore had a specific theory in mind when he enquired, "Were ten the entire number of clerks you hired in those few months before you were exposed?"

"No, there were another three or four but, once they were certified, they left for pastures new."

Mr Elliott's expression remained stoic despite having his theory confirmed and exceeded. Returning to the point of the nailed-down windows in his mind, he enquired, "How did Mr Perkins enter your home?"

"I have no idea," Mr Dorsey replied with a shrug of his shoulders and a shake of his head. "I heard no one breaking in, or even the front door unlocking."

"You couldn't have missed either?" Mr Elliott enquired, knowing the possibility of Mr Dorsey falling asleep was a probable one, especially given the fact he had been tied to a bed at the time.

"Absolutely not; it gets very quiet indeed once Mr Colby goes out."

Mr Elliott left his thoughts of Mr Dorsey's slumber unsaid as he decided to gather as much remaining contextual information as he could. He therefore enquired, "How did Mr Glasgow and Mrs Bonham treat Mr Perkins?

Can you think of any reason why someone would want him dead?"

"I don't have first-hand knowledge of how Mr Perkins was treated by his employers, but I'm certain it would've been highly appropriate," Mr Dorsey replied with a hard edge to his voice. "As for why someone would want him dead, I really have no idea, nor are there any grounds for you to think I'd know such a thing."

"It's a standard question," Mr Elliott retorted but wrote down his client's response, nonetheless. Closing his notebook once he was done and depositing both it and his pencil into his briefcase, he then stood and extended his hand to Mr Dorsey. "I will find out when you are due to appear before the magistrates. When I have the date and time, I shall make the necessary arrangements to provide you with counsel both before and during the hearing."

Mr Dorsey turned toward him, but Mr Elliott didn't alert him to his extended hand. Yet, his client found it regardless—without difficulty—and gave it a firm squeeze as he replied, "Thank you, Mr Elliott. And please thank the Society for me."

"I shall, Mr Dorsey."

THIRTEEN

"Mr Thaddeus Dorsey will be taken before the magistrate at Bow Street police court tomorrow morning to enter his plea. I shall recommend he plead not guilty," Mr Elliott said and closed his notebook. He had spent the last quarter of an hour recounting the interview with his client to his fellow Bow Street Society members comprising of Miss Trent, Mr Maxwell, Miss Dexter, Mr Snyder, Dr Weeks, and Dr Alexander. Sitting around a rectangular table in a compact parlour filled with immense furniture and an unfathomable amount of clutter, they were certainly shoe-horned in.

Miss Trent was at the head of the table with a notebook of her own in front of her and a pocket watch by her elbow. She clasped her hands together and rested them upon the table as she said, "In that case, I'm obliged to ask a question which some of you may find uncomfortable or offensive. It remains a necessary one that I'm obliged to ask, however. Mr Maxwell, Miss Dexter, and Mr Snyder, did you, at any point, tell Mr Thaddeus Dorsey Palmer was in fact Mr Perkins?"

"No, the last time we saw him was when we took the clay model to him," Mr Maxwell replied.

"Mr Maxwell and I returned to speak with the lamplighter, but we didn't speak with Mr Dorsey," Miss Dexter further explained.

"Nah, I've not met Mr Dorsey 'cause of havin' to stay with the cab," Mr Snyder said.
"What abou' Locke?"

"Yeah," Dr Weeks said. "Where *is* the flouncin' sonofab—?"

"Mr Locke is working on the Society's behalf as we speak," Miss Trent interrupted in a firm tone. Irritation was etched into her eyes and facial expression as she watched Dr Weeks take a swig from a palm-sized bottle of gin and set it down beside his feet on the table. "I've already asked him the same question, though," she went on whilst Dr Weeks took a cigarette and some matches from his trouser pocket, He put the cigarette into the corner of his mouth and lit it. Yet, when he blew out the match and flicked it over Mr Maxwell's right shoulder, she scolded, "Could you at least *attempt* to be tolerable, doctor?"

"Nah," Dr Weeks replied.

"Then—" Miss Trent began but was interrupted by the door opening and Mrs Dexter carrying a tray in containing cups of tea, a plate of homemade biscuits, and a bottle of cloudy lemonade. The men—aside from Dr Weeks—stood the moment they saw her. He continued to smoke instead and acknowledged her presence with a simple glance over his shoulder.

"Ma-Ma, we don't need tea," Miss Dexter reminded her mother.

"Allow me to take this from you, Mrs Dexter," Mr Maxwell said as he held the tray's sides. "It looks heavy."

"Thank you, sir," Mrs Dexter replied, allowing him to take the tray and place it in the table's centre. Mr Snyder and Mr Elliott took a cup of tea each before Mr Maxwell picked up his own and a couple of biscuits.

"Ooo, thank you, Mrs Dexter. A nice cuppa, jus' what I needed," Mr Snyder said and savoured a generous mouthful of the steaming-hot beverage.

"Good evening, Mrs Dexter," Dr Alexander greeted with his usual warmth as he, too, helped himself to a cup of tea.

"See? Your mother knows best, Georgina," Mrs Dexter told her daughter and patted her on the shoulder on her way out.

Dr Weeks tossed a coffee-stained paper folder onto the table. Exhaling a cloud of cigarette smoke that caused those around him to cough and cover their mouths, he said to Miss Trent, "There's yer report."

Miss Trent picked it up and tossed it back to him, however, saying, "You'll have to explain its contents, Doctor. We don't all understand Latin."

"Forget that shit," Dr Weeks scoffed with another pull from his cigarette. "It's in English." He rested the folder on his thigh and flipped it open. With a nod to the tray, he enquired, "She bring any coffee?"

Dr Alexander examined the remaining cups on the tray. "I'm afraid, not."

"Damn woman knows I like coffee…" Dr Weeks muttered under his breath with a shake of his head. Reading the contents of the file, he then continued in a normal tone, "Meat were on its stomach on the floor—"

"Mr Perkins' body," Mr Elliott corrected.

Dr Weeks turned his head toward the solicitor and allowed his cigarette smoke to drift into his face as he replied, "Yeah." Mr Elliott wafted the smoke away with one hand as the other stifled a cough. If Dr Weeks saw the glare that ensued he didn't acknowledge it. Instead, he turned his gaze back to his file and went on, "He were on the floor in a puddle of blood the size of a lake."

"The heart was still beating when he was fatally wounded, then," Dr Alexander mused aloud.

"Do y'all wanna give the report?" Dr Weeks growled as he looked between Mr Elliott and Dr Alexander.

"Sorry," Dr Alexander replied, lifting his hands in a calming motion. "Please, continue."

Dr Weeks flicked the excess ash from his cigarette and returned it to the corner of his mouth as he continued, "Perkins' throat were cut and, yeah," he looked to Dr Alexander, "he were alive when it were done."

Dr Alexander gave a soft smile of appreciation.

"His throat were cut from right to left and there were some small bruisin' on the underside of his chin," Dr Weeks resumed. "Reckon the murderer grabbed 'im from behind, held his chin, and cut his throat open. Were blood splattered up the door and its frame in front of 'im."

Miss Dexter gasped and covered her mouth as her complexion paled.

"Are you feeling unwell?" Miss Trent enquired, concerned.

"Y—yes, I mean… sorry, I'll be fine," Miss Dexter replied.

"Get outta the kitchen if ya can't stand the heat, darlin.'" Dr Weeks told her, his cigarette bobbing up and down as he did so.

"No," Miss Dexter replied and took a cup from the tray. "Thank you, Dr Weeks. Please… continue." She took a sip of sweet tea to ease her shock.

Dr Weeks grunted but continued with his report. "Perkins were lyin' with his arms up and his hands by his head, his head bein' in the doorway of the bedroom. Were some bruisin' on his forehead; reckon he knocked it on the door when he fell. A dagger with a fancy-assed handle were lyin' by Perkins' right hand. Bits of china were on the floor at his feet and on his legs, too. His clothes were old and cheap; his jacket cuffs had cyanide stains and dust on 'em, and dust were on the bottom of his shoes."

"What about how Mr Perkins and his murderer got in?" Mr Snyder enquired. "Windows woz nailed shut, back door's rusted shut, front door woz locked, and Dorsey woz tied to the bed."

"That's what Mr Locke is investigating," Miss Trent replied. "He's going to give me his findings first thing in the morning."

Mr Snyder settled back in his chair with a nod and drank some more of his tea.

"A knife were in his pocket. Blade were four inches long and 'bout an inch at its widest point," Dr Weeks continued and indicated the knife's length between his thumb and index finger. "Blood were on it but were too old to be from the murder."

"Human?" Dr Alexander enquired.

Mr Maxwell leant forward with a mouthful of biscuit, whilst Miss Dexter toyed with her fingers in her lap as she continued to listen with a mixture of anxiousness and intrigue.

"How should I know?" Dr Weeks replied. "I ain't exactly got cuttin' edge equipment to work with."

"May we see the knife?" Mr Elliott enquired.

"Nah," Dr Weeks replied. "'Cause if my bein' 'ere, tellin' y'all this, don't get me in trouble, takin' the knife outta the Yard *will*. Jus' have to take my damned word for it."

"Very well," Mr Elliott replied, maintaining his stoicism despite the profanity, and updated his notes. "I'll be requesting to view it anyway."

"Then why the *hell* did ya ask?" Dr Weeks demanded.

"Can we please return to the matter at hand, gentleman?" Miss Trent interjected with a warning look to them both. "And stop bullying everyone, Dr Weeks, or your membership will be terminated. Do I make myself clear?"

Dr Weeks mumbled his response as he crushed out his cigarette.

"What was that?" Miss Trent challenged.

"I said yeah," Dr Weeks snapped.

"Good," Miss Trent replied. "And you can take your feet off the table as well." Dr Weeks released a heavy sigh, but she kept her gaze on him until he did as she'd asked. Noticing Dr Alexander had raised his hand afterward, she enquired, "Yes?"

"I only asked the question because it may have been the knife used to kill, and cut open, Mrs Bonham's cat, Malcolm," Dr Alexander explained.

"Maybe we could ask Mr Glasgow's cook if one of her knives is missing? If it is, we could ask her to describe it," Mr Maxwell suggested.

"I agree," Miss Trent replied. "You may do that tomorrow."

"M—Me?" Mr Maxwell stammered.

"Is there any reason why you shouldn't?" Miss Trent probed with a quirk of her brow.

146

Mr Maxwell swallowed hard as he recalled his close encounter with the cook and maid. Unwilling to risk provoking Miss Trent's displeasure by revealing the incident, though, he replied in a voice strained with nerves, "No… Tomorrow it is."

"I'll accompany Mr Maxwell," Miss Dexter said and gave his hand a brief squeeze of reassurance under the table.

"Cab should be done tomorrow, too. I'll take 'em," Mr Snyder interjected.

"That's settled, then," Miss Trent said, making a note of the arrangement. "Please continue, Dr Weeks."

"Weren't any rips in his clothes," Dr Weeks resumed, referencing his report as he did so. "When stripped, apart from the huge slash to his throat, his body were free of wounds. No tattoos or scars. Dirt under his fingernails were dust and cyanide."

"You said there were cyanide stains on the cuffs of his jacket, too. Were the combined amounts a fatal dose?" Mr Elliott enquired.

"Ya don't need a lot to kill someone, a few grains. There were more than that under his nails and on his cuffs," Dr Weeks replied.

"Why?" Mr Maxwell enquired but cowered under the Canadian's glare. "Sorry… stupid question."

"Yeah, it is," Dr Weeks agreed, taking a swig of gin and resuming his report. "When I cut 'im open, there weren't much to write home 'bout." He flicked through several pages. "Weren't malnourished, weren't dyin' from disease, had eaten some beef, potatoes, and gravy in the hours before his death; they weren't unrecognisable so reckon it weren't that long before. He'd drunk some wine, too. A lotta wine." He smirked. "My kinda fella." Closing the folder, he tossed it back onto the table and pocketed his gin bottle. "The cutthroat were what killed 'im. Body were only a little stiff, still, so reckon he were killed between ten and eleven o'clock last night. Could've been a little earlier but no later."

Mr Elliott picked up the folder only for it to be snatched away by Dr Weeks.

"D'ya reckon I held somethin' back?" Dr Weeks challenged, glaring at him.

"I will need to read the report if I'm to defend Mr Dorsey," Mr Elliott replied in his usual monotone.

"Then ask for it in writin'," Dr Weeks said, pushing his chair back with his feet and slipping the report into his bag under the table. Rather than moving his chair back to the table, though, he put the bottom of one foot against the table's edge and tilted his chair back on its hind legs. Taking the bottle of gin from his pocket, he lifted it in mock toast to Miss Trent and had another swig from it. The clerk watched in irritation before standing, walking over to him, and pulling his chair back with one, hard tug. Dr Weeks' foot dropped from the table at once as his chair was forced back onto all fours. Although he cast a black look in Miss Trent's direction, she returned to her own seat and picked up a different paper-folder from underneath her notebook.

"You should all have a copy of my report about Malcolm's examination," Dr Alexander announced, looking around at the pristine, typed documents he'd handed out earlier. Waiting for his fellow Bow Streeters to open them up, he then continued, "It's my suspicion—and Mr Maxwell and Miss Dexter will agree—Malcolm was killed because he'd possibly swallowed something his murderer desperately needed back. I didn't find any traces of cyanide on the body though, Doctor Weeks. So, I don't know if Mr Perkins encountered the animal or not. But the killing and dissection were both intentional. I examined Malcolm's organs but, as with Mr Perkins, no symptoms of disease were found. Though Malcolm was an adult, he was a youthful one."

"Thank you, Doctor," Miss Trent said with a warm smile. "Mr Maxwell, you found some letters in Mr Perkins' room at the Glasgow-Bonham residence. Could you read them aloud, please?"

"Oh, um…" Mr Maxwell replied, sliding the pile of letters in front of him and taking one from the top. Having read its contents earlier, he felt his cheeks warm and his palms moisten at the thought of doing so in front of the others. Nevertheless, he took out the letter, slid his tongue over his dry lips, and cleared his throat. He was about to begin when a thought occurred to him. "Maybe Miss Dexter should—?"

"Miss Dexter is aware of the letters' nature," Miss Trent interrupted. "She'll leave the room if she feels the need to. Please, read them."

"Right…" Mr Maxwell replied, clearing his throat a second time. "Let me see…" He read the first line internally and felt his cheeks grow hotter as his complexion flushed a bright pink. Placing a hand upon his chest and toying with his cravat's bow, he read aloud, "My dearest, darling Palmer. I can't stop dreaming of our time together, of how you wrapped your arms about me, of how you tasted, and of how you felt as you…" Mr Maxwell cleared his throat, again. "…slipped inside of me and made our bodies into one."

"*Damn*!" Dr Weeks exclaimed, slamming his hand down upon the table and chuckling. "Yer sure this ain't yer personal stash?"

"Yes!" Mr Maxwell cried, horrified.

Dr Weeks laughed harder at this as he settled back in his chair and lit a cigarette with a shake of his head.

"Please, continue, Mr Maxwell," Miss Trent said with a disapproving glance at Dr Weeks.

"Yeah, I wanna see how long this fella lasted," Dr Weeks interjected, grinning as he took a pull from his cigarette and exhaled the smoke soon after.

"How crude," Mr Elliott remarked.

Beads of sweat had formed on Mr Maxwell's forehead and he wiped his palms upon his frock coat as he continued. "I know our love is forbidden, but I cannot stop the way I feel. You make me feel things I have never felt before, shared new sensations with me I've never

149

experienced before. When you kiss me, the rest of the world melts away and I see only you. Palmer, my dearest, darling, my body cries out for you when we are not together. I touch—" Mr Maxwell stopped and put the letter down. "Do I really have to read this out, Miss Trent? It's *very* detailed."

"No," Miss Trent replied, "Are all the letters like that?"

"Yes. And, I'm sorry, but I refuse to read those out," Mr Maxwell said.

"Let's see," Dr Weeks said, snatching the letter from Mr Maxwell and settling back to read the rest. A dirty chuckle left his lips while his eyes seemed to twinkle with delight. Holding it up a moment later, he enquired, "Can I keep this?"

"Absolutely *not*," Miss Trent replied, snatching it back from him and tucking it under her notebook. "There are plenty of Cat Houses where you can find those things, Doctor."

"Is the sender's signature on any of them?" Mr Elliott enquired with perfect stoicism despite the confrontation.

"No," Mr Maxwell replied as he wiped his face and hands with his handkerchief and straightened his cravat.

"You should also have a copy of Mr Locke's report regarding his search of Mr Perkins' apartment," Miss Trent said. "You'll see he also found some letters there. They, too, were unsigned."

"So, Perkins were makin' a stitch with a married woman," Dr Weeks said with a broad smile. "Dirty sonofab—"

"We don't know that for certain," Miss Trent interrupted. "But we must consider it as a possibility, yes."

"Mr Maxwell, you should find out if the other servants at the Glasgow-Bonham residence knew Mr Perkins had a lover and, if they did, whether or not they knew her name," Mr Elliott suggested. "I doubt anyone in that house knew of his other residence, though. Especially as he was on a footman's wage."

"We should go back to the apartment," Mr Snyder said as he put down his empty cup. "Mr Perkins' lass might go back there."

Miss Trent hummed in agreement and said, "After you've taken Mr Maxwell and Miss Dexter to the Glasgow-Bonham residence tomorrow, you can watch Brookbond House. You know what to do."

Mr Snyder nodded.

"Dr Alexander, I'd like you to speak to Mr Glasgow whilst Mr Maxwell speaks to his servants. Miss Dexter, I'd like you to speak to Mrs Bonham alone at the same time. Dr Alexander, you may take a moment to reassure Mrs Bonham you are doing all you can once Miss Dexter has spoken to her, if you wish."

"I will, thank you," Dr Alexander replied.

"Mr Elliott, please keep us informed about the progress of Mr Dorsey's case in the magistrate's court. Mr Locke shall question Mr Colby and visit Mr Timothy Dorsey to inform him of our progress thus far," Miss Trent said. "Now, if there are no further questions or objections, I'd like to close this meeting."

FOURTEEN

The night air was bitterly cold as Mr Locke crept down the
service alleyway and reached the gate to Mr Dorsey's
backyard. He'd taken the precaution of timing the patrols
of the constable on duty in the area to pinpoint the exact
moment when he could enter the alleyway unobserved and
uninterrupted. He had also foregone his expensive frock
coat for his stage one and coupled it with a black shirt, silk
cravat, scarf, bowler hat, and leather gloves. Positioning
himself to the left of the gate, he jumped and gripped its
ice-covered top. Swinging his long, slender leg upwards,
he then hooked his foot onto the wall's inner edge and
pulled himself onto and then over the wall. Similarly to a
gymnast on a pommel horse, he spun his hands 180° as his
body moved over the top of the wall and gripped the wall's
inner edge as his legs dropped down on that side.
Lowering himself the remaining distance, his feet made no
sound as he placed them upon the yard's frozen ground
and darted into a darkened corner. Light poured from the
kitchen windows and Mr Locke put his back to the wall so
he could see inside without being seen himself. Stilling his
body and slowing his breathing, he watched Mr Colby
perform several mundane domestic tasks before
extinguishing the lamps and going into the hallway.
Personally, Mr Locke would've dismissed him.

The backyard was overlooked by the neighbouring
houses' upper floors, but there were no lights in any of the
windows. Mr Locke therefore felt confident enough to
stride across the yard and grip a drainpipe to the right of
the back door. Using the ledge of the window beside it as a
foothold and keeping a firm grip of the pipe, he jumped
and placed his left foot on top of the doorframe. Suddenly
hearing the creak of the kitchen's interior door, he held his
position and listened. Footsteps sounded as someone
entered the room and then grew louder. Fearing he may be
discovered, Mr Locke used his upper body strength to lift

his right foot from the window ledge and dig his toes into the crumbling brickwork above. No sooner had he done so did light flood the backyard from the kitchen windows. Once again, he held his position as he listened to whoever it was move around the kitchen for several moments.

When the backyard was plunged back into darkness, and he heard the footsteps fade, followed by the thud of the interior door, he slid his hands up the drainpipe. Gripping it tight, he next wedged each foot in turn between it and the wall and pulled himself upward using the power of his upper body strength alone. Using this method, he scaled the drainpipe within seconds to reach a window on the first floor. Although it was in darkness, there was a curtain drawn over it, thus preventing him from seeing if there was anyone inside. Furthermore, the sash frame was impossible to open due to the nails driven into it. Swinging on the drainpipe to rest his body against the wall on the other side, therefore, he peered into the window there. An inspection of it drew the same conclusions, however.

Deciding to try further up but suspecting any windows accessible to Mr Dorsey would be nailed down, he scaled the drainpipe past the second floor whilst making brief inspections of its windows. As expected, they, too, were nailed down. He therefore completed his climb to the roof and pulled himself onto its tiles. The air was bitterer there so he covered his mouth and nose with his scarf and crawled across the roof to an attic window. The moment he peered into it, though, he saw the tell-tale black dots of nails and frowned. *This house is harder to break into than the Bank of England*, he mused.

He rolled onto his back and braced his heels against the curve of the iron guttering as he retrieved a narrow, cardboard box from his frock coat. Slipping a folded cut-throat razor from it, he returned the box to his pocket and exposed the blade. Whilst remaining on his back, he then slid the blade's tip under the corner of a nearby tile and pried it loose. With careful movements, and using his sense of touch alone, he reached across with his free hand and retrieved the tile before it could fall and alert Mr Colby to his presence. He then lifted his shoulders off the roof and reached down to place the tile in the gutting beside his feet. Repeating this precarious process several more times until he'd created a hole big enough to squeeze through, he then returned the razor to its box and rubbed the moss, soot, and grime from his gloves in disgust.

He entered feet first and dropped into the empty room. In wealthier households, such as his own, the attics were reserved for the female domestic servants. The fine layer of dust covering the floor was evidence that this hadn't been the case in Mr Dorsey's home for many years. Nevertheless, Mr Locke crept across the room and opened the first of two doors. Beyond was a second, equally empty and dusty, room with a fireplace engulfed by cobwebs. He therefore opened the second door and found himself at the summit of some narrow, yet steep, stairs leading to a closed door.

Listening for a few moments, he descended with as little noise as possible and opened the door a crack. Pitch blackness greeted him until his eyes adjusted enough for him to see the outline of a landing. He pressed his back against the wall and opened the door wider. A sudden slam from downstairs caused him to freeze, however, and he held his breath as he listened. He thought he'd heard the turning of a key, but it may have been his mind filling in the blank. He therefore remained still and waited for further sounds which would confirm the presence of someone in the house. When none came, he released a slow, deep breath and stepped out onto the landing. Crossing it and peering over the bannisters at the darkened hallway below, he saw the hat stand was empty. *Mr Colby has gone out, it seems*, he mused, and checked the time on his pocket watch; it was nine thirty p.m.

Now relieved from the threat of detection, he strode along the landing and opened the first door he came to. The room beyond was in complete darkness and a musty smell drifted into his nostrils. Allowing his eyes to adjust once more, he saw the outline of curtains at the window. Venturing further in, he took a box of matches from the other interior pocket of his frock coat and ignited one. As the tiny flame cast out its light though, Mr Locke couldn't believe what he was seeing…

FIFTEEN

Located a stone's throw from Mr Dorsey's home at the
north end of Bow Street, the police court had been the
chief petty court in London since the eighteenth century.
Attended by three magistrates in the current year of
1896—of whom the principle was Mr John Bridge—the
court had moved to its new location around 1880-81
following the building's completion. Prior to this,
proceedings were conducted across the road in No's 3 and
4 Bow Street where the Fielding brothers had famously
formed the Bow Street Runners in the 1700s. In addition to
this, John Fielding had formed a short-lived experiment in
which magistrates in 'Rotation Offices' worked under the
direction of the Bow Street 'Police Centre,' and kept
records of all criminals put before them. These records
were used to create a central register at the Police Centre
which was combined with army deserter lists. The
eventual product was published regularly in the police-
only publication—the *Police Gazette.* Though the
experiment collapsed due to lack of funds, the basic
formula of magistrates controlling permanent constables
from fixed offices was nonetheless at the heart of the
Middlesex Justice's Act of 1792.

The considerable size of the current four-storey
building dominated Bow Street. Its Italian architectural
style was depicted in its high doorways, tall, arched, sash
windows, and ornately carved roof sculptures. A set of
doors on its angular corner was both the first entrance one
came to when approaching from the direction of Covent
Garden and the entrance to the police court. Moving
further along the building's front took one past the
immense double doors which served as a means of entry
for Black Maria police vans transporting prisoners.
Finally, one came to a set of steep, stone steps which led to
the main entrance of the Metropolitan Police Service's E
(or Holborn) Division's station. Aside from sharing

156

premises with the court, Holborn Division was also notable for having the only white 'POLICE' lamp in London. This was at the request of Queen Victoria who, in 1861 when the standard blue lamps were introduced, didn't want to be reminded of the blue of Prince Albert's death room whenever she visited the Opera House nearby.

Mr Elliott was sitting opposite Mr Dorsey in a holding cell at the police court. The solicitor had been alarmed to see his client's blackened eye upon being let in by the Custody Sergeant. The wound's colouration suggested it had been inflicted recently, whilst its shape and size hinted at a fist. Mr Elliott wasn't medically trained, however, and he doubted the police would permit a doctor's examination when the wound wasn't life-threatening. Regardless of this, though, Mr Elliott was furious at his client's treatment and wanted answers. With a hard edge to his tone, he therefore enquired, "Which one of them was it?"

"I'm not sure." Mr Dorsey frowned. "Inspector Conway, I believe. There was a constable there as well though." He lifted and dropped his hands in exasperation. "I told them all I know, but they *wouldn't* believe me."

"Did they ask you about Palmer?"

"No, but they asked me why I'd hired the Bow Street Society, so I told them. They didn't ask me anything further about Palmer so I can only assume they thought him unimportant. I didn't volunteer information about him because that's *my* personal business."

"They're unaware of the link, then," Mr Elliott mused aloud.

Mr Dorsey's brow creased in confusion. "What link?"

Mr Elliott looked straight into his client's eyes as he replied, "Palmer and Perkins were one and the same."

Mr Dorsey's mouth fell open. "No… It—it can't be." His entire body trembled as tears slid down his cheeks. Slowly, he stood and took a few brief steps before dropping to his knees and crying, "*No!*" He crossed his shaking hands and covered his eyes as he gripped his bowed head and broke down into uncontrollable sobbing.

The hatch in the cell door slid back, and a concerned constable peered inside. Mr Elliott lifted his hand to signal all was well, and the hatch was closed once more. Whilst Mr Dorsey's apparent outpouring of grief masked the constable's fading footfalls, Mr Elliott watched his client with as much scrutiny as he had before. After ten minutes or so had passed, the strength of Mr Dorsey's sobs weakened enough for him to find his voice. "*How*? Wh—when did you find out?" His hands clenched into fists, and he twisted his body to glare at Mr Elliott. "*Why wasn't I told?!*"

"The day before Perkins' body was found. Our members were at Mr Glasgow's house the next morning to speak with Perkins and inform him of your concern. Our intention had been to bring him to you."

"You should've told me directly!"

"Why? If you had known, you wouldn't have killed him?"

"*I didn't kill him!*"

"No, but that is what the prosecution will ask should you make such a statement in open court."

"I don't *care* about open court!" Mr Dorsey lowered his hands and turned around on all fours. "My friend is *dead*! If I had known, maybe—"

"*No*," Mr Elliott interrupted. "You couldn't have done anything to save him, Mr Dorsey. You were tied to the bed at the time. Furthermore, Palmer only visited you when you were alone at night and gave no other means of contact."

Nothing about Mr Elliott's demeanour or voice was sympathetic, a fact Mr Dorsey was all too aware of. Sitting on his heels, he bowed his head and hunched his shoulders like a child who'd been scolded by his schoolmaster.

"Desist in concerning yourself with things which cannot be changed and focus upon the here and now; you will soon be taken before the magistrates and you *must* plead not guilty," Mr Elliott went on. "Speak clearly and with confidence. *Don't* let your emotions overwhelm you and, should you have a hallucination, do your utmost to ignore it." The minute inclination of Mr Dorsey's head was the only acknowledgement Mr Elliott was granted. He therefore enquired, "What else did Inspector Conway discuss with you?"

"He described the murder weapon to me," Mr Dorsey replied in a morose tone. "It was my letter opener, the one I keep in the study."

"Did Inspector Conway allow you to hold the weapon, so you could verify it was as he described?"

Mr Dorsey nodded.

The hatch slid back a second time and the constable announced, "Your turn, Mr Dorsey." As he slammed the hatch shut, unlocked the door, and swung it open, Mr Elliott stood and slipped his arm under Mr Dorsey's to lift him to his feet. Guiding his hand to his elbow, then, Mr Elliott walked in front as they were led into the court room.

The hearing was brief—around fifteen minutes— and Mr Dorsey's plea of not guilty was recorded by the court. A trial start date was also set for the following month and Mr Elliott was given just enough time to reassure his client that neither he nor the Bow Street Society would abandon him before he was taken back to his cell. When he left the court and went outside, though, he caught sight of Inspector Conway at the police station stairs. Seizing his opportunity for answers, he strode down the street toward him, and called, "Inspector!"

Inspector Conway stopped at the top of the stairs and looked down at him. "Can I help you?"

"Mr Gregory Elliott, Mr Thaddeus Dorsey's solicitor."

Inspector Conway turned toward the door with an impatient expression as he replied, "I've got nowt to say to you."

"Yet I have plenty to say to you," Mr Elliott retorted from the foot of the stairs. "There was no need to give him a black eye."

Inspector Conway looked back down at him and replied, "'E fell."

"You don't deny he has a black eye, then?"

Inspector Conway walked down one step and towered over him as he replied, "Your bloke's a blind nutta. 'E went berserk and fell."

"I shan't let this lie."

Inspector Conway went down one more step, but Mr Elliott stood his ground despite Inspector Conway's chest being mere inches from his nose. The policeman leant forward and, in a voice made rougher by its lowered volume, warned. "You'd do good to watch your gob." Mr Elliott's stoicism remained in place, but Inspector Conway's hard expression didn't alter either. "You can't prove out 'gainst me. But I've got shiploads 'gainst your bloke; forget about me and save 'im from the drop instead." He moved up the steps backwards before turning and entering the police station. Mr Elliott allowed him to go but knew it wasn't over; it was *far* from over.

* * *

"Get lost!" Mr Colby commanded upon opening the door to find Mr Locke standing on the porch. When he then stepped back and reached to close it again, though, Mr Locke's question caused him to pause.

"Why have all the upstairs' rooms been emptied of their furniture?"

Mr Colby shifted his weight from one foot to the other despite continuing to glare at the Bow Streeter as he replied, "They haven't."

"Very well." Mr Locke turned toward the street. "I am certain Inspector Conway will be interested to hear you have lied to me."

"You threatening me?" Mr Colby opened the door wide and stepped outside.

"Not at all; I am merely doing my duty as a law-abiding citizen."

Mr Colby advanced upon him. "I've not let you up there." He gave Mr Locke's chest a hard prod. "*You* must've broken in. What do you reckon the inspector would make of *that*?"

"So, the rooms *have* been emptied?" Mr Locke smirked. "I have no need to 'break in,' as you so crudely put it, Mr Colby. Not when I have your gullibility to rely upon. Besides, gentlemen such as I do not lower themselves to the level of common thieves. Now, shall you tell me here *why* the furniture was removed, or will you invite me inside? I recommend the latter. Perhaps you could even show me one of the rooms?"

"Get lost," Mr Colby growled, shoving him and returning inside. Before he could close the door on him, though, Mr Locke had caught himself with one foot and wedged his walking cane against the frame. Attempting to kick it away but failing due to Mr Locke's increased weight upon it, Mr Colby demanded, "Get your stick outta the door!"

"*Why* have all the upstairs' rooms been emptied of their furniture?"

Mr Colby pulled back a clenched fist, but Mr Locke seized the scruff of his shirt and dragged him closer, obliging the attendant to grasp the doorframe in surprise. When Mr Colby then attempted to step back, Mr Locke tightened his grip and drew him closer, still. Bent forward with his toes wedged against the frame, Mr Colby cried, "I'll tell you!" There was fear in his eyes as he added, "his brother, Timothy, emptied them. I can't tell you why."

Mr Locke quirked a brow and raised his walking cane.

"No, please!" Mr Colby cried when he caught sight of it out of the corner of his eye. "I can't tell you!

He'll get rid of me if I do, and I need this job! Please…
ask *him*!"

Mr Locke maintained a firm grip as he enquired,
"Has he visited the house since your patient was arrested?"

Due to his awkward stance, Mr Colby's nod was
more of a jerk.

"What did you discuss?" Mr Locke further
enquired.

"His brother being took by the coppers for
murder."

"Anything else?"

"Nah," Mr Colby replied. Mr Locke drew him
close enough for him to feel his breath upon his face, and
Mr Colby insisted, "I swear that's all!"

Mr Locke eased his grip a fraction. "Very well. I
shall assume the police showed you the murder weapon.
Did you recognise it?"

"It's the blind bugger's letter opener."

"Did he, or anyone else, have access to it?"

"Anyone coming to the house could've took it."

"I see," Mr Locke replied. "I cannot condone your
decision to allow a blind man, sick in mind, to carry
around such a sharp-bladed implement, however."

"He didn't," Mr Colby retorted as his fear changed
to anger upon seeing the pedestrians of Bow Street
gloating and pointing at him. "It was in his study. Let me
go!"

Mr Locke quirked a brow and replied, "I shall,
when you give me a satisfactory answer."

"Fine!" Mr Colby sighed. "He probably took it
when I was making his supper. I do let him wander,
y'know."

"Except at night when you wish to entertain
yourself elsewhere," Mr Locke drily remarked.
Nevertheless, he released Mr Colby, who straightened and
smoothed down his shirt. "Was Mr Timothy Dorsey aware
of your 'arrangements' for his brother?"

"Don't be daft. He wouldn't have allowed it."

Mr Locke looked over at the pedestrians and tipped his hat to them. Having been caught in their gawking, they drifted away with a mixture of embarrassment and amusement. "By the way, where *were* you, on the night of the murder?" he enquired upon turning his attention back to the attendant. "If you were not fulfilling the duty you were being paid for?"

"The Turk's Head pub on Edgware Road, if you must know."

"Oh, indeed I must," Mr Locke coolly retorted. "For considerable doubt has been cast over Mr Dorsey's guilt due to your claim of returning to the house the next morning and discovering Mr Perkins dead in the hallway and Mr Dorsey tied to his bed. I am curious; why did you not tell the police you found Mr Dorsey standing over the body with the dagger in his hand?"

"Because that's not what happened," Mr Colby replied and folded his arms across his chest. "And I don't fancy joinin' 'im in a copper's cell."

"It would have been simpler, though, and you would not have the cloud of suspicion hanging over you like you do now."

"What cloud?" Mr Colby eyed him. "I've not got any clouds over me."

"Were you aware that 'Palmer,' your patient's friend, was none other than Mr Perkins, footman to the Glasgow-Bonham residence next door?" Mr Locke enquired.

Mr Colby frowned. "Thaddeus' not got any friends."

"As you told us the first night we met. Yet we have since discovered you were mistaken. You had no knowledge of either Mr Perkins' visits to your patient or his alias of 'Palmer,' then?"

"Nah, I didn't, and I've said all I'm gonna. Now, leave me alone," Mr Colby retreated inside and slammed the door.

Mr Locke couldn't help but smirk at the uncouth man's brashness as he descended the steps, climbed into his carriage, and instructed his driver, "To the Bank of England, Mr Lambert."

SIXTEEN

Originally opened in 1694, the Bank of England had stood in its current location since 1734. Known as the Old Lady of Threadneedle Street, the immense structure impresses all who see it. Its Romanesque façade boasts several mighty columns, intricately carved stonework, and subtly deceptive windows. Toward the close of the eighteenth century, architect Sir John Sloane expanded the bank. The result was the Consol Office where business concerning the trade of Government bonds was handled. Modelled on ancient Roman baths, the office had a glass dome to provide natural light in addition to the standard supply of gas lamps suspended from the ceiling. On the day of Mr Locke's visit, however, the grey month of January was living up to its reputation and, as a result, very little daylight was to be had. At almost ninety feet long and fifty feet wide, the Consol Office was as impressive as the bank's exterior. Its arches had sunken panels with white rose decorations whilst ridged, column detailing upon the walls beneath enhanced one's sense of grandeur. Elbow-high mahogany desks lined both sides of the office and were manned by a small army of clerks who glanced at the clock above the door every so often to see if it was time break time yet.

It was almost noon when Mr Locke walked through the door and surveyed the clerk's faces in search of Mr Timothy Dorsey's. Upon finding him at the third desk on the right, Mr Locke approached and waited for him to finish serving the customer ahead of him. Timothy was sliding coins off the counter into his left hand using his right and saying the amended amount aloud as each coin was added. Once complete, he held open a small bag with the fingers of his right hand whilst his left dropped the coins into it. Straight afterwards, he retrieved a handkerchief from his trouser pocket with his right hand and wiped his nose, apologising to his customer as he did so. His customer gave a soft grunt in response and Timothy secured the bag, deposited it into a drawer, and then locked it. Next, he recorded the amount into a ledger whilst re-confirming it aloud for his customer's benefit. Satisfied his business was now complete, the customer bid him good day and departed, thereby allowing Mr Locke to step forward and take his place at the counter.

"Good afternoon, sir. How may I help—Mr Locke?" Timothy stared at him a moment before glancing over at his manager, and then enquiring, "Have you brought news?"

"I have been reliably informed Mr Elliott is doing his professional utmost for your brother. I am able to add identical sentiments of my own to that, too." Mr Locke took some paperwork from his frock coat relating to his own Government bonds and placed it upon the counter. "The purpose of my visit goes beyond that, however. Yet my intention is not to place you in an uncomfortable position with your employer. Thus, while we converse, you shall assist me with my bonds." He retrieved a small, leather bag containing ten guineas from the same place and added it to the paperwork. "And a deposit."

"Thank you," Timothy replied with earnest gratitude as he picked up the paperwork and put the sheets in order. "What's on your mind, then, Mr Locke?"

"Firstly, I am curious as to why you are working rather than attending your brother's hearing in Bow Street."

"Your Mr Gregory's there. I'm not needed." Timothy felt Mr Locke's eyes boring into him but still took a few moments to respond. "I'm not heartless when it comes to my brother, as you've seen. I wanted to be there, but I couldn't." He lowered his voice and shame crept into his tone. "I'm not a wealthy man, Mr Locke. I can't afford to miss a day's work."

"You have power of attorney over your brother's estate; do you not receive an allowance for your trouble?"

Timothy looked up, startled, and his voice waivered as he replied, "An allowance? No…" He frowned. "Such a thing is impossible."

"I do not see how or why he could object given all you have done for him," Mr Locke remarked.

"He wouldn't…"

"Then why, pray, is it impossible?"

"Because… aside from the fact the rules surrounding single-house confinement forbid me from profiting from it…" Timothy's frown deepened, "my brother is almost as poor as I am."

Mr Locke quirked a brow but was distracted momentarily by the neighbouring clerk coughing. Upon seeing he was engrossed in his work, Mr Locke resumed his conversation with Timothy, saying, "I see; a rather desperate situation, then." Timothy nodded. "It must have been devastating for you both when the furniture had to be sold."

"I beg your pardon?" Timothy's head shot up, and he stared at him in wide-eyed horror. "How did you…?" He dismissed the question with a shake of his head as desperation overwhelmed his features. "*Please*, I beg you not to tell anyone. Not even Thaddeus."

"He does not know?"

"No," Timothy confessed, his complexion turning pale. Though his fingers were resting on the paperwork, he wasn't reading it any longer. In a quiet voice strained with emotion, he enquired, "Who told you?"

"It was a lucky guess on my part," Mr Locke replied in a casual tone. "When I visited your brother's house this morning, I took a chance on an idea of mine and asked Mr Colby why the furniture had been removed from the upstairs' rooms. He was not intelligent enough to recognise when he was being toyed with so gave me the answer without intending to. He refused to relinquish the reason why, however. May I ask, was it Mr Colby who persuaded you to sell your brother's worldly goods?"

167

"No, it was my decision. After Mr Glasgow purchased my brother's half of the business, it became painfully clear how little money there was left in it. My brother, it seems, had been in denial over his worsening health and so had employed a veritable army of legal clerks to do his work for him and thus prevent anyone from finding out the truth. Thaddeus managed all the finances in the business and refused for Mr Glasgow to see the books until after the payment had been made. Mr Glasgow, believing the business to be sound due to the reputation my brother had built up over the years, agreed to the arrangement. Though Mr Glasgow paid a handsome amount for Thaddeus' half, the money didn't stretch much further than the coverage of existing debts and a year's worth of wages for Mr Colby and the same again for my brother's living costs. This was startling when it became obvious his health would never improve." Timothy sighed. "I arranged for Mr Colby to bring Thaddeus to my house for the afternoon whilst Mr Glasgow oversaw an auction house's removal of all the furniture from the upstairs rooms. The auction, held the next day, generated enough money for a further two years' worth of care for my brother but, again, finances are running low. Mr Colby does all he can but… Thaddeus would be devastated if he found out about the sale."

"You need not pay Mr Colby whilst your brother is incarcerated, though, surely?"

"I do," Timothy replied, forlorn. "He's the only one capable of keeping my brother safe; he recognises the onset of his 'episodes' and knows how to control him when he becomes violent—"

"By tying him to a bed and nailing down windows?" Mr Locke enquired in a sardonic tone.

"He had his reasons for doing that," Timothy replied without conviction.

"Is that what he told you?"

"No, I didn't ask him," Timothy admitted and continued his inspection of the bond certificates. His eyes kept darting back and forth to the money bag, however. "I *can't* lose Mr Colby. He's agreed to waiver half of his wages this month if I let him continue living in the house. Besides, Thaddeus will need him when he gets out."

"Your brother is being held on suspicion of murder, Mr Dorsey," Mr Locke reminded him. "At the current time, it is *very* unlikely he will ever leave prison alive *unless* reasonable doubt can be cast upon his guilt or the guilty party is brought to justice. Mr Colby could very well be that guilty party and *you* are allowing him to reside in the very house where a man was killed. He could be destroying evidence as we speak."

Timothy stared at him once more. "Really...?"

"Yes; really. My suggestion therefore is for you and me to visit your brother's house—tonight—and examine it for potential clues, *without* Mr Colby."

"But... Mr Colby wasn't there when—"

"We only have his word for it. In the same way we only have your brother's word he did not kill Mr Perkins, and your word you did not arrange for your brother to be arrested for murder so you could free yourself of his burden."

Timothy tightened his grip upon the certificates, crumpling them.

"Come now, Mr Dorsey. Surely you knew such a supposition would be put forward once you had disclosed your dire financial situation?"

"*No,*" Timothy said with a shake of his head and trembling hands. "I didn't... I wouldn't... How you could even think I...?" He pushed the paperwork across the counter toward him and mumbled, "Everything seems to be in order, sir..." Shaking his head, he emptied the money bag next and muttered, "I—I wouldn't..." Cupping his left hand beneath the counter's edge, he then slid each guinea into it with his right.

Being a magician, Mr Locke had spent many hours developing the dexterity of his fingers. As a result, he was naturally drawn to the hands of others and often compared their level of dexterity to his own. Most of the time he didn't realise he was doing it, and this was one such time. He watched Timothy press the fingertips of his right hand against the guinea as he slid it across the counter but kept his thumb free.

"Currently anyone connected to this case is a suspect," Mr Locke said. "Give us sufficient reason to doubt the possibility of your guilt by telling us the truth and you shall find the accusation will weaken and eventually disappear entirely. Now, in addition to searching the house for clues, I would also like to conduct an experiment in your brother's bedroom."

"Of course," Timothy replied, sliding the next six guineas across the counter and dropping them into his hand. "What time should I expect you?" He appeared to drop the next guinea into his hand, but Mr Locke wasn't certain due to it being hidden by the counter's edge.

"Seven o'clock," Mr Locke replied, watching him slide the penultimate guinea across the counter. Unlike with the others, though, he saw Timothy's thumb bend inward as the guinea was allegedly dropped into his palm. It remained tucked in even as the last guinea was added to the pile with a gentle chink. Timothy then retrieved a small bag from underneath the desk and dropped the pile of guineas into it from his semi-closed left hand. Afterwards, he took out his handkerchief, wiped his hands with it, and slipped it back into his trouser pocket before securing the bag. Yet, despite the apparent innocence of Timothy's actions, Mr Locke had seen his thumb was bent upon going into his pocket and straight upon coming out.

"I shall see you tonight, then, Mr Locke," Timothy said, securing the bag in the drawer and recording its amount in the ledger. "Ten guineas, correct?"

"Ten guineas," Mr Locke echoed with a smirk.

"I do agree with what you said—about us all being a suspect, but… what motives do we have?" Timothy enquired as he closed the ledger. "Neither Thaddeus nor Mr Colby had any reason to kill Mr Glasgow's footman."

"They do, when you consider Mr Perkins paid nightly visits to your brother under the alias of Palmer," Mr Locke replied.

Timothy swayed, gripped the counter's edge and held his forehead as he said, "Oh, my God… I—I didn't know that…"

"Neither did Mr Colby—or so he claims," Mr Locke remarked and, gathering up his Bond certificates, slipped them back into his frock coat.

"Did the police tell you… about Perkins being Palmer?"

"No. As far as we are aware, the police remain ignorant of the fact," Mr Locke replied. "The visits were part of the reason why your brother hired the Bow Street Society. 'Palmer' usually called upon Thaddeus once Mr Colby had tied him to his bed and left for the evening. Your brother requested our assistance when 'Palmer' did not visit as promised."

"But *why*? Why such secrecy—by both of them?" Timothy enquired, dumbfounded as his initial shock subsided. "Why even visit my brother at all?"

"As I understand it, Palmer visited your brother as a friend. Thaddeus does not have many of those, does he?"

"No…"

"I know it shall be difficult but, between now and our meeting this evening, please attempt to recall any instances in which your brother may have interacted with Mr Perkins beyond their nightly conversations," Mr Locke said. "I would also be most grateful if you could think of a reason why anyone would want either Mr Perkins or your brother out of the way. Until this evening, then. Good day, Mr Dorsey."

"Y—Yes… of course," Timothy replied. "Good day, Mr Locke."

SEVENTEEN

Having been brought to the Glasgow-Bonham residence by Mr Snyder in the new cab as arranged, Mr Maxwell had headed for the basement whilst Dr Alexander and Miss Dexter had sought out Mr Glasgow and Mrs Bonham, respectively. Cook and Betsy, the maid, were deep in conversation when Mr Maxwell approached the kitchen door like a man walking to the gallows. He'd evaded discovery during his previous visit, but he couldn't be certain neither woman had seen the back of him, at least. Knowing he had little choice but to proceed, he braced himself for a cool reception as he tapped on the door and peered around it. Cook was kneading bread at the table whilst Betsy was darning socks by the fire. Neither showed any hint they'd recognised him, but both were taken off guard by his unexpected arrival.

"Can we help you, sir?" Cook enquired in a formal voice reserved for guests.

Relieved, Mr Maxwell entered and flashed them a smile. "Yes, actually. I'm Mr Joseph Maxwell, an apprentice journalist with the *Gaslight Gazette* and—"

"Out with you!" Cook ordered. Plucking up her rolling pin, she moved around the table toward him and waved it in his face. "I said *out*! Your kind's not welcome here!"

"You don't understand. I'm not here looking for a story!" Mr Maxwell cried, shielding his face with his arms. "Well, not at the moment. That is, I—I will be, b—but not *now*."

"*Out!*" Cook yelled, advancing upon him with the rolling pin aloft.

"Wait! I'm here as a member of the Bow Street Society!" Mr Maxwell cried, wrapping his arms about his head and ducking. The anticipated blow didn't land, though. Fearing she may be waiting for him to expose his face, he lifted it just enough to peer past his arms at her.

172

She'd lowered the rolling pin and was looking at him with a confused expression.

"What's that when it's at 'ome?" Cook enquired.

"A group of people who investigate cases the police either can't or won't," Mr Maxwell replied. "We've been hired by your mistress to investigate the murder of her cat so, please, don't hit me." He lowered his arms and eyed the rolling pin with great trepidation.

"Here, haven't you lot been working for Mr Dorsey?" Betsy enquired.

"Yes," Mr Maxwell replied and swallowed hard. He didn't dare take his eyes off the rolling pin. "He wanted us to find his friend, Palmer, who turned out to be your fellow domestic, Mr Perkins."

"What are you talking about*?"* Cook enquired.

"Mr Perkins was paying evening visits to your neighbour, Mr Thaddeus Dorsey, using the alias of Palmer," Mr Maxwell explained. "When he didn't arrive one evening, though, Mr Dorsey hired us to find him. Soon after, Mr Perkins was found murdered in Mr Dorsey's house."

"How do you know this Palmer was our Mr Perkins though?" Betsy enquired.

Since Cook kept the rolling pin at her side, Mr Maxwell felt able to break his focus on it. Yet, he wished he hadn't when he saw the darning needle in the maid's hand. It wasn't as cumbersome as the rolling pin, but he was quite certain Betsy could cause some permanent damage to his person with it if he inadvertently upset her. Licking his dry lips, he replied, "Mr Perkins was renting an apartment in Chelsea under the name of Palmer. We found the tenancy agreement to prove it."

"I don't believe it," Betsy rebuked. "Why would Mr Perkins work as a footman if he had a nice place like that?"

"That's what we're trying to find out," Mr Maxwell replied.

Cook put down the rolling pin and lowered herself into a chair as she tried to comprehend what she'd been told. "It don't make any sense."

"You didn't know about any of this, then?" Mr Maxwell enquired, relieved the immediate threat of violence had passed.

"None of it," Cook replied.

"Is that why Mr Dorsey killed him? Because he found out who he was?" Betsy enquired.

"We don't know. There's doubt whether Mr Dorsey committed the crime at all. May I sit?" Mr Maxwell enquired as he reached for one of the chairs tucked beneath the table. At the Cook's wave of approval, he pulled it out and sat down. "Can either of you think of anyone who'd want Mr Perkins dead?"

"No, I can't," Cook replied.

"That Mr Colby might've. I heard they was courting the same girl," Betsy said,

"That's just idle gossip," Cook scolded.

"Billy from the butcher's shop told me and he never lies," Betsy retorted.

The feet of Mr Maxwell's chair scraped across the floor as he pulled it close to the table. Casting a sheepish glance to the cook, he mumbled, "Sorry," and rested his hands upon the table. Changing his mind, though, he put them into his lap, only to switch one of them back to the table. Cook reminded him of an old school mistress who'd taught him as a boy. She could put the fear of God into him with one look, too. Clearing his throat, he enquired from Betsy, "Do you know who the girl was?"

"No, no one does. Billy said he saw her with Mr Colby one day and Mr Perkins the next," Betsy replied.

"There's evidence that Mr Perkins was living with a woman in his Chelsea apartment, a forbidden lover. Do you know who that could be? Could it be the girl Billy saw Mr Perkins with, maybe?" Mr Maxwell enquired.

"Nah. Billy said this one was a right street rat; one that works by night, if you know what I mean," Betsy replied.

"No, I'm afraid I don't," Mr Maxwell said.

Betsy cast an uncomfortable glance at cook who said, "a fallen woman is what they say, sir. One with more than one fella to warm her bed."

"Oh," Mr Maxwell replied as his entire face flushed crimson.

"What's this got to do with the mistress' cat?" Cook enquired.

Mr Maxwell stared at her, dumbfounded, until his recollection of why he was there overcame his embarrassment. "Her cat!" He cried. "Yes... well, nothing on the face of it, really. We're just considering the possibility the two murders might be connected. You see, a knife was found on Mr Perkins' body that had blood on its blade. The blood was a few days old. It looked like a kitchen knife so we were wondering if it might have been one of yours?"

"It was," Cook replied. "The police were here the day poor Mr Perkins was found; they showed me the knife and I told them it was one of mine. It had gone missing two nights before."

"Sorry, two *nights* before?" Mr Maxwell enquired.

"That's what I said," Cook replied. "The knife was there when I went to bed but was gone when I got up."

"Was anything else stolen? Were there any signs of a break-in?" Mr Maxwell enquired as he took out some scrap paper and a pencil.

"No, nothing," Cook replied. "Door was still double bolted from the night before and the kitchen door's locked from the hall, too. Just in case any thieves do get in."

"And the windows?" Mr Maxwell enquired but realised there were none when he glanced around the room. "Never mind." He gave a weak smile and wrote his notes. "Have either of you ever been in Mr Dorsey's house at all?"

"No," Cook replied.

"Never," Betsy added.

"Did you hear or see anything out of the ordinary either last night or the night your knife was stolen?" Mr Maxwell enquired, but both women shook their heads. "And nothing overnight?"

"The Four Horsemen wouldn't have woken me up last night," Cook replied.

"Me either. Slept like a log I did," Betsy added.

"What time did you both go to bed?" Mr Maxwell enquired.

"The usual time," Cook replied.

"Midnight," Betsy said.

Mr Maxwell drew a flower on the corner of his ragged paper as he considered his next question. When he settled upon it, he poised his pencil in readiness of more note taking and enquired, "Did anyone in the house go out yesterday evening at all, apart from Mr Perkins, that is?"

"No. The mistress did her stitching in the parlour and the master was working up in his study," Cook replied.

"When did Mr Perkins go out?" Betsy enquired.

"We were hoping you could help us with that," Mr Maxwell replied.

"I don't know," Betsy said and shrugged her shoulders. "I never saw him leave."

"Me neither," Cook added.

"When *was* the last time you saw him?" Mr Maxwell enquired as he hurriedly updated his notes.

"It was after dinner had finished; he said he would help the master in his study," Cook said.

"Did he say what he would help him with?" Mr Maxwell enquired.

"No, and it wasn't our business," Cook replied.

"The last I saw him was at dinner," Betsy interjected.

Mr Maxwell frowned but added to his notes, nonetheless. He had some interactions with servants at his father's home, but he couldn't say either way what made for a good employee. He therefore enquired, "Was Mr Perkins a good servant? Did he get along well with your master and mistress?"

"Oh, *yes*." Cook smiled with a proud glint in her eyes. "He got on and *never* complained."

"Which is why the master kept him on," Betsy added with a nod.

"And Mrs Bonham?" Mr Maxwell ventured.

"She liked him, too. Got along like a house on fire, they did. He was always making her smile with a little joke or two," Cook replied with genuine warmth.

"Thank you, ladies," Mr Maxwell replied, putting away his paper and pencil. Clasping his hands on the table in front of him, he flashed a smile at them both and said, in a discreet tone, "Well, now that we're all friends, and you know I'm not going to print anything you say, why not tell me who Mr Perkins' mystery woman in Chelsea was, hmm?" Cook and Betsy exchanged glances and he continued, "Come on, you can tell me; I promise it will be off the record." His smile broadened as he leant forward and whispered, "Was it Mrs Bonham?"

"You dirty, little toe-rag!" Cook cried as she once more reached for the rolling pin and leapt to her feet. Betsy followed and both women advanced on Mr Maxwell.

"You want your mouth washin' out with soap, you do," Betsy warned.

Mr Maxwell clambered to his feet and stumbled on his chair as he retreated. Gripping it behind him, he then moved around it and took swift, backward steps to the door as he replied, "Thank you, ladies, for your help. If you, er, think of anything, we're, er, down… there." He pointed in the general direction of the Society office.

"Go on, out with you!" Cook ordered, closing the gap and brandished the rolling pin.

Mr Maxwell reeled backwards through the door, walked into the opposing wall with a grunt, and stumbled as he scrambled for the stairs with Cook close behind. Clambering up them on all fours, he then opened the door at the top and threw himself into the hallway. Seeing Dr Alexander there, he momentarily closed his eyes in relief before walking over to him in a haphazard line and gripping his shoulder as he tried to catch his breath. "Thank *God* you're still here, Doctor."

Dr Alexander scanned his chaotic appearance and enquired, "Did it not go well?"

EIGHTEEN

Mr Glasgow cradled his appointment book and turned its pages as he entered the waiting room of his photography business. Finding a well-dressed gentleman warming his hands by the fire, he enquired, "Dr Alexander?"

"Yes. Mr Lanford Glasgow, I presume?" Dr Alexander replied, leaving the fire and crossing the room with an outstretched hand.

Mr Glasgow closed his book and tucked it under his arm. "Indeed," he said, shaking his hand. "If you'll be so kind as to follow me, Doctor, we'll have your photograph taken in no time."

"Jolly good," Dr Alexander remarked and followed Mr Glasgow, first onto the landing and then to the next door along. Allowing his host to enter the room ahead of him, he enquired, "How long have you been a photographer as well as a lawyer?"

"Only a year."

The room was around twenty feet long and ten feet wide with a petite bureau in its far corner beside a window hidden by a heavy, burgundy-coloured curtain. Hanging from a rail fixed to the wall to Dr Alexander's left as he entered was an identical curtain that Mr Glasgow pulled back to reveal a second door. Going through it, he led Dr Alexander into an equally long but narrower room with a boxed camera and tripod in its centre. A black cloak that kept the photographer in pitch-darkness hung from the camera's back whilst a brass cap covered it lens. The light of four gas lamps caressed the darkness from their sconces mounted upon the walls, but it was insufficient for Mr Glasgow's purpose. Even a layman such as Dr Alexander realised a great deal more light was required to capture the perfect photographic print of his likeness. Having made his way to the other side of the room, though, Mr Glasgow tossed back another curtain and the room was filled by cold daylight in an instant.

The studio's back wall was adorned with a pastel-coloured mural of an English country garden with another burgundy curtain tied back by gold rope beside it. An immense rug of identical colour almost entirely covered the dark, lacquered floorboards. Standing on one side of it was a chaise lounge displaying an arrangement of sun-faded cushions, and sporting several large, vertical tears down its highest side. Narrow strips of fabric dangled from the wounds in a familiar way to Dr Alexander. Unless he could examine them further, though, he could neither confirm nor dismiss his suspicions, but he also wasn't willing to offend his host by doing so without his permission. He therefore continued his visual examination of the studio with the wooden column carved and painted to look like white stone, and the large-leafed plant in a round, dull-brass pot atop it. Against the back wall was a table laden with blank sheets of paper, glass plates, empty trays, and bottles containing chemicals, including cellulose nitrate, silver nitrate, potassium cyanide, and pyrogallic acid. A heavy, black curtain hung around the table, suspended from the ceiling by a brass pole, whilst a line of string was tied across the back wall above it. A series of pegs were clipped to the line and the distinct odour of burnt almonds lingered in the air. Flecks of what Dr Alexander presumed to be silver nitrate covered the floor, both under and around the table, along with several other unidentifiable stains.

"You wish to have just one copy of your portrait, correct?" Mr Glasgow enquired as he pushed the chaise lounge to one side.

"Yes, please." Dr Alexander smiled. "Where shall I stand?"

"Just here, please, Doctor." Mr Glasgow motioned to the space the chaise had occupied and Dr Alexander moved into it. Taking the opportunity to cast a discreet eye over the damage whilst he adjusted his tie and smoothed down his jacket, he realised he'd need to get closer still. Yet, in addition to the wounded fabric, he noticed the indentations of the chaise's feet and two long, deep scratches in the rug's pile. The latter had been previously hidden from view by the piece of furniture. Mr Glasgow's sudden question brought his focus back to the matter at hand, however; "Will the Bow Street Society be paying my fee for this photograph also?"

"No," Dr Alexander replied as he watched Mr Glasgow take a square, glass plate from the table. After a moment's consideration he conceded it had been foolish of him to think his host wouldn't know of his association with that group. He therefore asked the natural question; "Did your sister tell you I was with the Society?"

"She told me a veterinary surgeon by the name of Doctor Rupert Alexander had been enlisted by the Society to look into her blasted cat's murder," Mr Glasgow replied and closed the curtain over the window. Returning to the table, he prepared the plate with a mixture of soluble iodide and cellulose nitrate, carried it to the camera, and slipped it inside. "Pose, please," Mr Glasgow instructed as he let the daylight back in and ducked under the black cloak. Dr Alexander gripped his jacket's lapel with one hand, held his other in his pocket, and lifted his chin in a regal manner. Satisfied his client had settled upon his position, Mr Glasgow unscrewed the cap from the camera's lens, instructing, "Stay perfectly still, please, or the image will be blurred." Dr Alexander held his breath and body for several seconds until Mr Glasgow replaced the cap and emerged from beneath the cloak. "You may relax, now." Taking the plate from the camera, he carried it over to the table, pulled the curtain around, and undertook the process of developing the image. Hearing liquid being poured against a hard surface, Dr Alexander then smelt the scent of bitter almonds in the air become stronger.

With Mr Glasgow's view obscured by the curtain, Dr Alexander felt able to conduct his examination of the chaise lounge without reprieve. He therefore ran his fingers over the tears in the piece of furniture, finding some short strands of hair amongst them, as he enquired, "You don't agree with the investigation, then, sir?" Crouching upon the rug, he next followed its scratches with his fingertips and found they were both deep—they'd cut through to the ratting underlay—and *very* narrow. Some short strands of hair had also been caught by the rug's pile. Dr Alexander felt a great sense of satisfaction at having his suspicions confirmed but, as he rose to his feet, he noticed the light hit something in the corner of his eyes. Venturing closer to the spot, he saw a pearl was jammed between two floorboards and was partially covered by the rug's fringe.

"Of course not; it's an absolutely ridiculous exercise," Mr Glasgow replied from behind the curtain. "What will you do when you unmask the so-called 'killer?' Hang him?"

"If only I could," Dr Alexander remarked. "The poor creature was left in a ghastly state." He crouched down beside the pearl and gripped it with his fingernails. Unable to prise it free, though, he gave it several firm tugs coupled with a soft grunt or two.

"What are you doing?" Mr Glasgow suddenly enquired from above.

Dr Alexander ignored him for the moment, though, and instead gave the pearl another tug.

"What do you have there?" Mr Glasgow challenged.

Dr Alexander smiled as he felt the pearl slip free. Rising to his feet, he then held it up for his host to see. It appeared to be from a woman's gold earring—at least, that was what Dr Alexander had surmised.

"Give it to me," Mr Glasgow ordered, tossing aside the rag he'd been using to wipe his hands, and snatching the pearl from his client's fingers. Taking a moment to inspect it for himself, he then dropped it into his pocket. "Esta knows what I think on the subject, but she also knows I care about her," he went on as he continued to glare at Dr Alexander. "If it makes her happy to waste your time, and you're all happy to have it wasted, I shan't stand in your way. That's what you wanted to know, isn't it? It's the reason why you didn't volunteer the fact you were with the Society when you booked your appointment, correct? To relax me into a false sense of security so I would open up to you. Perhaps to even 'confess?'" He scoffed. "I had nothing to do with that animal's death—it never even came in here—and why you'd think she wouldn't have told me of you, I have no idea. I'm very close to my sister."

"That's clear to us," Dr Alexander replied, his curiosity piqued by Mr Glasgow's lack of explanation regarding the earring. He had formed his own ideas as to why, but it was clear Mr Glasgow wasn't prepared to discuss the matter further. Dr Alexander therefore continued, "I would've been surprised if she hadn't told you. The truth is, I do need a photograph as my wife keeps telling me she has nothing to remember me by. I work long hours." He smiled. "But I wanted to talk to you about Malcolm's murder—and Mr Perkins'—too. I've never 'investigated' an animal's murder before, Mr Glasgow, so the whole concept is new to me as well. That doesn't make the matter any less serious though." He checked the time on his pocket watch. "I won't take any more than ten minutes of your time. For your sister's sake."

Mr Glasgow studied him for several moments and released a soft sigh. "Very well," he began as he glanced at the chaise lounge but didn't invite his client to sit. "Like I said, the cat never came in here. I didn't go out of my way to spend time with it, either. If anything, it was an annoyance to me as it was always getting into places it shouldn't, getting under my feet, and damaging things with its claws."

"Such as your chaise?" Dr Alexander indicated the damage. "Cats do have a habit of scratching things they shouldn't; it gets rid of the old, outer husk of the claw, you see. I recognised the tell-tale scratching pattern in the fabric as soon as I saw it."

Mr Glasgow's expression became hard as he looked at the tears. "He did that when it was still out in the hall. I gave him a good kick for it."

Dr Alexander was horrified. "You *kicked* him?"

"I pushed him away, but he kept doing it. That's an expensive piece of furniture, Doctor, an antique." Mr Glasgow pulled on a piece of the torn fabric. "Just look at it." Upon seeing Dr Alexander's horror hadn't abated despite his explanation, he said, "The cat was fine. It was more like a firm nudge than a kick."

Dr Alexander gave a curt nod, but anger lingered in his eyes.

"Look, I know kicking him wasn't the best thing to do, but I didn't kill him," Mr Glasgow said.

Dr Alexander felt his anger ease despite the weak expression of regret and enquired, "Do you have any idea who did?"

"Mr Perkins."

"Why would he want to kill Malcolm in such a horrible, horrible way?"

"I don't know, but he's the only person in the house who had easy access to the creature aside from me, my sister, the cook, and the maid."

"You don't think the other servants could've killed him, then?"

"No, they're not of that character."

"But Mr Perkins was?" Dr Alexander enquired as his anger dissipated and intrigue took its place.

Mr Glasgow gave a soft sigh. "Perhaps. He always behaved decently around me, my sister, and the other servants, but who knows what darkness lies behind a man's eyes?"

"Indeed. I trust his previous employers never had any quarrel with him?"

"None at all. As far as I can remember, I never had any reason to complain about his work, either."

"Did Mr Perkins ever assist you with your photography work?"

184

"Yes; he'd develop the photographs whilst I operated the camera when I had a lot of clients to see."

"Was that a skill he came into your employ with?"

"No, it's something I taught him." Mr Glasgow tilted his head as he studied Dr Alexander with curious eyes. "What's his helping me with my photography work got to do with anything, Doctor?"

"Well, Mr Dorsey told us he'd smelt burnt almonds on the night Mr Perkins was murdered, and traces of cyanide were also found under Mr Perkins' fingernails. I noticed the smell of burnt almonds and the bottle of potassium cyanide on your table when I came in."

"I see," Mr Glasgow replied though continued to study Dr Alexander. "Huh," he added with a thoughtful air before returning to the table behind the curtain and checking on the progress of his client's drying photograph.

Dr Alexander approached the curtain but didn't go behind it. "As you spent a lot of time with Mr Perkins, did you know him rather well?"

"As well as any master knows his servant."

"Then why didn't you recognise him when Miss Dexter showed you the model?"

Mr Glasgow looked around the curtain in confusion as he enquired, "What model?"

"Miss Dexter's clay model of Palmer's face based on Mr Thaddeus' Dorsey's description and amendments," Dr Alexander replied. The craftsmanship of the piece had impressed him when he'd seen it in the newspaper. "You took a photograph of it at the Society's request. I was wondering why you didn't realise it was your servant."

"Because it looked *nothing* like him," Mr Glasgow rebuked and retreated behind the curtain. Unpegging the photograph, he held it flat to examine its surface. Finding it was still wet, he hung it back up and leaned on the table with his hands. "And they told me it was of a man named 'Palmer,'" he continued, "so it never occurred to me to look at it as if it were Mr Perkins."

Dr Alexander supposed it was a reasonable explanation, even if he thought most people would compare the image to those they knew as a matter of course. He ran his eyes over the studio and enquired, "Have you ever taken Mr Dorsey's photograph?"

"No. I have as little to do with Thaddeus as possible," Mr Glasgow replied with more than a hint of irritation. "Besides, he's not allowed to leave the house without Timothy's permission."

"Because he might hurt himself?" Dr Alexander enquired.

"Because he might hurt others," Mr Glasgow replied and took down the now dried photograph. Stepping out from behind the curtain, he held it out to his client. "Here."

"Marvellous," Dr Alexander complimented as he took it. "Agatha will be pleased with this. Hopefully, she'll stop asking me to pose for one, now. How much do I owe you?"

Mr Glasgow named the required amount and, whilst he was waiting for Dr Alexander to supply it, remarked, "Honestly, I'm surprised it took Thaddeus so long to kill someone. Thank you." He took the monies and wrote a receipt. "It's been coming for a long time."

"Why do you say that?"

"He's a violent man, possessed of great selfishness and an infinite capacity to deceive," Mr Glasgow replied, tearing off the receipt and giving it to Dr Alexander.

"Could you elaborate on that?"

Mr Glasgow's brow creased into a scowl as he replied with distinct bitterness, "Thaddeus claims to be blind yet admits to seeing, with great clarity—people, monsters, colours and patterns. He claims to be mad but can hold a conversation as well as you or I."

"The things he sees are part of his madness, as I understand it, for they're not there when others look."

"When others are *there*," Mr Glasgow retorted. "That could be a false pretence for their benefit."

Dr Alexander could see the merit in such a suggestion, but he wished to reserve judgement for when he could meet the man in person. Nevertheless, he knew it would be unwise to dismiss the possibility altogether. He therefore enquired, "Do you have any evidence?"

"No, but it's only logical, isn't it?"

"It's a logical supposition, yes," Dr Alexander conceded. Then remembering something Miss Trent had told him, he enquired, "You were business partners with him though, correct? Trust is important in such an endeavour."

A shadow of regret passed over Mr Glasgow's face as he replied, "I trusted him back then; he was the best criminal lawyer London had seen in years." He busied himself with cleaning up the mess on the table as he continued, "When I joined his firm, I was still new to the ways of the court room. He took me under his wing, helped me grow. I was ecstatic when he offered me partnership. When things started to fall apart for him, I wanted to help in whatever way I could." He paused in his activity to stare into the ether a moment as he added, "I could see the business had become a burden for him, so I bought his half." His features contorted back into a scowl, though, as he placed the bottles with loud thuds and said, "For years, the firm had been highly successful; people *trusted* him with their lives, as I had." He strode across the room and violently tugged the curtain back across the window. "It was only after the paperwork was signed, and I was finally able to look at the books, did I realise I'd been fooled by his deceit. The firm was almost bankrupt. With Thaddeus gone, the better-paying clients left, too. If Esta hadn't come to live with me when she did…" He spun around to face Dr Alexander. His calm demeanour highlighted the agitation of his own, though. He therefore took a deep breath and admitted, "Yes, I should've looked at the books before buying the business, but I *trusted* him because he'd given me no reason not to."

"But if he was going mad, surely you would've doubted his ability to make sound judgements?" Dr Alexander enquired whilst being careful not to use a judgemental tone.

"He hid the true extent of his illness from me, from all of us," Mr Glasgow replied. "When he lashed out and everything was exposed, I felt sorry for him. I didn't know he'd been unwell for *months* beforehand." Mr Glasgow folded his arms across his chest. "Well, he now *claims* he'd been unwell for all that time. Honestly, I think he just grew tired of having to take care of himself and the business. Blindness and madness are easy enough things to imitate, Doctor. I've seen plenty of cases at the magistrates' court wherein allegedly blind beggars have been exposed to possess perfect vision. Thaddeus knew how badly the business was doing and he needed a way out. Timothy and I were just too loyal, and naïve, to realise what he was doing."

"And when *did* you realise, Mr Glasgow?"

"When I saw one of his alleged 'episodes' for myself, he was shouting there was a demon in the room as he stared at the corner." Mr Glasgow put his hands on his hips. "He could move around the furniture without any difficulty to get to it, Doctor. He described the creature, but the way his eyes focused on that one spot convinced me of his deceit."

"I see," Dr Alexander said and took a moment to decide upon how best to word his next question. "Given what you've just told me, Mr Glasgow… and the circumstances of Mr Perkins' murder… please don't be offended when I ask for your whereabouts the night he was killed."

"I was here; *all* night, working in my study until I went to bed at about a quarter to ten."

"And where was Mr Perkins at that time?"

"I don't know; fulfilling his duties as our footman, I presume." Mr Glasgow opened the door into the smaller room but turned toward Dr Alexander when something appeared to occur to him. He said, "He did come to my study to ask if I required any assistance, though, so he *was* at home." His voice was cooler as he admitted, "Yes, I hate Mr Dorsey for what he is and what he did, but I wouldn't kill Mr Perkins to get my revenge on him. I avoid Thaddeus and speak as little about him as I can. For him to know *exactly* how little he means to me now, for him to *know* I know his secret, and for him to live with the burden of those things for the rest of his days. *That* is my revenge, Doctor. Not murder, *never* murder. Especially not of an innocent man such as Mr Perkins."

"Unfortunately, Mr Glasgow, Mr Perkins wasn't as innocent as you thought," Dr Alexander revealed, his chest feeling tight under the weight of what he was about to say. He knew it was necessary for the investigation—and he'd agreed to do whatever was necessary to find the truth—but, nonetheless, these thoughts did little to ease his discomfort. Mr Glasgow's questioning gaze didn't help matters either.

"What do you mean?" Mr Glasgow enquired.

"Well, for one he had an apartment in Chelsea in addition to his room here," Dr Alexander replied with a deep sigh.

Mr Glasgow frowned as he enquired, "And the second?"

"He was living there romantically with a woman, one who was forbidden to him," Dr Alexander replied.

Mr Glasgow went over to the chaise lounge and sat down. With a subdued voice, he enquired, "Do you know her name?"

"No, we were hoping you could help us with that," Dr Alexander replied.

Mr Glasgow looked up, confused, until the realisation of what was being insinuated crept onto his eyes. Once again, his features were mutated by a fierce scowl as he half-growled, "It wasn't Esta." He leapt to his feet and advanced upon Dr Alexander. "Aside from the fact I wouldn't allow such a thing to happen under *my* roof, my sister is a lady and thus, she wouldn't debase herself by accepting the courtship of a *footman*."

"One of our members searched the apartment, Mr Glasgow," Dr Alexander replied. "Mr Perkins and his lover seem to have met there regularly. So, it wouldn't have been under your roof…" Though his words were strong, his conviction had weakened beneath the weight of his discomfort and Mr Glasgow's offended response.

"*No*. It wasn't Esta. I make *damned* sure *no one* touches or speaks to her like that. *No one*."

"Mr Glasgow, I appreciate you're trying to be the protective brother but—"

"You're right; I *am*. She was almost forced into destitution by a man before; I shan't let that happen again. Mr Perkins wasn't having an affair with my sister. You'll need to look elsewhere."

"What man?" Dr Alexander enquired, feeling his courage return at the emergence of this new line of enquiry.

"Mr Samuel Regis," Mr Glasgow replied in disgust. "He was a soldier who attended a ball where I and my sister were. He approached her and invited her to dance; unfortunately, I was otherwise engaged with another young lady with whom I'd promised to dance. Within a month, he and my sister were engaged to be wed. I wasn't at all happy about it. She was completely in love, of course, so I had to take it upon myself to dissuade him. He confessed to what he was up to but ignored my threats and pleas, stating my sister had her own mind and her own money. I therefore sought the help of the police. A constable visited him at his barracks, and he was dismissed for misconduct. No charges were formally pressed, but his commanding officer wished to avoid the scandal. My sister immediately broke off the engagement for the same reason and the soldier went abroad. We've never heard from him again, but word is he died on some ship in the Atlantic."

"How can you be certain Mr Perkins hadn't seduced Mrs Bonham in the same way?"

"Because he knew of the story and he knew I wouldn't have hesitated to do the same to him. Furthermore, as I said before, I made sure no one spoke romantically to my sister. She's limited in the number of men she may encounter: me, Mr Perkins, Mr Colby, and the Dorsey brothers. She's *never* left alone in the company of men from outside our home. *Never.*"

*"*You allow her to see Mr Thaddeus Dorsey?" Dr Alexander enquired in surprise.

"Only because she insists upon it. I protect her, Doctor, I don't imprison her. She knows why I do what I do and she both respects and appreciates it. She would *never* break my trust and *never* degrade herself by having an affair with any of them. Certainly not with Mr Perkins."

"You trust her, then?" Dr Alexander enquired.

"Completely," Mr Glasgow replied.

Dr Alexander took in another deep breath, grateful the discussion which had caused him so much discomfort had been completed. He put his photograph into his bag and offered a weak smile to his host by way of a peace offering. He hoped Mr Glasgow understood his predicament, and how necessary his questions had been. Seeing some of the tension ease from Mr Glasgow's shoulders and facial muscles in response to his smile, he decided to move on and enquired, "What is your opinion of Mr Colby and Mr Timothy Dorsey?"

"Mr Colby is a hard man, but he has to be to keep Thaddeus under control," Mr Glasgow replied. His voice warmed and his expression soften as he continued, "Timothy is the complete opposite—kind, generous, naïve, and highly gullible. Unfortunately, he has yet to come to the same realisation about his brother as I have. He still allows Thaddeus to rule his life, despite my trying to persuade him of the truth."

"You and Mr Timothy Dorsey are good friends?"

"Very good," Mr Glasgow replied. "We each have responsibilities to our siblings; it's something we try to help one another with as much as we can." He checked his pocket watch. "And I believe your time is over, Doctor." He indicated the open door. "This way, please."

Dr Alexander left the studio ahead of him and passed through the smaller room to emerge back on the landing. When Mr Glasgow joined him there, they walked to the top of the stairs where they bid their farewell and shook hands. Yet, even as he descended, Dr Alexander felt Mr Glasgow's eyes upon his back. Deciding to wait for Mr Maxwell and Miss Dexter outside, therefore, he crossed the hallway only to hear the former's voice behind him.

"Thank God you're still here, Doctor."

Dr Alexander scanned his chaotic appearance and enquired, "Did it not go well?"

"It went *horribly*!" Mr Maxwell exclaimed as he dabbed at his pale face and hands with his handkerchief. "I narrowly escaped the kitchen with my life."

Dr Alexander stared at him in utter horror. Before he could enquire further about what had occurred, though, the parlour door opened, and Miss Dexter emerged. She looked between them with concerned eyes as she closed the door and enquired, "What's happened?"

NINETEEN

Miss Dexter thanked Mrs Bonham as she accepted the cup of tea from her. Resting its saucer upon her lap, she took a delicate, yet welcome, sip of the warm liquid. The pitter-patter of rain filled the parlour as an overcast sky and lack of interior light darkened the room. Mrs Bonham sat in the chair whilst Miss Dexter occupied the sofa. Yet, both positions made it impossible for the table in front of the window to contaminate their fields of vision. Mrs Bonham used a set of small, silver tongs to drop two sugar cubes into her cup and gave it a slow stir as she mused aloud, "Lanford will be grateful for Dr Alexander's custom." She tapped the spoon against her cup's rim and laid it on her saucer. "He's a very proud man, my brother."

"I believe most men are," Miss Dexter observed and placed her cup upon its saucer. Maintaining her perfect posture, she inclined her head toward her hostess and enquired with genuine concern, "but how have *you* been, Mrs Bonham?"

Mrs Bonham cradled her teacup and saucer as she replied, "It has been difficult, but one must keep one's dignity and continue onward."

"We *will* find out who killed Malcolm."

"I know you shall," Mrs Bonham replied with a weak smile. It soon faded, though, as a great unease descended upon her features. "But what of Mr Dorsey? Who is helping him?"

"We are."

"You are?"

"Yes, we have a lawyer amongst our members, a Mr Gregory Elliott, who has agreed to defend him," Miss Dexter explained. "We also believe Mr Dorsey is innocent so are doing all we can to find the person responsible. This… is the other reason I called upon you today." She bowed her head and looked to her cup as if hoping the tea leaves would give her the appropriate words to use. "Mrs

Bonham, I... I don't know quite how to tell you this, but..." *Why didn't I request Mr Maxwell to accompany me? Words are more his speciality than mine*, she thought and met her hostess' gaze. *You are here now, Georgie, and she's waiting to hear what you have to say.* Finding some resolution in her thoughts, Miss Dexter continued, "Mr Perkins... was Mr Dorsey's friend, Palmer."

"He was?" Mrs Bonham enquired, limiting the expression of her emotions to the surprise in her voice. "I now understand why you seemed to have difficulty in forming the words." She steadied herself with a sip of tea. "I had no idea."

"There is something else you should know," Miss Dexter began. "We've found some love letters." Mrs Bonham promptly met her gaze with a startled look in her eyes but didn't speak. Miss Dexter therefore went on, "Letters which were... very intimate and... seemed to be from a forbidden lover."

Mrs Bonham's cup and saucer at once toppled from her hands and onto her skirts, spurring Miss Dexter to attempt to catch them in vain. Whilst the artist then set aside her own drink to gather up the remnants of her hostess', Mrs Bonham sat in a state of shock that momentarily paralysed her. It wasn't until she felt the pressure of Miss Dexter's handkerchief against her skirts as she dabbed at the damp material that she was finally roused from her trance. "Oh... Forgive me," she said with a quiet voice and dazed expression.

"Are you well, Mrs Bonham?"

"Yes..." Mrs Bonham rubbed her temple. "Yes, of course." She allowed Miss Dexter to complete the tidying up as she gathered her thoughts and tried to suppress the panic growing within her bosom. "Where did you find these love letters?"

"Here, in Mr Perkins' bedroom, and at his apartment in Chelsea."

"I *beg* your pardon," Mrs Bonham said, blinking in surprise. "*What* apartment in Chelsea?"

"It would appear Mr Perkins was renting an apartment in Chelsea as well as living here."

"But…" Mrs Bonham began, stunned. "What were the letters doing *there*?" She lifted a trembling hand to her forehead. "They were private." She clenched the same hand and held it under her nose as she turned her head away, and the corners of her eyes glistened with unshed tears. "You shouldn't have read them."

"We had no choice," Miss Dexter replied in a meek voice. "Mr Dorsey's life depends upon us finding who really killed Mr Perkins. If it was his lover—"

"It wasn't," Mrs Bonham snapped as she stood. Going to the fireplace, she then turned back with a fierce glare and said, "Do you hear me? It *wasn't*."

Miss Dexter's lips parted, closed, and parted again as she fathomed her response to Mrs Bonham's outburst. Dumbfounded, she admitted, "I—I don't know what to say."

"Then don't say anything."

"I—"

Mrs Bonham cut off Miss Dexter's words with a sudden grasp of her hands. "I *beseech* you."

"But if you know who Mr Perkins' lover was—"

"Mr Perkins?" Mrs Bonham interrupted with a swift releasing of her hands. "Did you say, 'Mr Perkins' lover?'"

"Yes. She may hold the key to who killed him. *Please*, Mrs Bonham. If you know who—"

"I don't," Mrs Bonham snapped and turned back toward the fireplace. "I was confused by what you said, with all that has happened with Thaddeus and Malcolm, my mind is quite all over the place." When she faced the artist again, there was a large, albeit contrived, smile upon her face. "Please, forgive me."

Miss Dexter was speechless as Mrs Bonham returned to her chair like nothing had happened. She'd never seen such a dramatic to-and-fro of emotions in one person before, and she sincerely hoped she'd never see it again. Still confused, but compelled to speak by her curiosity, she enquired, "Who did you think I was speaking of?"

"No one." Mrs Bonham offered a more genuine smile. "Honestly, I was utterly confused. I thought you were speaking of Thaddeus—Being the one who killed Mr Perkins, that is."

Miss Dexter couldn't bring herself to accept such an explanation. Mrs Bonham's reaction to the letters' discovery had been so intense Miss Dexter had little choice but to consider an obvious possibility. She bowed her head and rubbed the handle of her teacup as she pondered how best to word the question she needed to ask. "I'm sorry, Mrs Bonham, but…" She bit her lip and met her gaze. "…Were you Mr Perkins' lover?"

"*Me?*" Mrs Bonham enquired, stunned. At Miss Dexter's nod, she rested her fingertips upon her bosom and urged, "It wasn't *I*." She gave a weak laugh. "Mr Perkins was a *footman,* Miss Dexter. *I* am a *lady*. The mere idea is *disgusting.*"

"Your reaction to the letters being discovered, though—?"

"I was shocked by the news of Mr Perkins having another residence—another life even," Mrs Bonham interrupted as she covered the damp patch on her skirt with her shawl. "I usually take absolutely *no* interest in the love affairs of my servants *unless* they are acting in a scandalous fashion. His forbidden affair was complete news to me."

Miss Dexter pursed her lips together as she realised she had no idea how to proceed despite her strong suspicion that Mrs Bonham wasn't being honest with her. Considering her next step carefully, therefore, she then enquired, "But you're a widower, aren't you?"

"Yes, but that doesn't mean I wish to start an affair with a servant. Aside from such a thing being scandalous, I wouldn't want to humiliate myself again or disappoint my brother."

Miss Dexter bowed her head and took another delicate sip of her tea as she replied in a meek voice, "I understand."

"No. You don't." Mrs Bonham shook her head. "My brother is *very* protective of me and with good reason. I've fallen foul of a conman pretending to be a suitor before. Neither I nor Lanford have any intention of letting it happen again." Mrs Bonham then settled back against her chair and rested her hands in her lap as a silence descended between them.

"Was Mr Perkins a good servant?" Miss Dexter enquired after several long moments.

"Yes. He was punctual, impeccably presented, well-liked by the other servants, and hard working." She nodded toward the door. "He assisted my brother more than I. I have Betsy, my maid, for my requirements."

"How did you come to hire him, may I ask?"

"He was recommended to us by a good friend of mine who was downsizing her staff because her children had left home, and she and her husband were moving to a smaller house. Perkins' references were excellent, so we took him on."

"May I ask how long he's worked for you?"

"It must be five years now." Mrs Bonham considered a moment. "Yes, five years."

Miss Dexter thought she'd heard Dr Alexander's voice in the hallway and glanced at the door. Unable to think of any further questions, she placed her cup and saucer upon the tray and rose to her feet, saying, "Thank you for your time, Mrs Bonham. Goodbye." She then gave her a gracious dip of her head and departed.

Stepping into the hallway, she founded Dr Alexander in conversation with Mr Maxwell. Upon hearing the latter speak of escaping the kitchen with his life, she looked between them with concerned eyes, closed the door and enquired, "What's happened?"

"Mr Maxwell's conversation with the servants didn't go very well," Dr Alexander explained.

"I was threatened with a rolling pin," Mr Maxwell added, feeling his cheeks warm as he realised how ridiculous it sounded.

Miss Dexter's eyes were wide with amazement, though, as she enquired, "Were you hurt?"

"No... But I could've been," Mr Maxwell replied.

Miss Dexter breathed a small sigh of relief and agreed, "Oh, yes, of course."

"Don't worry, Mr Maxwell. She could've thrown rock buns at you," Dr Alexander said with a smirk.

Miss Dexter chuckled at both the mental image of such an occurrence and Mr Maxwell's alarmed reaction to Dr Alexander's words.

"Rock... buns?" Mr Maxwell repeated in terror as his own mind conjured up images of being pummelled by jagged stones.

"Rock buns are a type of cake," Miss Dexter explained with a smile.

"Oh," Mr Maxwell replied. A sudden wave of relief and embarrassment swept over him, obliging him to look to his feet, clear his throat, and smooth down his frock coat to hide his crimson complexion. "I—I knew that."

"I'll just say goodbye to Mrs Bonham and let her know Malcolm's body is ready for burial," Dr Alexander told them in amusement. When he reached the parlour door, though, he took a moment to compose himself and adopt a more sombre expression. Having assumed Mrs Bonham would've heard their voices in the hallway, he just knocked once before entering the parlour. She immediately crumpled a piece of paper in her hands and turned in her chair toward him with a gasp. Upon seeing him, though, her surprise switched to anger as she hastily wiped her eyes and cried, "How *dare* you enter without an invitation!"

"My sincere pardons, Mrs Bonham," Dr Alexander replied, retreating into the hallway and closing the door.

"What's wrong?" Mr Maxwell enquired.

"I think we've outstayed our welcome," Dr Alexander replied, heading for the front door without stopping. As he then held it open for his fellow Bow Streeters, he resolved to inform Mrs Bonham of his news in writing later that day.

"What is it?" Miss Dexter enquired in a whisper once they were all on the porch and out of earshot of the house's occupants.

"Mrs Bonham was crying when I entered the parlour," Dr Alexander replied, keeping his voice just above a whisper. "And reading something, I believe—a single piece of paper."

"A let—" Mr Maxwell began in his usual tone, only to lower it when the others shushed him. "A letter, maybe?"

"I really couldn't say. She crumpled it up when I walked in. I didn't want to risk a confrontation by asking about it," Dr Alexander replied. "Whatever it was, we certainly have a great deal to report to Miss Trent."

* * *

"Git your hands off me!" a female voice demanded from Mr Dorsey's porch as Dr Alexander, Mr Maxwell, and Miss Dexter reached the street. The voice had an Irish twang that attracted the Bow Streeters' attraction and they crossed the road to gain a better—yet inconspicuous—view of the house. The owner of the voice was a fair-skinned brunette in her early twenties with fiery brown eyes and a narrow waist beneath a loose-fitting, dark-brown, tattered dress. She rested a thin hand upon her protruding, angular hip as she almost touched Mr Colby's nose with her pointed finger. "Ye stay away from me, ye hear?!"

"You wasn't there last night and now *you're* yelling at *me*?!" Mr Colby shouted back. "What's going on, Merla?"

"Ye know what ye've done, Jack. And ye're not having me! Not now, not ever!"

Merla turned to leave, but Mr Colby grabbed her arm. As he then pulled her back around, her open palm slammed against his cheek. Stunned by the sudden impact, Mr Colby's anger erupted a heartbeat later and he gripped her arms tight. Shaking her hard, he yelled, "Look here, you *whore*! I don't know what the bloody hell you're talking about, but you're gonna tell me!"

Alarmed by what they were seeing, Dr Alexander and Mr Maxwell hurried back across the road to intervene, whilst a nervous Miss Dexter remained behind. Yet, Merla didn't wait for their assistance, instead choosing to kick Mr Colby's shin as she yelled, "Git ye filthy hands off me!"

"Argh!" Mr Colby cried as a sharp pain shot up his leg. Releasing her at the same time, he gripped his shin with both hands as she ran down the steps to the pavement. "Come back, you *bitch*!"

"Stay away from me or I'll go to the coppers about what ye done, Jack! I swear to God heself!" Merla shouted back up to him before almost colliding with Dr Alexander and Mr Maxwell as she turned. Seeing their surprised expressions, she challenged, "What ye looking at?!" Neither Bow Streeter was given an opportunity to respond, though, as Merla had already stepped out into the road to cross the street, narrowly avoiding being run over by a cab in the process. "Watch where ye're going!" She yelled at the driver. Mr Colby, who'd followed her as far as the pavement, stopped when he saw Dr Alexander and Mr Maxwell and retreated inside.

"Miss?! Erm, miss! Please!" Miss Dexter called after Merla once she'd crossed to her side of the road. When Merla continued walking without acknowledging her, though, Miss Dexter hitched up her skirts with one hand and hurried after her, calling "Excuse me, miss!"

"*What*?" Merla said as she spun around. "If he's sent ye to fetch me, ye've wasted ye time."

"No, I, er, pardon," Miss Dexter replied and swallowed hard as she fought to regain her breath. "My name is Miss Georgina Dexter. I'm an artist and member of the Bow Street Society. Our client is Mr Thaddeus Dorsey—"

"Nah," Merla interrupted, shaking her head as she turned her back on her. "I'm not talking to ye."

"Please, miss, he's innocent," Miss Dexter said, going after her once more. "If you know anything that could assist him, then—"

"I don't," Merla interrupted without looking back at her.

"What's Mr Colby done that's so bad, then?" Mr Maxwell called after Merla as he and Dr Alexander caught up with Miss Dexter.

Merla spun around and strode over to Mr Maxwell until she was mere inches from his face. With a sneer, she replied, "None of ye fecking business, lad."

"We can pay you," Dr Alexander suggested with his hand in his pocket.

"I ain't no peach," Merla said with a hard prod to Dr Alexander's chest. To Miss Dexter, she added, "Ye wanna know what Jack did? Go ask him." Casting a black look to the men, she then muttered an insult under her breath about two-faced toffs and continued on her way.

"The street rat!" Mr Maxwell cried in recollection and pressed his hand to his forehead. Considering going after Merla for as long as it took to realise it would only bring him trouble, he said, "Miss Dexter, could you quickly draw Merla before she disappears, please?"

"Erm, y—yes, I think so…" Miss Dexter replied, taking out her sketchbook and pencil. "But why?"

"Betsy, the maid, told me a young woman was seen with Mr Perkins one day and Mr Colby the next. She described her as a street rat, a woman who worked by night," Mr Maxwell replied as Miss Dexter went to work.

"And you think Merla is the woman Betsy was talking about?" Dr Alexander enquired.

"Yes. Well, she does look like someone who lives on the streets," Mr Maxwell replied but frowned when he realised such a description could apply to a great many people in the city. "Might not be her but if Betsy shows Billy, the boy from the butcher's shop, the sketch, he might be able to identify her."

"And thus, help us confirm she was Mr Perkins' secret lover," Dr Alexander mused aloud. His sense of triumph was dashed by Mr Maxwell shaking his head, however.

"At least I don't think so," Mr Maxwell clarified, wiping his forehead and hands with his handkerchief. "I don't know. It's all just guess work." He sighed. "Why couldn't she just tell us what she knew?"

Dr Alexander hummed and suggested, "Perhaps another of our members could try getting the answers from her? We'll see what Miss Trent says."

"Finished." Miss Dexter turned her sketchbook around to show them the uncanny likeness of Merla staring back at them from the page.

"That's wonderful!" Mr Maxwell cried, embracing her without thinking about what he was doing until he'd done it. Horrified by his own inappropriate behaviour, he said, "Oh, pardon me! I—I shouldn't have… that is…" He cleared his throat. "Apologies, Miss Dexter."

"No apologies are needed, Mr Maxwell," Miss Dexter replied with a blush.

Dr Alexander chuckled at this rather awkward show of affection. Stepping around them both to head back to Endell Street and Miss Trent, he whispered into Mr Maxwell's ear as he passed, "When this case is finished, you should invite her to dinner, dear fellow." Mr Maxwell looked at him over both shoulders and then turned around as he walked away.

"I shall meet you at Miss Trent's office," Miss Dexter said.

Startled, and afraid she may have overheard Dr Alexander's words, Mr Maxwell faced her with wide eyes.

Processing what she'd said, though, he gave an awkward smile and replied, "Err, yes… of course." He accepted the sketch and felt his cheeks warm. "Goodbye." When she returned his smile and bid him the same, his heart melted. Unable to take his eyes off her, he watched her go after Dr Alexander and join him at the corner to Endell Street. "Dinner," Mr Maxwell said as he glanced at the sketch and approached the Glasgow-Bonham residence. "Yes." He smiled.

TWENTY

Dr Weeks tossed back the last of his ale and poked a passing barmaid's behind with his finger. "Same, again," he said in a slurred voice. He'd entered the *Turk's Head* five hours previously and secured a prime position on a bench under the window. He sat in its corner, with his arm resting on that of the bench, and his leg across the remainder of the seat. His early arrival seemed prudent in light of the crowd that had occupied the pub since—and he would readily agree with such an assumption—but the reality was he'd been in dire need of a drink. After the barmaid took his glass, he lit a cigarette and took a deep pull from it as he scanned the room. Miss Trent was sitting two tables over from his and he gave a soft grunt before enjoying another tobacco fix.

"Thanks, darlin'," he said as the barmaid set down his replenished drink a few moments later. Pressing the money into her hand with bloodstained fingers, he smirked at her worried expression. "I'm a doctor," he reassured, but her departure was a swift one, nonetheless. Chuckling into his glass at this, he then enjoyed a hefty mouthful of his drink.

The bitter heaviness of the ale slid down his throat and he gave a deep sigh of appreciation, followed by a few muttered words as the woman he was waiting for *finally* arrived. Lifting his arm, he shouted, "Merla!" When she didn't hear him over the din, he took out his cigarette and slipped two fingers into his mouth to give a loud, shrill whistle. Most people stopped talking for a moment to investigate the source of the noise before resuming their conversations. Merla, who'd done the same, smiled upon seeing it was Dr Weeks and strolled over to his table.

"Ye know how to get a lass' attention, don't ye, Percy?"

"It were that or get up and lose my seat and I ain't doin' that for anyone." He slipped the cigarette back into the corner of his mouth and put down his drink. Taking her by the hand, he guided her to the vacant spot beside him and enquired, "What ya drinkin'?"

"I'll get it."

Dr Weeks pulled on her hand to force her to sit as he replied, "Forget that. Let 'em come to ya." He snapped his fingers at the passing barmaid. "Another ale, darlin'!"

Merla chuckled and patted his knee, saying, "It's never dull with ye, Weeks."

"It'll be dull enough when yer dead," he replied, offering her his cigarette. As she enjoyed a small pull from it, he continued, "Heard ya met some of my friends earlier."

Merla passed the cigarette back with another chuckle and gave him a playful push. "*Ye* have friends?"

"Yeah." Dr Weeks gave her a weak push in return. "Yer my friend, ain't ya?"

"I'm just ye willing accomplice," she replied with a smile to the barmaid who'd put her pint down on the table.

"Same thing," Dr Weeks retorted as he paid for the drink. Waiting until the barmaid had gone, he then continued, "Anyway, my friends wanted to talk to ya and yer refused, remember? One were a sexy, shy thing, one were a Scottish doc, and the third were a clumsy little fella who don't know how to talk to folks without gettin' 'imself killed."

"*They're* ye friends?"

"Someone's gotta keep an eye on 'em," Dr Weeks replied, having another mouthful of ale and burping as a result.

Merla laughed as she picked up her own drink. "No one's ever gonna think ye're a Lord, Weeks."

"Good, 'cause it ain't somethin' I want folks knowin.'"

"Ye told me."

"Don't change the…" He hiccupped. "…damn subject." He settled back in his corner and looked at her bleary-eyed. "Tell me what ya wouldn't tell 'em."

Merla's features hardened as she took a small sip of ale and replied, "Ye are my friend, but that's none of ye business."

"Like hell it ain't," Dr Weeks retorted. Gripping the top of the bench, he learnt forward and pointed his finger. He was swaying so much it was hard to tell if he was trying to point at her or not. "I know yer involved with Jack Colby, and Jack Colby's in the runnin' for murderin' Arthur Perkins." When she turned her head away in annoyance, he added, "Society ain't workin' for the coppers—"

"But ye do." Merla glared at him with a slight shimmer to her eyes.

"I cut up bodies for 'em; I ain't a copper," he replied. "'Sides, the Society's workin' for Thaddeus Dorsey. Yeah, he's crazy, but they reckon he's also innocent so if yer've got somethin' that needs tellin' 'bout Colby, then yer'd better tell me b'fore the coppers *do* hear of it. Society's got a lawyer that can help ya out if it comes to that—"

"I can't afford to pay a lawyer."

"Nah, but *I* can."

She took a large swallow of ale and, putting the glass down on the table, stared at it with glazed eyes. After a while, she took a deep, shuddering breath and bolstered herself with another generous helping of ale. Finally meeting Dr Weeks' gaze once more, she revealed in a sombre tone, "Jack killed Arthur."

"Colby weren't at Thaddeus' house when Perkins were killed."

Merla brushed away a stray tear from her cheek and replied, "Yeah… he were with me when the murder were supposed to happen, but he could've done him in before he left."

"S'ppose," Dr Weeks conceded as he crushed out his cigarette against the sole of his shoe and dropped the stub into an empty glass on a neighbouring table. Taking a large swig from his own pint, he then sat back in his corner and enquired, "Why'd he wanna kill 'im though?"

"He saw us sitting in here and thought we were together. Jack knows Arthur's not…" She frowned. "…*Wasn't* a customer. We'd known each other for years. Jack thought Arthur was sweet on me and so he told him to get lost. They argued, but it was broken up before they threw punches." She pushed a strand of haie from her face. "Truth was…" she began through a sigh. "…I loved Arthur but to him, I were just a friend. God knows I tried to make him see otherwise, but he weren't interested. Hell, I can't remember any woman he were soft on."

"Ya knew Perkins for a long time, then?" Dr Weeks enquired.

"Since I were fifteen."

"Ya ever knew 'im as Palmer?"

"Yeah," she replied and smiled wistfully. "He had a right pair of sticky fingers on him when he were younger, so we all called him 'Palmer Perkins.'" Her smile faded. "When Jack found us talking, we were talking about him. Arthur wanted to know how things were going between us; he were the one who told me about Jack and how he were a nice fella." Merla cast her eyes downward. "Arthur… had wanted me to keep Jack away from Mr Dorsey's house every night."

"Why?"

"He never said."

"Did he pay ya to do that?"

"Don't be a bastard, Weeks." She scowled at him. "I did it because Arthur asked me to, which he knew I would. I suppose a part of me hoped it would make him finally see how much he meant to me and maybe, I dunno…" She looked up as she blinked away her tears. "…I were an eejit for thinking it would make him love me."

"Yeah," Dr Weeks agreed, inviting another glare from Merla. "What d'ya want me to say? I ain't gonna lie to ya." He nodded toward her pint. "Drink up; ya won't care 'bout anythin' then." Draining his own glass, he then nudged the barmaid's behind with it as she passed and said, "Same again, darlin'." As the barmaid plucked the glass from his hand, Merla gave a weak chuckle but only took a small sip from her own drink. Returning his attention back to her, Dr Weeks enquired, "Ya ever meet Mr Thaddeus Dorsey?"

"No. Jack talks about him sometimes but only to complain about him. Ye don't wanna know what names he calls him."

"Sure, I do; remember who yer talkin' to."

Merla gave another weak chuckle, but her mirth didn't reach her eyes. She replied, "Horse-shite, selfish bugger, liar when Jack's feeling polite."

"Why 'liar?'"

"Jack, when he's had a skin-full, says Dorsey can see but only when he wants to, and he doesn't want to often because he's got them all taking care of him. I'll tell ye one thing though." She pointed at Dr Weeks as she lifted her glass to her lips. "Jack's not a fool." She took a sip and put the glass back down. "He's got a plan."

"What kinda plan?"

"Skimming off the top what he thought he deserved for looking after the pathetic lunatic. He never told me, but he'd get the rounds in, buy me gifts, but talk of how little food Dorsey got, of how Jack rationed him to two lumps of coal a day. But," she released a deep breath, "it doesn't matter. Dorsey had nothing to do with Arthur's murder; Jack told me he'd tied him again when he met me that night. Nah, Jack done in Arthur because of me."

Miss Trent drained her glass and rose to her feet; she'd seen and heard all she needed. Stepping around her table, she gave Dr Weeks a subtle nod to signal her satisfaction with his work before turning toward the door. When she did, though, she caught sight of Polly entering the pub. Halting, Miss Trent saw her looking over the crowd—presumably for her so-called beau. Glancing back at Dr Weeks, who failed to notice Polly's arrival, Miss Trent then cursed under her breath and hurried to intercept her lover.

"Becky," Polly said with a broad smile the moment she saw her. Miss Trent didn't reply, though. Instead she took her by the arm and led her into the part of the pub where the crowd was at its most dense. Both confused and concerned, Polly enquired, "What's wrong?"

"Nothing," Miss Trent replied with a sweet smile.

Polly eyed her with suspicion and warned, "Don't lie to me."

Yet, even as Miss Trent tried to think of something to say, the crowd around them thinned and Polly saw Dr Weeks enjoying a drink with Merla. Her eyes narrowed at the sight and she moved forward with full intentions of confronting the pair. Miss Trent stepped in front of her, though, saying, "You can't go over there."

"Why not? He's carrying on with another woman!"

"I thought you were only with him for convenience?" Miss Trent challenged.

"It is…" Polly replied without conviction.

Miss Trent watched her with expectant eyes. When she didn't say any more, she probed, "But?"

"But… he told me he loved me, and Weeks don't say that unless he means it."

Miss Trent stared in disbelief at her lover's apparent manipulation of another until an idea so ridiculous it was almost inconceivable entered her mind. Initially dismissing it as such, her scrutiny of Polly's expression and body language gave her cause to reconsider and she felt a nausea build within her. "You… you love him, don't you?" Polly looked away and Miss Trent's heart fell into her stomach. "Oh, my God…"

"Becky…" Polly said, her voice and eyes tinged with regret. Reaching for Miss Trent's hand, she began, "I never wanted to hurt you—"

"*Don't* touch me," Miss Trent interrupted and yanked her hand away. Stepping closer to Polly so she could keep her voice low, she hissed. "You're supposed to like *women*!"

"I didn't plan it!" Polly hissed in return. "It just kind of happened."

"And you had the front to make *me* feel bad for neglecting *you*!"

"You *did*," Polly retorted as her regret shifted to anger. "Did you *really* think cheap words and a fumble would make things good between us? I'm better than that, Becky. At least Weeks treats me right—or he did! He's not ashamed to be seen with me, either."

"You *know* why we can't—"

"Excuses. You wouldn't care if I meant enough to you; plenty of girls live together and no one bats an eye. I was just your dirty, little secret, Becky; well, no more!" Polly yelled and shoved her way through the crowd to Dr Weeks' table. Picking up Merla's drink the moment she got there, she then tossed its contents into her face and warned, "Stay away from my bloke!"

Merla leapt to her feet and cried, "*Oi!*"

As Polly then tried to lunge for Merla, Dr Weeks took her by the wrists and demanded, "Ya gone crazy?!"

"No, but I'm not stupid, Percy!" Polly cried whilst attempting to pull herself free. "You're meant to love *me*! But now I find you carrying on with this *whore*!"

"I ain't carryin' on! I'm on Society business!" Dr Weeks replied, struggling to keep a grip on her in his inebriated state.

"She don't look like any doctor I've seen!" Polly yelled.

"*Bow Street* Society business! I'm a damned member!" Dr Weeks replied.

Polly's struggling ceased in an instant and she stared up at him, stunned. "What…?" She looked at Miss Trent, who'd now joined them, and back at Dr Weeks. "You're a member? But… so am I." She turned hard eyes to Miss Trent and said, "That's why you didn't want me to see them."

Dr Weeks' head spun from both the revelation and intoxication. Becoming light-headed as a result, he dropped down onto the bench and fought the urge to empty the contents of his stomach onto the table.

"What about me?!" Merla growled. "Look at my dress!"

"I'll buy ya a new one," Dr Weeks mumbled with a hand held to his head.

"You *knew* he was talking to her 'cause of the Society and said *nowt*," Polly said as she moved back around the table and closed the distance between Miss Trent and herself. "*That's* why *you* was here, too."

Miss Trent sighed and began, "You both knew those were the rules—"

Polly's sudden slap cut her off, however. Shocked, Miss Trent clutched her face and stared at her in disbelief.

"Get outta my sight, Becky," Polly warned.

Speechless at both her slap and anger, Miss Trent left the pub as fast as she could. Tears erupted from her eyes as she emerged into the street, but she told herself it was due to the bitterly cold night and not the ache in her chest.

TWENTY-ONE

Mr Snyder returned the flask of brandy to his jacket and, with a hard sniff, pulled his cloak back into place. He sat atop his cab opposite Brookbond House on the King's Road in the waning hope of seeing Mr Perkins' lover. Aside from driving some occasional laps of the street to ensure his horse's muscles remained loose enough to move at a moment's notice, he'd held his position all day. His presence had been unchallenged throughout but, similarly, he'd not seen anything of note either. The road was now quiet and shrouded in darkness between the patches of feeble light around the streetlamps. With this fact in mind, as well as his cold toes and numb nose, he contemplated calling it a night.

Suddenly, the sound of horses' hooves on the cobblestones sliced through the quiet. Moments later he saw another cab appear from around the corner in front of him and watched it slow to a stop outside Brookbond House. Due to his current location, Mr Snyder was unable to see the passenger as they alighted on the cab's other side. He therefore leaned over and listened.

"Thank you," a quiet voice uttered. Mr Snyder thought it sounded too deep to be a woman's, but he couldn't be certain. As his fellow driver reached down to take payment, Mr Snyder craned his neck but could see nothing of the passenger in the gloom. Having no choice but to wait until the vehicle had pulled away, he was pleased to see the passenger had lingered long enough for him to take a good look at him.

He was tall, around six feet, with a lean profile and broad shoulders. The impeccable fit of his black frock coat and dark-grey trousers reminded Mr Snyder of Mr Locke's attire, thereby marking the passenger as rich in Mr Snyder's mind. When he entered the porch, its extra light allowed Mr Snyder to see his fair complexion and neat, chestnut-brown beard lining his square jaw. Lacking in whiskers, the remainder of the gent's face was clean shaven. Finally, his small, brown eyes, soft cheekbones, and petite, narrow-bridged nose made his face look more like a woman's than a man's in Mr Snyder's opinion. Stood at his feet was a large suitcase.

The gentleman took out a key, unlocked Mr Perkins' letterbox, and removed a pile of envelopes from it. After securing the letterbox once more, he then picked up his suitcase and let himself into the building. Having seen many a man lift many a suitcase, Mr Snyder had come to recognise the body language associated with varying weights of luggage. The heavier a suitcase was, the more bent a man's arm became as he carried it. The gentleman's arm had been quite straight, though, suggesting to Mr Snyder it was either empty or holding little. Either way he was intrigued and muttered, "Whatcha got that for, then, mate?"

Ill-equipped to follow the gentleman for various reasons, Mr Snyder warmed himself with another snifter of brandy and settled down to wait. The gentleman had a key to Perkins' letterbox, so it was only right he'd have a key to Perkins' apartment, too. Whether he planned to leave that night or in the morning was unknown, but the suitcase's presence and late hour caused Mr Snyder to lean toward the former possibility. Gentlemen didn't visit the apartments of dead men at night unless they wanted to avoid being seen.

During the fifty minutes which followed Mr Snyder walked his horse up and down the street a couple of times whilst keeping a close eye on Brookbond House. By the time the gentleman emerged carrying the suitcase, Mr Snyder's cab was parked a few metres from the porch. He watched the gentleman remove the brass nameplate from Mr Perkins' letterbox, pocket it, and walk out onto the pavement in search of something. When he saw Mr Snyder and his cab, he strode over to them with his hand raised and enquired, "Pardon me, are you taking fares?"

"That I am, sir," Mr Snyder replied with a warm twinkle in his eyes. "Where'd you wanna go?"

"Victoria Train Station."

Mr Snyder nodded and, leaning upon a bent arm, enquired, "Time or distance?"

The gentleman looked down at the coins in his palm.

"Time's two shillin's for one hour or less, sir," Mr Snyder went on. "Distance's one shillin' for first two miles and then sixpence for every mile after that." He glanced at the suitcase. "You need me to wait at Victoria?"

The gentleman looked down at it, too, and replied, "Yes... I think so." His arm was markedly bent as he held it, suggesting to Mr Snyder that its contents were much heavier than before.

"It's eightpence for every fifteen minutes I wait, then," Mr Snyder said.

"You're very honest," the gentleman observed in pleasant surprise.

"That I am, sir. So, what'll it be?"

"Distance and... I'm not certain about the wait. I'll pay the fare in full once I've left Victoria."

"As you wish, sir. Hop in. Do you need that 'case puttin' up here?"

The gentleman frowned as he looked down at the suitcase, again. "No. No, I think I'll keep it with me, thank you."

"Very good, sir," Mr Snyder replied, waiting until the gentleman had climbed inside the cab and closed its doors before geeing on the horse and starting them on their way.

The journey was a short one and neither man spoke for the entirety of its duration. A small slot in the cab's roof, above his passenger's head, enabled Mr Snyder to keep an eye on him, though. It was a feature he'd added himself to safeguard his passengers' wellbeing; he'd never forgive himself if someone fell ill in his cab and he didn't notice. When they neared the station a few minutes later,

Mr Snyder was obliged to join a line of cabs queuing by a fence at the left side of the station's yard. The plethora of private carriages and omnibuses crowding the remainder of the yard meant there was no way he could drive his cab to the station door. He therefore pointed to the immense iron and glass-roofed porch in the yard's far corner and said, "Victoria Station's over there, sir."

One of the major terminuses, this Metropolitan and District Railway owned station connected travellers with the rest of London through the over-ground and underground railway networks. Due to this—and the additional on-site stations for the Chatham and Dover and Brighton and South Coast lines—it was as chaotic in the evening as it was in the afternoon. The throng of vehicles in the yard was forever on the move, whilst pedestrians risked injury by squeezing through the smallest of gaps and hurrying into the station in fear of missing their train. For those weary travellers departing Victoria Station, the sight of the Grosvenor Hotel towering above its roof was a welcome one.

"I shan't be long," the gentleman said as he climbed out with his suitcase.

"I'll be here, sir," Mr Snyder replied and watched his passenger make the perilous journey into the station building. Seeing a space open in front of his cab, then, Mr Snyder drove into it and manoeuvred the vehicle into a spot behind a driverless cab in the corner of the yard. Satisfied he'd parked out of the way of others, he once again settled down to wait. Several of his fellow cabbies hollered over their greetings, or whistled with a nod and a smile, as they recognised him upon driving past. The rest of the drivers gave him cold or fed-up glances due to being stuck in the chaos. Though it wasn't an uncommon occurrence at the stations, it was still a source of great frustration for the cabmen of London. It meant wasting time when time meant money; minutes lost at the station were minutes which could've been spent taking a better-paying fare. Fortunately, Mr Snyder was being paid twice-over; first, by the gentleman, and second, by the Bow Street Society.

Thirty minutes came and went with no sign of his fare, however. Mr Snyder sighed as he checked the time and muttered, "Don't tell me 'e's scarpered." Cursing himself for not insisting on the fare upfront, he picked up his horse's reins and was about to gee it into motion when the gentleman emerged from the throng. Jogging up to the cab with only a ticket in his hand, he cried, "a thousand apologies!" and climbed inside. Slamming the doors closed, he added, "there was a queue" before giving Mr Snyder a second address in Chelsea and catching his breath.

"Not to worry, sir," Mr Snyder replied, peering through the slot in the roof and seeing the gentleman slip the ticket into his frock coat. Calculating the full amount he should be owed, then, he looked back at the station and surmised where the suitcase had ended up. Deciding it would be wiser to inform Miss Trent and the others of his suspicions than attempt to retrieve it himself, though, he drove into the flow of traffic and eventually left the station yard.

Once again, the men were silent as they travelled to their next destination. The red-brick house they arrived at was several storeys high with a pristine façade. As the cab slowed to a stop outside, a butler and maid emerged to greet the gentleman, thus confirming Mr Snyder's earlier suspicions about his passenger's wealth. Nevertheless, he kept to their agreement as he said, "That's a shillin' for the wait, sir, a shillin' and sixpence for the journey there, and two shillin's sixpence for the journey here. So, five shillin's in all, please, sir."

"I thank you for your patience and discretion," the gentleman replied as he handed over the agreed amount with a tip.

"Thank *you*, sir," Mr Snyder said with a broad smile when he saw the additional coin.

"Good night," the gentleman said and went to meet his servants. His entire demeanour changed upon hearing his butler's words, however, prompting Mr Snyder to linger awhile. He watched the gentleman go into the house ahead of the servants but lowered his head when the butler looked out. Hearing the front door close, then, he returned his gaze to the house and saw a light in a ground floor window. Its curtains had yet to be drawn, thereby giving him an unobstructed view of the room beyond.

Judging by its furniture, Mr Snyder concluded it was a louge reserved for the private use of the residents rather than for the purposes of entertaining. Sat in a wheelchair by the fire was a sickly looking woman in her late thirties. She held out her hand and the gentleman took it as he walked into view. Giving it a gentle kiss, followed by a coy one to her lips, the gentleman then became hidden by his butler as he pulled the curtains closed. Deciding it was time to leave, Mr Snyder geed his horse forward and said, "Back to Bow Street." The horse nodded several times, and Mr Snyder chuckled, saying, "Yeah, I'm frozen, too."

TWENTY-TWO

"Good evening, Mr Dorsey. You already know Inspector Conway of Scotland Yard. This is Mr Gregory Elliott, the lawyer representing your brother, and Mr Bertram Heath, an architect. Both gentlemen are also members of the Bow Street Society like me," Mr Locke introduced. Timothy Dorsey looked at the faces of those gathered on his brother's porch with a mixture of concern and confusion.

"Pleasure to meet you, sir," Mr Heath said as he reached between Inspector Conway and Mr Locke to offer Timothy his hand. He was in his mid-twenties with combed-back, light-brown hair, green eyes, and a fair complexion. At only five feet four inches tall he was rather short. This coupled with his childlike features, meant he was often mistaken for being much younger than he was.

"I don't understand…" Timothy mumbled as he shook Mr Heath's hand.

"Then allow me to explain inside," Mr Locke replied, leading the others into the house, and scanning the hallway. "Mr Colby is not here, is he?"

"Er, no… He was going to be, but I paid him to go out," Timothy admitted.

Mr Locke rolled his eyes and enquired, "And why, pray, did you have to pay him?"

"Good question," Inspector Conway interjected.

"H—he was depressed; I don't know why," Timothy stammered. "And you said he couldn't be here tonight, Mr Locke." Timothy frowned. "*And* you said it would be only you, not Mr Elliott—though I am grateful for all you've done for my brother, sir— Inspector Conway, or a man who I've never met."

"I did not lie to you, Mr Dorsey," Mr Locke replied, taking off his hat and gloves and placing the latter into the former. "It was my intention for only I to be here this evening but, upon further reflection, I thought it an excellent opportunity to prove your brother's innocence to the fellow in charge of his case. As a natural addition to this, I knew I would require the legal expertise of Mr Elliott to grant advice as to our best course of action once I had, indeed, proven your brother's innocence. Mr Heath, on the other hand, is here purely to assist me in attempting to answer, once and for all, the question as to *how* Mr Perkins gained entry to this house at all."

"That does need answering..." Timothy conceded. "...Very well. If you think it's better to have everyone here, Mr Locke, I'll bow to your superior logic." Timothy offered a polite smile to the other Bow Streeters but was wary when his gaze fell upon the policeman. Keeping his distance from him, therefore, he told the others, "Forgive my rudeness, gentlemen. I'm pleased to meet you both, truly."

"Likewise," Mr Elliott replied as he took a sheet of paper from his briefcase. Referring to its contents, he then ran his eyes over the hallway and thought aloud, "...Mr Perkins' body was discovered over there..." Going over to the spot, he pushed open Thaddeus' bedroom door and looked inside. "Mr Thaddeus Dorsey was found tied to the bed in here?"

"Yeah," Inspector Conway replied, removing and holding his trilby as he strolled over to the lawyer, followed by Mr Locke and Timothy Dorsey. Mr Heath hung back, however.

Noticing his apparent reluctance, Mr Locke looked back at him and instructed, "Please commence your measuring, Mr Heath."

"Thank you, Mr Locke!" Mr Heath exclaimed and, putting his bag down on the stairs, took out a paper bag of hard-boiled, pear-drop sweets. Popping one into his mouth and sucking upon it, he next retrieved a tape measure, notebook, and pencil and began measuring the hallway.

Timothy frowned when he saw what Mr Heath was doing. From Mr Locke, he enquired, "What do you hope to achieve from this?"

"We must establish if there are any less obvious ways in or out of this house," Mr Locke replied. "Mr Heath has agreed to measure the rooms in an effort to achieve this. Now, aside from yourself, does Mr Colby have the only key to this house?"

"Yes," Timothy replied.

"Are there any secret passages, secondary external doors, or trapdoors into the basement or attic rooms?" Mr Locke enquired.

"No," Timothy replied, his frown deepening as he saw Mr Heath get onto his hands and knees and attempt to pin one end of his tape measure with a table leg.

"Are these the ropes Mr Colby uses to tie down Thaddeus at night?" Mr Elliott enquired from the bedroom. Timothy swallowed hard as he and Mr Locke entered the room and Mr Elliott lifted a length of rope attached to the bedframe.

"Yes," Mr Locke replied. "Mr Maxwell, Miss Dexter, and I found Mr Dorsey tied down with it when we first met him."

"My lads checked every inch of this 'ouse, Mr Locke. We found nowt; no secret doors, no trapdoors, nuffin.'" Inspector Conway said from his position by the fireplace.

"No offence, Inspector, but neither you nor I are architects," Mr Locke replied, removing his frock coat as he did so. "Clearly, if there is indeed another means of entering this house, it is highly concealed. Mr Heath is a well-respected and exceptionally knowledgeable man of his profession." He draped his frock coat over the frame at the foot of the bed and removed his suit jacket. "If such a means does indeed exist, the Bow Street Society is certain *he* shall find it. In the meantime, *we* must turn our attention to the question whose answer is long overdue." Sitting on the bed, he then unlaced his shoes and placed them side-by-side under it before lying down.

Shifting his body to the middle of the bed, next, he spread his arms and legs and said, "When you are ready, gentlemen, please tie me down as tightly as you can." Inspector Conway, Mr Elliott, and Timothy exchanged glances at the instruction but moved to fulfil it, nonetheless. Whilst Mr Elliott and Timothy secured Mr Locke's wrists and Inspector Conway secured his ankles, Mr Locke continued, "Thaddeus would have been covered by his blankets on the night of the murder, but I shall forego that factor to show you what it is I am doing. Logically, Mr Colby would never secure Thaddeus' limbs before placing the blankets upon him, either, so whether they are upon my person or not during this experiment is irrelevant."

"Thaddeus, my dear brother..." Timothy muttered with great sadness as he turned away from the bed and gripped the doorframe. "What have I put you through...?" Pinching the bridge of his nose, he fought to suppress his guilt. Knowing he must watch the experiment, though, he wrapped his arm around his stomach and gingerly faced the bed.

Mr Elliott, meanwhile, was taking a literal note of the ropes' positions, the bedframe's construction, and the materials which covered it. Tapping the frame's legs and running his finger along the minute gaps between them and the floor, he discovered they weren't attached. Inspector Conway, who'd perched himself upon the window ledge, lit a cigarette and followed Mr Elliot's every move.

"The bed's construction renders any attempt to slip the ropes free impossible," Mr Locke informed Mr Elliott.

"How'd you know?" Inspector Conway challenged with a slow exhaling of smoke.

"Because I have inspected it myself," Mr Locke replied, though intentionally neglected to clarify *when* this had been done. "Furthermore, despite Mr Colby possessing a greater degree of gullibility than is natural, he is intelligent enough not to tie his patient to a bed he may easily escape from. Especially when Mr Colby's blatant intention was to ensure he found his patient precisely where he left him on his return after enjoying himself elsewhere."

"Makes sense." Inspector Conway agreed. Standing, he gave each of the ropes a hard tug and found they held little to no slack. Nodding his satisfaction at the setup, therefore, he replaced his cigarette between his lips and said, "Let's get this over with, then."

"I shall prove to you, Inspector, it is humanly impossible for a man to escape without the aid of blades, careful tying of slip-knots, and slack," Mr Locke replied. Clenching his hands into fists, he pulled hard on the ropes binding his arms and legs. Next tugging on each rope several times, he then twisted his body as far as it would go to the left and right to apply intense pressure on the knots using his body weight alone. None of the strategies weakened the ropes' integrity, however. He therefore attempted to bite the knots, but the ropes' short lengths prevented his head from coming within inches of them. Final attempts to manipulate the knots with his fingers also failed for the same reason.

"Are you satisfied, Inspector, that Thaddeus Dorsey could no more escape from these ropes than I can?" Mr Locke enquired as he lay flat on the bed once more, his chest rising and falling rapidly from the exertion despite his high level of physical fitness.

Inspector Conway took another pull from his cigarette and, exhaling the smoke away from the others, approached the bed. He tugged on each rope in turn for a second time, but their knots remained secure. This drew a soft grunt from the policeman, and he crushed out his cigarette on the iron grate of the fireplace, replying, "Yeah. I am."

"Excellent!" Mr Locke said in triumph.

"Does this mean the charges against my brother will be dropped?" Timothy enquired with hopeful eyes.

"Provided you, Mr Locke, and Inspector Conway are willing to make written statements testifying to what

222

you've witnessed here this evening—and Mr Colby continues to insist he tied your brother down *before* he left him on the night of the murder—then, yes, it is possible," Mr Elliott replied without looking up from his notetaking.

"I do not believe there is even the smallest of chances we would refuse. Is there, Inspector?" Mr Locke enquired.

"Nah," Conway replied. "Be at the Yard first thing and I'll take 'em all." Walking around the bed, he then paused in the doorway to put on his trilby hat. "By the way, Perkins' body's being let go tomorrow for burial." His dark-blue eyes looked between Mr Locke's and Timothy's sombre faces and Mr Elliott's stoic one. "Thought you'd wanna know."

"Certainly, Inspector," Mr Elliott replied in his usual monotone. "Your consideration is appreciated, even if it doesn't extend to your prisoners." Inspector Conway's eyes hardened at that, but Mr Elliott didn't rise to the bait. Instead he walked past him into the hallway and returned his things to his briefcase. Returning to the bedroom door, he informed them, "I'll pay Thaddeus a visit in the morning to give him the good news. Good night, gentlemen." His cool gaze shifted to Conway. "Inspector."

"Bloody lawyers," Inspector Conway muttered under his breath as Mr Elliott departed. Turning to Mr Locke and Timothy, he warned, "First thing or I'll have the lot of you down in the cells with Dorsey." He, too, then left with a slamming of the door.

"Mr Dorsey, would you be so kind as to close the bedroom door and release me from these ropes?" Mr Locke enquired.

"Oh, yes, of course!" Timothy replied, feeling a little embarrassed he'd not thought of it earlier. Nevertheless, he had a broad smile on his face as he loosened the knot on Mr Locke's right wrist and said, "I can't thank you enough. I only regret we can't have my brother released tonight."

"You may thank me by discussing the *other* matter requiring our attention."

Timothy's hand shot back as if he'd been burnt and there was fear in his voice as he enquired, "W—What matter?"

Mr Locke slipped his hand free from the rope and untied his other. "Your deception at the bank, of course. It was rather ingenious."

Timothy recoiled from the bed. "I—I d—don't know what you're talking about, Mr Locke."

"Do not lie to me," Mr Locke replied and, sitting up, untied his ankles. "You pocketed my guinea and attempted to deceive me by pretending you had deposited it with the others. Your thumb had pressed it against your palm when you slid it over the counter's edge during your so-called 'counting' of the money. Your declaration of it being ten guineas, as I had informed you upon giving you the bag, was intended to strengthen the deception and, perhaps, provide you with an excuse should I, or another customer, ever challenge you on the deception. You could quite easily claim to be innocent of any wrongdoing as you had openly 'counted' the money in front of me, thus it must be *my* mistake, or, in the case of another customer, *their* mistake. It was most unfortunate for you, then, that I am a magician by profession and a master of sleight of hand. I knew what you had done the moment I saw your thumb bend inward."

"If you knew, wh—why didn't you expose me at the bank? Or tell Inspector Conway?"

"Because, Mr Dorsey, I am not in the habit of forcing a man's head under the water when he is already drowning," Mr Locke replied, getting off the bed and putting on his suit jacket and frock coat.

Dumbfounded, Timothy said in a quiet voice, "But I stole from you…"

"Yes, you did; a doubly foolish act when one considers how famous I am and thus how unlikely it was you did not know of my profession when I entered your bank," Mr Locke replied as he smoothed down his frock coat and tidied his hair.

"I wasn't thinking."

"That is as blatant as the nose on your face," Mr Locke retorted. "I also wager it was not the first time you had carried out such a deception. I shall even go as far as to say you had been taking an additional 'wage' for several months, if not years. Thus, the act has evolved into an unconscious habit you no longer notice you are enacting. Though you do not do it for yourself; you admitted you were in as much dire financial hardship as your brother, but that you were also desperate to keep Mr Colby as your brother's carer."

"You're right."

"But of course." Mr Locke smiled. "And, provided it is no more than a guinea here and a guinea there, I see no reason to ruin your life, or your brother's, by exposing you. Especially when things are on the up for Thaddeus." Mr Locke didn't wish to be branded a hypocrite, either, but it wasn't necessary to muddy the waters by mentioning it.

"Thank you, Mr Locke. You have no idea what this means to me," Timothy replied as both his heart rate and stomach settled.

"I do, Mr Dorsey, and *that* is precisely my point. Now, let us see how far Mr Heath has gone in his measuring, hmmm?"

"Yes, let's," Timothy agreed with a greater degree of contentment in his voice as he followed Mr Locke into the hallway. Finding it empty. Mr Locke called Mr Heath's name and the architect's voice sounded from the kitchen. The two men therefore entered that room but halted the moment they saw Mr Heath on his hands and knees by the wall with his tape measure in hand. Although he was intrigued by his methods and motives, Timothy felt reluctant to disturb him when he was amid the work. He therefore addressed Mr Locke as he enquired, "How will knowing the exact room sizes help you discover secret passageways? I would think examining the walls would be more useful."

"Indeed, it would, Mr Dorsey. I have already made a formal examination of the upper floor rooms and attic," Mr Locke replied. "But, alas, I found no clues whatsoever."

"Once I've measured each room, I'll be able to calculate the dimensions for each and, putting them together, come up with the dimensions of the entire house," Mr Heath interjected whilst continuing to measure. "This, coupled with my measurements of the chimneys and windows et cetera, shall highlight any inconsistencies. If a room happens to be smaller than the one above it, for example, with no obvious reason for it, we can mark the room as a potential contender for having a secret passageway within its walls. An examination of the original construction plans—I'll seek those out, don't worry—will highlight any intentional spaces in the walls for ventilation purposes though we can't rule out the idea of shoddy workmanship. You wouldn't *believe* the state of some of the houses I've seen in my time!"

"But each room has only one door, Mr Heath, leading to a landing or the hallway," Timothy replied. "Even if there was a secret passageway in the walls, it couldn't lead anywhere or have any form of entry point."

"Well, that's what I'm going to find out, Mr Dorsey," Mr Heath said. "You and your brother haven't made any alterations to the house since it was built, have you?"

Timothy shook his head but stilled as something seemed to occur to him. After a moment's contemplation, though, he dismissed it with a shake of his head and replied, "No, we haven't."

"What was it you were thinking of?" Mr Locke enquired, having caught the change in demeanour.

"I remembered a fireplace upstairs had to be examined by a chimney sweep once," Timothy replied. "Thaddeus kept insisting he'd smelt smoke one night. The sweep found nothing untoward though and couldn't fathom why my brother would've smelt smoke as the fire hadn't been lit in months. We put it down to my brother's illness and, fortunately, Mr Glasgow was kind enough to pay the sweep's fee."

"Did Thaddeus smell smoke again after that?" Mr Locke enquired.

"No," Timothy replied. "At least, as far as I know."

"And no alterations were made to the fireplace's structure by the sweep?" Mr Heath interjected.

"No, none," Timothy replied.

"Great!" Mr Heath exclaimed with a clap of his hands. Getting to his feet, he pointed to the ceiling and cried, "Now, to the upstairs rooms!" Whistling as he went, he paused on the stairs long enough to pluck another hard-boiled sweet from the paper bag before heading up to the landing. As he and Mr Locke followed, Timothy had to admit Mr Heath's idea was a brilliant one. He also hoped he'd find what he was looking for. Otherwise, they may have to consider the notion Mr Perkins was a ghost who'd slipped into the house under the doors. Timothy felt a shiver run down his spine at the mere thought.

TWENTY-THREE

Mr Snyder pointed at the sketch with his stubby finger and said, "His nose was narrower." He stood beside Miss Dexter, who sat before Miss Trent's desk, as they perfected a likeness of the Victoria train station gentleman. "Yeah, that's right," he added when she'd made the amendment. "And his eyes was smaller, too—and brown."

"Gentlemen, will you step aside, please?" Miss Dexter requested with a polite smile to Mr Maxwell and Mr Heath who'd leant over her sketch to gain a better view. "You're blocking my light."

"Sorry," Mr Maxwell mumbled and stepped back into the filing cabinet. An avalanche of papers fell from its top at once and scattered across the floor. Alarmed, Mr Maxwell dropped to his hands and knees and scrambled to retrieve them. As he was reaching under the desk, though, the office door opened behind him and sent him head-first into the front of the desk. "*Ow!*"

"Mr Maxwell!" Miss Dexter cried, reaching for his arm and helping him to his feet. "Are you hurt?"

"Just my head," Mr Maxwell replied as he held it.

"What's going on in here?" Miss Trent enquired with her head around the door. Mr Snyder dragged Miss Dexter's chair to one side, thus allowing the clerk to enter, and Miss Trent looked between them with a bemused expression. Seeing Mr Maxwell wince as he clutched his head, she enquired, concerned, "What happened?"

"Nothing, I'm fine," Mr Maxwell insisted, lowering his arm and plucking the pile of papers from the floor. "Just a little accident." He glanced down at the pile and stepped toward Miss Trent, saying, "Erm... here." He put the pile into her arms and recoiled with a sheepish expression. Looking to Miss Dexter's concerned one, he added, "Truly, I'm fine." He smiled. "But thank you for helping me."

Miss Dexter blushed but returned to her seat as Miss Trent went behind her desk and put the papers down. Deciding it would be unfair to scold Mr Maxwell given the limited space the office afforded them, she sat down and enquired from Mr Snyder, "Have you some news for us?"

"Yeah," Mr Snyder replied. "There was a gentleman at Mr Perkins' Chelsea place. 'E took a suitcase in, came out almost an hour later. After thievin' the nameplate from Mr Perkins' letterbox, 'e had me take him to Victoria station in the cab. Thought 'e'd scarpered when 'e'd not come back out after a while had gone by, but then 'e did and had me take him to another Chelsea address. From what I saw, I think it was his 'ome."

"I'm sketching the gentleman's likeness," Miss Dexter interjected.

"Which I'll arrange to have in the *Gaslight Gazette* again," Mr Maxwell added.

"Good," Miss Trent replied. From Mr Snyder, she enquired, "When you said he was a gentleman, did you mean he looked wealthy?"

Mr Snyder nodded.

"Mr Locke has connections amongst the upper classes through his illusionary work," Miss Trent continued. "Private performances at dinner parties and the like. I'll take the sketch and see if he recognises the man. Then we'll place it in tomorrow's evening edition of the *Gaslight Gazette* if he doesn't. I don't suppose Mr Locke told you where he would be?"

"Nah," Mr Snyder replied.

"Mr Heath?" Miss Trent enquired. "I presume he accompanied you to Mr Dorsey's house?"

"He did," Mr Heath replied and clasped his hands together. "An absolutely *marvellous* demonstration he gave, too! I didn't see it myself because I was measuring the hallway at the time, but it was certainly enough to impress the inspector for he immediately agreed to release Mr Thaddeus Dorsey! Mr Elliott made mention of statements needing to be made, but I really don't know anything about *that*. Architecture is my passion—well, you already know that. It's why I'm here!" He chuckled. "I—"

"And Mr Locke's whereabouts now?" Miss Trent interrupted.

"Yes! Quite!" Mr Heath smiled. "He said he had to travel to the Paddington Palladium as he was performing tonight. I've never seen any of his performances myself, but my wife keeps asking me to go with her. Perhaps we should all buy tickets once this gruesome case is over?"

"What a splendid idea," Mr Maxwell replied. "Miss Dexter, would you like to go?"

"Yes... I suppose I could..." Miss Dexter said with a bashful smile. Noticing Miss Trent's impatient expression, though, she added, "But I think we should try to focus on the matter at hand..."

"Have I made a faux pas?" Mr Heath enquired, concerned.

"Not at all," Miss Trent replied. "But Miss Dexter is quite correct; our social functions shouldn't be our priority at the moment. Were you able to get the measurements from the house, Mr Heath?"

"I was," Mr Heath replied. "I'll start working my way through the various archives tomorrow to find the original building plans."

"Good," Miss Trent said with a soft smile. "You may go home now unless there was something else? I know your wife worries."

"No, except to thank you for calling upon my services. I'm always happy to oblige wherever I can," Mr Heath replied and, putting on his bowler hat, bid them a goodnight.

"I presume Dr Alexander had to return home, too?" Miss Trent enquired from the others as Mr Heath made his way down the stairs to Bow Street.

"Yes," Miss Dexter replied and put the finishing touches to her sketch.

Miss Trent hummed her acknowledgement and said, "I'll also ask Mr Locke to investigate the matter of Mrs Bonham's mysterious piece of paper."

"How'd you get on with Miss Merla?" Mr Snyder enquired.

"Well," Miss Trent began through a deep sigh, "She and Dr Weeks are friends, so she opened up to him as we'd hoped she would. According to Merla, Mr Perkins had told her about Mr Colby and asked her to keep him away from Thaddeus' house *every* night. She didn't know why— Mr Perkins never told her—and she was never paid for doing it. Apparently, she loved Mr Perkins, but he never showed any interest in her. Despite this though, Mr Colby had become jealous when he'd caught Merla talking to Mr Perkins, about Mr Colby, at the *Turk's Head* one night. An argument broke out but didn't escalate to fisticuffs. Merla thus suspects Mr Colby of killing Mr Perkins, citing the theory Mr Colby could've killed him before leaving for the night."

"Why was Mr Perkins so keen for no one to find out about his visits to Mr Dorsey?" Mr Maxwell enquired, bemused. "It's not as if they were doing anything illegal. Unless…" His eyes widened. "…They *were*?"

"If anything illegal was going on, I don't think Thaddeus Dorsey was aware of it," Miss Trent replied. "After all, he'd have risked it being exposed when he called us in. Furthermore, the fact Mr Perkins was keen to have Mr Colby kept away shows Mr Colby wasn't aware of it either. I do agree with you though, Mr Maxwell; Mr Perkins was doing more than simply visiting a friend during those visits. He wouldn't have gone to such lengths by enlisting Merla's help otherwise. Exactly *what* else he was up to, I can't say, but someone else knew of it."

"The person that done him in?" Mr Snyder enquired.

"Exactly," Miss Trent replied. "And it might just be they didn't want Mr Perkins telling anyone about what they were doing."

Miss Dexter passed her sketch to Mr Snyder who gave it a firm tap and said, "That's him." Giving it to Miss Trent next, to take to Mr Locke, Mr Snyder enquired from her, "If it was being done in Dorsey's house though, don't that mean there could be something of it there still?"

"Yes," Miss Trent replied. "Which is why we must have Mr Heath's findings sooner rather than later." Her expression and voice became grave as she added, "Our client's life may very well depend upon it."

"But he was cleared…" Mr Maxwell pointed out, confused. A moment later, though, the penny dropped, and his face turned pale. "Oh…" He gave a hard swallow. "I see. It's not the hangman we should be worried about…"

"Precisely," Miss Trent replied.

TWENTY-FOUR

The perfect execution of an illusion followed by the riotous applause of his astounded audience was what the Great Locke thrived upon. They gifted to him the exhilarating high he craved and the melancholic low he cursed. He was untouchable amidst the fantasy of the stage but vulnerable amidst the reality of his silent dressing room. Although there was no replicating that feeling he had when he took his bow, he could at least have a taste with the help of a tourniquet and a needle filled with euphoria. He therefore lay upon his chaise lounge and tightened the tourniquet around his arm with his teeth, whilst his escape waited in the box at his side.

"Sorry to interrupt, but you're going to have to wait a little longer before you can indulge," Miss Trent said.

Mr Locke looked up and, seeing she was stood to the left of his changing screen, enquired, "And why, pray tell, is that?"

"I have a job for you. One you'll need your wits about you for," Miss Trent replied and closed the distance to grab his wrist when he reached for the needle. Meeting his gaze, she maintained her grip whilst closing the box.

"*No*," Mr Locke said as his other hand shot out to take it from her.

On this occasion, though, her reflexes were quicker than his and she pulled the box out of his reach before tossing it onto the dressing table. Standing between it and Mr Locke, she remarked, "I don't know why you insist on using it anyway."

"What is it you wish me to do?" he enquired, irritated, as he removed the tourniquet and rolled down his shirt sleeve. Fastening its cuff whilst he rose to his feet, he then further enquired, "I presume it has something to do with the Society's current case?"

"It does," Miss Trent replied, staying in his way. "Dr Alexander witnessed Mrs Bonham attempting to hide a document when they visited the Glasgow-Bonham residence earlier today. She was angry at the intrusion and told him such, but Dr Alexander could see she'd been crying. The single-page document, that Dr Alexander believes may have been a letter, could have some bearing upon Mr Perkins' murder, or even Malcolm's. I need you to 'work your magic' and find out what was in it."

Mr Locke rolled his eyes and put on his frock coat. "I will if you promise *never* to say that again."

"You have my word." She agreed with a smirk. Taking Miss Dexter's sketch from her bag and holding it out to him, she then enquired, "Will you look at this? It's a gentleman Mr Snyder saw visiting Mr Perkins' apartment in Chelsea. Afterward, he hired Mr Snyder and his cab to take him to Victoria station and then to a second address in Chelsea. Mr Maxwell is going to have the sketch put in the *Gaslight Gazette,* but I wanted you to look at it first. He had a suitcase with him when he went to the apartment and the station but left Victoria without it. Mr Snyder and I think he put it into the left luggage office." Mr Locke took the sketch with him to his dressing table but stopped halfway there. Noticing his change in demeanour, Miss Trent approached and studied his expression as she enquired, "You recognise him, don't you?"

"Yes. It is Lord Wendell Summerfield."

"I see. Well, if Mr Perkins were having an affair with his wife, or daughter, it's understandable he'd want to remove all evidence of it from the apartment. Such an affair with a lowly footman would certainly cause a scandal."

"No, that is not the case at all."

"How can you be so sure?"

"Lord Summerfield's wife is a cripple—she has been for years—and his only child, a daughter, is five years old."

Miss Trent stared at him, stunned. "*Excuse* me? Then what was in the suitcase?"

Mr Locke pursed his lips as he returned the sketch to her. Taking the box from his dressing table, he put it the top drawer, and retrieved the velvet roll of lock picks from the middle. Both drawers were then locked, and the key returned to its hiding place. "I suspect my suspicions may be similar to yours." He went on whilst combing his hair and applying his apparel for nighttime excursions; a black bowler hat, leather gloves, and a scarf to cover his mouth and nose. "If I am correct in my assumptions, any conversation with Lord Summerfield shall require the utmost discretion and delicacy. I have been his acquaintance for many years. I shall therefore broach the subject with him, privately."

"Thank you," Miss Trent replied, looking to his reflection.

"Inspector Conway informed me Mr Perkins' body shall be released tomorrow for burial. Lord Summerfield shall attend the funeral if he was connected to Mr Perkins as I suspect he was. For this reason, I shall also attend." He slipped the velvet roll inside his frock coat and opened the door. Indicating for Miss Trent to leave ahead of him, he added, "But first things first, yes?"

"Indeed." She went into the corridor and, once he'd joined her and locked the door, accompanied him through the stage door and into the service alleyway behind the Paddington Palladium. His private carriage and driver were already waiting for him, so he climbed inside and closed the door. Peering through its window, she said, "Good luck, and be sure to visit the office as soon as you're finished."

"I always do," he retorted and knocked on the ceiling. Miss Trent therefore stepped back, and the vehicle lurched forward. Watching until it had disappeared into the night, she gave a little smile of triumph and returned to the main thoroughfare where Mr Snyder would meet her with his cab.

* * *

Leather-clad hands eased down the window and drew the curtains, thus shielding the silhouette from the view of anyone in the street below. They then moved across the exposed floorboards and rug, without making a sound, and searched a chest of drawers, followed by the bedside cabinets, and bedding. The pillows were plucked from the mattress and returned when nothing was discovered beneath. Concealed compartments within the dressing table were also explored, along with the jewellery box and mirror. The room remained silent throughout, however. That was until Mrs Bonham's voice sounded from beyond the door, "I shan't hear of it, Lanford! It's absolutely disgusting!"

Footsteps hurried along the landing toward the room as a door slammed and Mr Glasgow yelled, "Esta, wait!" A second set of footsteps, presumed to be his, then hurried after the first.

"How could you, Lanford?! I shan't stay under this roof if *that* is going on!" Mrs Bonham cried as the sounds of hurried feet ceased.

Mr Locke, meanwhile, slipped across the darkened bedroom and opened the wardrobe doors.

"You're being ridiculous," Mr Glasgow said with disdain.

"Am I? It's shameful!" Mrs Bonham retorted as Mr Locke sifted through the gowns and turned his attention to the hat boxes on the shelf above. Taking the first one down, he opened it and felt around the inner edge of its base. He smiled as he discovered a lip. Lifting it, he slipped his hand underneath as he heard Mrs Bonham announce, "I'll be leaving in the morning."

"No, you won't!" Mr Glasgow commanded, followed by a grunt.

"You're hurting me!" Mrs Bonham cried in distress.

Feeling a bundle of letters, Mr Locke slipped his fingers underneath and pulled them out. Their envelopes were handwritten, addressed to Mrs Esta Bonham, and tied with red ribbon.

"Listen to me, dear *sister*, I know all about your sordid little affair so *don't* pretend you're the epitome of purity because you're *not*!"

"I don't know what you're talking—"

"*Don't* even *think* about lying to me, Esta. Perkins told me all about it before he died. I know *everything*."

"I… I'm still leaving!" Mrs Bonham yelled, and Mr Locke heard footsteps rushing toward him. Swiftly taking one of the letters from the bundle, therefore, he put the rest back into the hat box, returned the hat box to the shelf, and closed the wardrobe. No sooner had he slipped behind the curtains, though, did the bedroom door open and Mrs Bonham entered.

Mr Locke slowed his breathing and listened as she closed the door and sat at her dressing table with a sad sigh. Given the curtains' fabric was mere inches from his face, he was conscious of not doing anything that might make them twitch or sway. He therefore held himself as still as a statue as Mrs Bonham approached his hiding place with a rustling of skirts. The moonless, winter's night meant she was unlikely to want to look out the window, so he held little fear of her opening the curtains. Nevertheless, he felt easier when he heard a knock and Mrs Bonham retreated from the window with another rustling of skirts.

"Come in," Mrs Bonham called, and the door opened. "Oh, good evening, Betsy."

"Good evening, ma'am," Betsy replied, and Mr Locke listened as she assisted her mistress in preparing for bed. The sounds were quite familiar to him, due to having servants of his own, so, again, he was unperturbed.

"Will you need your draught tonight, ma'am?" Betsy enquired once several minutes had passed.

"Yes, please," Mrs Bonham replied, and Mr Locke heard the hiss of powder as it was dissolved in water, followed by the tap of a silver spoon against glass.

"Will that be all, ma'am?"

"Yes, thank you, Betsy. You may retire for the night."

"Good evening, ma'am." The maid then departed with a soft click of the door.

Mrs Bonham gave another sad sigh and pushed back her stool from the dressing table. Crossing to the wardrobe and opening its doors, she next retrieved the bundle of letters from the hat box and said in a soft voice, "My darling, what a mess we have made…" Mr Locke listened intently as he heard the sound of paper-against-paper as she pulled out a letter from the bundle, followed by a rustling as she took it from its envelope and unfolded it.

There was a few moments' silence whilst she read its contents but, rather than return it to the hat box with the others, she made a crumpling sound as she held it against her bosom. Mr Locke continued his silent surveillance of her even as she put the bundle into the hat box and then the hat box into the wardrobe. Considering it fortunate his envelope's absence had gone unnoticed, he listened to her take her 'draught' and get into bed. The room was then plunged into darkness as she extinguished the lamp at her bedside, but Mr Locke knew it was unlikely she'd fall asleep immediately. He therefore decided to wait a little longer before leaving the refuge of his hiding place.

Eventually, he heard Mrs Bonham's breathing become shallower as she descended into a deep sleep. Recognising this as his opportunity, he turned and eased the window open. Climbing out and sitting on the ledge, he then gripped the brickwork with one hand whilst the other reached back to close the window. He paused, though, when he thought he'd heard the bedroom door open. Deciding the risk of being discovered far outweighed the need to witness whatever was happening

238

inside, he slid the window down and began his descent to the ground.

TWENTY-FIVE

"Mr Maxwell and Miss Dexter are here," Mr Elliott announced upon returning to the parlour. Thaddeus Dorsey rose from his armchair at the news, but Timothy's hand on his shoulder compelled him to sit down again. Relaxing at his brother's reassurance that his visitors would come to him, Thaddeus then patted Timothy's hand.

"Welcome home, Mr Dorsey," Mr Maxwell said.

"Thank you; it's because of you I'm here," Thaddeus replied and gestured in the sofa's general direction. "Please, sit down."

"Would you like some tea?" Timothy enquired, still stood beside his brother as Mr Maxwell and Miss Dexter settled themselves upon the sofa.

"Yes, please," Mr Maxwell and Miss Dexter replied in succession.

The former couldn't help but scan the room, however, thereby catching the attention of Timothy Dorsey who said, "Mr Colby isn't here. I assume that's who you're looking for, Mr Maxwell?"

Startled at being caught, Mr Maxwell frowned and replied, "Yes. My apologies, I didn't mean anything by it. I just thought he would be here to take care of Thaddeus, that's all."

"I'm here," Timothy countered. "Besides, Mr Elliott explained it would be safer if Mr Colby stayed with his mother in Whitechapel, and I and Inspector Conway stayed here in his stead. At least until Mr Perkins' murderer is caught."

"Given the allegations of theft," Mr Elliott began, "in addition to his open admission of restraining your brother before he abandons him at night, I recommend you terminate his employ with immediate effect on the grounds of gross misconduct."

240

"He takes good care of me…" Thaddeus murmured. "…And endures a great deal; I'm not the easiest person to look after."

"You shouldn't defend such behaviour; whether your care is difficult or not, it is no excuse to bind you to the bed and leave you utterly helpless," Mr Elliott argued. "If there had been a fire, Mr Colby wouldn't have been on hand to inform others of your presence here. He put your very life at risk."

"Yes, there is *that*, but if *I* wasn't so unpredictable when I had one of my episodes, he wouldn't have had to do that," Thaddeus replied. "Everything he did to me was for my own good."

"*Everything* he did to you?" Mr Elliott enquired, concerned, as he moved closer to him. "What else did he do to you, Mr Dorsey?"

Mr Maxwell placed his hand upon Miss Dexter's to brace against what was to come. She withdrew hers, however, and clasped it with its fellow in her lap. Bowing her head and turning it away, she then returned her gaze to Timothy who'd put his hand back onto his brother's shoulder.

"Thaddeus?" Timothy encouraged.

"Nothing," Thaddeus mumbled.

"He can't hurt you now; we shan't allow it," Mr Elliott said.

"Please, tell us," Timothy urged.

Thaddeus dipped his head and rubbed his arm as he replied in dismay, "He'd be so angry if I told you and he *does* take care of me."

"I'm here to take care of you now," Timothy reminded him. "Thaddeus, *please*. What else has Mr Colby done to you? Whatever it is, we can make it better; *I* can make it better. Let me make it up to you; let me take *care* of you."

"You've always taken care of me," Thaddeus replied in surprise.

"No, I only *thought* I was," Timothy said with regret. "Leaving you alone with Mr Colby, to be abused and restrained, was never taking care of you. But I want to take care of you now, *proper* care of you. I can't do that though unless you tell me *everything* Mr Colby did to you."

Thaddeus released a sigh so deep it sounded as if it had been dragged from the depths of his soul. Putting his hand upon Timothy's, he shifted in his armchair to face him and said, "Mr Colby doesn't like it when I do things I'm not allowed to; the telephone conversation I had with Miss Trent, for instance. I'm supposed to ask his permission before I use it, despite knowing he always refuses. That's why I didn't ask him that day." His expression became grave as he continued, "He caught me using it. He was *so* angry, he beat me. He told me it was my fault—and it *was*! I shouldn't have used it without his permission."

"But it's *your* telephone!" Timothy cried in disbelief. Noticing the subtle shake of Mr Elliott's head, though, he bit his tongue and clasped his brother's hand to both reassure him and calm his own feelings.

"He was only looking after me, making sure I didn't do anything that could have me arrested," Thaddeus replied. "It's why he never takes me out of the house—not even into the garden."

"Does he often beat you?" Mr Elliott enquired.

"Only when I misbehave; I try not to misbehave as much as I can but, sometimes, I do things wrong without knowing I'm doing it," Thaddeus explained. "For instance, I picked up my spoon to eat my porridge when I wasn't supposed to. He struck me and reminded me *he* feeds me. I *knew* that, but I'd somehow forgotten."

"Have you told anyone else of this?" Mr Elliott enquired.

Timothy had paled and pursed his lips whilst his free hand gripped the back of Thaddeus' armchair.

"No," Thaddeus replied, unaware of his brother's distress. "I believe Esta suspects, but she's never challenged him on his behaviour, even when he's scolded me whilst she's been here. That makes it acceptable, then, doesn't it?"

"*No*, it *doesn't*," Timothy said, grief-stricken. "Can't you *see* that?"

"I can't see anything..." Thaddeus pointed out.

Timothy released his brother at once. Giving a hard inhalation as he did so, he then stifled his sobs with his hand as he fled the room.

"Did I upset him?" Thaddeus enquired, confused.

"Your brother just needs some time to comprehend what's happened, that's all," Mr Elliott replied.

"Where's Mrs Bonham?" Mr Maxwell enquired, deciding it was time for a subject change. "She was very upset when you were arrested so I thought she'd be here."

"I'll prepare the tea," Miss Dexter said as she stood. Leaving the room, she lingered in the hallway whilst watching Timothy's hunched figure on the stairs. Torn as to whether she should offer some words of comfort, she finally concluded it would be better to leave him alone and went into the kitchen. Aside from the fact she was merely an acquaintance, she had no clue what one ought to say in such situations.

"She's declined my invitation to visit," Thaddeus replied in the parlour. His fingers toyed with one another in his lap as he stared straight ahead. "I don't understand it. I thought she would've missed me... wanted to see me as much as I want to see her..."

"Well, there have been certain developments concerning Mr Perkins' murder—developments we'd hoped to confront Mrs Bonham about today—which, now that she's declined to visit, perhaps explain the reason behind the declination," Mr Elliott explained as he went to his satchel. Retrieving an envelope from it, he then removed the letter therein and unfolded it. Rather than read it aloud, though, he returned to Thaddeus and stood in front of him. With a grave tone, he revealed, "Mr Dorsey, we strongly suspect your friend, Palmer, whose real name we now know was Mr Perkins, was having an affair with Mrs Esta Bonham."

Thaddeus leapt to his feet. "No!" He cried, "No, it cannot be true! She—she couldn't! She—she wouldn't!"

"Mr Dorsey—" Mr Elliott began, alarmed by this unexpectedly passionate reaction.

"*No!*" Thaddeus interrupted. "It is a lie of the *foulest* kind!" He paced an area two square feet in size. "It *has* to be; neither would hurt me so, I know it." Tears streamed down his face as incoherent mutterings poured from his lips. Feeling around for his armchair, he then flung himself into it as his sorrow overwhelmed him and he descended into a fit of unadulterated sobbing.

"What's happening?!" Timothy demanded as he ran back into the room. Dropping to his knees at his brother's feet, he then placed a hand upon his arm and knee and watched him with great disquiet.

"Esta… she—she was having an… affair with—with… Mr Perkins!" Thaddeus exclaimed through a succession of sobs.

"*What?*" Timothy replied, stunned.

"When Dr Alexander, Miss Dexter, and I visited Mrs Bonham yesterday afternoon, Dr Alexander walked in on her reading something," Mr Maxwell explained. "When she realised he was there, she hid the document and yelled at him for not waiting to be invited into the room. Women in the Glasgow-Bonham house are rather intimidating, I can tell you."

"After some further investigation, we believe *this* to be the document she was hiding," Mr Elliott stated, offering the letter to Timothy.

Timothy took it as he stood and read it over. The moment he finished it, though, he sat on the arm of Thaddeus' chair, flabbergasted.

"There was a bundle of letters, hidden, in her bedroom," Mr Elliott went on. "If this wasn't the exact letter she was reading, it would've been similar. We believe all the letters in the bundle were from Mr Perkins." He stepped aside to allow Miss Dexter to enter the parlour. She was carrying a tray of tea things.

"Its spelling is certainly poor enough for a footman," Timothy murmured. "But why is it typed?"

"Perhaps he wanted to hide his identity?" Mr Maxwell suggested as he took the tray from Miss Dexter and placed it on the low table by the sofa.

"Typed?" Thaddeus enquired, lifting his head from his hands. "Quick, tell me what it says."

"I don't know if I should—" Timothy began.

"Tell me!" Thaddeus cried, throwing down his fist and unintentionally striking his brother's knee as a result. "*Please*, my happiness depends upon it!"

A sudden thought caused Miss Dexter to press her fingers against her lips. Glancing at her fellow Bow Streeters and realising it hadn't occurred to them, she made a split-second decision and snatched the letter from Timothy's grasp.

"I say! Give that here!" Timothy demanded.

Miss Dexter hurried to the window instead, though. Turning to the others, she then read aloud, "Darling Esta, my heart is a locket in which I hold our love and which only you have the key. In the darkest of nights, I am never alone, for your love keeps my heart, body, and soul warm and comforted. We cannot be together, my darling Esta, but our love shouldn't, or couldn't, ever die." Miss Dexter neared Timothy and her fellow Bow Streeters once more and, holding up the letter for them to read, enquired from Thaddeus, "Would you like to finish it, Mr Dorsey?"

"Yes…" Thaddeus replied and, straightening in his armchair, recited the letter word for word: "Though my body and mind are impaired, I know my heart remains pure and my heart loves you, dear Esta, now and forever."

"Mrs Bonham wasn't having an affair with Mr Perkins, she was having an affair with you," Miss Dexter said, addressing Thaddeus who nodded with a deep sigh of relief.

"Why didn't you tell me?" Mr Elliott challenged.

"I had to protect her; her brother is not a forgiving man when it comes to those who show any interest in courting her," Thaddeus replied.

"As we have discovered, but the affair could've created a barrier to you being cleared of Mr Perkins' murder," Mr Elliott countered.

"I don't regret what I did," Thaddeus retorted.

Mr Elliott's gaze hardened, but he remained silent nonetheless, as he gathered his papers.

"Mr Perkins typed the letters, under your dictation, whenever he visited, didn't he?" Miss Dexter enquired. "And you gave them to Mrs Bonham to read when she came."

"Yes," Thaddeus replied. "It was the only way I could write such letters. Palmer—Mr Perkins—was happy to do it and Esta never seemed to care they were so poorly written because she knew it was my love behind the words. She'd write her own response and read it aloud to me when we were alone."

"Did Mrs Bonham know who typed your letters?" Miss Dexter enquired.

"No, she never asked," Thaddeus replied. "I suppose she assumed I did it for she knew Mr Colby didn't know a thing about the affair. You must understand our love has never been physical; it runs far deeper than that. We are kindred souls, Esta and I. But now…" He sighed. "Mr Glasgow must have discovered the truth and forbidden her from seeing me."

"Because he wants to protect her?" Mr Maxwell interjected.

"I think that would be part of it," Thaddeus replied. "But his prohibition most likely stems from the fact it's I who loves her. He has a great hatred for me and is completely justified in harbouring it. You see, I... I wasn't entirely honest with Mr Glasgow about the financial health of the business when he looked to buy my half from me. I refused to let him see the ledgers because I knew how poor they were, and he'd never agree to the purchase if he saw them. He, trusting me, didn't fight me on the issue. I used his naivety, and unshakable trust and respect he held for me, against him so I might survive. I was selfish and I was a blaggard." He stood and, holding out his arm, ran his fingers along the mantel shelf's edge as he walked across the room. "But Esta is innocent in all of it; it's not fair to make her miserable because of a feud between us."

"Don't worry, Mr Dorsey. I'll try to speak with Mrs Bonham and ask her to visit you," Mr Maxwell said, prompting Mr Elliott and Miss Dexter to exchange troubled glances.

"Thank you, Mr Maxwell," Thaddeus replied. "If it's not too much trouble?"

"No trouble at all," Mr Maxwell said with a smile as he crossed the room. Stopping when he reached the door, though, he turned and added, "By the way, you said Inspector Conway was here. Maybe he should go with me?"

"He's attending Mr Perkins' funeral," Mr Elliott replied. "It's this afternoon."

Mr Maxwell's smile faded.

"I advised Mr Dorsey *not* to attend as, even though all charges against him have been formally reprieved, the true murderer has yet to be caught," Mr Elliott went on. "Any of Mr Perkins' family who may attend may be offended by his presence and thus may look to cause him physical harm."

"I've promised Thaddeus I'll take him to see Mr Perkins' grave once this is all over," Timothy interjected.

"Right..." Mr Maxwell turned toward the hallway. "Yes..." He straightened his cravat and rubbed the back of his neck. "Right." Stepping through the doorway, he then spun around with hopeful eyes as Mr Elliott's voice stayed him.

"Wait a moment," Mr Elliott called and joined him in the hallway. "I shall go and speak with Miss Trent. Mr Colby should answer to the allegations placed at his door."

Mr Maxwell's heart sank. "Oh, erm, okay." Frowning, he then enquired, "Wouldn't you like to come with me first?"

"Not particularly," Mr Elliott replied.

Mr Maxwell's stomach tightened as he watched Mr Elliott leave. Glancing back through the open doorway of the parlour, he saw Miss Dexter sat on the sofa and considered putting the same request to her. Dismissing it on the grounds it could make her feel obligated, and thereby put her in an awkward position, he instead offered her a weak smile. He then took his time in reaching the front door and was reluctant to open it.

"Shall I accompany you, Mr Maxwell?" Miss Dexter's sweet, wonderful voice enquired from behind him.

"Yes!" Mr Maxwell cried as he spun around. "I mean…" He cleared his throat and smoothed his waistcoat. "That would be most appreciated, Miss Dexter." He offered his arm to her and, with an amused smile and flushed complexion, she slipped her hand into its crook. Attempting to appear unfazed by the confrontation they were possibly walking into, he remarked, "I can go alone though." As he took a step forward, though, Miss Dexter's weight anchored him to the spot.

"I don't want to be a burden," Miss Dexter said when he looked at her.

"No! Oh, no, you wouldn't be," Mr Maxwell replied and patted her hand with a warm smile. "I *assure* you, Miss Dexter, you wouldn't be any such thing. In fact, I rather doubt you could *ever* be a burden to any man."

Miss Dexter's expression was a dubious one as she enquired, "Are you complimenting me so I will go with you?"

"Yes," he replied. "Is it working?"

Miss Dexter chuckled. "Indeed, it is," she put her other hand over his. "I would be afraid, too."

"*Afraid? Me*? Ha! I laugh in the face of fear—yes, you're right, I'm terrified," Mr Maxwell admitted and felt his cheeks warm at the sight of Miss Dexter chuckling behind her hand. "The cook and maid are terrifying enough. I dread what the others are like when they're angry." Miss Dexter laughed, and the back of Mr Maxwell's neck grew hot. "Anyway…" He cleared his throat. "Let's go."

Taking the lead to at least look like the courageous gentleman he aspired to be, Mr Maxwell headed next door with Miss Dexter and knocked three times upon the front door. There was still mirth in Miss Dexter's eyes when he glanced at her, but the touch of her hand on his arm remained a sign of her apparent fondness for him. Pleased to feel her lean into him when the door opened a crack and Betsy peered out at them, he puffed out his chest and said, "Hello again, Miss Betsy. We'd like to speak with Mrs Bonham. Is she available?"

"No, sir, miss," Betsy replied.

"Oh, what a shame. Well, perhaps we could arrange a time to return this evening?" Mr Maxwell enquired.

"I'm sorry, sir, miss, but mistress has given me orders not to admit visitors or forward any requests for her future company," Betsy said.

"But we have news regarding the murder of her cat," Miss Dexter interjected.

Betsy bit her lip as she considered. "Wait here a moment, please, miss, sir."

Once she'd closed the door Mr Maxwell leant closer to Miss Dexter and whispered, "What news?"

"We shall think of something," Miss Dexter whispered back, filled with as much trepidation as Mr Maxwell at the thought of outright lying to their client. Yet, both knew it was essential they gained access to the house and Mrs Bonham. After several long, agonising moments, the door opened, and Betsy peered out at them once more.

"Mrs Bonham has given me a message for you," Betsy began. "She wishes to cancel her commission with the Society but will pay for its time should Miss Trent write to her with a satisfactory quote."

"Did she give a reason why?" Mr Maxwell enquired.

"Did you tell her we had news for her?" Miss Dexter added.

"No, sir, and yes, miss. That was her answer. I'm sorry, but I must ask you both to leave. Good day to you sir, miss," Betsy replied and closed the door.

Thinking of putting his foot inside the door a heartbeat later, Mr Maxwell scolded the slowness of his intellect. He forgot this in an instant, though, when Miss Dexter knocked, again. "What are you doing?" he whispered in alarm. "She doesn't want to see us."

"Mrs Bonham adored her cat. I want to hear her turn us away herself," Miss Dexter replied with conviction despite the pounding of her heart. Yet, it wasn't Betsy or Mrs Bonham who answered but Mr Glasgow. Mr Maxwell and Miss Dexter immediately recoiled in fright.

"Leave my property or I'll fetch a constable," Mr Glasgow warned with one hand gripping the door and the other gripping the frame.

"W—We wish to see Mrs Bonham, sir," Miss Dexter said. "We have news regarding her cat's murder."

"What is it?" Mr Glasgow enquired through clenched teeth,

"I'm afraid I can't say as it's confidential," Miss Dexter replied, his fierce glare causing her heart to race.

"She doesn't want to see anyone," Mr Glasgow replied. "As our maid has already told you. If you refuse to give me the news, I suggest you write her a letter. Good day." The entire frame shook as he slammed the door.

"Well," Mr Maxwell began through a deep exhalation. "That was rather rude." He smiled at Miss Dexter, relieved the ordeal was over at least. "Back to Miss Trent?"

"Back to Miss Trent," Miss Dexter agreed and hurried down the porch steps with him. She didn't dare look back until they were almost at Thaddeus Dorsey's house. When she did, she was relieved to see no one glaring out at them. She therefore eased her grip on Mr Maxwell's arm and released the breath she'd been holding.

TWENTY-SIX

"So, will it be with the resurrection of the dead," the priest read aloud from 1 Corinthians in his bible. He stood at the head of an open grave, whilst the undertaker and grave digger conversed in hushed tones a few metres away. A lone mourner, attired in a tattered, black dress and hat, stood at the graveside. She held a discoloured handkerchief to her nose to catch her tears as a cocktail of anger and sorrow swelled within her bosom. *Arthur deserves more than* this, she thought. *Where were the other servants he worked with? Where was his employer?* She had half-hoped Mr Colby would be there to comfort her but, alas, she was obliged to shoulder this burden alone. Such was the story of her life, unfortunately. She clenched her hand into a fist around her handkerchief and her knuckles turned white. Yet, if she had looked further afield, through the disjointed landscape of monuments and gravestones, she would've seen another figure in mourning. They, like her, watched the proceedings in silence.

"The body that is sown is perishable, it is raised imperishable," the priest continued. "It is sown in dishonour, it is raised in glory; it is sown in weakness, it is raised in power; it is sown a natural body, it is raised a spiritual body. If there is a natural body, there is also a spiritual body." Closing his Bible, he held it against his chest and bowed his head. "Now, let us pray."

Merla dabbed at her eyes and bowed her head to repeat after the priest as he said, "Our Father, who art in Heaven, hallowed be thy name. Thy kingdom come. Thy will be done, on Earth as it is in Heaven…"

Meanwhile, the distant figure walked away and searched his coat for a handkerchief. When one was thrust in front of him, though, he halted and met its owner's gaze. "Mr Locke…?" he enquired, taken aback. "I didn't expect to see you here."

"I know. Please, take my handkerchief to dry your eyes, Your Lordship."

"But I'm not crying," Lord Wendell Summerfield denied with a weak laugh, but Mr Locke didn't withdraw his handkerchief. Lord Summerfield's smile faded, and he grimaced as he stated, "It's the cold, sir. Gentlemen don't cry."

"True; a gentleman does not show the weakness of tears in public but in private, as you believed yourself to be, he may freely express his inner emotions. We are friends, are we not?"

"We are," Lord Summerfield replied in a softer tone.

"Then you may consider your privacy untarnished, sir, and my discretion a certainty." Mr Locke held the handkerchief closer and, after a moment's hesitation, Lord Wendell took it with a grateful smile.

"Thank you, Mr Locke," he said. "I am in your debt."

"In that case, I ask for information by way of payment."

Lord Summerfield stilled and replied, worried, "But I have nothing you would find of value."

"I beg to differ," Mr Locke countered and blocked his view of the grave site by standing in front of him. "My promise of absolute discretion is bound by my word of honour as a gentleman, Your Lordship. You may therefore rest assured in the knowledge what you tell me shan't reach the ears of those who would mean you harm." He watched his friend's reaction as he then enquired, "What was the exact nature of your relationship with Mr Arthur Perkins, otherwise known as Palmer?"

"I know no one of that name."

"And yet, you weep at his funeral."

"Very well: he was a dear friend of mine," Lord Summerfield corrected.

"A Lord being dear friends with a mere footman is not only unheard of but utterly frowned upon," Mr Locke retorted.

Lord Summerfield's features contorted into a scowl. "You didn't know him; I did," he growled. "He was a servant by trade, yes, but he wasn't *my* servant—"

"No, he was your lover."

Lord Summerfield winced as if he'd been shot and turned away with his hand pressed against his heart. "Outrageous," he muttered before spinning around to glare at Mr Locke. Yet his voice lacked the conviction of his words as he went on, "And not to mention utterly disgusting. I suggest you take your sordid accusations back to the vile hole from which you crawled, sir."

"Take me to the left luggage office at Victoria station, then. Prove to me the contents of the suitcase, which you deposited therein, are not what I suspect them to be," Mr Locke replied.

Lord Summerfield stared at him in horror. "How do you know of that?"

"It matters not, Your Lordship. What does matter is the murder of one man and the near hanging of another for the crime. Whatever secrets your heart holds, however socially unacceptable they may be in this narrow-minded world of ours, I beseech you to confide them in me. I have already assured you of my trustworthiness and discretion, but I will assure you a thousand times more if it will convince you to do what is necessary to find Mr Perkins' murderer."

Lord Summerfield turned sharp eyes to the grave as he heard dirt hitting wood. Seeing the grave digger was filling in the hole, he clutched his chest over his heart and strangled his grief long enough to mutter, "Very well…" He sat on a nearby bench and felt the first spots of rain upon his face. "We *were* lovers," he admitted in a hushed voice. "I met Mr Perkins—Palmer as he called himself— quite by chance. I was in Holywell Street—" He momentarily met Mr Locke's gaze. "I'm aware of the thoroughfare's reputation, Mr Locke. I wasn't there for *that* but was instead, on my way to the old Globe Theatre."

He cleared his throat and continued, "I was passing *Sherburne's Bookshop* when Palmer hurried from it and ran directly into my person. He apologised, naturally, but we both saw it in one another's eyes, the longing for one like ourselves and the realisation we may have found them. All in a moment, one single moment, we *knew*." He placed his cane between his knees and rested both hands atop its handle. "We arranged to meet, again outside of *Sherburne's Bookshop*, the next afternoon under the pretence of settling the matter of my dirtied coat. He had managed to smudge some dust upon it from his hands."

He rubbed his hands together upon the cane as he resumed, "I have an apartment, also in Chelsea, where I hide my shame. When he met me, the next day as planned, I took him there. We had some wine, talked for hours— though it felt like mere minutes—and found we had a great deal in common. He held no judgements against me, despite my being many years his senior. In all the encounters we shared, he never once chastised, or humiliated, me. He *loved* me."

"Would you always meet outside of Sherburne's?"

"No; we were afraid someone may see us together and become suspicious," Lord Summerfield replied. "Most of the time, we met at the apartment unless he requested, specifically, to meet at Sherburne's."

"Was that very often?"

"Perhaps once or twice a month, nothing more."

"How long ago did you first meet?"

"Around six months."

"And when did you put the apartment's lease in Mr Perkins' name?"

"I didn't. I gave the letting agent written authority to create a new agreement with Mr Palmer recorded as the primary tenant. I told the agent he was my cousin."

Mr Locke quirked a brow and said, "I have seen the agreement of which you speak, and it records Mr Perkins' true name in addition to his alias of Palmer. Did you never read it?"

"No, I trusted what he told me."

"And yet, you do not seem shocked to discover his name was not Palmer?"

"I knew it wasn't Palmer; men like us rarely reveal our true names unless we can be certain of the other's discretion. Arthur never told me his true name but, you're right, I'm not shocked," Lord Summerfield admitted. "I read the truth in the *Gaslight Gazette* shortly after his death. I *was* shocked then, not by his deceit of his true name, but by his lying to me with regards to his profession."

"What did he tell you his means of employment was?"

"Nothing, but he allowed me to assume he was a gentleman of some means" Lord Summerfield extended his hand as he felt the rainfall become heavier. Satisfied a downpour wasn't imminent, he continued, "Of course, now I understand why he didn't tell me he was a footman for Mr Glasgow; he wanted to protect us both."

"Is that what he told you?"

"No, but he was that kind of man, Mr Locke. Kind, considerate, and far too generous for a man of such little means. He could never do enough for me, and I could never do enough to repay the favour."

"Do you know Mr Glasgow?"

Lord Summerfield averted his gaze to look upon the grave digger at work as he muttered, "No." Rising to his feet with the aid of his cane a moment later, he walked along the mud-path that led out of the grave yard. Glancing at Mr Locke as he fell into step beside him, he scanned the area for any other people. Seeing no one, he continued in a low voice, "There was no mention of an affair in the newspaper article about Arthur's murder so I thought I still had a chance to keep the whole thing concealed; my wife is a cripple, as you know. Aside from legal repercussions for myself—which I greatly fear even now—it would literally kill my wife to learn her husband is not as he seems."

"Understandable," Mr Locke observed.

"I therefore went to the apartment and used my key to let myself in. I own it, you see, even though it was Arthur's name on the tenancy agreement." His expression became grave. "You know the rest."

"Indeed," Mr Locke agreed. "The driver of the cab you took to Victoria works for the Bow Street Society in addition to his usual cab work. It is in my capacity as a Bow Street Society member I come to you now, Lord Summerfield, and it is the reason why I can guarantee absolute discretion in this matter. Now, we shall need to retrieve the suitcase to avoid it falling into the hands of the police. Will you therefore accompany me to Victoria?"

"The Police...?" Lord Summerfield enquired, horrified. As he glanced back at the grave site, though, he gripped Mr Locke's arm, pointed with his cane, and cried, "Look! It's Inspector Conway! He's here!"

Mr Locke spun around and, sure enough, there was the grizzled policeman at the graveside, staring straight at them. "Then we must act quickly," Mr Locke replied and the two hurried down the path toward the gate. Inspector Conway stepped around the grave at once and jogged across the grass to intercept them. A second, much larger funeral procession entered the graveyard and passed Mr Locke and Lord Summerfield, however, obscuring them from the policeman's view. Six pallbearers carried the coffin upon their shoulders and walked a slow march along the path. They were followed by a group of weeping women and sombre men. Attempting to go around them, Inspector Conway discovered there was insufficient room between them and the graves. He couldn't find any gaps within the procession itself, either. He therefore had no choice but to push two of the men aside and run for the gates. The mourners grunted and scolded the inconsiderate man, but Inspector Conway had already emerged onto the street. He looked up and down it but saw no sign of either Mr Locke or Lord Summerfield. Cursing at the top of his voice, he then punched the church yard's ancient stone wall. Stone fragments and dust, mingled with fresh blood, crumbled away as a result.

TWENTY-SEVEN

Heavy feet ran up the stairs to Miss Trent's office and Inspector Conway threw open the door. Crossing to her desk, he put his hands upon it, and leaned forward as he demanded, "What the *bloody* 'ell are you playin' at sendin' Locke?! 'E's scarpered with a suspect!" Miss Trent tilted her head to the right and darted her eyes in that direction several times. Bemused by her behaviour and irritated by her silence, Inspector Conway barked, "What?!"

"Afternoon, Inspector," Mr Elliott greeted behind him.

Inspector Conway straightened and came face to face with the lawyer. Catching movement out the corner of his eye, he then saw Miss Dexter perched upon the window ledge with Mr Maxwell standing by her side.

"We *were* having a meeting," Miss Trent said as she stood. "As for Mr Locke, *where* was he supposed to have been exactly?"

"Perkins' funeral," Inspector Conway replied.

"He was attending on behalf of our client, Mr Thaddeus Dorsey," Miss Trent told him and placed her hand upon her hip. "Who was he? This 'suspect' Mr Locke is alleged to have run away with?"

"I don't know that, do I?" Inspector Conway growled. "They scarpered before I could talk to 'im."

"Perhaps they didn't see you," Mr Elliott suggested.

"They saw me all right," Inspector Conway scoffed. "That's why they scarpered."

"I wonder why," Mr Elliott replied, drily.

"Watch it," Inspector Conway warned, pointing his calloused finger at him.

"I'm not one of your prisoners, Inspector; you can't intimidate me," Mr Elliott replied, pushing his finger aside. "If you are sincere in your threat though, I suggest you take a moment to rethink it. After all, you have three witnesses who would be willing to testify against you." As he stepped closer to him, Inspector Conway's hand dropped and Mr Elliott added, "a wise decision."

Inspector Conway continued to glare at him but slid his hands into his overcoat's pockets and sat on the corner of Miss Trent's desk.

"If Mr Locke met someone at the funeral—someone who he wished to converse further with—it's his right to leave with them if he so chooses," Mr Elliott went on. "If you being there convinced him this was the right course of action, I, for one, don't blame him."

"'E's messin' with police business," Inspector Conway pointed out. "If that bloke's Mr Perkins' killer, and Locke helped 'im get away, then I'll have 'im nicked."

"Which is your right, Inspector," Miss Trent interjected, "if you had some evidence. If Mr Locke did indeed assist the suspect in escaping from you, there must've been a good reason for doing so. Either way, you have my word I'll speak, personally, with Mr Locke and get at the truth of the matter. I'll pass on my findings to you, deal?" She held out her hand.

Inspector Conway sniffed hard and stood as he contemplated the offer. Muttering a curse under his breath when he saw her hand, he then sighed, and shook it. "Fine," he conceded, "but I wanna know soon as."

"And you will," Miss Trent assured. "In the meantime, there is someone else who requires your unique attention." She gestured to the empty chair by her desk and the policeman dropped down into it. Mr Elliott joined his fellow Bow Streeters by the window and hid his dislike of the man behind a mask of stoicism.

Meanwhile, Inspector Conway had rested his elbow upon the chair's arm and was in the process of lighting a cigarette as he enquired, "Who's that?" Tossing the spent match toward the bin, he missed by a small margin.

Miss Dexter reached for it at once but was overturned by Mr Maxwell who informed her he'd do it as he plucked it from the floor. Watching him place it beside her on the window ledge, she mumbled, "Inspector Conway is very rude."

"Aren't all policemen?" Mr Maxwell enquired.

"No, not *all* of them," Miss Dexter replied and, at his questioning look, leant closer and whispered, "Chief Inspector Jones is most polite and approachable."

"Have you met him, then?" Mr Maxwell enquired.

"Only once," Miss Dexter revealed.

Parting his lips to delve further, Mr Maxwell then reconsidered upon hearing Miss Trent's next words. Nevertheless, he made a mental note to speak to Miss Dexter about it, again, later.

"He's been physically, and mentally, abusing Mr Thaddeus Dorsey for months, if not years," Miss Trent said.

"Dorsey tell you that?" Inspector Conway enquired.

"He did and we believe him," Mr Elliott interjected.

Inspector Conway kept his eyes fixed upon Miss Trent as he took another pull from his cigarette, slowly exhaled its smoke, and enquired, "You see any bruises on 'im?"

"No, but I'm certain if a doctor were to examine him fully, some would be found," Mr Elliott, again, replied for her, adding, "We also suspect Mr Colby has been stealing from his employers."

Inspector Conway shifted in his chair to look directly at Mr Elliott and enquired, "What makes you think 'e has?"

"Miss Merla, a friend of his, told us Mr Colby had been taking small amounts from the allowance Mr Timothy Dorsey gives him for his brother's care," Miss Trent replied.

"He needs to be arrested and forced to answer the allegations set against his name," Mr Elliott added.

Inspector Conway finished his cigarette with a thoughtful expression. As he crushed it out against the sole of his shoe and tossed it into the bin—hitting his target this time—he enquired, "'E's in the Chapel, isn't 'e?"

"We believe so," Mr Elliott replied.

"I'll get his mum's address off Timothy Dorsey when I go check on 'em," Inspector Conway said. "Mr Maxwell, I'll need you to stay with the Dorseys when I'm gone."

"Oh," Mr Maxwell replied and glanced at Miss Trent who nodded her approval. Offering a weak smile to the policeman, he added, "Very well, then. I'll keep an eye out for any trouble."

"Fetch a copper if there's any trouble," Inspector Conway instructed.

Mr Maxwell's smile faded as he realised there was a strong likelihood of Mr Perkins' murderer returning to silence Thaddeus Dorsey. He couldn't defend him; winning at fisticuffs wasn't amongst his skillset. *The police are nearby*, he remembered and the knot in his stomach loosened as he replied, "Yes, of course…"

"I'll be waiting at the Yard to speak with Mr Colby once you've brought him into custody," Mr Elliott told Inspector Conway.

"Not bloody likely," the policeman retorted.

"Allow me to speak with Mr Colby, Inspector, and I guarantee I will leave his cell with a full confession," Mr Elliott replied.

"Thought you was above all that," Inspector Conway remarked.

"Violence is an abhorrent and ill-conceived method of coercion," Mr Elliott replied. "My approach shall garner a full confession of his abuse of his patient; one Mr Colby shan't retract at the earliest opportunity."

"And will he also confess to Mr Perkins' murder?" Miss Trent enquired.

"He didn't do that," Inspector Conway replied with a shake of his head. "I spoke to the landlord at the *Turk's Head* and 'e said Colby was there when the murder was done. 'E was there with that Merla woman."

"He may not have been present when it was committed, Inspector, but he may have been privy to the crime," Mr Elliott pointed out. "If that's the case, I shall ensure it's included in his confession."

Inspector Conway stood and, glancing over Mr Elliott, squared his shoulders and replied, "You can try, but if 'e don't talk, I'll be havin' a go at 'im." Glancing at Miss Trent, who folded her arms across her chest in disapproval, he then left the office and descended the stairs. Mr Elliott, though irked by the policeman's promise, remained silent in the knowledge anything more would've fallen on deaf ears.

"You'd better go to Mr Dorsey's house as well, Mr Maxwell," Miss Trent said. "Miss Dexter, you may accompany him if you wish."

"Oh, right, er… Miss Dexter?" Mr Maxwell enquired.

"I'll come with you," Miss Dexter replied, slipping her hand into the crook of his arm and following him to where Mr Snyder waited with his cab.

"Let's hope Mr Colby is in a fit state to talk by the time he reaches Scotland Yard," Mr Elliott mused aloud before bidding Miss Trent goodbye and taking his leave.

TWENTY-EIGHT

"Argh!" Mr Colby cried as pain erupted in his cheek. Attempting to move his head, a hand then drove it into the brick wall and held it there whilst another gripped his wrist. Mr Colby released another cry of pain as his arm was twisted and his hand pinned between his shoulder blades. Terrified the pressure could break his arm if he struggled, he demanded, "Get off!" Yet, his attacker responded by pressing their entire body weight against his back and digging an elbow into his shoulder.

"You're nicked," Inspector Conway growled into his ear.

"What for?!" Mr Colby yelled, releasing another cry as the policeman twisted his wrist some more.

"You've been hittin' Thaddeus Dorsey and tea-leafin' off his brother," Inspector Conway replied. "And if you helped to do in Mr Perkins, I'll take you to the drop myself." Applying the handcuffs and dragging him away from the wall by the scruff of his shirt, he then shoved him into the back of a Black Maria and slammed the door.

"Oi! What's your game?!" a voice yelled from across the street as Inspector Conway slid the bolt into place. Turning to see a constable approach, he reached into his overcoat and took out his warrant card to show him.

"Sorry, sir, I didn't realise," the constable replied. "Constable Gredlin, sir." He frowned, "forgive me if I talk out of turn, sir, but what are A Division doing in Whitechapel? And who'd you put in there?"

"Yard business," Inspector Conway replied, walking around him, and heading for the front of the vehicle.

"But this 'ere's H Division's patch," Constable Gredlin retorted as he followed. "You've gotta get permission from the inspector."

"Orders of Chief Inspector Jones," Inspector Conway said, climbing up and sitting beside the driver. "If

Leman Street's got a problem with that, get 'em to talk to 'im." He tapped the driver's arm and pointed ahead of them.

As the vehicle lurched forward, though, Constable Gredlin continued to walk alongside, saying, "Wait a minute! Stop!" The horses shifted into a trot and Constable Gredlin broke into a jog. "Oi! Slow down!" The driver flicked the reins, though, and the horses sped up, leaving a breathless Constable Gredlin behind. "Come back!"

* * *

It was over an hour later when Mr Elliott stepped inside Mr Colby's cell. The moment he saw him, Mr Colby leapt to his feet from the wooden shelf and begged, "You've gotta help me!"

Mr Elliott ran emotionless eyes over his scratched and bruised face. In his usual monotone he enquired, "Are your injuries the result of resisting arrest?"

"Nah. Coppers don't give you a chance to fight back when they wanna rough you up." Wincing when the door was slammed and locked, Mr Colby moved closer to Mr Elliott and implored, "You've gotta get me out of here like you did for Dorsey."

"That I cannot do," Mr Elliott replied. Sitting down on the shelf masquerading as a bed, he took his notebook and pencil from his satchel and waited for Mr Colby to join him.

"Why not?" Mr Colby demanded; his hands clenched into fists.

"Because, unlike you, Mr Dorsey was innocent."

"The bastard's not even blind!" Mr Colby yelled, but Mr Elliott's stoicism remained. Infuriated even more by this, Mr Colby challenged, "You'll help a devious bloke like that, but you won't help me?! What kinda bloody lawyer are you?!"

"A very good one," Mr Elliott replied. "And I didn't say I wouldn't help you. I said I wouldn't arrange for you to be freed. That's not because I helped Mr Dorsey, but because you *are* guilty of not only beating and mentally abusing the patient placed into your care, but also stealing from him and his brother. No magistrate worth his salt would allow such a man as you to walk free. Of course, if you can convince me of your innocence, I will endeavour to do everything within my power to ensure you are freed. However, if you're guilty—which I strongly suspect you are—a full confession is your best course of action so you may throw yourself upon the mercy of the court. I would also recommend showing some remorse for your actions but, given the look in your eyes, I sincerely doubt you are capable of such."

"I've got nowt to be sorry about. I'm not confessing to something I didn't do."

"Then I can't help you," Mr Elliott replied and gathered his things. When he stood, though, his path to the door was blocked by Mr Colby. "Stand aside, sir."

"I can't do that, not until you say you'll help me," Mr Colby replied.

"Admit your guilt and I shall," Mr Elliott said.

"That's blackmail, that is."

"No, it's an olive branch. I've already laid out my plan to help you but, if you choose to decline it by insisting on lying to me, there's nothing more I can do."

"I'll get someone else."

Mr Elliott consulted his pocket watch as he replied, "You can't afford anyone else; my fees, however, are being paid by the Bow Street Society."

Mr Colby closed the distance between them and, with a haunted look in his eyes, admitted in a fraught tone, "I won't be able to afford anything if I confess. Then what'll happen to my mum, aye? I *can't* lose my job, Mr Elliott. I *won't* lose it, do you hear?"

"You've *already* lost it."

Mr Colby dismissed the news with a shake of his head and replied, "Nah, you're lying."

"I *never* lie; Mr Timothy Dorsey would be a fool if he allowed you back into his brother's home after you confessed to tying him to a bed," Mr Elliott informed him. "Therefore, stop holding onto this false idea you still have a job and allow me to help you limit the damage your actions may have caused." His gaze softened as he continued, "You asked what would happen to your mother. Is she the reason you stole the money from Mr Timothy Dorsey?"

Mr Colby clenched his jaw but dropped onto the shelf. With a loud sigh, he nodded and held his head in his hands.

"You could've asked him for a pay rise," Mr Elliott observed. Due to Thaddeus not being classed as a qualifying "pauper" on the basis of his apparent wealth and lack of visits by a union medical officer, Mr Elliott saw no need to make enquiries with Mr Colby about monies Timothy may have received from public funds for his brother's care. In short, for the reasons stated above—revealed by Timothy himself—Mr Elliott knew Timothy wasn't entitled to any.

"He wasn't gonna give it to me," Mr Colby scoffed. "Thaddeus would've lied to his brother to stop him from giving me anything and Timothy always cried poverty whenever I asked for extra. It was only a few pennies here and there, maybe the odd lump of coal or loaf of bread, things my mum can't buy for herself."

"Didn't you believe Mr Timothy Dorsey when he told you he was poor?"

Mr Colby released a deep sigh and replied, "I knew he wasn't lying because I helped him get Thaddeus out the house when he needed the furniture sold, even kept the blind buggar from going upstairs so he wouldn't find out. But my mum's worse off than both of them put together; she'd die without the money I send her."

"I presume you are the sole provider for your family, then?"

"Yeah," Mr Colby replied.

"In that case," Mr Elliott continued, "I may be able to argue for your release based on mitigating circumstances. You'd be sent directly to the Convict Office at Scotland Yard, who would monitor your movements, but at least you'd be free to earn money for your family. Unless you are guilty of assisting Mr Perkins' murderer, of course."

"*I* didn't kill him!"

"You don't have to be the one who wielded the knife to be responsible," Mr Elliott pointed out. "Besides, Miss Merla is convinced of your guilt."

"She's mad; I wouldn't kill anyone. And I was with her when it happened."

"She thinks you may have murdered him before you left the house and, possibly, used her as an alibi for your whereabouts," Mr Elliott said as he retook his seat, retrieved his notebook and pencil from his satchel, and wrote down some key points. "She informed a fellow Bow Street Society member of an argument you had with Mr Perkins at the *Turk's Head* Pub. Do you say she is lying?"

"Nah. That happened, but I'm not going to kill a bloke over that, or over her, like she thinks. And I wouldn't make it so that a blind man took the drop, either. He's my money earner; he goes, and I lose my job." Mr Colby frowned. "I only hit him because he drove me mad; not doing what he's supposed to and turning violent. He's given me a few black eyes over these past few months, too. I had to make sure he knew who was in charge, didn't I?"

"His sickness of the mind prevents him from being in control of his actions at times. That is what you should've reminded yourself of when you decided to direct your anger and frustration at him," Mr Elliott replied, putting away his things. "You were the carer and the only sane person in the house; it was your job—nay, your duty—to ensure he was kept comfortable and secure. Whilst you did the latter—albeit via the employment of questionable means—you did all you could to make his existence as uncomfortable, even as painful, as possible."

It was unfortunate for all concerned that Thaddeus Dorsey's condition hadn't been checked at regular intervals by a medical officer during his confinement, or that the Lunacy Commission hadn't made enquiries after the same. Mr Elliott knew Thaddeus' home had been defined as 'private' under its single-house status due to Timothy taking no profit from his brother's confinement. As a result, the commission hadn't considered it their right to intrude upon the arrangement by implementing such visits. If it had, Mr Colby's ill-treatment of his patient may have been prevented.

Considering it redundant to enquire after potential visits from medical professionals on this basis, Mr Elliott instead informed him, "It is your fault you have lost your position and only means of supporting your mother, not his." Mr Elliott stood and crossed the cell to knock upon its door.

"You're right about what I did to Thaddeus," Mr Colby replied in a quiet voice. "But I didn't kill Perkins."

"I believe you," Mr Elliott said. "Do you know who did?"

"Nah," Mr Colby replied.

The door was unlocked and opened by the Custody Sergeant. As he stepped out and turned back toward his client, Mr Elliott said, "I'll inform Inspector Conway you're ready to make a formal statement."

"You gonna be there?" Mr Colby enquired with fear in his eyes.

"I wouldn't dream of leaving you to the mercy of the 'good' inspector."

"Thank you, sir," Mr Colby said, relieved, and winced as the cell door was slammed again. Rising to his feet and standing by it once it was locked, he listened to their footfalls until they'd faded; the Sergeant to his desk and Mr Elliott to Inspector Conway upstairs to deliver upon his promise.

TWENTY-NINE

The fire crackled in the hearth and warmed Mr Maxwell's back. Hooking his finger into his cravat and loosening it, he then wiped the sweat from his forehead with his handkerchief. Jutting out his lower lip and blowing upward to cool himself, he frowned when it made little difference. He therefore stood and, reaching behind him to grip the top of his chair, moved it to the left a little. Inadvertently obliging Miss Dexter to do the same on account of the limited space he left her with, he offered her a sheepish smile and apologised.

"How long we gotta wait?" Dr Weeks enquired from the armchair to the hearth's right. Slouched in it as he was, the only part of his anatomy visible to the others was a mud-caked boot whose heel rested on the fireplace's tiled base. The sound of liquid sloshing around a glass vessel then sounded as he lowered his bottle of gin after taking a swig.

"I've already told you; until Mr Locke arrives," Miss Trent replied.

"Yeah, but I don't find it so easy to trust yer word these days," Dr Weeks retorted, followed by another swig of gin.

"I'm not going to apologise for enforcing the rules of this Society. If you don't like it, you can leave," Miss Trent replied and looked over at the armchair. When Dr Weeks didn't respond, she stood and placed herself in front of the inebriated surgeon. She waited until he was taking another incredulous swig to grab the bottle's base and yank it from his grasp. Tipping over within her hand, its clear liquid poured over him and he clambered to his feet. "Either you get your drunken self over to that table, *Doctor*, and participate, or *leave*," Miss Trent warned, putting the bottle on the mantel shelf with a thud. Turning back to him, she put her hands upon her hips and resumed, "I don't care how much your ego is hurting—as *large* as it is. It's my job to run this Society but, most importantly, to keep its members *safe. That* is why none of its members may know who all the other members are. *You* knew that so *don't* act like a spoilt child when you're reminded of the fact." Returning to her chair at the head of the table, she'd just sat down, again, when Mrs Dexter entered with the tea things.

Mr Elliott held the door open for her whilst Dr Alexander took the tray and placed it upon the table. Smiling at them with appreciative eyes, she thanked them both and pointed to the tray as she announced, "I've got your coffee for you this time, Dr Weeks—oh my, you're all wet," Dr Weeks muttered a profanity and sat on a vacant chair at the table. "I'll fetch you a towel," Mrs Dexter informed him. Hurrying from the room and into the kitchen, a knock on the front door then brought her back past the parlour's open doorway. "It's all go, this evening," she remarked. "Oh, how *lovely*! For *me*?" she cried in delight after opening the front door. "What *will* my Henry say? *Thank* you, sir! Please, come in... Let me take your coat for you... They're in the parlour, sir. I'll just put these into some water." Another glimpse of Mrs Dexter was seen through the doorway as she went back down the hallway carrying a bunch of flowers.

A moment later, Mr Locke entered the parlour carrying a large suitcase. Mr Snyder recognised it as soon as he laid eyes upon it and gave Miss Trent a subtle nod to inform her of this fact. Taking the towel from Mrs Dexter when she returned with it, he then passed it to Dr Weeks, thanked Mrs Dexter for her hospitality, and closed the parlour's door. Meanwhile, Mr Locke had placed the suitcase upon its side on the opposite end of the table to Miss Trent, whilst Miss Dexter served the tea. When she came to Dr Weeks' cup of coffee, she handed it to him and waited with some trepidation as he tasted it.

"Thanks," Dr Weeks mumbled upon finding it was prepared to perfection.

"You're welcome," Miss Dexter replied in relief.

Dr Weeks pressed the towel against his sodden shirt to absorb most of the gin. Knowing he'd be unable to get rid of it all, though, he tossed the towel onto the armchair soon after and returned to his coffee.

Mr Heath, who'd been people-watching throughout, thanked Mr Maxwell as he passed him one of the toasted English muffins Mrs Dexter had brought in. They both leant forward, though—along with everyone else—when Mr Locke opened the suitcase and turned it around in one fluid motion.

"This is what that gentleman put in the left luggage office at Victoria?" Mr Snyder enquired.

"Yes. I accompanied him when he retrieved it," Mr Locke replied, removing his gloves.

"Whose are they?" Mr Maxwell enquired whilst chewing on a mouthful of muffin.

"His," Mr Locke replied.

Mr Maxwell took a sharp intake of breath and inhaled the morsel of muffin as a result. Coughing as soon as it slipped down his throat, he then drank several gulps of tea to wash it down before he stared at Mr Locke, red-in-the-face, and exclaimed, "*His?!*"

"Well, I never…" Mr Heath remarked, stunned.

"Are you absolutely certain?" Miss Trent enquired.

"He confirmed the fact to me in absolute confidence," Mr Locke replied.

"Yer discretion didn't last long, did it?" Dr Weeks remarked as he lifted a lady's lace night-gown from the suitcase with one finger.

"The gentleman in question is aware I am also a member of the Bow Street Society and gave me permission to show this suitcase, and its contents, to its members but *only* its members," Mr Locke clarified and tossed his gloves onto the table. "He would wear these clothes when he and Mr Perkins were alone in the apartment in Chelsea. They would refer to him as

'Wendy.' Thank you, Miss Dexter." Mr Locke smiled as she gave him his tea.

"I have encountered very similar scenarios before," Mr Elliott said with his usual stoicism. "It is a great deal more common than one may presume and is very much a hidden practice."

"What's yer woman's name then, Elliott?" Dr Weeks enquired with a smirk. "Ya seem to know a lot about it."

"Dressing as a woman, when one is male, is an offence all of its own, Dr Weeks. As such, I've encountered criminal cases about it at court," Mr Elliott replied, coolly. "Additionally, males who are willing to enter a sexual relationship with other males are committing the crime of sodomy in the eyes of the law. You shouldn't mock what you don't understand, Doctor. Many a man has committed suicide, or has been murdered, following his conviction for something he can neither prevent nor resist. Though they usually express a degree of shame, they all agree they find it incredibly difficult to suppress the feelings wider society deems to be unnatural. I assume it to be the case here, hence the gentleman's blatant attempt to distance himself from a relationship that, otherwise, he was happy to be in. Am I correct?"

"You are," Mr Locke replied. Having taken a seat at the table, he balanced his teacup upon his saucer and put them both down. "Inspector Conway saw the gentleman and I at Mr Perkins' funeral. Fortunately, I was able to assist the gentleman in his escape before the good inspector could confront either of us."

"We know," Miss Trent replied. "He came to the office afterwards; he wasn't very happy about it."

"If Mr Perkins was engaged in a homosexual relationship with this gentleman, whoever he is, why didn't you find evidence of it in his autopsy?" Mr Elliott enquired from Dr Weeks whose eyes narrowed above the rim of his coffee cup.

273

"'Cause there weren't any," Dr Weeks replied, plonking down his cup and causing some of its contents to slosh out over its sides. "If Mr Perkins were always on top, I'm not gonna find semen in his ass, am I?"

"Oh, my…" Mr Heath muttered, shocked, whilst Miss Dexter and Mr Maxwell's complexions flushed for the same reason.

"Thank you, Doctor, for that most… vivid explanation," Miss Trent said with a roll of her eyes. Taking a moment to calm her annoyance at his behaviour, she then enquired from Mr Locke, "Did Mr Perkins' lover tell you anything else?"

"He described how he and Mr Perkins met; Mr Perkins had accidentally bumped into him whilst leaving the *Sherburne Bookshop* on Holywell Street," Mr Locke replied. "For most subsequent meetings, they met at the Chelsea apartment."

"That's when old Joe from the St. Clement Danes Church shelter must've taken Mr Perkins in his cab," Mr Snyder mused aloud, recalling the conversation with his friend.

"Indeed," Mr Locke agreed. "For the rest, perhaps once or twice a month, they met at Sherburne's before continuing on to the Chelsea apartment."

"Sentimental reasons, do you think?" Dr Alexander suggested.

"Holywell Street hasn't enjoyed the cleanest of reputations—" Mr Elliott began.

"Nor's half of London," Dr Weeks interrupted.

"In the past," Mr Elliott finished with a glare to the Canadian. Waiting until Dr Weeks had resumed his drinking of his coffee, to ensure he wouldn't be interrupted again, Mr Elliott continued, "Though this reputation is still merited in many of the stalls and shops there, which continue to sell indecent and immoral literature of the most criminal kind, there are pockets showing some improvement."

"It's known as *Booksellers' Row* by a couple of the booksellers and publishers there. Particularly booksellers who offer new publications at twenty-five percent discount of their published price," Mr Maxwell said, and everyone looked at him with a mixture of surprise and amusement. Feeling the back of his neck become hot as he realised the unintended insinuation he'd made regarding his shopping habits, he added, "Only place I can afford to buy them—respectable books that is."

"The fact Mr Perkins felt the need to break the otherwise discreet arrangement with his lover though, to visit *Sherburne Bookshop*, suggests there may be more significance attached to the shop than mere sentimentality," Mr Elliott mused aloud.

Mr Maxwell, having hidden his embarrassment with a sip of his tea, saw a further opportunity to dismiss the implied obscenity of his reading material and revealed, "I know both *Sherburne's Bookshop* and its owner rather well; they're not at all immoral. I can pay them a visit tomorrow if you'd like?"

"I'd like to go with him," Miss Dexter said and placed her hand over Mr Maxwell's. "Mr Sherburne must be a very honest man if he's friends with one of our own."

"Well, we're more like acquaintances, really," Mr Maxwell replied.

"I'll drive you there," Mr Snyder interjected. "Now that the cab's fixed."

"Very well," Miss Trent agreed and made a note of the arrangement. "Holywell Street's not far from St. Clement Danes. Was Mr Perkins with anyone when he hired a cab from either there or Bow Street?"

"Nah," Mr Snyder replied. "Joe said Mr Perkins woz always on his own, so his bloke must've taken 'em both to Chelsea in his own carriage, then."

"I concur," Miss Trent said. "It would also explain why Mr Perkins was never seen on any of the omnibuses or trams." Mr Snyder hummed his agreement, and Miss Trent consulted her agenda for the next item. "Mr Elliott, you visited Mr Colby earlier; may you please tell everyone what happened?"

"This is Mr Colby's formal confession for his physical, and mental, abuse of Mr Thaddeus Dorsey and the theft of monies from Mr Timothy Dorsey," Mr Elliott began, passing a pile of identically, typed documents to Dr Alexander on his left. "Please, take one and pass it along," he instructed, having kept a copy for himself. "As you will read, Mr Colby claims he took the money so he could send it to his impoverished mother in Whitechapel. Some investigation on my part showed this was indeed the case. Mr Colby is the sole provider for his mother and siblings following his father's death, by drink, two years ago. He had no real excuse for the abuse he inflicted upon Mr Dorsey but insisted he wasn't involved in Mr Perkins' murder and the attempt to frame Mr Dorsey. Given the evidence, combined with this confession, I'm inclined to believe him."

"But Miss Merla was convinced he was guilty," Mr Maxwell pointed out.

"Merla were angry," Dr Weeks retorted as he leaned back in his chair and lit a cigarette.

"Maybe she killed Mr Perkins and tried to frame Mr Colby? Before the landlord saw them both at the pub," Mr Maxwell suggested.

Dr Weeks shook his head and, exhaling the smoke into the table's centre, replied, "She loved the bones of Mr Perkins; she were angry 'cause he were murdered and she thought Mr Colby could've done it 'cause he was one of the last in the house. Only reason why she were seeing Mr Colby regularly were because Mr Perkins asked her to."

"But she said Mr Perkins never showed any interest in her," Miss Trent pointed out. "She could've killed him in a moment of passion."

"And it *was* she who Billy, the boy from the butcher's shop, saw with Mr Colby one day and Mr Perkins the next," Mr Maxwell interjected, putting Miss

Dexter's sketch onto the table. "She was definitely connected to them both."

"Somethin' she ain't denied," Dr Weeks said and took another sip of coffee despite the cigarette in the corner of his mouth. "And don't forget; Mr Perkins weren't killed earlier. When he were killed, she and Mr Colby were seen at the *Turk's Head*."

"She could've assisted the murderer, then? As we thought Mr Colby had done," Mr Maxwell suggested.

"She was at Mr Perkins' funeral," Mr Locke announced, having picked up the sketch to take a closer look. "Aside from the gentleman, she was the only other mourner at the grave side. She would have believed herself to have been the only one as the gentleman stood several feet away. Thus, the grief she showed was, I believe, expressed with that assumption in mind and as such was genuine."

"See? She ain't guilty," Dr Weeks retorted.

Mr Maxwell frowned, "We're as far away from discovering the truth as ever."

"On the contrary, Mr Maxwell; we have eliminated three suspects from our list," Mr Elliott replied as he gathered in the copies of Mr Colby's confession.

"Mr Elliott is right, and we've still got lots more to investigate," Miss Dexter reassured with a gentle squeeze of Mr Maxwell's hand. "So please don't be disheartened."

Mr Maxwell's expression softened, and he placed his other hand over hers.

"Thank you, Mr Elliott," Miss Trent said, keeping her own copy of Mr Colby's confession for the Society's file. "Mr Heath, could you now present your findings?"

"Oh, *yes*!" Mr Heath exclaimed in joy. Standing, he unrolled a large piece of paper and laid it out upon the table. "These are the original plans of the Dorsey house. As you can see, it is very much a modern design in that—"

"Your measurements, please, Mr Heath," Miss Trent interrupted.

"Of course!" Mr Heath replied with a chuckle. "I get so easily distracted you know; sometimes my wife has to remind me to finish eating my dinner if I see a particularly interesting article in the newspaper—"

Miss Trent cleared her throat to interrupt this time.

"But, yes, the measurements," Mr Heath said with a sheepish smile. Taking out a second piece of paper from beneath the first, he pointed to a room with a chimney and fireplace marked upon it. "This is a room on the third floor, and this chimney is set against the wall adjoining the Glasgow-Bonham residence. Now, mark these measurements here." He pointed to those on the plan and, taking his notebook from his satchel, then pointed to a second set, saying, "Now mark the incredible difference in measurements of the same room when I took them the other day."

"They're smaller," Mr Elliott observed as he picked up the notebook to double-check the figures.

"*Exactly*!" Mr Heath cried in excitement. "In fact, they're *considerably* smaller. Both Mr Timothy and Mr Thaddeus Dorsey say they've never had any work done to the house so *where* have those two feet disappeared to?"

"A secret passageway," Mr Locke replied.

"*In one*!" Mr Heath exclaimed. "You are thinking like an architect, Mr Locke!"

"No," Mr Locke replied with a polite smile. "I am thinking like a magician. Did you notice any inconsistences in the chimney breast's construction, or in any of the walls, when you measured the room? I could find none when I examined them, but that does not mean they were not there."

Mr Heath's smile faded and, lifting his hands to drop them, again, replied, "I'm afraid not. But one of the attic rooms was also smaller in size than its counterpart on the original designs. The attic room was also directly above the third-floor room."

Mr Locke took another sip of tea as he recalled his late-night visit to the property. "I believe I saw the room to which you refer," he began. "It was covered in dust and did not seem to have been used in years. Mr Heath, if you would be so kind, I would like you to accompany me to the Dorsey residence tomorrow so we may examine the fireplace and walls of the third floor in more depth."

"Of course!" Mr Heath cried in delight.

"Be certain to return to the Society's office once you're finished," Miss Trent instructed them. "The same applies to you, too, Mr Maxwell and Miss Dexter. Mr Elliott, I expect you will attend Mr Colby's plea hearing at the Bow Street magistrates' court as promised?"

"I will," Mr Elliott replied.

"Good," Miss Trent said. "We'll await an update regarding his sentence once it's complete. Dr Alexander, Mrs Bonham has recently refused to see Mr Dorsey and has removed her commission to the Society to find Malcolm's killer. After our investigations of the house and Holywell Street are completed, everyone here shall visit Mrs Bonham at home to speak to her in person. I think we already have a strong idea as to who murdered her cat, don't we?"

"Indeed, we do," Dr Alexander confirmed. "And I'm confident the kitchen knife found on Mr Perkins' body was used to kill Mrs Bonham's cat and search its corpse."

"Then she has a right to know the truth even if she no longer wishes to pay us for our work," Miss Trent said.

"I wholeheartedly agree," Dr Alexander replied with a firm nod of his head.

"Then it is settled," Miss Trent said, closing her notebook. "Thank you, everyone. This meeting is now over."

THIRTY

Beginning at the northeast corner of St. Mary-le-Strand Church and running along St. Clement Danes' Church's right side on the Strand's east end, Holywell Street lacked the same virtuous status. Ironic when one considered the supposition that its name came from a religiously significant well allegedly located under the *Old Dog Tavern.* The Elizabethan, overhanging, gabled houses sheltered the narrow thoroughfare from sunlight; thus, granting it an appearance as filthy as its reputation.

Yet, for some, this seedy notoriety and gloomy atmosphere offered a cheap, and largely discreet, thrill amidst the drudgery of their everyday lives. Therefore, it wasn't uncommon to see clerks, on their lunch hour, huddled around a low window displaying questionable artwork. Such was the case when the Bow Street Society visited the notorious street. The focus of these clerks' attention, though, was a piece that was simultaneously innocent and provocative in the way a sheet covered its nude female model. Located behind the window's grimy glass, it took pride of place amongst tattered books and faded prints. The jangle of the shop's bell then distracted the group's attention, however, as their fellow emerged holding aloft a notorious volume.

"You never!" A clerk cried amongst the group, attempting to snatch it.

"I did. Dirty bits an' all," the book's owner replied, moving his prize away from the others' reach.

"Give it 'ere, then!" a third clerk cried as he tried reaching for it, nonetheless.

Turning sharply to prevent him from taking it, the book's owner grunted as he collided with Miss Dexter. The force of the impact sent them both stumbling backward; she into the arms of Mr Maxwell and he into the shop front.

"Apologise at once, sir," Mr Maxwell demanded.

The book's owner straightened and hid his prize behind his back as he replied, "Y—yes, of course. My apologies, miss."

"Look who's got it, now!" Another of the clerks declared as he slipped the book from its owner's fingers.

"Oi, give that here!" The owner demanded in surprise. As the thief, accompanied by his fellow clerks, hurried off in the direction of Wych Street, though, the owner mumbled a "pardon me" to the Bow Streeters and ran after him.

"Ruffians," Mr Maxwell remarked once they were out of earshot.

"Thank you," Miss Dexter said, her free hand resting upon his.

"No need to thank me," Mr Maxwell replied and squared his shoulders. "Someone had to remind him of his manners."

"Maybe you ought to get that book off 'em," Mr Snyder suggested from behind.

"*No*. I mean…" Mr Maxwell cleared his throat and held his frockcoat's lapels. "I think I frightened him enough for one day. I wouldn't want to be responsible for rendering him a nervous wreck."

"Nah, you do right not to go after him," Mr Snyder replied with a chuckle and stepped around them to head for *Sherburne's Bookshop*.

"I would, you know," Mr Maxwell insisted as he followed with Miss Dexter at his side.

"Not sayin' you wouldn't," Mr Snyder replied.

"But you don't have to; he learnt his lesson," Miss Dexter interjected. "I saw it in his eyes."

"Of course, he did," Mr Maxwell remarked with a firm nod. "He knows not to trifle with me again." Another chuckle from Mr Snyder caused him to glare at the back of the cabman's head, however. Parting his lips to confront his fellow Bow Streeter on the matter, the sight of the *Sherburne's Bookshop*'s sign up ahead caused him to push it aside, instead, as he pointed through the crowd and announced, "Over there, *Sherburne Bookshop*."

Its spotless windows displayed works by Dickens, Shelley, and Austin amongst prints of paintings depicting English country landscapes. The bright greens of the façade's wooden elements suggested a recent paintjob, whilst the entire frontage was clean and well-maintained. Leading the others inside, Mr Maxwell heard the gentle tinkle of the bell above his head as he entered. The interior was small but tidy. A Kerosene lamp standing on the end of the narrow, dark-wood counter also kept it well-lit. Bookcases lined the walls and, in the far corner on the right, a second door was marked *Employees Only.*

It was from this door that a fair-skinned man in his late sixties with a wrinkled, sagging complexion emerged. His grey eyes squinted through brass-rimmed pince-nez perched upon a bulbous nose. Tuffs of white hair jutted out from behind his ears despite the top of his head being bald. His dark-brown, shin-length coat exaggerated his short stature, whilst his loose-fitting, dark-grey trousers highlighted his lean build. The remainder of his attire—a white shirt, black waistcoat, and dark-brown cravat—was faded and worn. Yet, his most noteworthy feature was his swollen lower lip that looked as if it had been stung. He sucked upon it as he lifted his pince-nez and peered at the Bow Streeters through their lower halves.

"Ahh, Mishter Maxshwell," the man said as he stepped forward. Shaking Mr Maxwell's hand, he then looked past him to the others and enquired, "And friendsh?"

"Yes," Mr Maxwell replied. "This is Miss Georgina Dexter and Mr Samuel Snyder. Miss Dexter, Mr Snyder, this is Mr Ernest Sherburne."

"Pleash—ure to meet you both," Mr Sherburne said, smiling at their silhouettes. "How can I be of shervish?"

"Well," Mr Maxwell began, "I don't know if you've read the *Gaslight Gazette* lately—"

"I shaid I wouldn't read it again until your work wash in there," Mr Sherburne interrupted. "And I've kept my word."

"Yes… so you did," Mr Maxwell said with a weak chuckle. Glancing at Mr Snyder's amused expression and Miss Dexter's questioning one, he felt his cheeks warm. "But you really *must* read it, even if my articles are not in there, as it does feature some very interesting stories." He rubbed his palm against his frock coat's skirt. "Such as a man by the name of Arthur Perkins being murdered in Mr Thaddeus Dorsey's house. You'd sympathise with him because he's blind too."

"Of course, he ish, shon; he'sh dead," Mr Sherburne replied.

"No, I was referring to Mr Thaddeus Dorsey," Mr Maxwell clarified.

"I shee," Mr Sherburne said with a nod. Tossing a confused look Mr Maxwell's way, then, though, he added, "But I'm not blind."

"A—aren't you?" Mr Maxwell enquired.

"If I wash, I wouldn't need theesh," Mr Sherburne replied, momentarily taking off his pince-nez in the process. Rolling his shoulders as he replaced them, he then enquired in a cooler tone, "Why are you ashking me about a bloke called Perkins anyway?"

"We think he came here—more than once," Mr Snyder interjected.

"No, don't remember him," Mr Sherburne said.

"Perhaps if you saw his face?" Miss Dexter suggested, taking the *Gaslight Gazette* from her satchel and holding up the photograph of her clay model. "It's rather important we find out why he was here."

"To buy booksh," Mr Sherburne retorted. "Thish ish a bookshop."

"Please, look at the photograph to be sure?" Miss Dexter requested.

Mr Sherburne sucked upon his lip some more but, as he looked at the photograph, the sucking ceased. Staring at it for several moments, he then said, "No, I've not sheen him here before."

"But we *know* he was here only a few days ago," Mr Maxwell replied. "Maybe you've just forgotten?"

"I shed I don't know him, Mishter Maxshwell," Mr Sherburne retorted. Opening the door he'd emerged from earlier, he shuffled into the room beyond, and added, "I'm a very bishy man. Goodbye!"

"Why are you lying?" Mr Maxwell called.

Mr Sherburne spun around at once. "I'm not."

"I believe you are," Mr Maxwell retorted.

"Well, I'm not," Mr Sherburne countered.

"You *are*," Mr Maxwell insisted as he approached him.

"Am not."

"Are too."

"Am *not*!"

"Are *too*!"

"Gentlemen, *please*!" Miss Dexter interjected, causing both men to turn toward her. "We are getting nowhere." Approaching the pair, she waited until Mr Maxwell had stepped aside before addressing the bookshop's owner. "Mr Sherburne, Mr Perkins is dead—murdered—and his visits to your bookshop may be connected to his death but, then again, they may not. We can't say for certain either way, however, unless you tell us what it is you're hiding from us. Please, we don't mean you any harm."

Mr Sherburne ran his tongue over his swollen lip as he looked into her eyes. "You're a good woman, Missh," he said, taking a step back. "But I can't help you."

The door slammed shut in her face and Miss Dexter cried out in pain as her toe became caught underneath. Yanking it free with a soft gasp, she then slapped the wood and shouted, "Open this door at *once*, Mr Sherburne!"

"Allow me," Mr Snyder said as he laid a gentle hand upon her shoulder.

284

Miss Dexter moved away from the door and joined Mr Maxwell by the window display. Several passers-by who'd heard the shouting peered in at them from the street, obliging Miss Dexter to turn her back upon them in embarrassment. She was relieved her mother hadn't been there to witness her unladylike behaviour.

Meanwhile, Mr Snyder had walked backwards until he'd felt the bookcases bhind him. At which point, he then ran across the floor, jumped, and threw his entire body weight against the door using his shoulder. Its old lock yielded at once under the force and the door slammed against the inside wall, sending Mr Snyder with it. Miss Dexter gasped in horror but then breathed a sigh of relief when Mr Snyder gripped the doorframe and caught himself. Overjoyed, Mr Maxwell rushed into the adjoining room—congratulating Mr Snyder as he went—and discovered Mr Sherburne by a lit fireplace with a pile of photographs in his arms.

"Stop!" Mr Maxwell cried, running toward him.

Yet, Mr Sherburne threw the pile into the flames nonetheless and ran for the open doorway.

"Come back 'ere, you," Mr Snyder growled, grabbing hold of Mr Sherburne's coat and dragging him back inside.

"Don't hurt me!" Mr Sherburne cried.

At the same time, Mr Maxwell had leapt back in dismay when he'd seen the photographs land in the hearth. Filled with panic, he searched around for something to extinguish the flames with until he saw a kettle hanging from a hook above the fire. When he tried to pick it up though, its hot metal burnt his fingers and he recoiled in pained surprise. Shaking and sucking upon his fingers, he glanced around for a cloth. Seeing none, he sighed in frustration but then had an idea. Removing his frock coat, he twisted and wrapped it tight around his hand before plucking the kettle from its hook and dousing the flames with its dark-brown contents.

"What are they?" Miss Dexter enquired as she neared the now damp hearth.

"Photographs, I think," Mr Maxwell replied. Setting the coat and kettle aside, he crouched beside the fireplace, and retrieved the coffee-soaked and charred photographs. Gathering them into a pile, he rose to his feet and allowed Miss Dexter to examine them with him. The moment he saw what they depicted, though, he covered her eyes with his hand and cried, "Don't look, Miss Dexter!"

"I'm afraid I already have," she admitted, less shocked than Mr Maxwell had expected.

Mr Snyder dragged Mr Sherburne over to a chair and, putting his hand upon his shoulder, pushed him down into it. Keeping a firm grip upon him, he said to the others, "Give 'em 'ere."

"Prepare yourself," Mr Maxwell warned as he handed the photographs over.

"Blimey…" Mr Snyder remarked upon seeing their contents.

In two of the photographs Mrs Bonham and Mr Perkins were lying, alone and naked, upon a chaise lounge. Whilst she appeared to be sleeping, he was awake and posing with a bunch of grapes in his hand and a Roman-style helmet on his head. The remainder of the photographs depicted other nude men and women in provocative poses. The models ranged in age from early twenties through to late forties.

Arranging Mrs Bonham's and Mr Perkins' photographs side-by-side on the table, Mr Snyder enquired, "Do they look the same to you? What they're lyin' on."

"Let me see," Miss Dexter replied, easing Mr Maxwell's hand from her eyes, and peering down at the two images. "Yes, and I also think I recognise it."

"You do…?" Mr Maxwell enquired; uncertain he wanted to hear her answer.

"*I* haven't lain upon it, Mr Maxwell," Miss Dexter admonished. "I recognise it because I saw it in Mr Glasgow's house."

"I—I never meant to insinuate—" Mr Maxwell began.

"Are there any more of these?" Mr Snyder interrupted, looking to Mr Sherburne who shook his head. Following his line of sight, though, Mr Snyder realised he was staring at a blanket-covered mound in the corner. He therefore crossed the room and pulled off the blanket to reveal a veritable mountain of erotic photographs. Again, the models depicted ranged in age from mid-twenties to the middle-aged. The photographs were piled atop a narrow table with wooden crates beneath. The address for *Sherburne's Bookshop* was written on labels attached to the crates' sides. Amongst the crates were small, shallow, boxes made from papier-mâché. Each was sealed with private addresses written upon labels affixed to their lids.

"Where'd you get these from?" Mr Snyder enquired as he crouched down and took yet more photographs from the crates.

"No, no, no," Mr Sherburne replied.

"I know all the cabbies, and most drivers, in London, mate. So, you either tell me or I get the truth from 'em and take it to the coppers," Mr Snyder warned.

"It's jusht bishnessh!" Mr Sherburne insisted. "I've got to eat, haven't I?"

"But you have a respectable business here. Why would you risk it by dealing in such filth?" Mr Maxwell enquired, confused.

"Have you looked around, Shir? Filth shells here" Mr Sherburne replied. "And there'sh plenty of gentlemen who like to enjoy the urgesh of the body. They can't come here for fear of being caught, but my pictures allow them to indulge at home. I'm providing a shervice, meeting demand."

"Did Mr Perkins bring his photographs to you?" Miss Dexter enquired.

Mr Sherburne pursed his lips.

"*Please,* tell us," Miss Dexter urged. "It may be the reason why he was murdered."

"No, itsh not true!" Mr Sherburne retorted. "You jusht want me to loosh my bishness!"

Mr Snyder advanced upon him, saying, "If Mr Perkins brought these to you, and 'e was workin' with someone, they was probably the one who done him in. They could do you in, too, and then you won't have to worry about losin' your business anymore."

Mr Sherburne swallowed hard as he stared up at the larger man. "Very well," he finally agreed after much, frightened, contemplation. "I'll tell you."

THIRTY-ONE

Mr Locke's slender fingers smoothed over the cold tiles as his green eyes peered across their surface. Knelt upon the floor, he lifted his cheek from the fireplace's dark oak surround and traced the edge of its base with his fingertips. Stood at his side, watching proceedings with great interest, was Mr Heath who offered his handkerchief and remarked, "You've got dust on your cheek." Sitting on his heels, Mr Locke declined his fellow Bow Streeter's offer in favour of using his own handkerchief to wipe away the dirt. When he then resumed his position and continued his minute inspection of the fireplace, Mr Heath enquired, "What are you looking for?"

"A component with the potential to trigger a hidden mechanism," Mr Locke replied.

"I *see*," Mr Heath said, tucking his handkerchief into his pocket and popping a cherry-flavoured, hard-boiled sweet into his mouth. Moving around Mr Locke to reach the fireplace's other side, he then ran his finger along the mantel shelf and inspected it. Finding it smudged with dirt, he wiped it clean with his handkerchief and enquired, "Did you forget to inspect it the last time you were here?"

Mr Locke remained silent.

"Out of all the places to look, I would've started with the fireplace if I was looking for a secret passageway. Look around…" Mr Heath continued, scanning the room. "There's no furniture in here, or rugs to hide a trapdoor and the windows are nailed shut. Though I suppose there *could* be a very cleverly concealed trapdoor in these floorboards…" Mr Heath moved into the centre of the room and pressed the floorboards' corners with his foot.

A sudden click sounded, and Mr Heath's face lit up with glee. "Did you hear that?" he enquired. "Mr Locke, did you—?" He froze upon seeing the entire fireplace had swung away from the wall like a door. "I say, did *I* do that?"

"No, I did," Mr Locke replied, allowing Mr Heath to peer through the gap between the wall and the faux fireplace. Behind was a low, square hole large enough for someone to crawl through. Beyond this was a rather narrow, dark room. "I pressed each of the brass grate's frontal bars; the first twelve remained rigid, but the thirteenth slanted inward and released the lock keeping the fireplace-come-door against the wall." Taking a step back, Mr Locke closed the 'door' until he heard a click and ran his finger along the narrow gap between the rear of the faux fireplace and the wall. "The surround is not flat against the wall," he observed, "and, if you look closely, you may see the iron rods keeping the 'door' locked into the brickwork."

Mr Heath peered into the minute gap and, with a broad smile, exclaimed, "I see them!"

Unless one knew of its existence, the 'door' was too well-concealed to discover by accident. Even the falsified alcoves either side of the fireplace were perfect replicas of the genuine ones behind, right down to the wallpaper. The only hint was to be found on the floorboards in front of the faux fireplace. Unlike their counterparts in the adjoining room, these were swept clean of dust.

Mr Locke released the mechanism with a click and swung open the 'door' once more. Crawling through the hole, he then looked around. Its ceiling was that of the wider room so there was ample space for him to get to his feet. Directly opposite the hole was the opening into the chimney and Mr Locke felt a cold draft coming from it. The genuine alcove on the chimney's left also provided some additional space for movement, whilst the one on its right was occupied by a narrow table. Approaching it, Mr Locke found a candlestick holding an unlit candle and covered with hardened, melted wax. Beside it were piles of photographs depicting a familiar face. Picking one up for a closer look, Mr Locke quirked his brow and said, "I want you to tell no one of what we have found here."

"Pardon?" Mr Heath enquired from the hole.

Mr Locke slipped the photograph into his frock coat, went around to the alcove on the left, and looked up. Finding signs of what he'd suspected was there, he dropped back onto his hands and knees and crawled through the hole to join Mr Heath on the other side. "At least until I return," he said as he closed the 'door' with another click. "Also, do not allow anyone to enter this room under *any* circumstances, not even Inspector Conway."

"But what should I do if he asks what I'm doing?" Mr Heath enquired in alarm. After all, the grizzled policeman was downstairs at that very moment guarding Mr Thaddeus Dorsey against Mr Perkins' murderer.

"Tell him you are measuring the room, again," Mr Locke replied.

"If it's *absolutely* necessary, then of course I'll guard this fireplace—with my very life if needed!" Mr Heath replied.

"That is being a little dramatic," Mr Locke remarked with a smile and headed for the landing.

"Perhaps… but where are you going?" Mr Heath enquired as he followed.

"There are still some questions which require answers before we may return to Miss Trent. I shall not be long; you have my word."

Mr Heath frowned at his fellow Bow Streeter's elusive response but remained on the landing, nonetheless, as Mr Locke went downstairs and left the house. Whilst Mr Heath then went back into the room and closed its door, Mr Locke climbed into his private carriage and instructed his driver, "To Chelsea."

* * *

A nude photograph of Mr Arthur Perkins was slid across the table and placed before Lord Summerfield. His eyelids flickered and the corner of his mouth twitched in response, but the remainder of his features retained their cold mask of stoicism. He then sat in rigid silence as the photograph was withdrawn at the arrival of his maid. She brought a tea tray over to a nearby sideboard and, after setting it down, filled two cups from the pot. Sugar and cream were added to taste as she served the cups to their intended recipients and left the room at her master's curt nod of dismissal.

"Where did you find it?" Lord Summerfield enquired once they were alone.

"With many others in a concealed room," Mr Locke replied. "You do not seem surprised by either its existence or subject matter."

"Where was this room?" Lord Summerfield countered.

"You were aware of his posing for photographs in such a manner, then?"

"Don't be ridiculous, of *course* I wasn't."

"Why is it ridiculous? You and he were close—intimately so. There was never a moment when he confided this 'additional activity' to you? Perhaps during a conversation about fine art, or as you lay in one another's arms—?"

"*No.*"

"I do not believe you," Mr Locke said. "Additionally, lying to me is somewhat disappointing considering how well I have kept your confidence thus far—at great risk to myself. You are aware, are you not, impersonating a woman is as much of a crime as sodomy?"

"*Don't* call it that."

"Forgive me, I was only stating the correct legal term for it, but I see you find it offensive," Mr Locke said in a softer tone. "My request for absolute honesty still stands, however."

"I've been as open as I can, Mr Locke," Lord Summerfield replied, taking a mouthful of tea and replacing the cup upon its saucer with a gentle chink of china.

"What is preventing you from being completely open with me, then?"

"Ignorance; I can't tell you what I don't know," Lord Summerfield murmured.

"No, you know more than you are telling me, and I want to know *why*," Mr Locke challenged. "Does someone have a hold upon you?"

"*Certainly* not," Lord Summerfield snapped without conviction.

"Your words are deceitful, yet your eyes tell me the truth." Mr Locke placed the photograph back in front of Lord Summerfield. "You shall admit your prior knowledge of this photograph's existence and the identity of whomever is controlling you from afar." His features softened as his voice became sympathetic. "I did not come here to trap you. I came here to help you."

Lord Summerfield put his hands either side of the photograph and leant back in his chair. Staring at the vision of his dead lover for several moments, he then flipped the photograph over and covered his face with his hands. He released a deep sigh as he rubbed his face and let his hands drop to his lap.

"I knew of its existence or, rather, that others very much like it existed. I *was* ignorant of them though for most of our relationship," Lord Summerfield admitted with great reluctance. "I only found out when he told me of them the afternoon before he died." His shoulders sank as if they were made of lead as he continued, "He also explained about how he'd work within a room hidden in Mr Thaddeus Dorsey's house and it was this work which enabled him to see Mr Dorsey whenever his attendant left him for the night." Sadness then crept into his eyes and voice as he said, "He openly wept in my arms; he felt tremendous guilt over what they were doing to the poor man." Lord Summerfield took another large mouthful of tea to calm his emotions. "He told me he'd decided to end the work and tell Mr Dorsey everything. He considered him a friend, Mr Locke."

"You said 'they.' Did Mr Perkins have the assistance of another in his endeavours?"

"Yes," Lord Summerfield replied, turning the photograph over and gazing into his dead lover's eyes. "After Mr Perkins' murder was announced, he contacted me. He knew everything; about my relationship with Arthur, about the apartment, even who I was and where I lived. He said Arthur had told him before he'd died." He lifted desperate eyes to meet Mr Locke's gaze. "He threatened to ruin me if I didn't give him what he wanted."

"Which was?"

"That which most men greed after—money." Lord Summerfield sunk down in his chair. "And I paid it without thought; £500 was all my beloved was worth to me in the end." Leaning his elbows upon the table, he then held his head in his hands as he mumbled, "I don't deserve your kindness, Mr Locke, or your discretion."

"You have a great deal to lose, as well as a desire to spare your loved ones the pain of a scandal. Mr Perkins would not have begrudged you for what you did. When I think upon what I have been told of Mr Perkins, by you and Mr Thaddeus Dorsey, I feel able to say, with a great degree of certainty, that Mr Perkins would be enraged by your treatment at the blackmailer's hands. He would have undoubtedly encouraged you to pay whatever price was necessary to allow you to keep your secret hidden. I have no intention of doing the same, however. Instead, I beseech you to trust in me so I may set you free."

"I shan't divorce my wife," Lord Summerfield muttered as he lowered his hands.

"I neither ask nor expect you to," Mr Locke replied. "Tell me who is blackmailing you. I give you my word that I shall do all in my power to break the shackles he has you locked into." Mr Locke held Lord

Summerfield's arm as he then urged, "*Please.* If not for your own sake, then for Mr Perkins'."

Lord Summerfield's eyes dropped to the photograph and Mr Locke released his arm. A great sorrow etched itself upon Lord Summerfield's features as he caressed his dead lover's face. Covering it with a gentle hand, he then replied, his voice hoarse with grief, "Very well… I'll tell you everything I know."

THIRTY-TWO

Betsy moved back from the open front door and intercepted Mr Glasgow who'd come downstairs from his photography studio. "I tried sending them away, sir. Honest, I did," she said, holding clasped hands aloft like a beggar.

Mr Glasgow's scowl didn't ease, however, and she hurried alongside him as he strode across the hallway and demanded, "What's the meaning of this, inspector?"

"Murder," Inspector Conway replied, stepping into the house.

"I don't recall inviting you in," Mr Glasgow said, following the policeman as he went further into the hallway. "You have no right to barge your way in here. This is my home."

"This says I do," Inspector Conway countered, showing him his warrant card as he turned to face him. Glancing back to the porch, he added, "And they're with me."

Mr Glasgow's scowl deepened upon seeing Dr Alexander, Mr Locke, Mr Maxwell, Mr Elliott, Mr Snyder, Mr Heath, and Miss Dexter entering his home. Returning to the front door, he demanded, "And you can all *leave* again. A man has a right to privacy in his own home." Noticing movement out the corner of his eye, then, he looked out into the street and saw two uniformed constables standing on the steps.

"It won't be a long visit, sir," Inspector Conway said. "Then we'll be on our way."

Mrs Bonham's meek voice then pulled everyone's gazes to the landing at the top of the stairs as she enquired, "Lanford?"

"It's just the meddlers again, Esta," Mr Glasgow replied, closing the front door. "Go back to your room and rest."

"We have news about Malcolm's murder we thought you'd want to hear, Mrs Bonham," Dr Alexander told her.

Mrs Bonham's gaze darted to her brother as her grip tightened upon the handrail and she replied, "I cancelled my commission with the Society, Doctor."

"It's fortunate, then, that the truth is given free of charge," Mr Elliott interjected.

Mrs Bonham's eyes remained fixed upon her brother. Seeing the intense scowl upon his face, coupled with a subtle shake of his head, she said, "I'm sorry… but that's my decision."

"The truth also has a habit of surfacing," Mr Elliott remarked, causing Mrs Bonham and Mr Glasgow to simultaneously look at him and then at each other.

Once again, Mrs Bonham sought silent counsel from her brother who, realising he was being given little choice in the matter, said, "*Fine*. Esta, please come and join us in the parlour." He indicated the door to that room. "This way, everyone."

As he led the others into the parlour, Mrs Bonham hurried down the stairs, took her maid's hands in her own, and instructed her, "Go to the kitchen and stay there."

"Y—yes, ma'am," Betsy replied with a bob and hurried through the basement door.

When Mrs Bonham entered the parlour, she found Mr Maxwell, Miss Dexter, and Mr Heath seated upon the sofa, and Dr Alexander and Mr Elliott seated at the round table by the window with Mr Snyder and Mr Locke standing between them. Meanwhile, Mr Glasgow was stood behind the armchair by the fire and Inspector Conway was stood behind the door. The latter closed it upon her entering and stood in front of it whilst she crossed to the armchair and sat down.

"Come on, then," Mr Glasgow encouraged. "Now that you've got our unbridled attention, what is it you want to say?"

A knock sounded from the hallway and Inspector Conway lifted his hand at Mr Glasgow's movement, saying, "Stay where you are, sir."

"This is *my* home," Mr Glasgow retorted.

"Won't be a moment, sir," Inspector Conway replied and slipped out of the room.

Infuriated by his apparent disrespect, Mr Glasgow strode after him into the hallway. Although he closed the door behind him, his voice was heard saying, "You forget yourself, Inspector. Continue as you are and you'll *all* have to leave—come now, this is *too* much! That man is *not* welcome in my home; you've gone *too* far, Inspector!"

The parlour door opened, and Inspector Conway entered, replying, "Mr Dorsey's here at my invitation, sir. Soon as we're done, 'e'll go."

"Thaddeus?" Mrs Bonham whispered and rose to her feet.

Mr Glasgow followed Inspector Conway into the room and, seeing his sister standing, ordered, "Sit down." Watching her until she'd done so, he then turned toward the door as Timothy guided his brother into the parlour. Glaring at Thaddeus as he passed, he growled, "How did you manipulate your way into this one, hmm?"

"Lanford—" Mrs Bonham began.

"Be quiet," Mr Glasgow interrupted, glaring at her. "And *don't* defend him."

"I wasn't…" Mrs Bonham mumbled and bowed her head.

"Sit down," Inspector Conway ordered both Mr Glasgow and the Dorsey's.

Whilst Mr Heath and Mr Maxwell stood to provide space for Timothy and Thaddeus on the sofa, though, Mr Glasgow folded his arms across his chest, and said, "I prefer to stand."

"I'll go as soon as I've heard what they have to say," Thaddeus said in a quiet voice once he and Timothy were seated.

"Damn well you will," Mr Glasgow retorted, causing his sister to gasp in shock.

"Enough of that," Inspector Conway warned him. Keeping his back to the parlour door, he looked to the Bow Streeters and said, "Better get started."

"This murder wasn't the most brutal I've ever come across, but it was certainly one of the more intriguing ones. A man was found with his throat cut mere feet from a bed whereupon a blind man was bound," Mr Elliott began as he retrieved a thick, bound document from his satchel and held it up. "This, ladies and gentlemen, is the case in its entirety. Its contents is comprised of reports written by Bow Street Society members following their interviews of witnesses and suspects alike, signed statements from key witnesses, and affirmations signed by the Bow Street Society members involved. You may rest assured that, as soon as the murderer's identity is laid bare, this case file shall be passed onto Inspector Conway of Scotland Yard to initiate the proper legal proceedings against them."

"On the night of the murder, Mr Thaddeus Dorsey's house was, by all appearances, impenetrable," Mr Locke began. Taking the document from Mr Elliott, he turned to the relevant section and continued, "all windows were nailed down, and the backdoor's lock was rusted shut. Mr Colby had locked the front door when he departed for the night; as he had done every night for the past few weeks." He placed his hand upon Thaddeus' shoulder and felt it tense at his touch. "As my esteemed colleague touched upon, Mr Colby bound Mr Thaddeus Dorsey to his bed with rope prior to leaving. This had, again, been part of Mr Colby's routine for the past few weeks—assuming both men told the truth when questioned, of course.

"Yet what if they were not? What if they were accomplices in Mr Perkins' murder and had lied to provide one another with a perfect alibi? Thaddeus could have lied when he attested to Mr Colby departing the house, and Mr

299

Colby could have lied when he attested to both tying down Thaddeus and finding him in the same condition the following morning.

"This scenario lacks credibility for several reasons, however. First, Mr Colby detested Thaddeus and Thaddeus feared Mr Colby; a good recipe for accomplices in murder this does not make. Whilst it is true both men could be excellent actors, I and my fellow Bow Street Society members agreed this was unlikely. Second, Mr Colby had nothing to gain by becoming Thaddeus' accomplice in murder, or by being dishonest about tying him to the bed. Timothy Dorsey's shocked reaction to Inspector Conway's revelation regarding Mr Colby's method of containment for Thaddeus proved Timothy was unaware of it. Remember, Timothy is the man paying Mr Colby's wages. Thus, by stating he had tied Thaddeus to the bed, Mr Colby risked immediate dismissal by his employer. He would not have taken this risk if he had not been obliged to tell the truth. Furthermore, if he *were* Thaddeus' accomplice in murder, he would have also knowingly put his employment at risk by assisting Thaddeus in committing a heinous crime."

"Mr Colby could've murdered Mr Perkins before he left the house," Mr Glasgow pointed out. "Have you thought of that?" He glanced around the room. "I also noticed he's not here, about the only person you've not invaded my home with."

"He's commenced a period of supervision under the Convict Office at Scotland Yard," Mr Elliott informed him. "He pleaded guilty to multiple counts of theft, in addition to his consistent physical and mental abuse of Mr Dorsey. He was granted leniency, however, because he is the sole provider for his family. Otherwise, he would have been given the noose."

"You had a man convicted, and his name tarnished, on the word of that liar?!" Mr Glasgow cried, pointing at Thaddeus.

"No. His current situation is due to his own actions and willingness to take responsibility for them," Mr Elliott replied. "You have my word as a gentleman, Mr Glasgow, that Mr Colby's confession wasn't forced in any way." Mr Glasgow's gaze shifted to the policeman, prompting Mr Elliott to add, "Inspector Conway had no part in the retrieval of said confession apart from his writing it down whilst I was in the room with the two of them."

"And Mr Perkins' murder? Did he confess to that?" Mr Glasgow asked.

"No," Mr Elliott replied with a shake of his head. "The reason why Mr Colby committed the theft was, as I've already stated, because he was his family's sole provider. Knowing of Mr Timothy Dorsey's dire financial situation, he knew any request for a pay rise would've been denied. Thus, theft was the only other option open to him. As a result, though, it meant Mr Colby needed to continue as Mr Thaddeus Dorsey's attendant so he may retain constant access to funds. He knew how poor Mr Thaddeus Dorsey's finances were also, so there was little chance of a monetary gift in Mr Dorsey's will when he died. Thus, it made no logical sense for Mr Colby, working alone, to murder Mr Perkins, frame Mr Thaddeus Dorsey for the crime, and lose is only source of income."

"Even though he had a motive for wanting Mr Perkins dead," Mr Maxwell interjected.

"What motive?" Thaddeus enquired. "He didn't know of Mr Perkins' visits."

"No…" Mr Maxwell began and, clearing his throat, took the case file from Mr Locke. "But a friend of your maid's, Billy from the butcher's shop, saw a woman called Merla with Mr Colby one day and Mr Perkins the next."

"I don't understand," Timothy said.

"Well, Merla was the reason why Mr Colby left your brother every night," Mr Maxwell replied. "According to her, she was asked to befriend Mr Colby by

Mr Perkins, but she was never told why." Glancing down at the heavy document, he then looked around for somewhere to put it. Giving a weak smile to Dr Alexander when he offered to take it, he then passed it over and clasped his hands behind his back. Deciding this was uncomfortable, though, he relaxed his arms at his sides and resumed, "Mr Colby caught Miss Merla speaking with Mr Perkins one day and the two men argued. Because of that fight, Miss Merla's thoughts were the same as yours, Mr Glasgow; that Mr Colby must've murdered Mr Perkins before he left the house. But, as Mr Elliott has explained, Mr Colby would've risked his livelihood by framing Mr Dorsey."

"We have established why it is unlikely Thaddeus and Mr Colby were accomplices in Mr Perkins' murder and why it is unlikely Mr Colby acted alone," Mr Locke said and retrieved the thick document from Dr Alexander. "Let us address the possibility of Thaddeus murdering Mr Perkins on his own. First, let us examine his motive: he had none. In fact, he considered Mr Arthur Perkins a friend, albeit under the alias of Mr Palmer.

"Second is the opportunity Thaddeus could have had to commit the crime. As attested to by Mr Colby, he tied Thaddeus to his bed before leaving the house on the night of Mr Perkins' murder. I, Miss Dexter, and Mr Maxwell saw an example of his handiwork during our initial meeting with Thaddeus on another night prior to the deed being committed. Now, it would be logical to suggest Thaddeus had discovered a way to somehow free himself from the ropes to murder Mr Perkins *and* provide himself with a perfect alibi. Therefore, it became vitality important to prove whether this was possible.

"Yes, I, Miss Dexter, and Mr Maxwell could swear under oath to seeing Thaddeus tied to the bed, but eyewitness testimony may be undermined in a court of law. An unbiased, scientific experiment was therefore required." He opened the document once more. "As witnessed by Inspector Conway, Timothy Dorsey, and Mr

Elliott, and recorded in this document, I conducted such an experiment using Thaddeus' bed and the ropes attached to it. No application of contortion or sheer physical strength could loosen the ropes binding my wrists and ankles, however. This was due to one simple fact: the ropes were too short to provide sufficient slack. Without slack, I was unable to reach for the ropes' knots, either with my fingers or my teeth. I was also unable to gain sufficient leverage with my limbs to apply enough pressure to the ropes to pull them loose. I therefore concluded, with my witnesses' agreement, that it was impossible for Thaddeus to free himself."

"So, he *did* get someone to untie and re-tie him after all," Mr Glasgow said.

"I would never do such a thing!" Thaddeus cried. "Nor would I murder Mr Palmer!"

"How did they leave the house? As I have already explained, it was secured and only Mr Colby and Mr Timothy Dorsey had keys," Mr Locke pointed out. "Unless you know of another way?"

"Of course not," Mr Glasgow replied. "Someone could've stolen the key from Timothy."

"Was your key stolen?" Mr Locke enquired, and Timothy shook his head.

"Maybe Mr Perkins untied him, and Thaddeus killed him in a fit of madness; he's more than capable of it," Mr Glasgow accused as he pointed at the blind man.

"Again, how did Mr Perkins enter the house to untie him?" Mr Locke enquired. "Granted, I succeeded in gaining entry, but Mr Perkins had neither the skills nor the time to do as I did. Furthermore, if Mr Perkins had untied Thaddeus, who re-tied him once Mr Perkins was dead? It was certainly not possible for him to re-tie himself."

Mr Glasgow sighed and diverted his gaze as he mumbled under his breath.

"Thaddeus Dorsey is not guilty of this crime," Mr Elliott said with his usual stoicism. "I have encountered deceptions in the courtroom. His reaction to the news it was his friend, Mr Palmer, who had been murdered was genuine."

"Then he's fooled you as he fooled me," Mr Glasgow remarked.

"A fact you're very bitter about," Dr Alexander observed as he accepted the thick document back from Mr Locke.

"I've made no secret of it," Mr Glasgow replied with a shrug of his shoulders. "Thaddeus Dorsey is a devious, manipulative blaggard who's made not only my life a misery but also his brother's. He's almost bankrupt the both of us."

Thaddeus had his head bowed and his clasped hands pressed against his mouth.

"Indeed, he has," Mr Locke agreed. "To the point where Timothy has been obliged to employ as much deception as Thaddeus has been accused of."

The colour drained from Timothy's face like water from a sink as Thaddeus enquired, "What does he mean?"

"I…" Timothy said, his voice subdued by fear.

"The deception was used to protect Thaddeus, though, not to destroy him," Mr Locke resumed. "You are lucky to have a brother like Timothy, Mr Dorsey. He has risked everything so you may live a comfortable, and relatively happy, existence."

"What's 'e done?" Inspector Conway enquired.

Mr Locke met Timothy's desperate gaze and replied, "I cannot break a confidence, Inspector."

Timothy released the breath he was holding and collapsed against the sofa.

"You can't say sumin' like that and then nowt else," Inspector Conway told Mr Locke. "Either you tell me now, or I'll have 'im dragged down Bow Street station."

"You have my answer," Mr Locke replied.

"And 'ere's mine," Inspector Conway retorted, taking a firm grip of Timothy's arm and dragging him to his feet.

All at once, Mr Glasgow blocked the door and Mr Elliott blocked Inspector Conway. The latter warned, "You can't arrest him simply because you feel like it, inspector."

"I never said out 'bout arrestin' 'im," Inspector Conway retorted.

"Wait!" Timothy cried. "*Please*! I'll—I'll tell you what you want to know. Just, *please*, I can't leave my brother."

Inspector Conway released him with a push and, as Timothy sat on the sofa, said, "I'm listenin'."

"It's as Mr Locke said, I did it for my brother," Timothy replied.

"Did *what*?" Inspector Conway demanded.

"I stole monies from the bank!" Timothy cried, dropping his head to his hands as his emotional state disintegrated into violent trembling fuelled by shock and tears born from anguish. "I swear it was only the occasional guinea here and there, Inspector, and every penny was spent on my brother's care." Timothy gripped the top of his head. "Check my bank account if you don't believe me... You'll find it's empty with several outstanding debts attached to it."

Inspector Conway scanned the room; the only person who didn't appear taken aback by Timothy's confession was Mr Elliott. Yet, the policeman had come to realise that stoicism was the lawyer's default expression. Considering Timothy's criminal act, then, he decided it wouldn't be easy to prove and a mess to investigate as a result. He therefore set it aside for the moment in favour of another question and enquired, "Enough debt to wanna sell the 'ouse?"

"No!" Timothy cried as his head shot up. "I'd never do that to my brother!"

"Might if you was hard-up enough," Inspector Conway suggested.

"And send my brother to an asylum?" Timothy enquired in disbelief. "All I have done, the stealing, the selling of furniture, has been to keep him at home."

"What furniture did you sell?" Thaddeus enquired.

Timothy's gaze darted to his brother in horror before the realisation of his mistake caused his face to crumple. Stifling a sob with his hand, he then slid off the sofa and knelt at his brother's feet. "Thaddeus... please forgive me..." he said as he took his hands in his. "I had no choice; you *must* understand that."

"Our father's furniture... passed down the generations... sold?" Thaddeus enquired, stunned.

"Yes, but I did it for you," Timothy replied. "All of it was for you."

"Not if you wanted rid of 'im, it wasn't," Inspector Conway interjected as he stood over them.

"Wh—what?" Timothy enquired, looking up at him in confusion.

"You was in debt and burdened with your brother's care," Inspector Conway replied. "Doin' in Mr Perkins and framin' your brother gets 'im off your back and gives you a way of gettin' monies."

"That's the most disgusting thing I've ever heard!" Timothy yelled as he scrambled to his feet. Standing face to face with the policeman, he then insisted, "I *love* my brother; I wouldn't do that to him."

"Timothy Dorsey is not guilty of committing this crime, Inspector," Mr Locke began, stepping in between the two men. "Aside from his devotion to Thaddeus making it highly unlikely he would wish to frame him, Timothy's sensitive nature would never permit him to slit a man's throat."

Inspector Conway recalled Timothy's tense demeanour during their first meeting and conceded Mr Locke's point with a soft grunt of acknowledgement. He therefore moved back to his prior position by the door, saying, "But if Mr Colby, Thaddeus or Timothy Dorsey didn't do 'im in—"

"A woman called Merla was mentioned earlier," Mr Glasgow interrupted, gripping the sofa's back to tower over the Dorsey's. "Is she a suspect? If she is, she's also conspicuous by her absence."

"She was, for a time, yes, but she's not now," Mr Maxwell replied.

"Why not?" Mr Glasgow enquired.

"She loved Mr Perkins, but he never loved her," Mr Maxwell replied. Realising that didn't answer the question, though, he went on, "She could've murdered him out of revenge and tried to frame Mr Colby for it, yes, but... Mr Locke, you saw her at Mr Perkins' funeral, didn't you?"

"I did," Mr Locke replied. "She was the sole mourner at his grave side and her grief was undoubtedly genuine."

"She related her version of events to a mutual friend of ours who is also a Bow Street Society member," Mr Elliott said. "Their conversation was also witnessed by a second Society member, whose testimony you will find in the case file. Both members concluded she was telling the truth."

"She also had no opportunity to commit the crime, for she was seen at the *Turk's Head* public house, drinking with Mr Colby, at the time of the murder," Mr Locke pointed out. "Correct, Inspector?"

"Yeah," Inspector Conway replied. "Spoke to the landlord myself; they was loud and couldn't keep their hands off each other."

"Thus, Miss Merla has been eliminated as a suspect for Mr Perkins' murder," Mr Maxwell declared in triumph and smiled at first Mrs Bonham and then Mr Glasgow. Upon seeing the latter respond with a glare though, Mr Maxwell wiped the smile from his face, cleared his throat, and went to the window.

Mr Glasgow, meanwhile, turned his irritation on the policeman and enquired, "Why didn't you mention her testimony before?"

"Because they was already ruled out as suspects," Inspector Conway replied, looking from Mr Glasgow, to Mrs Bonham, and back again. "But you two's not."

THIRTY-THREE

"I didn't murder him!" Mrs Bonham cried as she leapt to her feet. "Lanford, tell them!"

"Don't trust him to help you, lass," Mr Snyder said.

"But he must, I'm *innocent*," Mrs Bonham replied. "Lanford, *please*. I didn't murder Mr Perkins; I wouldn't—*could not*—do such an awful, awful thing." Noticing Miss Dexter had approached, Mrs Bonham looked at her in confusion before catching sight of a white piece of paper in her hands. "What are you…?"

"You can't trust your brother to help you because of this," Miss Dexter replied.

"What is it?" Mrs Bonham enquired.

"Please take it and see," Miss Dexter requested.

The sympathetic look in her eyes reignited Mrs Bonham's fear and her hand trembled as she took the paper from her. Even in the parlour's dim light she could see the vague outline of furniture coming through from the paper's other side. Lowering herself into the armchair with the demeanour of someone who'd been informed of a death in the family, she then rested the paper on her leg and placed her hand upon it. Her fingernails dug into the chair's arm as, with a cool voice, she enquired, "Lanford… is this what I think it is?"

"No, of course not, Esta," Mr Glasgow replied in mild surprise. "There's no way they could have gotten it."

Mrs Bonham turned over the paper and saw the photograph she'd dreaded: her, nude and asleep, on the chaise lounge in her brother's photography studio. Crumpling it into a ball, she tossed it at him and cried, "Take a look for yourself and *then* tell me you never gave it to them! You *promised* me no one would see it if I did as you asked!"

Mr Glasgow caught the ball and, opening it out, frowned upon seeing the photograph. "*I* didn't give it to them. They must've stolen it." The cynicism in his sister's eyes reignited his anger, though, and he insisted, "I swear to you, Esta; I haven't given, or told, them *anything*!"

"You're a liar!" Mrs Bonham yelled, lunging at him. Thaddeus at once scrambled to his feet, though, and clumsily put himself between Mrs Bonham and her brother. She immediately threw herself into his waiting arms and broke down into violent sobbing. "You *swore* on my *life* you wouldn't show it to *anyone*, Landford…" She said against Thaddeus' shoulder. "I gave you *everything* I had…"

With Timothy's assistance, Thaddeus guided Mrs Bonham to sit beside him on the sofa. The two continued to hold one another and Mr Glasgow clenched his hands into fists at the sight. Attempting to advance upon them, with the intention of dragging his sister from Thaddeus' clutches, his path was then blocked by Mr Snyder's broad frame. Glaring at him, he ordered, "Get out of my way."

"Don't believe a word this bloke says, lass," Mr Snyder said, standing his ground. "We got that from Sherburne's on Holywell Street; 'e was gonna sell 'em. Your brother told him to. But that's not all you done, is it, Mr Glasgow? Mr Perkins posed for you, too. And 'e was the bloke that delivered the filth to Sherburne's."

"I don't know anyone by the name of Sherburne," Mr Glasgow replied through gritted teeth. Glancing at the others, he continued, "And Mr Perkins had access to my camera and chemicals; he could've easily arranged for another to take the photograph of him and make prints."

"Bit difficult to do beyond the grave; Mr Sherburne said he received delivery of the photographs of Mr Perkins and your sister only yesterday," Mr Maxwell revealed. "Also, you'd sent word to him, ahead of time, to let him know the crate would arrive in a hansom cab."

"And we have a signed, written statement attesting to the fact," Mr Elliott revealed as he took the thick document from Dr Alexander. Turning to the required page, he folded over the others, and held up the file so Mr Glasgow could read it.

"He's the owner of a morally unsound business," Mr Glasgow retorted with a smirk after casting a brief glance over the statement. "No court would deem his evidence as credible."

"Mrs Bonham, please may I invite your maid, Betsy, to join us?" Mr Locke enquired.

"Whatever for?" Mr Glasgow demanded.

"Of course," Mrs Bonham replied.

"Thank you," Mr Locke said with a bow of his head. "Excuse me for a few moments," he then left the room.

"This is *ridiculous*," Mr Glasgow muttered and folded his arms across his chest. Nevertheless, he paced the room until Mr Locke returned with Betsy. At which point he attempted to approach his servant but was, again, prevented by a physical intervention by Mr Snyder. Sighing, he therefore resumed his pacing but at a distance from the maid.

"Betsy, did Mr Glasgow receive any clients whenever Mrs Bonham was not around?" Mr Locke enquired.

"Yes… and at night, sir," Betsy replied.

"And Mr Glasgow received them *personally*?" Mr Locke enquired.

"He did," Betsy replied.

"Were you aware these same people were posing for nude photographs?" Mr Locke enquired.

Betsy's eyes widened as she replied, "*No,* sir. I assumed they were the master's regular customers; people who could only come after working hours."

"Thank you, Betsy. You may return to the kitchen," Mr Locke said.

Miss Bonham gave a nod of agreement and the maid hurried away.

"She's lying," Mr Glasgow said. "Servants are known for being deceitful."

"True. Mr Perkins lied to me when I enquired if he had ever visited Mr Thaddeus Dorsey's home during our first visit here. Miss Dexter and I were struck by his similarity to the clay model, you see. Nevertheless, I suggest you read another of our signed statements," Mr Locke said, taking the thick document from Mr Elliott, and turning to a two-page statement signed, *Lord S—*. Holding it close enough for Mr Glasgow to read but far away enough so he couldn't snatch it, Mr Locke went on, "This is a signed, written statement from an individual whose identity shall remain confidential. You will see it is signed 'Lord S,' but we shall neither confirm nor deny this is their actual title and initial. Although you, Mr Glasgow, are already aware of his identity for it was *you* who contacted him following Mr Perkins' murder to blackmail him over his romantic involvement with the deceased." The corner of Mr Glasgow's mouth twitched, and Mr Locke smiled as he continued, "You knew of the affair because Mr Perkins had told you of it the day before he was murdered. He also told you of the apartment in Chelsea. What you did not know, however, was that Mr Perkins had told this individual—this 'Lord S'—about him posing nude for several of your photographs, about him delivering those same photographs to Mr Sherburne, and about *you* being the one who supplied them."

"You weren't at all surprised when I told you about the apartment in Chelsea, Mr Glasgow," Dr Alexander said.

"Whereas Mrs Bonham, Mr Colby, and the Dorsey's were," Mr Maxwell added.

"Mr Perkins confided in you that he intended to confess all to Mr Thaddeus Dorsey," Mr Locke said. "Like your sister, he placed his trust in you. Unfortunately, this trust was misplaced and he, like her, had to be dealt with to avoid losing your income."

"Mere conjecture," Mr Glasgow retorted. "And ludicrous besides."

"You murdering an innocent creature was ludicrous, and for what? An earring I found between two floorboards," Dr Alexander said. "You were terribly angry when I did that. You hated him—you admitted that much to me. There were scratches and cat hairs on both the chaise and the floor underneath. The scratches were consistent with those inflicted by a cat when it sharpens its claws—as we discussed at the time. The indents of the chaise's feet in the carpet made it obvious it had been there for a long time. You therefore lied to me about the chaise's location when Malcolm had scratched it. I had to ask myself why and, coupled with your angry reaction to my discovery of the earring, I could form but one conclusion: you thought Malcolm had swallowed the earring, but you couldn't wait for him to pass it, so you killed him to retrieve it."

"This is absolute lies, all of it!" Mr Glasgow exclaimed. "I wouldn't kill your cat for a lost earring, Esta."

"You would if it belonged to your nude model and *not* your sister," Mr Locke pointed out. "The earring's discovery was the day before I overheard you and Mrs Bonham arguing. While I have yet to receive confirmation of my theory from Mrs Bonham, I suspect she was unaware of your additional photographic 'work' when Malcolm had allegedly swallowed the earring. Both Betsy's testimony and the argument lend some weight to this."

"You were afraid Mrs Bonham might find the earring if Malcolm passed it, either through defecation or vomiting," Dr Alexander said. "Mrs Bonham had told my fellow Bow Streeters of Malcolm's ill health in the days leading up to his death. Yet, when you did kill him and cut up his body, you couldn't find the earring. Nevertheless, you attempted to place the blame on Mr Perkins by leaving the knife you'd used to cut up Malcolm's body on his. You also suggested to me that you thought Mr Perkins had the temperament for such brutality."

"Your sister has been under your control ever since the scandalous affair with the soldier though, has she not?" Mr Locke enquired, and Mr Glasgow pursed his lips. "I suspect she has also been supporting you financially during that time. When she walked in on you taking a photograph of a nude model, she would have been shocked. During the argument I overheard, she threatened to leave. I presume you also intended to financially cut off your brother in the process?"

Mrs Bonham nodded.

"Why didn't you?" Mr Elliott enquired. Although they suspected the answer, it was important for Inspector Conway to hear it directly from the source.

"The morning after the argument, Lanford showed me that photograph," Mrs Bonham replied as she glanced at the crumpled piece of paper in her brother's hands. "I take a sleeping draught so wouldn't have awoken even if a coach and horses had driven through my bedroom. He'd… carried me to the studio and taken the photograph whilst I was asleep. He threatened to publish it if I didn't grant him power of attorney over my financial affairs. He said… it was the least I could do to repay him for protecting me for all this time. He was already receiving an allowance from my bank account, but he demanded full access to it all."

"You've told everyone how Thaddeus Dorsey left you in a poor financial situation, Mr Glasgow," Dr Alexander said. "You were in the house when the auction house collected Thaddeus' furniture because Timothy had taken you into his confidence. You therefore knew he couldn't lend you any money."

"You were reliant upon your sister's money and the income from the sale of erotic photography through *Sherburne's Bookshop*," Mr Locke said. "As I stated earlier, Mr Perkins threatened the latter because of his intention to confess all to Thaddeus. Yet, why would such a confession to a blind, mad man make any difference to you and your operation?" Mr Locke closed the distance between him and Mr Glasgow. Both his expression and voice were grave as he continued, "Because Mr Perkins was storing your photographs in a concealed room within Mr Dorsey's house. It is why he came to be in the house whenever Mr Dorsey was alone and bound to his bed. Mr Perkins told you he had been speaking with Thaddeus, under the alias of Palmer, when he revealed his intention of confessing the truth to him."

"You weren't surprised when I told you Mr Perkins was also Mr Palmer, either," Dr Alexander interjected, and Mr Glasgow glared at him with clenched teeth.

"The statement by 'Lord S' reveals Mr Perkins had told him about his visits to Thaddeus and his feelings of sympathy toward him," Mr Locke said as held up the thick document once more and addressed Mr Glasgow. "Mr Perkins became Thaddeus' friend and typed up his love letters to your sister. During your argument with her, you revealed Mr Perkins had told you of the affair. You murdered Mr Perkins to stop him from revealing your concealed storage room upstairs and thereby destroying one of your sources of income. You then attempted to frame Thaddeus for the crime for two reasons: as revenge for his deception about the law firm's true worth that left you in dire financial straits, and to prevent your widowed sister from marrying him. If she had, she would have left your home and taken her considerable wealth with her."

"Even if Mr Dorsey had seen or heard you murder Mr Perkins, you knew you could blame it on a figment born from his madness," Mr Maxwell said.

"I have *never* heard such ridiculousness in all my life," Mr Glasgow said. "*None* of this would *ever* stand up in court; you have no proof other than the words of a bookseller of questionable reputation, a self-confessed sodomite, and a blind mad man. You also forget I was at home *all* night. Ask my sister, ask my servants; I *never* left."

"It is true you did not depart via the front door, yes," Mr Locke confirmed.

"He *was* at home… all evening," Mrs Bonham added with a sniffle.

"But just in case my sister is lying," Mr Glasgow said, looking at the policeman in triumph. "Inspector, did anyone *see* me enter Thaddeus' house?"

"Nah. We spoke to the neighbours and the copper on patrol that night; no one saw you."

"*Precisely*," Mr Glasgow replied as his smirk broadened into a smile. "You have no case against me, Mr Locke. Even you said it was difficult to release the front door's lock if one didn't have the skill; *I* don't have the skill."

"True, but the murderer did not enter the house via the front door," Mr Locke revealed.

Mr Glasgow's smile vanished.

"I don't understand," Timothy said.

"How else could he have gotten in…?" Mrs Bonham enquired.

"If you would all be so kind as to follow me, I shall demonstrate how he entered Mr Dorsey's house without stepping a foot outside," Mr Locke replied. "Provided I have your permission, Mrs Bonham?"

"*Don't*, Esta," Mr Glasgow growled.

"Of course, Mr Locke," Mrs Bonham replied, allowing Timothy to guide Thaddeus whilst she rose to her feet and headed for the door. When Mr Glasgow gripped her arm and stayed her, though, she turned hard eyes upon him and warned, "Take your hand off me, Lanford."

Both stunned and angered by her defiance, Mr Glasgow tightened his grip upon her until Inspector Conway joined them. Releasing her with a push of her arm, he warned, "We shall discuss this *later*, Esta."

"And I'll be *very* keen to hear what you have to say for yourself," Mrs Bonham retorted and left the room.

"After you, sir," Inspector Conway said.

Mr Glasgow followed his sister, muttering, "The sooner we get this farce over and done with, the better."

THIRTY-FOUR

Mr Glasgow had his arms folded across his chest and a resentful expression on his face as he looked to the Bow Streeters gathered opposite him on the third-floor landing. Meanwhile, Thaddeus was standing behind him, book-ended by Mrs Bonham and Timothy, whilst Inspector Conway occupied the stairs. "I see nothing unusual here," he observed.

"That is because we have yet to reach our destination," Mr Locke replied.

"Then let's get on with it," Mr Glasgow snapped. "I'm a *very* busy man."

"When we talked in your photographic studio that day, Mr Glasgow, you told me you were at home all night in your study until you went to bed at about a quarter to ten," Dr Alexander said.

"And? What's that got to do with anything?" Mr Glasgow enquired. "Aside from proving I *never* left the house."

"You also said Mr Perkins was at home that night as he came to your study to ask if you required any assistance," Dr Alexander replied. "Something Mr Perkins had told the cook who later told Mr Maxwell."

"Yes, *and?*" Mr Glasgow enquired with increased irritation.

"By the way, Mr Glasgow, is your bedroom in the attic?" Mr Locke enquired as he broke away from his fellow Bow Streeters and approached a nearby door.

"*No.* My bedroom is on this floor," Mr Glasgow replied.

"Therefore, under normal circumstances, you would have little reason to enter the attic?" Mr Locke enquired.

"Yes," Mr Glasgow replied. Releasing a sigh and glancing up at the ceiling, he enquired, "What's the *point* of all of this?"

"Aside from the storeroom, there's only cook's and Betsy's bedroom up there," Mrs Bonham interjected, confused.

"All we ask is for you to humour us," Mr Locke replied to them both as he opened the door to reveal a set of steep stairs beyond. "Ladies first."

Mrs Bonham cast a concerned glance from Mr Locke to her brother and then to the stairs. After taking a moment to gather her courage, though, she passed through the open doorway and climbed the stairs. Miss Dexter went after her, followed by Mr Locke and the remaining Bow Streeters, and then the Dorsey's.

"After you, sir," Inspector Conway instructed Mr Glasgow who climbed the stairs whilst muttering something about meddlers. The policeman closed the door behind him as he followed.

At the stairs' summit was a narrow, dimly lit corridor with a door on either side at its far end. Mr Locke and his fellow Bow Streeters had gathered in the room beyond the door on the left, whilst Mrs Bonham and the Dorsey's were huddled in the corridor. Slowing at the sight of them, Mr Glasgow walked down the corridor toward them but stopped when he saw where the Bow Street Society members were. Rather than join them, though, he opened the door on the right and stepped inside. Meanwhile, Inspector Conway remained at the top of the stairs.

"The servants' room," Mr Glasgow said with outstretched arms. "Satisfied?"

The room in which he stood was rather plain-looking. It contained two single beds with a table in between, a wardrobe, and a tattered, old rug.

"Not quite," Mr Locke replied. "You are in the wrong room. I suggest you join us in here."

Mr Glasgow frowned and dropped his arms to his sides with a firm slap. Considering refusing the request, he then pinched the bridge of his nose and crossed the corridor to pass through the other door. The room beyond was filled from floor to ceiling with all manner of furniture, boxes, and trunks. There was a thin layer of dust on everything except the floorboards.

Mr Locke was at the rear of his fellow Bow Streeters gathered in the cramped space by the door. Their position meant Mr Glasgow was unable to venture further into the room, a fact that intensified his irritation. He growled, "And *this* is just a storeroom."

"Indeed it is," Mr Locke replied as he scanned the room's perimeter. Spotting a large wardrobe stood against the wall shared with Thaddeus' house, he then squeezed through a gap in the boxes to examine it further. When a brief tug of its doors informed him it was locked, he enquired, "May I have the key to this wardrobe, Mr Glasgow?"

"It was lost years ago," Mr Glasgow replied.

"Then I have no choice but to let myself in," Mr Locke remarked with a smile. Slipping a thin piece of metal from his frock coat's sleeve in a blink of an eye, he then inserted it into the lock and manipulated its mechanism until it released with a soft click. "The lock is remarkably loose despite not being used in years," he observed in a sardonic tone. Pushing a box aside once his pick was returned to its hiding place, he opened the doors to reveal a two feet-by-three feet hole in the brick wall where the wardrobe's rear panel ought to have been.

"I… I can't believe it…" Mrs Bonham whispered from the corridor. "Lanford…?"

"Be *quiet*, Esta," Mr Glasgow hissed.

Meanwhile, Mr Locke had gotten onto all fours and was backing into the wardrobe. Gripping the wardrobe's bottom edge as he lifted each leg into the hole, he then walked on his hands to move further back into the wardrobe until it was occupied by his torso and only his head poked out. His fellow Bow Streeters, Mr Glasgow, and Mrs Bonham edged closer for a better view of his actions, whilst the Dorsey's and Inspector Conway were obliged to observe from the doorway. Unbeknownst to them, though, Mr Locke had reached a second wall with his feet. Perpendicular to the first, it stood about a foot-and-a-half's distance away. He therefore bent his knees to draw his torso further into the wardrobe whilst reaching behind him to grip the bottom edge of the hole. Flashing a smile to his audience, he then pulled his entire body backward and disappeared through the hole.

"Mr Locke!" Mrs Bonham cried.

Mr Elliott, Dr Alexander, Mr Maxwell, and Mr Heath rushed forward at once to move aside the boxes and furniture. Seeing they were otherwise occupied, Mr Glasgow withdrew to the door but was prevented from leaving by Mr Snyder's hand upon his shoulder.

"Don't go yet, sir," Mr Snyder told him.

Once the way was cleared, Inspector Conway pushed past the others, climbed into the wardrobe, and peered through the hole. He remarked, "Blimey…"

"Is Mr Locke hurt?" Miss Dexter enquired.

"Nah," Inspector Conway replied.

"Why not join me, Inspector?" Mr Locke's voice echoed from below.

"How're am I gonna get down there?" Inspector Conway enquired. Mr Locke's reply was too muffled for the others to hear. Nevertheless, it seemed to satisfy the policeman as he climbed backwards through the hole without hesitation. Hooking his elbows onto the wall either side of the hole, he then allowed himself to drop a short distance before gripping the wall. Only then did he pull his head and shoulders through the hole and drop fully out of sight. Again, the other Bow Streeters rushed forward and saw his calloused fingers were still gripping the wall. A moment later, though, they, too, disappeared and the group heard a loud thud.

"It's a secret passageway…" Mr Maxwell said in awe.

"Send Glasgow through next!" Inspector Conway shouted from below.

"Go on, sir," Mr Snyder said as he shoved Mr Glasgow toward the wardrobe. "Don't wanna keep 'em waitin'."

Mr Glasgow glared at Mr Snyder and glanced at the door behind him. When Mr Snyder closed the distance, though, he recoiled and said, "*Fine*." Smoothing down his waistcoat as he faced the wardrobe, he then released a soft sigh and traversed through the wardrobe and its accompanying hole in an identical manner to Inspector Conway. Upon landing, he found himself in the very place he'd expected: the narrow room concealed behind the faux fireplace in the third-floor room of Thaddeus' house. On this occasion, though, Inspector Conway and Mr Locke were waiting for him.

"Wanna explain what you're doin' with a secret way into Thaddeus' 'ouse?" Inspector Conway enquired and gave the 'door' a shove. It swung open and Mr Glasgow stepped back as if the gallows were on the other side. The sudden touch of Mr Maxwell's feet upon his shoulders caused him to leap forward, however, and he lunged for the hole. Crawling through it, he then scrambled to his feet but was soon dragged down, again, by the full weight of Inspector Conway who had tackled him to the floor. He struck his chin upon impact but was kept pinned by Inspector Conway who made short work of applying the handcuffs. "You're nicked, *sir,*" he growled into Mr Glasgow's ear before stepping off him and pulling him to his feet.

A confused Mr Maxwell emerged from the concealed room a moment later and enquired, "Why is there a door at all?"

"It was a safety precaution," Mr Locke replied. "As you have seen, the room is rather small and claustrophobic. Mr Perkins was expected to work by candlelight amongst piles of paper. Such a material would be perfect fuel for a fire. In fact, it is my suspicion a fire did break out and, although Mr Perkins successfully extinguished it, he realised he would not have been able to make a swift escape back through the ceiling had the fire taken hold. Remember, there was an incident, related by Timothy, wherein Thaddeus had insisted he had smelt smoke and Timothy was obliged to bring a chimney sweep into the house to inspect the fireplace."

Emerging from the concealed room after Mr Maxwell and catching the tail end of Mr Locke's statement in the process, Mr Elliott said, "A sweep you recommended, Mr Glasgow." He brushed the dust from his coat and enquired, "Did you pay him to say all was well with the fireplace?"

Mr Glasgow glared at them and spat onto the floor at their feet. Inspector Conway immediately lifted him off his feet and slammed his face into the wall as a result.

"That'll do, Inspector," Mr Elliott warned, prompting Inspector Conway to ease the amount of pressure he was applying to keep Mr Glasgow pinned against the wall.

"Anyway," Mr Locke resumed. "Mr Perkins— naturally alarmed by this occurrence—would have insisted on an easier escape route. The faux fireplace would have been installed during the concealed room's construction, so it was simply a matter of cutting around it, fixing hinges to one side, and applying the locking mechanism."

Timothy Dorsey crawled out of the concealed room and rose to his feet. Shocked by what he'd heard, he stared at Mr Glasgow and said, "That day when you were alone in the house, waiting for the auction house to collect the furniture… You would've had plenty of time to construct the room."

"You know what he did to me, Timothy!" Mr Glasgow yelled as he struggled against Inspector Conway. "He ruined me!"

"We were *friends,* Lanford! I *trusted* you!" Timothy cried.

"You lured Mr Perkins into this house under the pretence of supporting his decision to confess to Thaddeus," Mr Elliott began with his usual stoicism. "You allowed him to walk downstairs and approach Thaddeus' bedroom before you brutally murdered him and left his body for Mr Colby to find the following morning. You had ample access to the letter opener due to the passageway. Your hatred for Thaddeus is what compelled you to frame him for murder, however."

"Where *are* the Dorsey's?" Mr Maxwell enquired, confused, as he peered back into the concealed room.

"Mr Maxwell!" Miss Dexter cried from above.

"Miss Dexter!" Mr Maxwell cried in return, crawling into the concealed room and leaping to his feet. Seeing Miss Dexter's lovely face peering down at him through the hole, he waved and said, "I'm fine! We're fine! Mr Glasgow's been arrested!"

"Good," Miss Dexter replied in relief. "I, Dr Alexander, Mr Heath, and Mr Snyder will bring Mrs Bonham and Thaddeus Dorsey around to you the old-fashioned way." She smiled. "In case you were worrying about us."

"Worrying? Me? *No,*" Mr Maxwell replied.

"Oh…" Miss Dexter said, frowning.

"That is—*yes*! Terribly, *terribly* worried," Mr Maxwell said.

Miss Dexter's smile returned, and she replied, "We shall be there soon." Retracting her head from the hole, she then poked it through again to say, "I'm glad you're unhurt." As she disappeared for the final time, Mr Maxwell felt his cheeks grow hot and he returned to Mr Glasgow and the others with a broad smile upon his face.

EPILOGUE

Mr Thaddeus Dorsey savoured the warmth of the fire and the touch of his beloved's hand in his as he listened to the gentle pitter-patter of rain against the parlour's window. Sitting on the sofa with Mrs Bonham's head resting against his shoulder and a bellyful of tea, he felt an odd sensation. Its alien nature took him aback until he realised what it was: he was content. After enduring so much—at the hands of Messiers Colby and Glasgow—he had emerged into a better life and a brighter future.

"Would you like another cup of tea, Thaddeus? Mrs Bonham?" Timothy enquired.

"No, thank you," Mrs Bonham replied as Thaddeus shook his head.

"That will be Miss Trent," Timothy said at the sound of knocking coming from the hallway. "Excuse me."

"Excellent," Thaddeus replied and leaned forward to place his cup and saucer upon the low table. Mrs Bonham's gentle touch on his wrist then guided him back on track as he almost missed it. Putting the cup and saucer down with a smile, he said, "thank you."

"You're welcome, my darling," Mrs Bonham replied with a soft kiss on his cheek.

"Miss Trent, brother," Timothy announced upon his return.

Thaddeus stood and, keeping the back of his knees against the sofa, held out his hands in the direction of Timothy's voice as he said, "Thank you for coming, Miss Trent."

"I wouldn't have dreamt of refusing," Miss Trent replied, taking his hands in hers. "I'm relieved to find all is well with you, still; your note had me concerned."

"How so?" Thaddeus enquired.

"Well, the Society has received payment for both commissions, so I hadn't expected to hear from you again so soon," Miss Trent replied.

"Thaddeus and I have joyous news we wanted to share with you," Mrs Bonham interjected.

"We are to be married!" Thaddeus announced and lifted a finger as he added, "But! I have other business to discuss that needed the *personal* touch." He held his hand out. "Please, sit. Would you like some tea? We are due a new pot."

"No, thank you," Miss Trent replied with a polite smile and sat in the armchair. "Congratulations on your engagement; everyone at the Bow Street Society wishes you a long and happy marriage."

"Thank you," Thaddeus replied as he lowered himself back onto the sofa. "Naturally, the Bow Street Society is invited to the ceremony."

"And our members shall be delighted to attend," Miss Trent said.

"Good," Thaddeus replied with a smile. Allowing Mrs Bonham's hand to slip into his once more, he then gave it a soft kiss and held it upon his knee as he continued, "We've decided to move away from London; too many awful memories and far too chaotic for me. What little money Mrs Bonham's brother left her with will help to buy a little cottage for us in Bournemouth."

"The coastal air is very rejuvenating," Mrs Bonham interjected. "We feel it will do Thaddeus' health the world of good."

"And hopefully reduce the likelihood of my having another episode," Thaddeus added.

"But even if he does have another, he knows he'll have my love and support to help him through it," Mrs Bonham said, placing her other hand upon his.

"Indeed," Thaddeus replied and gave her hand another soft kiss. "We now need to decide what to do with this old place, however. Which brings me onto the business I referred to, Miss Trent. We'd like to gift it to the Bow Street Society."

"*Pardon*?" Miss Trent enquired, stunned. "But… wouldn't the money from its sale be welcome to you both, to you three?"

"My brother and I have discussed this at great length," Timothy began. "We agreed that, without the Bow Street Society's assistance, he would've been falsely taken to the gallows and I would've been imprisoned in Newgate. It's true we don't have much, but what we do have is thanks to you and your Society."

"I'm—we're—grateful for the offer, Mr Dorsey," Miss Trent replied to Timothy and, looking to Thaddeus, repeated, "Mr Dorsey." Addressing them then, she went on, "but we can't accept such a generous gift."

"And if it wasn't a gift?" Thaddeus enquired.

"The Bow Street Society is still in its infancy, sir," Miss Trent replied. "Thus, our current funds are insufficient to purchase a house of this size."

"But if an arrangement could be made for monies to be passed onto us…? From the fees you collect from clients," Thaddeus suggested. "We don't make this offer lightly, Miss Trent. We want some *good* to come from all this bad. The Society having possession of this house would be the best thing I could hope for it. Otherwise who knows what might become of it? We are all in agreement. *Please,* Miss Trent. You may even have Mr Elliott see to the necessary paperwork if you're concerned about the legality of it all."

"We shan't take no for an answer," Timothy interjected.

"In that case… we have no choice," Miss Trent replied with a weak smile. "But I want the allowance arrangements in place *before* the deeds are signed over to us. I'll also require separate, signed, written statements from you both—validated by two independent witnesses—confirming you're consenting to the house being passed into the Bow Street Society's care."

"Of course, anything you want, Miss Trent," Timothy replied.

"We know you'll take excellent care of it," Thaddeus added.

"You have my solemn word we will, Mr Dorsey," Miss Trent said. "*Thank you.*"

* * *

"That was delicious, Mrs Dexter," Mr Maxwell complimented as he placed his knife and fork side by side upon his plate.

"Thank you, Mr Maxwell. It's a pleasure to dine with a gentleman who appreciates my culinary skills," Mrs Dexter replied, looking to her husband sitting opposite.

"It was mutton stew," Mr Dexter remarked and unfolded the evening newspaper.

"Do you have to do that *now*, Henry?" Mrs Dexter enquired.

"I like to know what's going on," Mr Dexter replied from behind the broad sheets of the *Gaslight Gazette*.

"We have a journalist at the dinner table, Henry," Mrs Dexter pointed out as she gathered up the plates. "He can tell you what's going on."

"*Apprentice* journalist," Mr Dexter corrected.

"Actually," Mr Maxwell began and cleared his throat. "My editor liked my article about Mr Glasgow's arrest so much he's made me into a full-fledged journalist with the *Gaslight Gazette* and given me a pay rise."

Mr Dexter dipped his newspaper to peer over both it and his pince-nez as he enquired, "How *much* of a pay rise?"

"A couple of pounds," Mr Maxwell admitted as his face flushed under Mr Dexter's scrutiny. "B—but I also get more hours, access to an assistant and the newspaper's camera, and further opportunities to see my work on the front page."

"I think it's wonderful news," Miss Dexter interjected with a smile.

"Thank you, Miss Dexter," Mr Maxwell replied as his cheeks turned a darker shade of pink.

"Hmm," Mr Dexter replied, unconvinced, and returned to his newspaper.

"Will you help me bring out the tea, Georgie?" Mrs Dexter requested.

"Yes, Ma-Ma," Miss Dexter replied, taking some of the plates, and going into the kitchen with her mother.

Mr Maxwell admired Miss Dexter as she left but, upon returning his attention to the table, was taken aback by Mr Dexter watching him intently.

"You're fond of my daughter, aren't you?" Mr Dexter enquired.

"I am, sir," Mr Maxwell replied with a swallow.

"Hmm," Mr Dexter said as he cast a glance over him.

To Mr Maxwell's surprise, though, he returned to his newspaper without elaborating further. Uncertain as to what was being expected of him as a result, Mr Maxwell waited for several moments whilst listening to the sounds of the Dexter women preparing the tea. When it became apparent they would be awhile, Mr Maxwell cleared his throat and said, "Mr Dexter—" He was interrupted by Mr Dexter's disapproving glance to his elbows on the table, though. Removing them at once and tucking his hands beneath the table, Mr Maxwell went on, "I'm actually more than just fond of your daughter. In fact, I think I'm in love with her."

"Hmm," Mr Dexter replied from behind the newspaper.

"Mr Dexter… I want to ask for your daughter's hand in marriage."

Mr Dexter put down the newspaper and stared at him. "I *beg* your pardon?"

"I… I want to marry your daughter," Mr Maxwell replied. "I love her and believe I can provide for her. Sh—

She's an amazing young woman, and I know we'd be happy together. All I ask for, Mr Dexter, is your permission to make that a reality."

"We *are* talking about *my* daughter, aren't we?" Mr Dexter enquired.

"Indeed, we are, sir," Mr Maxwell replied. Mr Dexter's silent scrutiny caused the back of his neck to warm, however, and the palms of his hands to moisten. Hearing the pounding of his heart in his ears as well, he waited with tense anticipation for the man's answer.

"Very well, Mr Maxwell," Mr Dexter finally agreed. "You have my permission."

"Permission for what?" Mrs Dexter enquired as she entered the dining room carrying a tray of tea things.

"Mr Maxwell's going to marry Georgina," Mr Dexter replied as he returned to his newspaper.

A sudden thud sounded from the doorway as Miss Dexter dropped the sponge cake she'd been carrying.

"Georgie, you must be more careful!" Mrs Dexter scolded as she dropped to her knees and retrieved the pieces of cake. Seeing her daughter lower herself to help, Mrs Dexter shooed her away, saying, "Never mind this! Go and get out the best china. We must celebrate this *marvellous* news!" She got to her feet and set down the cake and its plate upon the sideboard. "Come here, Mr Maxwell, allow me to embrace you!"

"I'm glad you approve," Mr Maxwell replied as Mrs Dexter flung her arms around him before he could stand.

Yet, when he looked to her daughter, he saw the corners of her mouth had dipped and her eyes were glistening with unshed tears. Worried, he enquired, "Miss Dexter…? What's the matter…?" Rather than answer him, though, she instead went to the dresser and took out the best china. This caused his concern to deepen and, approaching her, he attempted to place a gentle hand upon her arm as he enquired, "Georgina?"

"I need some air," Miss Dexter snapped, withdrawing from him as she hurried from the room.

"M—Miss Dexter?" Mr Maxwell enquired, stunned. Glancing at her parents to garner their permission to go after her, he then also left and found her in the garden. Confused and alarmed, he enquired, "What's the matter?"

"*How* can you not *know* the answer to that, Mr Maxwell?!" She cried through a sob as she turned towards him with tears streaming down her face. "You have just asked my Pa-Pa for my hand in marriage!"

"B—Because I love you—" Mr Maxwell began, taken aback.

"We hardly know one another!" Miss Dexter interrupted.

"Yes, I—I know, but I want to get to know you better, Georgina."

"Then do so through courtship, not through engagement!"

"Oh…" Mr Maxwell replied as the terrible realisation of what he'd done dawned upon him. "I—I'm sorry… I never intended to upset you. I'll go back inside and tell your father the engagement's off."

"And *shame* me and my family?" Miss Dexter enquired in disbelief. "That is *worse* than being engaged." Taking her handkerchief from her pocket, she dried her eyes and dabbed at her nose. "I never wanted to be dependent upon a man, to be his child bearer. I wanted to be like all the other women artists—to be financially independent as they are."

"You still can be—"

"George Dexter cannot be married to a man, Mr Maxwell!"

"Who's George Dexter?" Mr Maxwell enquired, confused.

"*I* am George Dexter," Miss Dexter replied with her hand pressed to her bosom as she walked up to him. "It's the name under which I exhibit my work. And now…" Her lips trembled as she fought to contain her grief. "…he shall be no more." Despite her best efforts, fresh tears slipped down her cheeks as she continued, "My *dreams* shall be no more. You have *trapped* me with your ignorance, Joseph." She stepped around him and went back into the house, adding, "I shall *never* forgive you for it!"

* * *

Miss Trent opened her office door, but the lit kerosene lamp on her desk prevented her from going any further. Certain she'd extinguished it prior to leaving for her meeting with the Dorsey's, she scanned the room and relaxed upon seeing a familiar figure stood by the window. She therefore entered the office, closed the door behind him, and crossed over to the lamp to increase its intensity with a turn of its knob. As she removed her coat and draped it over the back of her chair, she said, "I should have more locks fitted to that door or stop inviting men who can pick them." She smiled and, perching upon the corner of her desk, folded her arms across her chest and remarked, "I'm surprised you came."

"No one knows I'm here," her visitor replied and placed his bowler hat upon the desk beside her.

"I didn't think for a moment they would," Miss Trent replied with a playful twinkle in her eyes. "I have great news. Mr Thaddeus Dorsey has gifted his house to the Bow Street Society out of appreciation for what we've done for him."

"*Really?*" the man enquired, taken aback. His surprise soon shifted to cynicism, though, as he probed, "What did you promise him in return?"

"Absolutely nothing, Richard," Miss Trent replied as she stood and sat down behind her desk. "I tried to refuse, but he proposed an allowance, from the Society to him, in exchange for the lease on the house. It will be a small percentage of the total amount we receive from clients' commissions. I thought it was a reasonable proposal so agreed to his terms." She pointed at him as he opened his mouth to argue, saying, "We need new premises and *you* know it..." she lowered her hand, "...unless you have somewhere else in mind?"

"No," the man replied.

"I thought not," Miss Trent said with a smile. "It's a fair arrangement, for everyone, and the extra space will be invaluable to our expansion plans."

"I agree but—"

"Then it's settled." She rose to her feet once more and straightened his tie. "You put me in charge of running this Society, Richard. Which means you'll have to stretch your faith in me a little from time to time."

The sound of heavy feet on the stairs then caused them to step back from one another.

"I don't care *what* he paid you," the man said. "Your Society interfered with a police investigation!"

"You're only angry because we embarrassed the so-called 'good' inspector," Miss Trent retorted with a hand upon her hip.

"Now listen here—!" The man began.

"Only me," Inspector Conway interrupted as he entered the office.

"For goodness *sake*, we thought you were one of the others," Miss Trent said.

"What are you doing here, anyway?" the tweed-suit wearing man enquired. "No one's supposed to know I'm here."

"They don't, sir," Inspector Conway replied. "I come to tell Miss Trent that Mr Glasgow sung like a canary once we got 'im down the station. Also, to show her this." He tossed the evening edition of the *Gaslight Gazette* onto her desk. The front-page headline read, *SOCIETY SOLVES CASE THAT BAFFLED POLICE.* Whilst Miss Trent and the tweed-suit-wearing man read it, Inspector Conway closed the door and lit a cigarette, saying, "Lads're not gonna like this, sir. We got it tough with the public as it is; this won't make it better."

"I know," the man replied with a deep frown. "But your cooperation with the Bow Street Society should, hopefully, help to ease relations, the friendly face of policing."

Miss Trent's eyebrow quirked as she said, "We only did what Mr Thaddeus Dorsey paid us to do; we found Mr Arthur Perkins. The police weren't going to investigate a case put to them by a blind madman, so we had to step in. The fact Mr Perkins was murdered, and our client falsely implicated in the crime, made us obligated to find out the truth."

"Don't argue," the tweed-suit-wearing man said. "The only way this can work—for everyone in London to have access to the justice they deserve—is if we work *together*." He tossed the newspaper down. "I won't stand for this squabbling."

"Sorry, sir," Inspector Conway replied.

"Me too," Miss Trent added.

"Now, I'm going home to my wife," the tweed-suit-wearing man said. "Inspector, I suggest you do the same. Miss Trent, what are your plans?"

"I'm going to the Palladium with the Heaths tonight. To see Mr Locke perform," Miss Trent replied.

"Very good. Be sure to wait ten minutes before you leave after we're gone, though," the tweed-suit-wearing man said.

"Of course," Miss Trent replied.

Inspector Conway bid her goodnight and left via the stairs whilst the tweed suit-wearing man remarked to Miss Trent, "They did exceptionally well with this case; be sure to tell them so."

"I will."

"Good. Good night, Miss Trent."

"Good night, Chief Inspector Jones."

Enjoyed the book? Please show your support by writing a review.

DISCOVER MORE AT…
www.bowstreetsociety.com

Notes from the author

Spoiler alert

Thaddeus Dorsey, the curious client at the centre of this mystery, is fictitious. The malady he suffers from, however, is fact. Termed Charles Bonnet Syndrome by modern medicine, it is a condition in which an individual has visual hallucinations due to a severe loss of sight.

In Thaddeus Dorsey's case, this loss of sight is caused by Age Related Macular Degeneration. Though most commonly found in people in their sixties and seventies, Age Related Macular Degeneration can also occur in people in their forties—Thaddeus is forty-five. This particular condition affects a small part of the retina, called the macular, at the back of the eye. Sufferers lose their central field of vision but retain their periphery. As a result, those with Age Related Macular Degeneration don't tend to go completely blind.

Charles Bonnet Syndrome is named after a Swiss natural philosopher of the same name who, in around 1760, noticed how his elderly grandfather, Charles Lulin, was having "visions". Lulin had experienced severe loss of sight due to cataracts—a condition in which a white film forms over the lens at the front of the eyes and prevents light from entering. Bonnet knew his grandfather was in otherwise good health and, most importantly, didn't suffer from any mental health problems. Bonnet concluded, therefore, his relative's hallucinations were connected to his loss of sight. It wasn't until the 1930s, however, when the syndrome was given its official name.

In 1896—the year in which this novel is set— organised optometric medicine was only a year old and widely considered to be a pseudoscience. Someone like Thaddeus Dorsey wouldn't have seen an optician when he began to lose his sight, therefore, but rather a physician. As Thaddeus himself states, his sight deteriorated over a long period of time, a common characteristic of Age-Related Macular Degeneration.

He also describes how he hid the fact he had begun to see things until the day when he lost all emotional control whilst at work. Some sufferers of Charles Bonnet Syndrome hide the existence of their hallucinations—even in modern times—due to a fear they have a mental illness and/or other people may think they have one. This latter attitude would have been the most common in 1896 as hallucinations were, as they are today, associated with illnesses of the mind. Such is the case with Thaddeus Dorsey and those around him; not only does he believe himself to have a mental illness but so, too, do his brother and his love.

Mr Colby and Mr Glasgow, on the other hand, believe Thaddeus could be lying about the hallucinations and even his blindness. Thaddeus himself tells the Bow Street Society members, "For most of the time, I'm able to see only vague shapes and colours through a thick, white fog. There are times when I'm able to see with crystal clarity, however." He also goes on to describe how he knew his friend 'Palmer' was real because he *couldn't* see him. Additionally, prior to the Society members speaking to him, he asks a non-existent entity why it never speaks. Both the clarity of the hallucination and the lack of sound are characteristics of Charles Bonnet Syndrome which sufferers have described experiencing.

A theory put forth about why the hallucinations are so clear—and the cause of the Syndrome itself—is the brain is filling in the gaps in vision by supplanting them with stored images collected when the sufferer could see. Put simply, the sufferer is seeing a projection of an image created within their mind's eye. A suggested reason for why sighted people don't have these kinds of hallucinations is the idea the perfect sight itself prevents the brain from creating them. This would certainly explain why sufferers never experience any sound with their hallucinations as their hearing hasn't degenerated in the same way as their sight.

During the course of a visit by the Bow Street Society Thaddeus experiences one of his "episodes". Observant readers may have noticed how the parlour in which he sat was dimly lit. This detail was intentionally included as dim light is considered to be one of the triggers for Charles Bonnet Syndrome hallucinations. In light of this, Mr Colby's action of closing the curtains could be considered crueller than first thought, as it would've had the potential to make Thaddeus' hallucination worse.

Unfortunately for Thaddeus, he never receives an explanation for his condition but is at least granted a better quality of life in the end. Prior to this he was confined to his own home and cared for by Mr Colby—his attendant. Such an arrangement was a reality for some, usually wealthy, individuals suffering from a mental illness in 1896. Termed a "Single House" confinement during the period, it was different to madhouses in there was only one patient being cared for, or guarded, by a paid attendant. Mr Elliott describes the arrangement in reference to Timothy Dorsey's responsibilities to his brother. He says Timothy is "the party accountable for ensuring Thaddeus Dorsey is kept in a state of comfort within the confines of his own home, as a voluntary boarder, without the prospect of profit for Mr Timothy Dorsey. Such obligations are stipulated in the terms attached to the formal arrangement of a single-house confinement, as outlined by the Lunacy Commission, in accordance with the Lunacy Act of 1890."

"Single houses" didn't require a license and weren't visited upon by members of the Lunacy Commission. The main reason for this being the commissioners didn't think they had a right to. This is highlighted in the novel by the following passage:

> It was unfortunate for all concerned that Thaddeus Dorsey's condition hadn't been checked at regular intervals by a

medical officer during his confinement, or that the Lunacy Commission hadn't made enquiries after the same. Mr Elliott knew Thaddeus' home had been defined as 'private' under its single-house status due to Timothy taking no profit from his brother's confinement. As a result, the commission hadn't considered it their right to intrude upon the arrangement by implementing such visits. If it had, Mr Colby's ill-treatment of his patient may have been prevented.

In other words, patients like Thaddeus who were in the care of a paid attendant within a private, single-house, also faced the possibility of being abused by the only person they had contact with. In *The Case of The Curious Client,* even Timothy—the one responsible for his brother's comfort— is unaware of the abuse Mr Colby inflicts upon Thaddeus. He is also ignorant of the windows being nailed down and the backdoor's lock being rusted shut.

Admission of a patient into a single-house arrangement didn't require a certificate. Nonetheless, Thaddeus is described as being a "voluntary boarder"— further evidence of his own belief in his 'madness'.

Though Timothy doesn't live with Thaddeus, he is named, by Mr Elliott, as being the one who "holds the power of attorney over his brother's—Thaddeus'— financial affairs." Throughout the book it is explained to the reader, however, that Thaddeus' business wasn't as healthy as it could've been at the time of his confinement. This, coupled with the fact Timothy can't take any profit from Thaddeus' confinement, leads to Timothy's own financial hardships. Such a scenario was feasible in 1896, given the realities already outlined above.

The alternative of placing Thaddeus within an asylum, such as Bethlam Royal Hospital (aka Bedlam), wouldn't have been any more favourable. Due to there being very little understanding of mental illness in the latter half of the nineteenth century, asylums were more akin to places of punishment than places of treatment. Submersion in freezing cold water, restraints, and isolation were but some of the 'treatments' offered within the walls of such establishments. Little wonder, then, Timothy is willing to do (almost) anything to keep his brother from being admitted into one.

A famous Sherlock Holmes story, The Resident Patient, alludes to a "Single House" confinement in its title. Physicians would often recommend attendants, or "Keepers" as they were known in the early part of the nineteenth century, for a fee. Therefore the fact the aforementioned patient is resident within the upper rooms of a doctor's clinic is far from coincidental.

Thaddeus' sight loss and living arrangements created the perfect conditions for a locked-room mystery—particularly one where even a client's credibility is questioned. Thus the curious element of this novel is given a meaning beyond Thaddeus' own curiosity about Palmer's whereabouts—Thaddeus himself becomes a curiosity. In portraying the characters' reactions to Thaddeus' "insanity" as I did, I also hoped to portray a faithful representation of society's attitudes towards such a thing in 1896. I also wanted to highlight a lesser known aspect of mental health care from the era—as most assume there were only asylums—and bring attention to a condition that can be both frightening and confusing to those who have experienced it.

I first discovered the existence of Charles Bonnet Syndrome many years prior to researching this book. It was explained to me by a local charity, who assist people who are either blind or severely visually impaired, when I was attending one of their open days. One anecdote they gave, which has always stayed with me, was a severely visually impaired person who thought they had two people sitting in their house, talking, for several hours. Such is the vividness of the hallucinations, and the fact they *can* last for several hours, this person thought the people were real. Fortunately, in most cases, the hallucinations subside and disappear up to eighteen months after the loss of sight has occurred.

My primary reason for including a semi-blind person at all in this book was the fact I was writing about what I knew. Though I don't have Age-Related Macular Degeneration or Charles Bonnet Syndrome myself, I do have a degenerative eye disease which affects my peripheral vision. I therefore felt able to create a visually impaired character that was a) believable, but also, b) wasn't a two-dimensional embodiment of his condition. Furthermore, Thaddeus is a character that goes against the widely held misconception a person is either perfectly sighted or perfectly blind. The reality is very few people living with sight loss lose their sight completely. Even in my own case it's unlikely. The final point I want to leave you with is, as Thaddeus has shown, disability doesn't define a person. I know it certainly doesn't define me.

~T.G. Campbell
July 2020

MORE BOW STREET SOCIETY

The Case of The Lonesome Lushington
(Bow Street Society Mystery, #2)
NOVEL

In this sequel to *The Case of The Curious Client,* the Bow Street Society is privately commissioned to investigate the murder of a woman whose mutilated body was discovered in the doorway of the London Crystal Palace Bazaar on Oxford Street. Scandal, lies, intrigue, and murder all await the Society as they explore the consumerist hub of the Victorian Era & its surrounding areas, glimpse the upper classes' sordid underbelly, and make a shocking discovery no one could've predicted...

On sale now in eBook and paperback from Amazon.
Also available for free download via Kindle Unlimited.

The Case of The Spectral Shot
(Bow Street Society Mystery, #3)
NOVEL

When Miss Trent, is paid a late night visit by a masked stranger, the Bow Street Society is plunged into its most bizarre case to date. New faces join returning members as they encounter unsolved murders, the contentious world of spiritualism, and mounting hostility from the Metropolitan Police. Can the Society exorcise the ghosts of the past to uncover the truth, or will it, too, be lured into an early grave...?

On sale now in eBook and paperback from Amazon. Also available for free download via Kindle Unlimited.

The Case of The Toxic Tonic
(Bow Street Society Mystery, #4)
NOVEL

When the Bow Street Society is called upon to assist the
Women's International Maybrick Association, it's
assumed the commission will be a short-lived one. Yet, a
visit to the *Walmsley Hotel* in London's prestigious west
end only serves to deepen the Society's involvement. In an
establishment that offers exquisite surroundings,
comfortable suites, and death, the Bow Street Society must
work alongside Scotland Yard to expose a cold-blooded
murderer. Meanwhile, two inspectors secretly work to
solve the mystery of not only Miss Rebecca Trent's past
but the creation of the Society itself…

On sale now in eBook and paperback from Amazon.
Also available for free download via Kindle Unlimited.

SOURCES OF REFERENCE

A great deal of time was spent researching the historical setting of *The Case of the Curious Client* prior to my even starting to write it. This research covered not only the physical setting of London in 1896 but also transport, communication technology (such as typewriters and telephones), medicine, the Metropolitan Police, the City of London Police, servants, working conditions & opportunities for female artists, Victorian locks & locking mechanisms, and even magicians and illusions of the period, to name but a few. Thus a great deal of information about the period has been gathered, so as to inform me of the historical boundaries of my characters' professions and lives, which hasn't been directly referenced in this book. Where a fact, or source, has been used to inform the basis of descriptions/statements made by characters in the book, I've strived to cite said source here. Each citation includes the source's origin, the source's author, and which part of The Case of the Curious Client the source is connected to. All rights connected to the following sources remain with their respective authors and publishers.

BOOKS

Jackson, Lee Daily Life in Victorian London: An Extraordinary Anthology (Victorian Ebooks)
The following two citations are from the above book.

"Bar-Maids" Chapter – Extract from Cassells Household Guide, 1880
Subterranean/underground bars, the barmaids' working hours & practices.

"At Homes" Chapter – Extract from Cassells Household Guide, 1880

Proper tea preparation when providing for guests, correct placement of a gentleman's hat & gloves upon being seated, proper etiquette surrounding unmarried women giving handshakes to men whom they are only slightly acquainted with.

1897 Sears Roebuck & Co. Catalogue

The following six citations are from the above book.

"Telephones." section, specifically entry No. 6310, p.478.

Image and description used as historical reference source for basis of description of Miss Trent's telephone in the Bow Street Society's office.

"Wallpaper Department" section, specifically entries for Colour Papers and Borders, Gilt Paper, Gold Parlor Paper, Gilt Embossed Papers, and High Grade Embossed Papers, p.317

Descriptions of available colours and styles used as historical reference sources for basis of descriptions of walls in both Mr Thaddeus Dorsey's house and Mr Lanford Glasgow's.

"Regular ANNUAL LAMP SALE" section, specifically entry No. 95007, "Study Lamp", p.623

Description of "Study Lamp" used as historical reference source for basis of description of Mr Thaddeus Dorsey's bedside lamp.

"THE BEST IRON BEDS AND THE CHEAPEST" section, specifically entry No. 9394, "The Massive and Rich Appearing Iron Bed", p.599

Description used as historical reference source for basis of description of Mr Thaddeus Dorsey's bed.

"Lace Bed Sets." section, specifically entry No. 23283, "Three Piece Lace Bed Set", p.316
Description used as historical reference source for basis of description of Mr Thaddeus Dorsey's bed linen

"Our Clock Department" section, specifically entry No. 62947, "Ceres", p.465
Description used as historical reference source for basis of description of ornament in Mr Lanford Glasgow's house.

Fido, Martin and Skinner, Keith <u>The Official Encyclopedia of Scotland Yard</u> (Virgin Books, 1999)
The following two citations are from the above book.

"Bow Street" entry, p.25
Explanation of history of police court & police station, in addition to the explanation as to why Bow Street Police Station has a white lamp rather than a blue one outside, used as historical reference source for basis of description for the same in book.

"Trial of the Detectives" entry, p.269
Historical reference source used as basis for Mr Gregory Elliott's and Mr Thaddeus Dorsey's reference to this case during their discussion.

Goodman, Ruth <u>How to be a Victorian</u> (Penguin Books, 2014)
The following three citations are from the above book

"Getting Up" chapter, specifically the Deodorants and Body Odour section, p.18
Mention of soaps having lavender and rose scents used as historical reference source for Mr Percy Locke and Mr Joseph Maxwell having these scents in their physical descriptions.

"Getting Up" chapter, specifically the Importance of Cleanliness section, p.21-22
Text on miasma and germ theories used as historical reference source for basis of description of open windows and enclosed shelves in A.B.C Tearoom description. Mention of carbolic soap and quotation "a maidservant who smelt of carbolic soap came to be one whom mistresses had faith in, one whom they were much more likely to employ"(p.22) used as historical reference source for Mr Perkins, Footman to the Glasgow residence, smelling of carbolic soap. Explanation of carbolic acid being "one of the most popular disinfectants" (p.22) also used as historical reference source for the description of Dr. Weeks having this scent, also.

"Getting Up" chapter, specifically the Teeth-cleaning section, p.23
Description of three dentifrice recipes, taken from early editions of the Englishwoman's Domestic Magazine, (specifically recipe for American tooth powder) used as historical reference source to form basis of the description of items on Mr Thaddeus Dorsey's washstand.

* * *

MAPS

Shire Books (inc. Old House Books)
http://www.shirebooks.co.uk/old_house_books/
The following two maps were published by the above

Booth, Charles <u>Booth's Maps of London Poverty East</u>
<u>& West 1889</u> (reproduced by Old House Books)
Used as historical reference source for the location of Bow
Street and for the basis of the locating of Mr Perkins's
apartment in Chelsea

<u>London Railways 1897</u> (reproduced by Old House
Books)
Used as historical reference source, in conjunction with
the "CABS" article in Reynolds' Shilling Map of London,
1895, as the basis for the description of Sam Snyder's
search for 'Palmer' on the trams and omnibuses

* * *

VIDEOS

Magneto Era (1876-1900) by PHONECOinc
Published on 23rd August 2013 on www.youtube.com
Information on American Triple Box design telephone and
double box design telephones used as basis for description
of Miss Trent's telephone in the Bow Street Society's
office.

* * *

WEBSITES

Lee Jackson's *The Victorian Dictionary*
http://www.victorianlondon.org/index-2012.htm
The following sources are all taken from The Victorian Dictionary website

"CABS" – Reynolds' Shilling Map of London, 1895
Fares by Distance, Fares by Time, Extra Persons, Luggage & Waiting.

"OMNIBUSES" – Reynolds' Shilling Map of London, 1895
Omnibus running times, fares, colours, and routes.

"TRAMWAYS" – Reynolds' Shilling Map of London, 1895
Tram times, routes and fares.

Dickens, Jr. Charles. "CAB-CHA" – Dickens' Dictionary of London, 1879
Cabmen's shelters' locations & opening times.

Dickens, Jr., Charles "Police Force" Dickens' Dictionary of London, 1879
List of police divisions and stations

Dickens, Jr., Charles "Law Society (Incorporated)" entry Dickens' Dictionary of London, 1879
Basis of reference to Mr Thaddeus Dorsey's, and Mr Elliott's, involvements in the Law Society. Also, the costs associated with Clerks and the Law Society cited by Mr Elliott.

Photograph of a Hansom Cab, 1896.
Description of a Hansom Cab

Wey, Francis <u>A Frenchman Sees the English in the Fifties,</u>
1935
*The size of an omnibus, passengers preferring the upper
deck.*

<u>Punch, September 28,</u> 1861
Omnibus Conductors referred to as 'Cads'

Greenwood, James. <u>The Seven Curses of London</u>, 1869
*Dishonesty of Omnibus Conductors, Omnibus Drivers' &
Conductors' working hours & wages.*

Cassell & Company Limited, <u>The Queen's London. A
Pictorial and Descriptive Record of the Streets, Buildings,
Parks and Scenery of the Great Metropolis in the Fifty-
Ninth year of the reign of Her Majesty Queen Victoria,</u>
1896
*Photographs and descriptions of the Bank of England,
Euston Station, Bow Street Police Court, The Strand with
St. Mary's Church looking East, Sloane Square, and St.
Clement Danes used as reference sources for the in-book
descriptions of the Bank of England, Euston Station, Bow
Street Police Court, Holywell Street's location, and
Chelsea.*

Fry, Herbert, <u>London,</u> 1889
*Origins of Holywell Street's official name, the origins of
its unofficial name as 'Booksellers' Row', its reputation
for selling questionable literature, and the discount
provided for new, cheap books.*

<u>R.D.Blumenfeld's Diary, October 23,</u> 1900
*Holywell Street's description, Holywell Street's location,
description of Clerks crowding the street during their midday rest hour.*

"Correct likeness! Only a shilling!" - The Leisure Hour, 1859
Collodion process photography as cheap, individuals from other professions taking up photography to supplement income, night photography.

"Criminal Photography" – All the Year Round, November 1, 1873
Photographing of prisoners and regulations surrounding thereof.

*****

"The British Monetary System before Decimalisation" article by I. Van Laningham
http://www.pauahtun.org/Calendar/money.html
Monetary symbols and definitions used as historical reference source for clarification of monetary symbols/numbers described in contemporary sources of the time, e.g. "CABS" from Reynolds' Shilling Map of London, 1895.

"Maskelyne and Cooke – House of Mysteries" article by magic, Oct 11, 2011, located on The Magicians Scrapbook website.
http://www.magicians-scrapbook.co.uk/maskelyne-and-cooke-house-of-mysteries/
Source of reference for poster advertising Maskelyne and Cooke at the Egyptian Hall in the underground station. Existence of Maskelyne and Cooke was brought to the attention of the author during a guided tour of The Magic Circle Headquarters, London, England (please see acknowledgements at beginning of this book for further information).

Victorian London Cabmen Shelters article, Posted 10th December 2012 by Jsac
http://dustyburrito.blogspot.co.uk/2012/12/victorian-london-cabman-shelters.html
Reference source for description of Clement St. Danes cabmen shelter

Historical Eye - London Then and Now: Victoria Station circa 1896
http://historicaleye.com/1896%20London%20then%20and%20now/victoria%20station.html
Photograph & Description of Victoria Station used as reference source for description of Victoria Station.

Patient.co.uk "Charles Bonnet Syndrome" article
http://www.patient.co.uk/doctor/Charles-Bonnet-Syndrome.htm
Description of syndrome, its causes, its symptoms, and patients' reluctance to disclose these symptoms used as basis for Thaddeus Dorsey's "madness".

Royal National Institute of the Blind (RNIB) website
The following two articles are from the above website.

"Charles Bonnet Syndrome" article
Description of syndrome, its causes, and its symptoms used as basis for Thaddeus Dorsey's "madness".

"Age-Rated Macular Degeneration" article
Researched in connection with above article to help form basis of Thaddeus Dorsey's "madness".

Andrew Roberts's Mental Health Timeline
http://studymore.org.uk/mhhglo.htm
Lunacy Acts, Lunacy Commission, classification, regulation & licensing of 'Single Houses', definition of 'home care', law distinction between 'paupers' & 'non-paupers' and how they were defined/supported.

The Mail on Sunday - "The Wider View: Facelift for the Bank of England reveals a tale of two Cities" article by Mail on Sunday Reporter.
Updated: 22:04, 20 September 2008
http://www.dailymail.co.uk/news/article-1058798/The-Wider-View-Facelift-Bank-England-reveals-tale-Cities.html
Historical facts & photograph used as basis for in-book description of the Bank of England's Consol Office's interior.

Photograph of the exterior of the Bank of England, located on the Pictorial Gems website.
http://www.pictorialgems.com/public/upload/producti mage/1995-2739-4.jpg
Photograph used as historical reference source for basis of description of the exterior of the Bank of England in the book.

The Victorian Ironmonger "Old Door Locks" article
http://www.antiquedoorfittings.co.uk/page_1589551.html
Definitions of various traditional locks used as reference source for Thaddeus Dorsey's front door lock as described by Mr Percy Locke.

"British Phone Books" Information sheet
www.BT.com – specifically the BT Archives
First phone book for the entire country was published in one volume in 1896. The length of this phone book and number of entries.

**The Typewriter Museum – "Salter 5 (Improved)"
Article & "Instructions for using the Salter Standard
Typewriter No.7"**
*http://www.typewritermuseum.org/collection/timeline/ind
ex.html*
*Used as basis for description of Miss Rebecca Trent's
typewriter and its operation (see acknowledgements for
further information).*

**The Royal Veterinary College – "History of the
College" article**
http://www.rvc.ac.uk/About/Museums/Index.cfm
*Reference source for the historical establishment of the
Poor People's Out-Patient Clinic that Dr. Rupert
Alexander is an employee of in the book.*

**"A LOOK AT THE COUNTRY HOUSE SERVANT –
The Footman" article by Maggi Anderson, Fri, May 31,
2013.**
*http://maggiandersen.blogspot.co.uk/2013/05/a-look-at-
country-house-servant-footman.html*
*Reference source for basis of Mr Perkins' bedroom within
the Glasgow household.*

Encyclopaedia Britannica website
http://www.britannica.com
The following two articles are from the above website

**"DEVELOPMENT OF PHOTOGRAPHY" article by
Helmut Erich Robert Gernsheim**
http://www.britannica.com/technology/photography#re
f416380
*Specifically the section entitled "DEVELOPMENT OF
THE WET COLLODION PROCESS" used as historical
reference source for the basis of the description of the
process used by Mr Lanford Glasgow when he takes, and
then develops, a photograph of Dr. Rupert Alexander.*

"Wet-collodion process" entry
http://www.britannica.com/technology/wet-collodion-process
Used as historical reference source for the basis of the description of the process used by Mr Lanford Glasgow when he takes, and then develops, a photograph of Dr. Rupert Alexander.

"BRITISH SLANG – LOWER CLASS AND UNDERWORLD" article by I. Marc Carlson, 26th January 1994
http://www.tlucretius.net/Sophie/Castle/victorian_slang.html
Used as historical reference source for slang used by Inspector Conway, specifically the terms "Derbies", "the Chapel", and "copper".

"17 Euphemisms for Sex From the 1800s" Mental Floss article by Adrienne Crezo published on September 4, 2012 https://www.mentalfloss.com/article/12399/17-euphemisms-sex-1800s
Dr. Weeks' mention of "makin' a stitch" when referring to Perkins' affair. Definition of this term in the article is: "similar to having a brush, "making a stitch" is a casual affair."

Printed in Great Britain
by Amazon